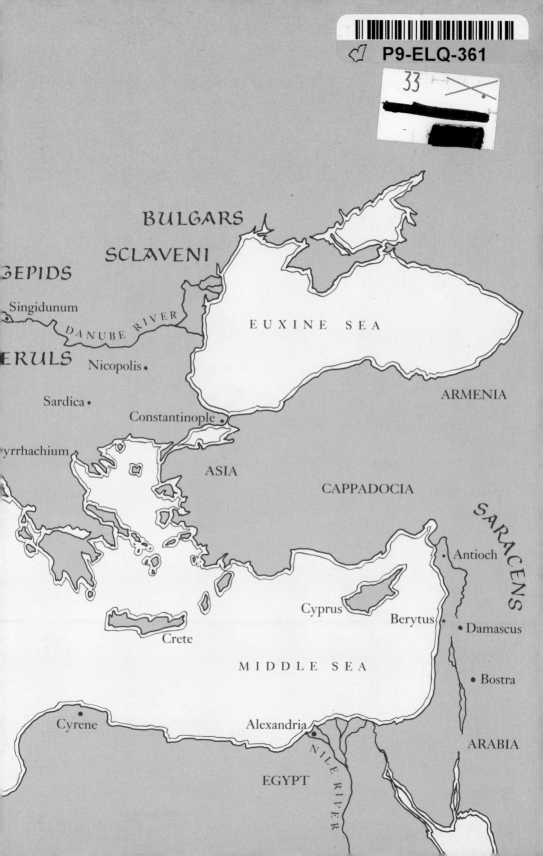

BULGARS

SCLAVENI

GEPIDS

Singidunum

DANUBE RIVER

ERULS

Nicopolis

Sardica

Constantinople

yrrhachium

ASIA

EUXINE SEA

ARMENIA

CAPPADOCIA

SARACENS

Antioch

Cyprus

Berytus

Damascus

Crete

Bostra

MIDDLE SEA

Cyrene

Alexandria

ARABIA

EGYPT

NILE RIVER

The
BEARKEEPER'S
daughter

The
BEARKEEPER'S
DAUGHTER

—

GILLIAN
BRADSHAW

HOUGHTON MIFFLIN COMPANY · BOSTON · 1987

Library of Congress Cataloging-in-Publication Data

Bradshaw, Gillian, date.
The bearkeeper's daughter.

1. Theodora, Empress, consort of Justinian I,
Emperor of the East, d. 548 — Fiction.   2. Byzantine
Empire — History — Justinian I, 527–565 — Fiction.
I. Title.
PS3552.R235B44   1987   813'.54   87-2924
ISBN 0-395-43620-6

Printed in the United States of America

V 10 9 8 7 6 5 4 3 2 1

The display type is sixth century Roman Calligraphy from *Arthur Baker's Historic Calligraphic Alphabets* (New York: Dover Publications, Inc., 1980).

Endpaper map by Jacqueline Sakwa.

TO JUDY
in gratitude for the equine advice
and much else

While it is the condition of our birth to die, it is unendurable to descend from imperial power to the state of a fugitive. God forbid that I should ever be without this purple robe; may I not outlive the day when I cease to be greeted as empress! If safety is what you want, my emperor, it's easily had. We have plenty of money; there's the sea; there are our ships. But look out that when you are safe, you don't discover that death would have been preferable. For my part, I like the old saying, "Empire is a fine winding sheet."

— the Empress Theodora
Procopius B.P. I.xxiv.35–8

The
Bearkeeper's
daughter

1

The Empress Theodora

CONSTANTINOPLE WAS BIGGER than he had ever imagined.

The ship approached it slowly, wallowing over the low swell in the hot September sun, her patched brown sails tugged intermittently by the light breeze. The small group of passengers clung to the railings amidships, shouting with excitement and pointing out gardens, a portico of shops, a harbor; the gilded cross glittering from the high dome of a church; an emperor's statue perched upon a column. *It's like a mirage in the desert,* John thought, gripping the railings like all the rest. *Shimmering around the edges, too vast and too beautiful to be real.*

"That's part of the Great Palace," said the master of the ship, coming to John's side and pointing at a building on the water's edge. John stared at it, and a cold lump settled in his stomach. Two wings fronted with white marble columns flanked a central building which was covered with polished stone tiles: it glowed among its surrounding gardens like a precious jewel in a wrapping of silk. The towering sea walls of the city made an additional bend around it, cutting it off from the common houses, protecting it, a city of its own. John shook his head and looked down. He studied his hands on the ship's railing. Thin hands, yellow from illness; the fingernails were dirty. He tried to imagine them touching things in the jeweled palace and couldn't.

"In fact, most of this end of the city is part of the palace complex," the shipmaster went on, grinning. "The empress gave that bit to some of her monks. She has a couple of other houses for herself, each the size of a cathedral, and the emperor has four or five. And then there are the chapels, and the barracks for the guards — it's a big place, the Great Palace. Who was it you were going to talk to?"

"An official of the empress's household," John murmured. It was what he had been saying all through the voyage, whenever anyone asked. He wished now that it were true.

"Well, you'll have to ask the guards at the Bronze Gate where to go. That's the only entrance to the palace. We'll be docking at the Neorion Harbor on the Golden Horn. To get to the palace, you walk up to Constantine's marketplace, then go left along the Middle Street to the Augusteion market; the Bronze Gate of the palace is at the other end of the marketplace. Just tell the guards your business and they'll let you in. You have somewhere to stay while you're in the city?"

John ducked his head and muttered assent.

I suppose I'll have somewhere to stay by tonight, he thought, as the master went off to supervise his ship. *Lord of All, I wish it were tonight already! Immortal God, what will I do with my things? I can't walk into the Great Palace, into the empress's household, carrying a sack full of old clothes!*

When the ship had turned into the Golden Horn and docked, he asked the shipmaster if he could leave his belongings aboard it for the night.

"Why don't you leave them at your lodgings?" asked the ship-master reasonably.

"I . . . I'd like to go to the palace first," said John.

The shipmaster shrugged. "If you like — but are you likely to be admitted, straight off like that? Officials like to keep people waiting."

"I don't know," said John. "I might be. Can I leave the things here for now, anyway?"

"Oh, certainly; it's no trouble. But it will be quite late this

afternoon before you can get to the palace, you know. You'll
have to get a license to enter the city from the customs official
first."

"Why? I'm not going to sell anything here."

The shipmaster chuckled. "In this city, everyone has to have
a license. You even need a license to beg — and it isn't easy to
come by, either! They won't give one to people from outside the
city, not without a hefty bribe they won't. Everyone who comes
to Constantinople has to show that he either has business in the
city or has some means of supporting himself. If he doesn't, he's
sent back home at once — unless they need workers for some
public project, in which case he'll be offered a job and enrolled
on the spot. Even though you're a gentleman and don't need to
worry about that, you'll still have to get a license."

"I see," said John, looking at his hands again. They were
smooth hands, uncalloused by manual labor. Only a shiny patch
of skin on the right middle finger hinted at his hours of office
work. *I am a sort of gentleman,* he told himself, silently and
bitterly. *A gentleman's bastard. Well, I hope I look gentlemanly
enough that the customs official is polite; I don't have the
money to support myself here for more than a week, and I don't
want to end up enrolled in a public bakery or repairing a cistern.*

"Of course, if you're in so much of a hurry, I could get the
official to see you before the cargo or the others . . . ," the shipmaster added, grinning at John expectantly.

John swallowed a sigh, reached slowly into his purse, and
handed the man a large bronze coin, then added a second one.
The shipmaster grinned again and slipped them into his own
purse. "I'll see what I can manage," he said.

Now I don't even have enough to live on for a week, John
thought bitterly. *That was a stupid thing to do; I could have
waited till tomorrow. And it was stupid to ask for a private cabin
on the ship — only it seemed ridiculous, traveling to the court
of Their Sacred Majesties under a canvas tent with six other
passengers, a mob of children, four goats, and some camels. But
if I'd suffered it and kept my mouth shut, I'd have had enough*

to last a month or so — time to look for a job, if I'm not received at the palace.

But if I'm not received, I'm unlikely to want a job either.

The customs official showed up promptly: a small, dark, grizzled man in a short tunic and knee-length red cloak. The shipmaster seemed to know him — they shook hands and slapped each other on the back, exchanging news while John watched in motionless impatience from the railings. Then the shipmaster gave a grin and showed the official over. "This is one of my passengers," he told the man, "and he's in a hurry to do some business at the palace; you can talk to him first." He stood back to watch them with a proprietary smile, like a host who has introduced his two most interesting guests at a dinner party.

The official surveyed John with a sour, assessing eye. *Aged twenty to twenty-five,* he decided, setting it out in his mind as though writing the certificate. *Short and slight; black hair, clean-shaven, dark eyes; slight scar at corner of left eye. Pale complexion — a bit yellow, in fact; has he been ill recently? That cloak and tunic are meant to be black, I'd guess, for all that they're more of a mud color than anything else: he's in mourning. I know, he's from one of the plague-hit areas. Good-quality cloth, though, and the border on the tunic's real silk: he's not poor. That headcloth with the braided cord round it is Saracen in style, and the ship's come from Berytus. So we have here ... I'd guess some kind of Arab, come to sort out some business over an estate left at somebody's death.* He smiled drily at John, taking out his stylus and wax tablets. "Your name?" he asked politely.

"John, son of Diodoros," John replied nervously. "Of the city of Bostra in the province of Arabia."

The official smiled again, gratified. "And your business in Constantinople?"

"I've come to see an official in the household of the empress on ... on some personal business."

"In the household of the *empress*?" the official asked, lowering his stylus and lifting his eyebrows.

"Yes," said John, and swallowed. "You see ... you see, the

person knew my father once, and when my father was dying he
. . . he asked me to take a message, a personal message." He
felt the cold lump in his stomach again at the lie, remembering
the hot dark room, the stink of illness and corruption, and his
father's voice croaking, "You must never go there. Promise me
you won't go there." He shivered.

The official's eyebrows came down again. "I see. Some personal business of your father's with an old friend." *I was close,*
he thought to himself, satisfied. "And when did your father die?"

"June," John said shortly. "It was the plague."

There was a moment's silence in the hot autumn sun, a stillness brought on by the bare word: *plague.* The shipmaster's
proprietary smile drooped; the official's sour look ebbed into
grimness. *No one ever mentions it,* John realized. *I shouldn't
have. Too many people have died of it; it disturbs them to hear
it named.*

"We had it here in June, too," the official said softly. He
glanced down the harbor northward. "There was no room in the
city to bury all the dead. They heaped them in the watchtowers
of the city wall. When the wind was from the north you could
smell them there, rotting. It was as though the world itself was
falling to bits. I thought everyone on earth must be dying. I
lost a brother to it, and nearly a son as well."

"I almost died of it," returned John. He couldn't bear to add,
*It was my father who nursed me through it. He saw me through,
and then died of the plague himself.*

"So you survived it!" The official stared at John a moment.
Survived it well, he thought to himself bitterly, picturing his
ten-year-old son, whom the plague had left half crippled and
unable to speak clearly. *But the boy's recovering,* he told himself
earnestly; *he'll get better; he's so much better now than he was
last month! Maybe in another month he'll be like this, a bit
yellow, but normal.*

He sighed, and gave John a tired smile. No reason to question
this one. He set a piece of parchment down on top of his tablets,
slipped the stylus into the pen case slung about his neck, took

out a pen, dipped it into the inkwell at the side of the case, and wrote out a certificate. "No point in giving you any more trouble, then!" he said, handing it to John. "That gives you permission to stay in the city while conducting personal business at the court. Keep it with you at all times; if you lose it, report to the office of the quaesitor at the Augusteion. That's all; enjoy your stay in the city. Who's next?"

It was still only early in the afternoon. John left the ship, his feet sounding hollow and hesitant on the wooden gangway. He walked up the stone docks, showed the new license to the officials at the harbor gate, and went on into the city. The streets were narrow, lined with tall houses whose overhanging balconies almost touched, shutting out the light. A few women sat on the balconies, spinning and watching the world go by, and the clothes hanging out to dry flapped brightly in the breeze; apart from that everything was still, sleeping away the noontide. Slowly he climbed the hill away from the harbor; as he drew nearer to the summit the houses grew grander, their high walls hanging over the street. When he reached the marketplace, the sunlight was almost blinding after the shadowed back alleys. He stood on the corner catching his breath. The wide expanse of the market was almost deserted; the splash of water from the fountain in its center carried clearly through the silence. Gold on a column of porphyry, a statue of the emperor Constantine gazed down on the marble colonnades, on the sirens and hippogriffs of gilded bronze, and on the shuttered shops that sold silver, perfumes, and jewels.

Left, the shipmaster had said. John looked left across the marketplace. The colonnades of white marble opened into a street wide as a parade ground, the porticoes topped with statues: emperors and empresses, heroes, senators, and pagan goddesses, comfortable amid the magnificence. Further away, a church rose like a hill, its face of rose-colored marble giving way to a towering gilded dome. Despite the bright sunlight he felt cold. He took a deep breath and started walking.

The shops were just beginning to open when he reached the

Augusteion market. The dome of the church loomed over him to his left; on his right stood the towering columned front of the hippodrome, and next to it, on the other side of the market-place, stood a massive building roofed with gilded bronze and gated with bronze, set deep into frowning walls: the Bronze Gate of the Great Palace. John stood on the other side of the square staring at it. The chill he felt had made his hands quite numb, and he was afraid to go on.

I must be mad, he thought. *I could have asked my half-brothers to help me find a job; they wouldn't have refused; it was just pride and obstinacy, not wanting to be indebted to them. I could have got a place as a scribe on the city council; the salary wasn't so awful, I could have lived on it, and maybe been promoted in a couple of years. Father was right: I shouldn't have come here. Even if it's true, I'll probably be killed for it, and how can I be sure it's true? He was half delirious when he told me. The letter might have been a forgery, or a joke. Oh God, I should go back now, right now; go home . . .*

But he remained standing where he was. *If I don't go on, I'll never know,* he told himself. *I'll spend the rest of my life wondering who I really am, too much of a coward to find out. And I don't have any real home to go back to, with Father dead.*

He walked slowly across the wide public square.

The great bronze doors were half open, and a troop of guards stood leaning on their spears in the entranceway, watching the marketplace with expressions of unutterable boredom. In a painted frieze above their heads the emperor Constantine, crowned with the imperial diadem and the Christian cross, trod on a dragon. The emperor's stern eyes seemed to fix John accusingly as he approached the gateway, but the guards paid him no attention until he was nearly touching the great door. Then one of them leaned his spear across the path, spat, and drawled, "Business in the palace?"

"Yes," whispered John.

"Got an appointment?"

"No . . . that is —"

"Well, go on into the gatehouse and tell the guards there where you want to go." The spear came back up and the guard took a half-step back. John blinked at him uncertainly, then walked past him through the outer gate. Beyond it was a steep archway with another bronze-sheathed gate at its far end, this one closed. Halfway along the arch on the right was a closed door, also plated with polished bronze. He stopped, glanced back through the half-open outer gate into the marketplace. No one paid any attention. He went on, turned the handle of the door. The hinges creaked as it opened slowly.

The room beyond was rectangular, domed, and magnificently decorated with mosaics. Pictured barbarian captives knelt amid a jumble of exotic cities: "Carthage" John read on one wall, and "Ravenna" on another. In the center of each wall a purple-cloaked king offered his crown to the emperor, triumphant in the central dome. Next to the emperor stood the figure of a woman in a purple cloak and diadem, surrounded by the sacred aura of an empress: her face, masklike with dignity and power, was still the face of a real woman. It was a beautiful face, narrow, pale, long-nosed, the cheeks and chin slightly rounded, the lips firm. The heavy-lidded, intense dark eyes, ignoring the mosaic kings, seemed to stare directly into John's own. He stared back, entranced.

"Your business?" a voice demanded.

John tore his eyes from the mosaic and saw that some more guards were lounging at the other end of the room, and that a crowd of men and women were waiting on a bench below the captive barbarians. One of the guards had spoken; he wore a gold collar around his neck and appeared to be the captain. He now watched John expectantly.

"I . . . I want an audience with the empress," John answered. "A private audience." And all at once he felt sick. He had said it.

"With the *empress*?" asked the soldier incredulously. All his fellows, and all the people waiting in the room, sat up and stared. They were waiting to see the praetorian prefect's secretary about their tax assessment, waiting to see the master of the offices' scribe about a job for a friend, waiting to see the emperor's chamberlain with a notice of evictions on one of the imperial estates; waiting for appointments with any one of a dozen imperial officials and underlings. They stared at the young man in the mud-colored cloak who wanted an audience with the empress.

"Who are you?" asked the captain of the guard. "Do you have an appointment?"

"I have a message for her," John told him, ignoring the first question and trying desperately to keep his voice steady. "About a friend of hers, an old friend, who's dead." Unable to keep his numb hands still, he fidgeted with the silk border of his tunic, miserably aware of how it had faded. It had been his best tunic, green with red-and-white borders, and even when he had first had it dyed black it had looked very distinguished. Now . . .

He took his hands off it. *The tunic wouldn't have impressed anyone here anyway,* he told himself. *If I were a patrician dressed in white and purple, sweeping up to the Bronze Gate in a carriage with a couple of dozen attendants, I could expect the guards to be impressed, but they'll hardly pay attention to anything less, not here, in a city like this. If I look presentable, that should be enough. And I do look presentable.* He straightened his shoulders and tried to ignore the staring eyes.

He's a monk, decided the leader of the guards. *Wearing black, with that nervous fanatical look, all flashing eyes and determination. Oh yes, he's some damned heretical Monophysite monk from one of the eastern provinces, one of the empress's darlings, with news from one of her precious "spiritual fathers" in Egypt or Syria. And if we do anything to hinder him, we're in trouble: she protects her heretics better than the emperor protects his guards. Well, I'll have him shown in. And if he's not one of her monks, her attendants can deal with him.*

He forced himself to smile, though he hated heretics. "Very well, good sir. Dionysios." He beckoned to one of the guards. "Show this . . . gentleman . . . to the household of the most serene Augusta, in the Daphne Palace."

Stunned by the ease of this victory, John followed the guardsman from the gatehouse into the first green silent courtyard of the Great Palace.

He could not remember afterward which way he went — barracks and gardens, chapels and porticoes, domes, columns, and fountains all blended into one overmastering impression of magnificence through which he moved helplessly, like a mouse scuttling through a church. But eventually he found himself in a reception room hung with purple curtains and lit by lamps of pure gold. A boy — no, a man, but smoothly beardless: a eunuch — sat at a writing desk making notes in a book. The guardsman banged the butt of his spear on the mosaic floor and the eunuch looked up. "Yes?" he asked. His calm voice was high-pitched, like a woman's.

"This gentleman wants a private audience with the most pious and holy sovereign Augusta, Theodora," said the guard formally. "He doesn't have an appointment."

The eunuch laid his pen against his lips and surveyed John. "You are?"

"My name is John," he croaked, and tried to clear his throat. "I . . . I have some news for the empress. A death . . . an old friend of hers is dead."

"What 'old friend'?" asked the eunuch politely.

"Diodoros of Bostra — my father. She . . . she knew him a long time ago. I thought —"

"That she would be interested? Did she know him well?"

John swallowed. He reached into his purse and took out the folded letter he had been carrying since his father's death. With shaking hands he gave it to the eunuch, who read it silently. John didn't need to hear the words aloud; he knew them by heart. "To Diodoros of Bostra from Theodora, empress, Augusta, consort of the Sacred Majesty of the emperor Justinian. Yes, my dear, it is me. But if you ever presume to come here to Constantinople, or even claim any knowledge of me back in your hole in Bostra, I swear by God who hears all that it will be the last journey or the last boast you ever make." That was all.

The eunuch frowned at the letter and checked the seal. He read it again. "She does not sound as though she considered him a friend," he said at last, carefully. "I think, sir, it would be better if you did not trouble her. If you like, I will inform her of his death at some appropriate time."

"I have to see her." John clenched and unclenched his numb hands. The eunuch fixed him with a gaze of inflexible and imperturbable inquiry. John swallowed again, faint and sick with fear, and said clearly, "My father told me that she was my mother."

The smooth face changed. It glanced quickly at the letter again, then studied John. Behind him he could hear the guardsman moving, trying to see his face again, to compare it with the other face, the one that had gazed into his from the mosaic.

"Wait here," said the eunuch. Taking the letter, he disappeared behind the purple curtains.

John stood in the purple-draped reception room for what seemed an eternity. He wondered if he should sit down; his legs felt weak and unsteady. But the only seat was the eunuch's place at the writing table, and he was nervous of taking that. He looked around again. The guardsman from the Bronze Gate was standing by the door, watching John with a fixed, fascinated stare. John gave a rather sickly smile back, and the guard looked away quickly.

It could not really have been more than fifteen minutes before the eunuch reappeared. His face was slightly flushed and he seemed short of breath; he gave John a brilliant smile and announced, "She will see you at once!" John wondered if he would faint.

The guardsman struck the floor with the butt of his spear and prepared to go, but the eunuch stopped him with a quick gesture. "You had better wait here for further orders." The guardsman looked alarmed, but John had no time to wonder why. The eunuch took his arm and hurried him through the curtain and down a corridor.

"Have you ever had an audience before?" he asked John.

"No, of course not! She . . . she'll see me? Now?" *It's too fast*, he thought. *I don't have time . . .*

"When you are admitted to the presence, you must take three steps forward and then prostrate yourself," the eunuch instructed him, still hurrying him along. They passed through an anteroom with couches of cedarwood; several richly dressed men, one in white and purple, glared at John as he was rushed through. "Go right down to the floor, like a priest adoring the altar during the sacred mysteries," the eunuch continued, ignoring them. "Keep your arms above your head. The mistress will extend her foot toward you, and you may kiss the instep of her slipper; after that you can stand or kneel, but don't sit down. Don't speak until she gives you permission. And another thing, don't call her 'empress,' call her 'mistress,' like a slave. It's the custom."

"Yes, but . . ." They were at the end of another corridor, and in another room. Everything in it seemed to shine: the paintings on the walls, the gold tiles in the mosaic floor, the gleaming tapestry rugs, the purple silk of the curtains at the far end. A crowd of eunuchs circled him at once, nodding and whispering to each other in their strange high voices. Some of them, he noticed, carried swords; one wore the white and purple of a patrician. There was a smell of incense. John's attendant let go of his arm, nodded to him, then drew back the curtain on the far side of the room. There was a wash of light, diffuse but brilliant sunlight from some hidden window, and at the same time a scent of myrrh. John hesitated, and the patrician eunuch gave him a slight push between the shoulder blades. He staggered to the edge of the curtain and looked into the eyes of the empress Theodora.

Three steps forward, he thought, going calm. *It's almost over now.*

He took the three steps and went down onto the polished marble of the floor. He lay a moment with his cheek pressed against the cold stone, feeling his heart beat twice; then a purple sandal, studded with gold and jewels, appeared before him. He

touched the instep with his lips — the leather was new, soft as
wool — and rose to his knees, looking again into the dark eyes.

The picture in the mosaic had been better than he realized:
kneeling before her, he saw the empress first, then the woman.
The imperial diadem, a band of purple silk stitched with gold
and jewels, completely covered her hair and dripped pearls down
to her shoulders. Her purple cloak was thickly edged with gold
and jewels and fastened with an emerald clasp. Even the long
tunic beneath it seemed to be made half of gold. She half sat,
half reclined on an elevated couch of purple and ivory — an
attitude of indolent grace. But she was leaning forward to study
him, and one thin pale hand held the arm of the couch so
tightly that the manicured fingernails had gone white. She saw
him notice it, and her lips went white too; the eyes glittered as
they moved to the eunuchs who stood motionless behind him,
then back. The letter he had given the eunuch lay on the couch
beside her.

"Who are you?" the empress demanded. Her voice was low,
even, with the sharp accent of Constantinople which pronounced
everything on the teeth.

"My name is John, mistress," he answered. The chilling panic
was gone, and his mind felt clear again. Now that the moment
had come, actual and irreversible, he could speak, could even
remember the eunuch's instructions. Only one catastrophe could
overtake him now, not the thousand of his imaginings. "I am
the son of Diodoros of Bostra. He told me that you would remember him."

She gave a snort. "Why have you come here?"

He knelt a moment staring up at her. The soft light of the
hidden window washed about him; from somewhere beyond her
came the sound of a fountain. "He also told me that you were
my mother," he said at last.

"Did he indeed?" The voice was harsh. "Has he told this
story to many people? And who have you told it to?"

"Mistress, he told it only to me, and only when he was dying
of the plague. If he was raving, do not hold him to blame for

it, but set it down to the disease. As for me, I've told no one. I was afraid to believe it. The only people who have heard it, apart from yourself, are your own attendants."

She sat back on her couch, her eyes still fixed on him. Picking up the folded letter, she tossed it to her attendants. "Destroy this," she ordered; then, to John, "What did you say to the guards at the gate?"

"That I wanted an audience with you, mistress, on a personal matter."

"Did any of them escort you here?" At his nod, she looked back at the eunuchs.

"I commanded him to wait in the reception room for further orders," the attendant said at once.

"Good." The empress smiled.

The patrician eunuch gave an embarrassed cough and added, "There were also, unfortunately, several people waiting on your sublime presence in the second anteroom. They have seen that the young man was admitted in a hurry and are almost certainly trying to discover why."

Theodora shrugged. "They'll ask the guard who he was. And you must tell the guard that the young man was lying, and that I commanded him to be taken away and severely punished for his insolence. Say I told you to flog him, take him out of the city by the private harbor, and put him on a ship that is to leave him in a dungeon in Cherson. Say that I am displeased with the guard and with his captain for admitting someone with such a frivolous insult, and they are both to be posted elsewhere."

John felt the blood draining again from his face and hands. *But the letter was real,* he thought, *it was plain that it was real. And she did seem to know my father. It must be true . . .*

The eunuchs hesitated, watching him; he heard the slight rasp as one of them loosened his sword in its sheath. There was no escape. But he'd known that from the moment he entered the Bronze Gate.

He pressed his fingers against his knees. *Father said that she would have me killed, that she had none of a mother's feelings*

— after all, she abandoned me when I was only a few months old. And she can't want to have her bastard by another man before the emperor's eyes.

But, he thought with a surge of pain, *she might at least admit that it's true. Even if she does have me killed afterward. Simply to have me whipped for insolence and then . . . oh God.*

"Well?" said Theodora. "What are you waiting for? Go deal with the guardsman."

One of the eunuchs bowed. "And do we take the young man out and punish him as you said, mistress?"

She stared a moment, then put her head back and laughed. "Holy God, Holy Almighty, Holy Immortal! What do you think I am, a Fury? No. Leave him here — leave me alone with him. And keep your mouths shut about it; tell no one, not even your friends in the emperor's household. Do you understand? Not one word. A young man was insolent; he has disappeared, never to be seen again. And another young man may do very well in the world, with my help — but no one is to say that he is my son. You may go."

Stunned, disbelieving, John saw that the eunuchs smiled — not formal smiles, but looks of real pleasure and affection. They prostrated themselves to the empress and backed away. "And tell those idiots in the second anteroom to go home!" the empress called after them, and they bowed again, still smiling, and left silently. Behind them, the purple curtain rustled shut.

The empress sat up, swinging her feet under her, and took off the diadem. The hair beneath it was thick and very black. She was younger than he had thought — forty-five at the oldest.

"Stand up, then," she told him, and he did so. She set the diadem down in her lap, holding it between her delicate hands, watching him. "When did your father die?"

"June," he said, and swallowed, not sure how to address her now.

"June. My husband had the plague in June, too, but he survived it, thank heaven. Strange that the two men I've loved most should both be ill at the same time." She watched him another moment, her head tilted slightly to one side, and then she commanded, "Come here."

He came, uncertainly. It seemed improper to stand over her, but he didn't dare sit on the imperial throne. He dropped back to his knees, compromising. One of her hands left the diadem and quickly touched the side of his face, dropped to his shoulder, fell to the heap of gold in her lap. "John," she said, and shook her head.

"It's true, then?" he asked, wanting desperately to hear her say it.

"Oh, yes. If it weren't, would you still be here? I do not tolerate insolence and insults. You are my son. My son!" The quick hand touched his face again, and again leapt away. "Who did your father say your mother was, before he told you the truth?"

"He said I was the son of a whore, a comic actress from the circus, a bearkeeper's daughter he met while he was studying law in Berytus."

She gave a delighted smile. "That's perfectly true. Oh Lord of All, that's exactly like him! How he could lie while still telling the truth! But that's what lawyers are for." She giggled. "But of course he wouldn't have known I'd become any different from that, until I sent him that letter." She stared at him, almost wistfully. "And I suppose he told you that when he wanted to take me back to Bostra with him, I walked out on him and abandoned you?"

"Yes." John hesitated.

The corners of her mouth pulled down, the wistful look hardening. "What else did he tell you?"

John thought of everything he had heard about her, from his father or from his father's friends and acquaintances: conversations overheard or even carried on in front of him, the merciless laughter about "Diodoros' little slut, his bastard's mother." "She hitched up her tunic at a drinking party and walked on her hands down the table, wriggling her buttocks with everything plain as daylight. Shameless bitch, but my God, I envied Diodoros!" "I wouldn't have minded a few shots at that target myself — after all, enough men have hit it!" "Rabbelos was visiting them in Berytus and he made a pass at her; she didn't want him, so she went straight for him and damn near tore his balls off. She joked about it afterward in front of her lover. Diodoros just laughed, but afterward he told Rabbelos that if he tried anything like that again he'd kill him." "I heard that when she left him she took five gold pieces and three dresses of real silk he'd given her, all the jewelry and most of the furniture, but she couldn't manage the baby!" "She told me once" (his father's account, detached and bitter, prompted by some miserable bold question from John) "that she had done a burlesque of Leda and the swan on the public stage in Constantinople, with thousands watching. She said that she scattered grain over herself and put some under the leather girdle round her private parts, which was all she wore. Then they brought in a goose, which proceeded to eat all the grain off her while she writhed about on the ground and cried rape. Then she gave birth to an egg. She swore the crowd loved it. 'They just roared!' she said. Would you really like to have her here? For all the people of Bostra to roar at? I was infatuated enough to want to bring her here. Be glad she never came."

But before the woman who sat in her imperial purple watching him with fierce eyes, these descriptions, which had tormented him for years, seemed fables, senseless and insane. "He said," John told the empress carefully, "that you had meant to give up a wild career when he met you, that you were faithful to him, that he had promised you that he would marry no one as long as he was keeping you, and that you left when you found out that he had perjured himself and was going to marry the daughter of Elthemos."

She raised her eyebrows. "He must have been in an uncommonly honest mood to admit that."

John looked down. The admission had followed the story about the goose, when John had turned and walked away, sickened, his ears ringing with the half-heard chorus that had always followed him: "whore's son, bastard." His father had run after him, saying, "No . . . wait!"

"He was trying to be fair," he said. "But he hated you for leaving him."

She gave a snort, half laughter, half disgust. "Oh, I'd bet my life he hated me for that! He thought we were in love, and because of that I should be ready to go live in some stifling little shack on a backstreet in Bostra, raising his child and hoping that he would spare me the odd hour from his wife! My husband," raising her head, "is worth a dozen of him, even leaving rank aside. *He* wasn't ashamed to marry me."

"He said that he loved you," John whispered, confusedly aware that he was trying to defend his father, the magistrate of Bostra, upright and respectable, with the very fact that had always been the chief blot on his character. "He said that you were the only woman he had really loved — that he'd only married his wife for her family's influence and money."

She smiled, but this time the smile drooped. "He said that to me too. And I believed it. But why he thought the fact that he preferred money and power to love would convince me to come to Bostra with him, I don't know." She rubbed her hand under her eyes. "Well, so he's dead now. Poor Diodoros!" The hand dropped, fingered the jewels on the diadem. "I did love him," she added after a moment. "As much as I'd loved anyone. But in the end I wasn't sorry to leave him, and it wasn't hard." She shook her head, then looked back at John. Once more she lightly touched his face. "It was hard to leave you, though. God, how I cried over you — I think I wept into every bit of sea between Berytus and Constantinople. My poor little baby, left behind! But now, here it is twenty-three years later, and here you are!" She gave him a look of sheer delight. "My own son." Then the eyes narrowed quickly and she asked, "Why did you come here?"

"To . . . to see you."

"Yes, of course, but wanting what? Money? Position? Revenge on someone?"

"I wanted to see you!"

She gave him a cynical look. "And it never even crossed your mind that I might do something for you? Be honest with me if you want my help."

"It crossed my mind," John admitted. "But I couldn't really think about it. I couldn't believe it, you see. I didn't know if it was true, if . . . if you'd be offended at my coming."

"You thought I might have you killed?" she asked, amused.

"You'd threatened my father."

She looked at him thoughtfully. "And perhaps, if I were threatened myself . . . but you haven't tried to threaten me. So, if you thought I might kill you and you hadn't given any thought to advancement, why did you come?"

John bit his lip. "I wanted to see you," he repeated, after a long silence. "With my father dead . . ." He swallowed, meeting the cool eyes again. With dread he realized that he would have to go on, saying things that it hurt even to think, that he had been ashamed to say to anyone else before. He stopped, trying to nerve himself for it. The empress, the diadem in her lap, waited, leaning against the arm of the couch, resting her chin on her hand and watching him. *Giving me rope to hang myself,* he thought.

"A bastard lives by other people's tolerance," he told her at last. "I knew I could have been left to die at birth, or sold or abandoned when you left me. There were plenty who said that that's what should have been done. Instead, my father got me a nursemaid, had me raised in his own house, had me educated almost as well as his legitimate children. But I was . . . no, not hated; even my father's wife doesn't really hate me. Disapproved of. A whore's son shouldn't be treated like the legitimate children of a respectable woman. And dependent, because I had no rights in the house. You don't have rights if you're only alive because of someone's charity. I worked for my father, as his secretary; he kept saying that he would find me a proper job with a salary and some prospects somewhere else, but nothing came of it. He never had the money ready to buy a decent position for me, or if he did, he couldn't spare me just then. I thought — well, that he couldn't be bothered, and that he expected I would fail if he did get me a proper job. He *could* be generous with me, and kind, but usually he was irritable and impatient.

"But when the plague came to Bostra and I caught it, my father dropped everything and looked after me. No one else was willing to — my old nursemaid was sick with it herself, and no one in the house, not even the slaves, thought I was worth the risk of catching it. But my father stayed beside me right through it. "You're my favorite son," he said. "Damn the others; live!" So I did. I was just recovering when he came down with it. I looked after him as well as I could, in my turn — but you've seen the disease, you know how . . . how many have died of it.

"And when he was dying, my father told me about you and showed me your letter. Immortal God, the empress, the sacred Augusta! I had always been . . . despised, because of you. But if you were . . . You see, it changed what I was too, turned me into something completely different from what I had been.

"And when Father died, the tolerance he had given me was gone. My half-brothers would have respected his wishes enough to find me some kind of work, but their mother wanted me out of the house. I felt as though I really had died of the plague. I was like a ghost in that house. I didn't know who I was anymore, or what I should be doing. So I decided to leave Bostra and to come here, to this city, and to see you."

She watched him a moment longer, then sighed and lifted her head. "My poor little boy. So you know it too, what it is to be despised. Never mind." The eyes brightened. "We can make up for it now." The teeth gleamed in a smile. "In a few years you can ride back to visit those half-brothers and their bitch of a mother, wearing the purple stripe on your cloak, with a thousand attendants waiting on you. You can make them *crawl* to you then. Just let them wait!" She brushed her hair away from her eyes, rested her hand on his shoulder, and added, "I'll see to it. Trust me."

He didn't know what to say. She would see to it that one day his half-brothers and their mother would come crawling to him?

He tried to picture that, and his mind recoiled in horror from the image of his father's wife, her stiff, sour, disapproving face crumpled with terror, pawing at his knees. There was no point in going back, and certainly no point in humiliating others and embarrassing himself. But he met the empress's brilliant gaze and nodded.

"I trusted Diodoros to look after you," she told him after another moment. "Knowing him, he must have had you trained in something useful. Tell me about yourself. What were you taught, what would you like to do?"

John blushed and looked down. "He didn't . . . that is, I haven't studied law, as he did. Nor rhetoric, nor philosophy. My half-brothers were learning things like that . . ."

"Damn things like that, then. If there's much of me in you, you wouldn't like them anyway. You said you were your father's secretary: you must know how to write letters, anyway — and maybe some accounting, yes?"

"Accounting and shorthand," he admitted.

"Shorthand! Mother of God, I can get you a job tomorrow! What the hell use is law, compared to shorthand?" She laughed, jumping up from the couch; John gaped at her. "Don't you know how many offices of state there are in this city? And half the high officials have lost their private secretaries in the plague, and can't find anyone sufficiently *confidential* to replace them. Now, where to try . . ."

"I don't know that I want to be a secretary," John said, climbing to his feet in alarm.

"Don't be ridiculous. This won't be like writing letters for your father about dike taxes on the estates or whatever. No, we'll get you a position with someone good, and if you can distinguish yourself with him . . . Let me see." She pushed aside the curtain, opened the door to the corridor, and clapped her hands. Almost immediately one of the eunuchs bowed himself in. It was the patrician — he must be her head chamberlain, the chief of her staff.

"Eusebios," she said, smiling, "have one of the secret rooms prepared for this young man, and find some clothes for him. I have decided that he will be a secretary to some high official of state. Make me a list of which officials need one, what each would want one to do, and if they want something in return for giving someone the job, what they would want. Bring it to me tomorrow morning."

"But . . ." said John helplessly. "I don't know whether —"

"Trust me," said Theodora, giving him a ravishing smile. She picked up the diadem and put it back on her head, tucking her hair under its gleaming shield. "I am dining with my husband this evening; there's no more time to talk now. You will have breakfast with me tomorrow morning, and we'll decide then where you should go."

He stood facing her, afraid again. He had put himself in her hands and he had to trust her, but he felt as though he were driving a chariot at full career and the reins had snapped. She stood there, an image of purple and gold, with the remains of the smile fading from her lips. She was beautiful, she had been pleased that he had come — the most serene Augusta, co-ruler of the world. He must continue to please her. He bowed. "Yes, mistress. But I don't . . . I don't know what my position here is. Please explain it to me. I don't want to do anything stupid."

She gave him a sharp, suspicious look, then, reassured by his confusion, laughed. "Ai! My dear boy, at the moment you have no position here. If it were to become known that you were my son, you never would have a position here. Oh, no one would kill you; at least, I don't *think* anyone would. But I had a daughter — your half-sister. I kept her, my acknowledged bastard. Of course, it's easier with a girl; it's expected that a respectable girl will be kept in. But I not only had to keep her out of sight, to avoid offending the delicate sentiments of the senators, who believe that whores belong in brothels; I had to marry her young to someone of lower rank than I would have liked. So that she wouldn't embarrass us, you see. But she was really too young, and she died in childbirth. If I publicly acknowledged you . . ." She moved a step nearer to him. She was a small woman, he realized. He hadn't noticed it before. "You would be sent out to some estate in the country and kept there quietly, in obscure luxury, and that would be the last anyone heard of you. Because it is embarrassing for an emperor to have his wife's bastards about the place — particularly when he has no children of his own. Do not embarrass us, I warn you." The voice had hardened again. John swallowed and bowed.

"If we keep it quiet who you really are, you should have a position soon," Theodora went on, relenting. "I'll pass off my interest in you by saying that you're some friend's cousin, and see to it that you have everything you need to do well. You can trust my staff here; they can keep secrets. And until we get you a job, you are a secret. You can forget everything that happened before you entered the Bronze Gate. You're a new man now."

"I . . . I left my things on the ship," said John uncertainly.

"Don't go back for them. Remember Orpheus, and never ever look back. 'Heu, noctis propter terminos Orpheus Eurydicen suam vidit, perdidit, occidit . . . quidquid praecipuum trahit perdit, dum videt inferos.' Eusebios!" The eunuch bowed. "Look after the young man."

The eunuch bowed again, and the empress swept from the room.

When the eunuch was showing him to the "secret room," John managed to stir himself enough to ask, "What was it she said in Latin? It was Latin, wasn't it?"

"It was," returned the eunuch, smiling. "She learned the language to gratify the Augustus. She said, 'At the limits of the night Orpheus saw, lost, killed his Eurydice. Whatever distinction one achieves, he loses when he looks below.' Here is Your Honor's room. I am sorry it hasn't been prepared for you; wait and I will fetch the slaves."

Waiting, John sat on the unmade bed. A *secret room*, he thought. It was quite large, lit indirectly by a window high in the wall, and it could be divided in two by means of curtains; icons of Christ and his mother covered one of the walls. One of the secret rooms, the empress had said. How many were there, and who else were they used for?

He put his head in his hands, feeling limp with exhaustion, blind with bewilderment, and, he admitted to himself, very frightened. Yet the thing he hadn't dared to believe was true, and the empress was pleased, was eager to help him, was even urging him to 'achieve distinction'; everything was turning out far better than he had ever imagined. So why did he wish he was back in Bostra?

I mustn't fail, he told himself, trying not to think of Orpheus. *She's the daughter of a man who fed bears for the circus — an actress, a prostitute, and now she's empress. And I'm her son. I must be able to achieve some kind of glory. It would please her, and I must please her.* He clung to the memory of her smile and sat up as the slaves came in to prepare the room.

II

The Chamberlain's Secretary

JOHN SLEPT BADLY, and woke before the first gray light slid from the high window over the roof. Unable to go back to sleep, he lit one of the lamps on the golden lampstand and prowled about the room, not quite daring to leave its confines. The previous night he had noticed a book rack under the icons, and he now examined all its contents. A collection of gospels, a collection of epistles, a psalter; the writings of Basil of Cappadocia, of Severus of Antioch, of John Philoponos — nothing but theological works. He frowned for a moment; then, at last understanding the purpose of the secret room, he smiled. It was well known in Bostra that the empress sympathized with the Monophysite theology — or, as they put it in the eastern provinces like Arabia, was "a lover of piety and orthodoxy." The emperor, however, and most of the population of Constantinople were Dyophysites, adhering to the creed of the council of Chalcedon ("the godless heresy," as the bishop of Bostra called it, "which divides the nature of the Most High, and strips from our Lord's mother her honor as the Mother of God.") "Piety and orthodoxy are proscribed in Constantinople!" the monks shouted in the streets of Bostra. "Pious and holy monks, godly bishops, are imprisoned and executed by orders of the godless emperor

— unless the sacred empress protects them." And this was how the sacred empress protected them: secret rooms, private harbors and ships to take them elsewhere, and a personal staff who knew how to be discreet. And, he realized, palace guards who knew what was going on but turned a blind eye. *So that*, he thought, *was why they let me in so quickly yesterday*.

Immensely cheered by this small victory of understanding, he sat down and read the psalter until the slaves came in to tell him that his bath was ready.

The sun was high before he was summoned to breakfast with the empress. The slaves had given him a bath and a haircut and had brought him fresh clothes. They were extremely rich clothes; the short red tunic had medallions of silk worked with patterns of gold, the shoulders of the long cloak were stiff with brocade, and the fabric of both was shot with silk. Moreover, there were trousers. No one wore these in Arabia, and he felt awkward and self-conscious in them; and the back of his neck, too, felt strangely bare without the headcloth he was used to. But when the summons finally came and he was led down more corridors to a private breakfast room, the empress was delighted.

"Let me look at you!" she said, jumping up from her couch. Her hair was loose, damp from her bath, and the purple cloak hung abandoned on her couch. In her embroidered tunic she looked lithe, young, and even smaller than she had the day before, and she was smiling. The breakfast room opened onto a garden where a fountain played beneath a fig tree and birds sang in the bright sunshine.

"Lord of All!" said Theodora when she had walked right round him, admiring the effect. "I've done all right for children! You look much finer than that bitch Passara's son. I wish I could introduce you to her! He's an ugly hulking brute, her boy, with a skull as thick as a dinner pot, but *she* thinks he'll be the next emperor. We'll see about that! But sit down here, next to me, and have some breakfast."

He sat down awkwardly on the couch; she sat on the other end, curling her legs up. The golden table was set with white bread, sesame cakes, goat's milk, and fresh figs. Theodora helped herself to a fig, munching it with small bites and evident enjoyment.

"Who's Passara?" asked John nervously.

She giggled. "Wife of my husband's cousin, Germanus. You've heard of Germanus? He's a complete bore, and his wife is the worst snob in Constantinople. Anicia Passara, descendant of emperors! She fancied herself as an emperor's wife too, back when old Justin wore the purple. But it's *my* husband who's emperor, while Germanus does what he's told. She can't stand me and I can't stand her. Let's forget about her. Go on, help yourself!"

John helped himself to a fig and reached for a cup; one of the slave girls at once jumped over and fetched it for him, filled it with goat's milk, and bowed as she put it into his hand. John stared at it uncertainly. He was far more accustomed to filling cups himself than to having them fetched for him.

"I've thought what to tell people about you," Theodora said, finishing her fig and rinsing her fingers in a silver basin of rosewater. One of the slaves held out a towel for her to dry them. "I'll say that my father, Akakios, had a respectable half-brother who settled in Berytus, and that you're his grandson." She picked up a sesame cake and bit into it.

"What was your uncle's name?" John asked cautiously.

She shrugged, her mouth full of sesame cake. "How about Diodoros? He didn't exist, my love. I don't have *any* respectable relations, except those I've acquired since my marriage. But no one except my sister will know that it isn't true, and Komito will go along with the story if I tell her the reason for it." A giggle. "Komito will be able to tell you the whole history of our respectable Uncle Diodoros by the time you meet her." She shoved the rest of the sesame cake into her mouth and dusted off her fingers.

John took a piece of white bread. *My Aunt Komito,* he thought; *my grandfather, Akakios. He must have been the bear-keeper. Strange to have a whole new set of relations.* "I'd like to meet her," he told Theodora.

She smiled, holding up a finger for him to wait until she had finished chewing. "In due time," she said, after swallowing noisily. "First we have to get you a position. Though I'll send Komito a note about you this morning." She snapped her fingers and the slaves jumped to attention. "Run and find Eusebios," she told one of them. "Ask him to bring that list I requested yesterday."

In a few minutes the eunuch appeared, carrying a scroll of parchment. He prostrated himself to Theodora and kissed her foot. John flushed, realizing that he had forgotten to do this. But she'd jumped up so quickly . . . Well, at least she didn't seem to resent the omission.

Theodora took the scroll and unrolled it, studying the list of names. "Theodatos — God no, all you'd learn from him would be embezzling. Addaios — no, he's a probing, inquisitive creature, and belongs too much to my husband. Tch!" She paused, looking up at John and cocking her head to one side. "What sort of official would you like to work for?"

John licked his lips. "I . . . I would like to go into the army. The cavalry. I learned how to ride, and some archery, while I was in Bostra . . ."

Theodora laughed. "A real Persian education — how to ride, how to shoot, and how to tell the truth. Do all young men want to be dashing cavalry officers? Every male under thirty I've spoken to recently seems to have a burning ambition to jump onto horses and flourish swords. Well, I suppose it looks impressive. And if you can do well in it, it's a royal road to advancement. Eusebios," she said, turning to the eunuch, "Belisarius' secretary caught the plague, didn't he? Did he die?"

John sat up straight, his face going hot. Belisarius! The greatest general alive, the conqueror of the Vandals and the Goths, the terror of the Persians!

But the eunuch was shaking his head. "No, mistress. I believe the fellow had a particularly mild case and recovered."

"A pity. The sour, two-faced, boot-licking back-biter would be better dead. I don't know why Belisarius tolerates him. I suppose he doesn't know what the man says about him behind his back.

He's easily deceived — his wife certainly finds him so." She giggled. "Still, I suppose it's for the best. Belisarius *says* he can conquer Italy with just his private attendants and his own money, but I'll believe that when I see it done, and being associated with a lost war never helped anyone. We'll find someone else." She studied the scroll again.

John slumped, keenly disappointed. He remembered with a stab of pain the horse his father had given him: a beautiful light gray Arab mare, a gift from the tribe of Ghassan in Jabiya. He had raised her from a foal, trained her, ridden her every chance he had. She had still been in her prime when he rode her to Berytus and sold her to buy his passage to Constantinople. He remembered the armies of the duke of Arabia passing through Bostra on the way north, armor gleaming, the light on their spears like a host of stars, their horses dancing along the crowded streets. Off to fight the Persians and their allies, to defend the empire. The rest of the world bought and sold and hoped for their success; they acted, put their courage to the test, and either secured their fellow citizens by a victory or died. That was glory. Not sitting in an office in Constantinople making notes in shorthand.

"Here!" said Theodora sharply. She thrust the scroll at him, pointing out one name.

"*Prae.s.cub.* Narses," John read. "Asks only for efficiency." He had no idea what the abbreviation meant; the name, Narses, was foreign. Persian, he thought, or maybe just Armenian. It wasn't familiar.

"I thought Narses had found someone already," Theodora said, turning to Eusebios.

Eusebios coughed. "The man he found proved unequal to the work, and was given a place elsewhere."

"Yes, I suppose it's a very demanding job. What does your secretary do, Eusebios?"

"Oh, there's no real comparison between my job and Narses'," said the eunuch. "I serve Your Serenity; he serves the whole empire."

"It would be ideal," said Theodora. She took the scroll back from John and gazed at it, her eyes narrowed. "We'll try it," she said after a moment. "If he thinks you can't do the job and turns you down, we can try someone else." She handed the scroll back to Eusebios.

"Who's Narses?" John asked helplessly.

Both the empress and her attendant gave him looks of astonishment.

"I didn't understand the abbreviation," he added defensively.

"*Praepositus sacri cubiculi,*" Eusebios supplied at once. "Head chamberlain. My own title, in fact, but in the emperor's household, and with additional responsibilities."

"I would have thought you'd have heard of him," Theodora put in, "but I suppose that in a place like Bostra, nobody knows who's running the empire. I'd be very pleased if you could keep a job with Narses. You'd be under Peter's eye too, and that's important. I'll send you round as soon as you're officially here."

"Oh." John bit his tongue to keep himself silent. *Why does she consult me,* he wondered, *if she's already made up her mind that I'm to draft letters for the emperor's chief eunuch? Not much of a job for a man. I suppose in a year's time I'll have learned to give people slimy smiles and ask for bribes. Sit on your balls and get rich — work for a eunuch.* "Who's Peter?" he asked unhappily.

"My husband." The empress's chamberlain offered her a notebook of appointments to look at, and she glanced through it.

"Your husband? But I thought —"

She looked back up, smiling. "You thought his name was Justinian Augustus? Augustus is a title, and he called himself Justinian when his uncle, the emperor Justin, adopted him as his heir. His *name* is Petrus Sabbatius. But don't you try to call him that. Nobody calls him that now but me."

He stared at Theodora. Her dark head was bent over another paper that Eusebios was showing her; pearl earrings glowed against her neck. She smiled at her chamberlain and asked some question, then nodded. The eunuch smiled back and took out a pen case, asked one of the slaves to fetch parchment: some petition was about to be answered, or some piece of business decided. John was suddenly overwhelmed, ashamed of his resentment. Here he was, Diodoros' bastard from Bostra, sitting at breakfast with the empress, watching her settle affairs of state. He was ignorant and unskilled; he might prove an embarrassment to her. He should be grateful that she was willing to help at all. He must do his utmost to succeed in whatever job she found for him, to show himself worthy of her attention.

He finished his breakfast, trying to listen to what the empress said, trying to relish his position. But again he had an image of himself as a charioteer, the reins gone, clinging helplessly to the fragile shell of his chariot as the horses took it wherever they wanted to go.

It was in fact a week later that he was taken to an interview with the emperor's head chamberlain. The intervening time was spent in suspending his presence on a tissue of lies. John found himself transformed: his nationality, parentage, education, and history were all changed. The empress considered changing his name, but decided that Johns were common enough that she didn't need to bother. But he was required to grow a beard, to put off any chance acquaintances. "And it's fashionable now anyway," she told him. "None of the young men in Constantinople shave anymore; they're all trying to look like Belisarius." He was to be legitimate, the son of a municipal scribe in Berytus; he had lost both parents to the plague and appealed to his second half-cousin, whom the family had previously ignored; she had received him at her summer palace in Herion; he had "arrived from Herion" six days after his real arrival, and was duly given a guest room, with less confidential slaves attending it, in another part of the palace. On the next morning, Eusebios collected him early and escorted him to another building within the Great Palace.

"Your new position has been explained to Narses," the eunuch told him as they walked down a colonnade of variegated marble through a garden of spent roses and sweet-scented thyme. "And the sacred Augusta has written him a letter, saying that it would gratify her if he would consider you for the job. But I'm afraid that that does not really settle the matter. Narses does have control over his own office, and he does insist on a high degree of efficiency. Since his own secretary died he has taken two young men on trial, one of them on the mistress's recommendation, but both proved inadequate for the job and were found work elsewhere. It's a pity you don't know Latin; that would help."

John nodded wordlessly. The web of deceit had left him disoriented and depressed, and after a week of observing Theodora and her staff, he felt more out of his depth than ever. Though she preserved an appearance of indolent luxury, she was no mere lady of fashion: she was a real and effective ruler, second only to the emperor himself. Governors in every corner of the empire wrote to her, soliciting her support or referring complex administrative problems to her sacred and august decision; her responses were immediate, cunning, and decisive. She received ambassadors, gave audiences, issued directives to the offices of state. She controlled vast estates in Asia and Cappadocia, and she used the income from these to maintain an army of spies and agents. Over her own servants her authority was supreme; even the emperor couldn't enter her palace without her permission. *It would have been better,* John thought, *if she had just acknowledged me and sent me off to the "obscure luxury" of some country estate. God knows, I never thought of becoming rich and powerful before I came here. I came because I wanted to know who I really was — and instead of finding out, I'm being turned into a complete sham. And I don't have a chance at this job. What do I know that prepares me for being private secretary to a minister of state? A man as powerful as this Narses seems to be can have his pick of learned and eloquent secretaries. He won't want me, and she, the Augusta, will be disappointed. Still, they scarcely expect me to get the job; they won't be that disappointed.*

He held his head up and tried to look confident as Eusebios led him into the section of the Great Palace called the Magnaura.

The head chamberlain's office was in the middle of this: on the side of it that faced the Bronze Gate were the labyrinthine offices of the imperial administration; on the other, inner side were the audience rooms and private quarters of the emperor and his household. All business from the outside world to the emperor had to pass through it. Theodora's palaces, however, lay on the inner side, and Eusebios showed John through half the emperor's house before arriving at the office of his chamberlain. After the lavish magnificence of the private apartments — the lampstands like gold trees with jeweled birds sitting in them; the hangings of purple silk and the tapestry carpets strewn over the floor; the priceless collection of statues and paintings — the chamberlain's office seemed plain. Its walls were painted with scenes from the *Iliad,* and the floor was decorated with an abstract mosaic in red and green. In one corner hung an icon of the Mother of God; at a desk under this a man in a purple-striped white cloak sat writing. Two scribes sat at a writing table near the door, copying something into a book.

Eusebios dropped the purple curtain that screened off the emperor's quarters, and at its rustle they all looked up.

"My dear Eusebios!" said the man in the patrician's cloak. He jumped up, came round his desk, and took Eusebios' hand warmly. He was a small, frail-looking eunuch, with a high sweet voice like a child's. He had fine dark hair frosted with white, dark eyes, and might have been any age between thirty and sixty — it was impossible to look at the smooth face and say more precisely than that. The unnatural voice and looks made John uncomfortable: he had never liked freaks. "And you must be John of Berytus," Narses went on, smiling at him. "Thank you for coming so early — I'm afraid most of the morning is already packed with business. If anyone needs another helper, it's me."

One of the scribes sniggered. He and his fellow were not eunuchs, John was relieved to note, but simply well-dressed young men of about his own age. They reminded him a bit of his half-brothers.

"The most serene Augusta informed me that you are her second half-cousin," Narses told him. "She said that you had some training as a secretary and could take shorthand — which is, of course, very useful, and uncommon in men applying for this position. Do you have any languages?"

"I don't know Latin," John said uncomfortably.

Narses smiled politely. "Perhaps it would be more helpful if you told me what you *do* know. If you're from Berytus, perhaps you're acquainted with Syriac?"

"A little," John replied. He had had to use the language on his father's business trips to Berytus. "And a little Aramaic and Persian. And Arabic."

Narses' eyebrows rose. "Persian?"

"Yes, my father used to do some business across the frontier — back before the war, of course! I used to handle the letters for him. That's why I learned the Aramaic as well." He began to feel nervous. Bostra was a trading city, and his father, like most of his fellows, had invested in the caravans. He had also indulged in smuggling silk and spices, but only since the war with Persia had begun. At that time the legal supplies had dried up and with them the caravans that had been Bostra's lifeblood, and the illicit trade was almost essential for the city's survival. But it was dangerous to admit any knowledge of it, and more than that, it was not something that a scribe's son from Berytus would have any experience of.

Narses paused, and then asked in Persian, "Was it the silk trade, young man?"

"Yes, Excellency," John replied in the same language, after gaping for a moment. "Only until the war, of course. We ship silk from Berytus; the caravans come from Bostra and from Damascus, and my father wished to supplement his earnings with a little investment in the trade." The Persian phrases were ones he had used often in correspondence with his father's partners, and they slipped off his tongue easily.

"I am surprised at your knowing Arabic, however," Narses went on, still in Persian. His accent was different from that of the Persians John had met in Bostra. "Was that for business purposes as well?"

John blushed. "Yes. One had sometimes to . . . to make arrangements with the king at Jabiya, you see." Arabic was his native tongue, the language he had learned from his nurse and spoken at home more often than Greek.

"With the king?" Narses asked, faintly puzzled.

"Al-Harith ibn-Jabalah of Ghassan," John explained. "The king of the Saracens of Jabiya."

"The phylarch Arethas!" Narses said, resuming Greek in a tone of amusement. "I wouldn't call him king here."

John bowed an apology. "You have to call him king there."

"I am sure of it. Well, a secretary who knows Persian and Arabic would undoubtedly be useful. Latin you can always learn here — there are plenty of men to teach it to you — but Persian is harder to find. And you can write it?"

"Not shorthand," John said hurriedly. "I can only do short-hand in Greek."

Narses smiled. "I believe there is no form of shorthand for Persian. I can't write the language at all, though I learned to speak it before I learned Greek. It's a nuisance sending to the master of the offices for a translator every time I want to send a letter. Well, well. What else can you do? I suppose you were trained in rhetoric at the school in Berytus?"

John blushed again. "No, Illustrious. My father was not so ambitious for me as that. I went to work for him when I finished elementary school at fifteen. I had a little private tuition in letters, but apart from that . . ." He made a dismissive gesture. *Apart from that*, he thought, *I'm scarcely better educated than a domestic slave. Perhaps I should pretend that I was trained as my brothers were: two or three years of rhetoric, and then law. But I don't know either subject, and could never keep up the pretense.*

"Apart from that?" asked Narses, still smiling.

"Apart from that, I learned only what a secretary learns. Shorthand, filing, a few languages, accounting."

Narses raised his eyebrows and gave a long sigh. He turned to Eusebios, who stood by the purple curtain smiling with satisfaction. "Convey my deepest regards to the sacred Augusta, and express to her my gratitude for her interest in the matter. I will be delighted to take on her kinsman, starting with a trial period of a week, and I have hopes that we will work well together. And thank you for coming over so early in the morning."

Eusebios bowed. "It's always a pleasure to see you. The mistress, foreseeing your decision, has invited you and her kinsman to dine with her this evening. Shall we see you then?"

"I am honored by the invitation, and delighted to accept it."

The two eunuchs shook hands again, and Eusebios withdrew behind the purple curtain, to go back to the household of the empress.

A *trial period of a week*, John thought. *What does that mean? He can't very well refuse me a trial period, since the empress asked him to take me on — but Eusebios looked so pleased! Was he just impressed by the Persian? And what does Narses mean? I can't tell whether he's pleased or annoyed with me.*

Narses gave him an encouraging smile. "Now, let me show you where you'll work," he said.

On the outer side of the large office was a smaller one, similarly decorated, where John and Narses found an overworked scribe struggling with a massive appointment book. He was older than the two in the inner office, a grizzled functionary long experienced in the palace. In an adjoining anteroom, a crowd was waiting. Narses took the appointment book, checked it, and called two names; two fine gentlemen came running, each followed by two or three attendants. "Admit the next names in the book when my door opens," Narses told John. "Anastasios can explain some of your other duties."

The overworked scribe looked at John gloomily. *Another young idiot*, he thought, studying the brocade on John's cloak. *When, oh when, will His Illustriousness manage to get a real secretary? We've been doing all the work between the two of us, and I don't know about him, but I've had enough of it. There was the first one, who spent all his time composing elegiac couplets — he was bad enough, but at least he didn't try to interfere with things. The last one, God rot him, ruined a year's filing in an afternoon with his 'rationalization.' I wonder what this one will try?* "I don't suppose," he asked John, hoping against hope, "that you know how to keep files?"

"Of course." John flipped through the massive book. "But I don't understand any of the abbreviations in here; you'll have to explain them."

By lunchtime John was exhausted and the scribe, Anastasios, was smiling.

The appointment book was divided into two columns: those who wanted an audience with the emperor and those who just wanted an appointment with the chamberlain. Certain categories of person were allowed in directly without an appointment; others were allowed to jump the queue to a greater or lesser extent. ("Or, if you must," Anastasios told John gloomily, "you can let them bribe you and put them in first.") Beside each name in the book was an abbreviation directing the reader to the file containing that person's business. The filing system was enormous, cumbrous, and complex, and spread out over the whole of the sacred offices that ran the empire. *I shall never understand it,* John thought, frightened.

He'll have mastered it inside a week, Anastasios thought happily. *He knows the principles of it, he knows what it's for, he's actually done a job of work. Thank God! I just pray he doesn't get too many ideas into his head — but he seems cautious enough now. Afraid, even — not used to being close to the emperor, I suppose. Thank God! Now I can sort out the damage caused by his predecessor.*

John looked again at the appointment book, wincing at the names. Patricians and bishops, senators and consuls, envoys from great cities, governors of provinces, ministers of state jostled one another in the chamberlain's anteroom. "Is it like this every day?" he asked Anastasios.

"Oh, most days it's worse," the scribe replied. "But the master hasn't been seeing as many people as usual; he's still recovering from his illness. When it comes to making new appointments, bear that in mind and try to head them off."

The master was not Narses, but the emperor. "Head them off?" asked John helplessly. "How? If a senator wants to see the Augustus, how is a chamberlain's secretary going to stop him?"

"Oh, there are ways," Anastasios said comfortably. "You'll learn."

It was almost a relief when Narses wanted John to take down a letter in shorthand, even though one of the letters he wrote out that morning had to do with the enormous sum of money promised to a barbarian king (the treasury had failed to release it) and the other with an appeal against a criminal sentence by a governor. Writing letters and transcribing them from shorthand was work he was used to, and the two scribes in the inner office did all the copying.

At around noon the stream of appointments dried up, and finally Narses came to the door of his office and found no one waiting. He gave one of his polite, ambiguous smiles. "You can go to lunch now," he told John — then stood aside as the two scribes pushed past him.

"What a morning!" one of them exclaimed cheerfully. "My thumbs ache!"

The other grinned at John. "We're going out to a tavern in the market," he said. "They do wonderful sausages there, and the wine's not bad either. Care to join us?"

"Ummm . . . ," John replied, looking uncertainly from Narses to Anastasios. Neither seemed to think the offer unusual; neither offered either to join them or to go elsewhere. Feeling lost, he nodded at the scribes. "Yes. Thank you." He slipped the pen he had been using back in its case and used the case as a paperweight for the half-transcribed letter, and the three young men set off for the tavern.

Narses went back into his office. Anastasios sat down at his desk and took out a lump of bread and a flask of watered wine.

His eye fell on the letter, and he pulled it over and looked at it. Nice, neat, clean book hand, properly laid out and correctly spelled. The wax tablets beside it were covered with the unintelligible scrawl of shorthand. He approved of it — a wonderful, complex system of abbreviations, so erudite and useful. He flipped the tablets over and saw on the back that the new secretary had made notes about the filing system. He studied them a moment, smiling an increasingly satisfied smile, then glanced at the door to the adjoining office. Taking the tablets, he rose and went over.

The emperor's chamberlain was lying prostrate before the icon of the Mother of God, praying. Anastasios had expected this and coughed quietly to attract his superior's attention, and the slight figure in the white and purple cloak sat up, rubbed his forehead, and gave the clerk a look of mild inquiry. Anastasios lifted the wax tablets.

"He's already working out my filing system," he said. "You're keeping him, aren't you?"

Narses smiled. "I think so, don't you?" And when Anastasios nodded, he added, "He knows Persian."

"Does he, now? How did you find him?"

"It seems he is a relation of the sacred Augusta, who has resolved to further his career."

"A relation of the mistress! Well! I wouldn't have guessed it."

"A distant relation." Narses smiled his unreadable smile. "For my part, I think there is a resemblance. Quite a strong resemblance, really. And I think perhaps something of her intelligence as well, though he hasn't realized it yet." The smile softened and became almost human. "I'd watch out, if I were you. The young man may yet have ideas about how things should be done."

"I hope not," Anastasios said fervently, but he smiled back. He bowed and slipped out the door to eat his lunch.

The tavern chosen by John's companions was a superior establishment, the sort of place he had only visited before when his father had wanted him to make notes of a business meeting. He had never had much money, and the heavy purse Theodora had given him felt strange at his belt. The two scribes seemed at home in the luxury, however, and asked the host for "the usual" with boisterous familiarity. In moments John found himself sitting at a marble-topped table by a window with a wine cup in his hand. A mixing bowl of water and a pitcher of wine stood on the table, and a serving girl set down a dish of sausages, a plate of bread, and a bowl of some vegetable indistinguishable under a rich sauce.

"How strong do you like it?" asked one of the scribes, picking up the pitcher. He was a tall, athletic-looking young man, brown-haired, blue-eyed, and self-consciously handsome.

"Not very strong, not at lunch," John replied quickly. "I can't work properly if I have it more than half and half."

The young man shrugged, but obediently poured only half the wine into the bowl. His fellow scooped the mixture into the three cups, then, smiling sheepishly, topped his own cup up with the wine. "I don't like it weak," he explained. He was of average height, plump, and dark. "My friend's name is Diomedes, by the way, and I'm Sergius — but everyone calls me Bacchus. Like the blessed martyrs, you see." He chortled.

John looked at him blankly.

"Sergius and Bacchus, you know! The church near the hippodrome."

"I . . . I'm sorry," John said, embarrassed. "I'm afraid I don't really know Constantinople yet. I only arrived yesterday."

The other two snorted. "That's something!" Diomedes said wistfully. "Arrive in Constantinople one day and get a job like yours the next! What it is to have relations!"

"They did say you were the mistress's second cousin, didn't they?" Sergius, or Bacchus, put in. "How much did your most illustrious cousin pay for the job, do you know?" He helped himself to some bread and sausage.

"No," said John, horrified by the thought of what she might have paid for it. "I don't know."

"I'll bet it was at least five hundred," Sergius said authoritatively. "My father paid two hundred fifty for my job, and yours must be worth at least twice that."

"At least," agreed Diomedes, nodding.

Five hundred, two hundred fifty what? wondered John. *Gold solidi? Lord of All, that's as much as all the officials in Bostra put together make! It can't be* solidi. "What does your father do?" he asked cautiously, helping himself to bread.

"He's a banker." Sergius scooped up some sausage with his bread and continued to talk through his mouthful. "Demetrianos — they give him the nickname Golden Thumb, but that's a joke; he came by his money fairly. He was very reasonable about my job; he said that two hundred fifty pieces of gold isn't that much if you think of it as an investment that pays a handsome return."

"Trouble is, it doesn't," said Diomedes. "His Illustriousness doesn't mind earning a bit on the side selling positions like ours, but he doesn't like *us* taking bribes."

"He gets really annoyed if you try to sell access to the master, or alter a document when you're copying it," Sergius explained, "even if it's really just a trivial alteration, a few hundred *solidi* more to a friend. He goes all cold and formal and reads you a lecture, and if you do it too much, you're out. But all eunuchs are mean."

"And we should warn you." Diomedes leaned over the table and rolled his eyes. "He always, *always*, finds you out. He has eyes in the back of his head."

"He just works like a damned soul," Sergius corrected. "He comes into the office before it's light and stays after it's dark, and hardly stops in between."

"Is that what he's doing now? Working?" asked John.

"No, at lunchtime he prays for a bit first, and then works," said Diomedes.

"Devout, he is." Sergius pronounced the term with distaste. "And not entirely orthodox — though I suppose, you being from the East, I shouldn't say that. You're none of you orthodox

south of Antioch. I don't mind. Who gives a damn about the
nature of God?"

Almost everyone, thought John in surprise, but he only asked,
"What about Anastasios?"

"Oh, he just sits in his office mumbling dry bread and admiring
his files," said Sergius with contempt. "He's nobody. He
was the other side of the corridor, in the offices, for years and
years as a junior clerk. He's somebody's bastard, and was bought
the junior position, then abandoned. He could never afford to
buy himself promotion. It was His Illustriousness who moved
him to the imperial household. He paid the fee himself, just so
as to have someone who could do files. He's pleased with you
because you don't know rhetoric; he'd much rather have shorthand." The voice had taken an edge of malice, and Sergius
stopped suddenly and got himself more to eat. *Should have kept
off the subject,* he thought. *I've got to keep the fellow sweet if
I want any advantage from him — can't let him see I think he's
an ignorant peasant.*

John looked at the dish of vegetables, noting the malice and
guessing its reason, unsurprised by it. He wondered whether the
vegetable was cabbage or wild greens. He dipped some bread in
tentatively and tried, and still wasn't sure.

"His Illustriousness is mad on work," Diomedes said, and
laughed.

Sergius sniggered. "Well, what else can he get out of life?
What was it you were saying to each other in Persian, by the
way? I hope we're not stuck with copying letters in that gib-
berish!"

"He just asked me about the silk trade," John said. "Where
is he from? Armenia?"

"Persian Armenia," Sergius replied at once. "But he's been
in the imperial household a long time — bought up as a slave
when he was still a boy, and God alone knows how old he is
now. Older than he looks. The master trusts him with his life,
and they say the mistress likes him as well."

"What's she like?" asked Diomedes. "The good thing about

working for His Illustriousness is that you meet absolutely everybody who's anybody — but I've never met the Augusta. They say, though, that she's the best patron in the world, and God help her enemies!"

John could think of no answer at once. Everything to do with the empress left him in a morass of confused and conflicting emotions. He took a mouthful of sausage, though his mouth was dry, and chewed it to disguise his hesitation. "She's been very kind to me," he managed to reply at last.

"I'll say she has!" agreed Sergius. "She got you a marvelous job." *And,* he added privately, *made you a gentleman. I bet you didn't wear a cloak like that when you were a town clerk's boy in Berytus.*

"I didn't know she had any relations in Berytus," said Diomedes. "They say that her family was Paphlagonian, but that she was born here in the city."

Sergius tittered. "In, ah . . . let's say, circumstances best left obscure. Like all her life before her marriage. I heard a story yesterday . . ." He stopped, looking at John sharply.

John felt his face go hot. "She has been very kind to me," he repeated angrily. "My side of the family was quite content not to know her before her marriage, but as soon as she was Augusta, they wanted favors. She cut them off cold. I fully expected that she would do the same to me, but she's treated me far more graciously than I could have dared to hope, and I am grateful." *And I'm telling lies to defend her,* he thought gloomily. He shook himself, aware of the others' assessing, wary gaze. They would be careful what they said about her before him in the future, he knew; they would be afraid that he might complain to her about them. "Maybe we'd better get back to work," he added, shamefaced. "Here, let me pay for the lunch."

It wasn't until he returned to Theodora's palace an hour before sunset that John remembered that he had been invited to dinner with the empress that evening. Dinners with the Augusta, he already knew, were something quite different from breakfasts.

She generally shared them with her husband and at least half a dozen others, and he had not yet been admitted to one: she had wanted to protect him from any dangerous attention before the dew on his new-spun position had dried. It was now considered to have done so, and he entered his allotted room to find yet another magnificent set of clothes laid out and a slave waiting to prepare him for the feast. He groaned, suppressing a strong desire to turn and run.

Oh God, he thought, submitting. *Hasn't there been enough for one day? It should have been enough, just finding the job, trying to work out what to do, trying to know what to think about Narses and Sergius and Diomedes — how am I supposed to meet all these other people now? Who else will be there? The emperor? Oh God, I hope not. She'll be there, of course. Expecting — what?*

"Is it customary to give something to the Augusta when you're invited to dinner with her?" he asked the slave abruptly.

The slave, a middle-aged man resigned to the vagaries of guests, paused for an instant in whetting his razor. "It is not expected," he said primly; then he added, as he stropped the blade on a piece of damp leather, "Though a gift of flowers might be received as a gracious gesture."

"Can you get me some flowers, then?" Desperately, John felt in his purse and dug out a handful of coppers. "Roses, if there are any."

The slave smiled and collected the coins. A very satisfactory amount, he noted. "If Your Eminence wishes. Could Your Honor just sit still a moment while I trim your hair? That's right . . ."

Fifteen minutes later, changed, trimmed, and carrying a chaplet of late roses, John was escorted to the banquet.

"Do you know who else will be there?" he asked the slave, miserably nervous.

"I am sorry, sir, but Her Serenity's arrangements for other guests are not my affair," the slave answered smoothly. "I believe the master will be present, but apart from that, I can't say."

John groaned. He looked down at the wreath of flowers. The fragile pink-white petals of the roses were circled with blue asters. Flowers from her palace, and bought with her money, he thought, disheartened. "What should I do?" he asked the slave. "Do I make the prostration and then give her the flowers, or give her the flowers first? And do I bow to the master first, and then the mistress, or the other way round? Oh Lord, you should have got a bouquet, not a wreath; she won't be able to wear it."

"Why shouldn't she wear it?" the slave replied imperturbably.

"She'll be wearing the diadem."

The slave gave a superior smile. "Not at a private dinner. I will bring you to the door of the dining hall, where the master and mistress will be standing to receive their guests. When I stop, you should make the prostration to the master and mistress together. Don't kiss their feet — it's an informal occasion. Get up at once, and hand the mistress the flowers, with a few suitable words if you wish. The dining room staff will then show you to your place. Very well?"

"Thank you," said John, and tipped him.

The palace staff had arranged it so the imperial couple did not have to stand in the doorway greeting guests for very long. John arrived in the courtyard to find another couple of guests just rising from their prostrations, and Narses waiting politely a few steps back to make his. The eunuch gave him the already familiar ambiguous smile and nodded, then, as the first arrivals entered the dining room, himself went down before the imperial majesty. When he was rising, the emperor took his hand and helped him up. Justinian the Augustus was a man of average height and stocky build, with a round, high-colored face drawn and yellowed by his recent illness. Worry lines circled his mouth and crossed his brow, though he smiled warmly at Narses. John tried not to stare. *My mother's husband,* he told himself, and the thought went through him like a shock of ice. He saw his father standing beside the door of the dining room of the house in Bostra, welcoming guests, with his wife at his side — the sour-faced, eminently respectable Agatha. Whenever John had come to one of the parties, she had given him a look as though she'd eaten unripe grapes. "Why do you have to bring the bastard in to our dinner parties?" she would demand of her husband afterward. "By all means have him looked after, but it's not proper having him here with our own children."

Narses had entered the next room. John went down onto the clean-swept tiles of the porch, careful not to crush the flowers, and rose again. The emperor gave him a slightly mystified look; the empress smiled.

Say a few suitable words, John thought, again feeling sick with fear. "Mistress," he managed, "please accept these as a token of my gratitude — a very feeble token." He offered her the flowers.

She gave a smile that was sweet with surprise and took them. "This is Narses' new secretary," she told her husband. "A distant cousin of mine — John of Berytus."

"A cousin of yours?" asked the emperor in a surprised tone. "I didn't know you had any family in Berytus."

"Oh, our father's half-brother Diodoros went there before we were born," said a voice behind John. He glanced back quickly, and found a court lady looking at him with cheerful curiosity. Her gold cloak was fringed with a widow's black. She was taller than Theodora, and older, but the resemblance was plain. *My Aunt Komito*, he thought.

"We never had much to do with them until this one appealed to Theodora," Komito went on. "Well, at least you look well enough." She gave a teasing smile and swept down and up in a rather perfunctory bow before going to Theodora and kissing her on the cheek.

"Oh," said the emperor, looking at his wife a shade doubtfully. "And you got him a job with Narses?"

"He can do shorthand," said Theodora. She took her husband's arm and turned to the dining room. "Can't he, Narses?" Komito shot John a sideways look and another smile before slipping past him; John followed her.

In the blaze of gold and glass that surrounded them, the

eunuch was nodding. "The young man has some experience as a secretary. It is a very useful qualification."

The emperor smiled, taking a place on the top couch with his wife beside him. John found himself escorted to the couch on the left, which he shared with Narses; Komito and the first arrivals were on the emperor's right. These last were a depressed, nervous-looking man of about forty and a woman, clearly his wife, who seemed a bit older.

"When did you appeal to my wife then, young man?" the emperor asked John in a friendly tone. Slaves hurried behind him, pouring chilled white wine into goblets of red and green glass, sprinkling the mosaic floor with flower petals and fragrant saffron. The couches and table were of ivory and gold, the dinner service set with jewels.

"This summer, master," John replied. His voice was not faint, as he'd feared it might be. "She received me at Herion last month, and called me to Constantinople when she'd found this job for me. I started today."

Justinian nodded and sipped his wine. "And do you like it?"

"It seems a very demanding job, master. I hardly know yet whether I'll be able to manage it at all."

This brought a smile. "I hope you do well in it," said the emperor. "What was your experience with the work?"

"I was a municipal scribe in Berytus, like my father," John responded humbly. "It is far more trivial work than serving a minister of state, I know. But some of the methods are the same."

"I expect he will manage," said Narses.

"Good, good," said the emperor. Then, turning back to his wife, he added, "I am surprised at your turning up relatives in Berytus, though!"

"They never wanted to know me before I was Augusta," replied Theodora. "I never wanted to know them afterward." She slipped the garland of roses onto her head and curled her legs up onto the couch.

"They were respectable," put in Komito. "*Dreadfully* respectable." She pulled a sober, disapproving face. "When Theodora was in Berytus, she tried calling on them and asking for a loan — it was after that time she was dropped in Alexandria, and she had no money to buy her passage home. They shut the door in her face."

"So I had nothing more to do with them," said Theodora, "until John here wrote this summer, and said that his parents were both dead of the plague last year and he was trying to pay off their debts — on a municipal scribe's salary. I thought, 'Poor boy — it wasn't *his* fault. He wasn't even born at the time.'"

"I am grateful to the Augusta," John found himself saying, looking at her. "Deeply grateful."

"Why were your parents in debt?" asked Justinian with interest. The slaves offered him a dish of fish eggs, which he waved away down the table.

"My father had invested in the silk trade," John replied immediately. "He lost a lot of money when the war broke out with Persia."

The emperor sighed, and frowned unhappily. "It has been a bad time, the past five years; a very bad time. War with Persia, revolts in Africa, and that unspeakable disease sent to punish us for our sins. I think God is angry with us."

The man across from John stirred. "We conquered Italy," he said.

Komito gave him a look of contempt. "It doesn't look conquered at the moment. Or why are you so keen to go conquer it again? I heard yesterday that the Goths have retaken Naples."

The man winced. He was lean, bearded, and had the remains of what must have been dashing, military good looks. "I did conquer Italy," he insisted querulously. "If we'd been able to keep the troops there just a few more months —"

"The troops were there for too long as it was," snapped Justinian. "I was wrong not to make peace earlier. If I'd recalled you and your men six months before I did, the great king wouldn't have taken Antioch. Or do you think Ravenna matters more?"

The man looked down and said nothing. *Is he Belisarius?* John wondered incredulously. *"I conquered Italy"* — *he must be. Mother of God, him? That sad-looking man? Count Belisarius, conquerer of the the Vandals and the Goths?*

"Antioch mattered more," said Theodora, leaning on her husband's shoulder.

Belisarius started nervously and gave her an anxious look. She smiled at him. She had taken a spoonful of fish eggs, and nibbled it before continuing. "What did we need Ravenna for? The empire had effectively managed without Italy for a hundred years. But Asia, the East, Egypt — those are part of us. We shouldn't have committed all those troops to reconquer the West. Not with the great king Chosroes looking for a war in the East."

"I agreed to an eternal peace with Chosroes," said Justinian unhappily. "How was I to know it would only last seven years? And the West used to be a part of us."

"The West ought to be a part of us!" cried Belisarius, picking his head up again. "We call ourselves Romans, but for fifty years we left Rome sitting in the hands of one tribe of barbarians while another set of savages divided the Western Empire among themselves. We were bound to restore it to Roman rule. And the Goths invited the war. They were the ones who murdered their lawful queen, your ally, with total disregard for your wishes, Augustus. And they were punished; God gave us victory over them. I conquered them, as you know; their king is your prisoner at this moment."

"Their ex-king," said Komito with a snort. "This fellow Totila who just took Naples with his Gothic army has rather more claim to the title than Justinian's prisoner."

"We do not need the West," Theodora repeated. "Yes, we should reclaim it; I would be the first to agree to that. But not at the cost of putting the whole East at risk! We do not have the troops or the money to hold both, not now."

Belisarius again started unhappily. *He is afraid of Theodora,* John realized with astonishment.

On the couch beside her husband, Belisarius' wife waved the argument aside. "This present war with Persia is almost settled. Chosroes has been asking for negotiations all summer."

The count nodded, heartened by his wife's support. "If you let me go back to Italy, I'll subdue it for you within a year," he told the emperor.

"Chosroes signals for negotiations with one hand and sacks cities with the other," said Justinian bitterly. "I'll believe the Persian war is over when I have his seal on a peace treaty, not before. I cannot spare you from the East."

Komito snorted again. "I don't think much of Italy, as you know, but you could spare him; you've already spared him. He didn't manage much on the Persian front, and you've replaced him with Martinus."

Belisarius winced again.

"That was only a temporary measure," said Theodora, smiling graciously. "Required by some . . . domestic problems in Constantinople. I am sure the most esteemed count could manage better on the Persian front in the future."

"The command was divided before," Belisarius put in eagerly. "A divided command never produces a victory." He shot a venomous look across the table at Narses.

The eunuch sighed. "I agree, most excellent Count. And I am sure that your allied troops were unreliable . . ."

"Those Saracens think of nothing but plunder!" agreed Belisarius vehemently.

"No one is ever unfailingly victorious in war," the emperor told Komito reprovingly. "I don't expect it. Even your lamented husband had his failures. I am confident of your abilities, Count."

Belisarius bowed his head. "Let me go back to Italy, then," he pleaded. "I can't bear it, seeing all my work there undone. I know I can reconquer it, Augustus."

"I would far prefer it if you could give the Persians one really stinging defeat," Justinian said in exasperation. "That would make Chosroes negotiate in earnest. Why is it always Italy,

Italy? My wife is right: our first concern must necessarily be to protect our own territories, not to conquer new ones."

"Italy *is* our territory. We conquered it and we're responsible for it," said Belisarius. "The Italians supported us in our first conquest, and now we've betrayed them to the Goths! The Goths have taken Naples and most of the southern cities, and they'll try for Rome itself. If we tolerate that, we're not Romans — we're nothing more than what the Goths call us: perfidious Greeks."

Justinian shook his head. "Yes, yes, yes, I know, I used to say that myself . . . but we let the Persians take Antioch. *Antioch!* A city that was certainly mine when I claimed the purple, and the third city of the empire. And the Persians have destroyed it, burned it to the ground; all its inhabitants are slaves in a foreign land. It should never have happened!"

"It wouldn't have happened if the count had obeyed your orders," said Komito. "You ordered him to make peace with the Goths and come back at once when the war broke out with Persia. And what did he do?"

"He defeated the Goths and brought their king and his treasure back to Constantinople," said Belisarius' wife, glaring at Komito.

"Defeated the Goths!" exclaimed Komito, and made a rude noise. "They don't look defeated to me!"

"No one foresaw that they would recover and elect a new king so quickly," said Narses soothingly.

"*You* would have foreseen it, if the count had been content to keep you with him and take your advice," Komito told him sharply. "You were sent out there to give him the benefit of it."

Narses sighed again. "The most excellent Belisarius was, however, quite correct. Divided commands are not efficient. That particular one ended disastrously, and His Sacred Majesty very wisely recalled me." The slaves came round, offering a dish of snails raised on milk, and the eunuch took one. "And that story is, fortunately, over and done with."

John looked at Narses with surprise. This frail court eunuch had been sent to Italy to share a command with Belisarius? It seemed incredible.

"Unlike the conquest of Italy," said Komito. "Just why is the count so eager to get back there? How much land does he own there? Or does it have anything to do with the fact that the Goths offered to make him Augustus of the West?"

The invincible Count Belisarius went white.

"Komito!" said Theodora in angry reproach.

Justinian shook his head.

"If you will think a moment," Belisarius' wife said sharply, "you will see that my husband is the one person who cannot be suspected of wanting that title. He was offered it on a platter and he refused it. 'Never while Justinian Augustus lives will I take such a title,' he said."

"Quite so, quite so," said the emperor. "I do not doubt your loyalty, Count. But I wish you were as eager to defend the East as you are to recover Italy."

"I've sunk years of my life into Italy," said the count earnestly. "There are others who can command in the East — Theoktistos, Germanus, Marcellus, Isaac the Armenian — all capable generals. And Martinus, of course. But I'm the one who's known in Italy; if I go there, I can achieve something that no one else could. Let me go, Augustus. I've told you, I'll take just my own retainers; it doesn't need to cost you anything, and no troops need to be moved from the East. We can't let the Goths take Rome away from us."

Justinian hesitated, biting on his lip, then shrugged. "We will have to consider this at some other time," he said finally. "My wife's dinner party is not the best place to settle affairs of state." He turned to Theodora and added, "I'm sorry for the quarrel, my dear."

"Never mind," she replied. "My sister started it."

Komito shrugged. "I'm sorry if I offended anyone. But you all know me: I've always had to speak my mind."

"Such a mind as it is," said Theodora maliciously; but after a moment she smiled at her sister and raised her cup to her.

Belisarius slumped unhappily back onto his couch, but his

wife leaned forward and began to ask about the appointment of some governor of Africa.

John remembered that dinner to the end of his life. After the argument there was no further discussion of political issues, but even the gossip was frightening — high officials appointed, found to be corrupt; alliances broken or mended; great fortunes made and lost. And all the while the slaves kept bringing round dishes of exotic foods, half of which he couldn't even recognize, and filling his glass with one priceless vintage after another. He said nothing more. His head was spinning with the wine and the confusion of the long day, and he wanted only to go to bed. To go home to bed. Home. But where was that? The guest room in this labyrinthine palace where even the slaves condescended to him?

It has to be that, he told himself sharply, *because the room you're thinking of, that little, plain, upstairs room in Bostra, isn't yours. And you're not who you thought you were. That woman at the head of the table, whom the great Belisarius is afraid of, is your mother. So you must belong here.*

But at last the final rich dish had been brought round, the slaves poured out the last of the wine, and Theodora yawned. At once Belisarius' wife, Antonina, rose, smiling sweetly. "It has been a lovely dinner," she said. "And thank you, my dear Augusta, for asking us."

"My pleasure," said Theodora. "I hope the little disagreement earlier hasn't spoiled your evening?"

No, no, of course not; no, it was useful to have such a frank discussion of the issues, and Antonina was grateful. She took her leave, and her husband prostrated himself to the emperor and followed her. Narses and Komito followed them, and John, after a glance at the empress, went with them. One of the slaves met him at the door and escorted him back to his guest room, where he collapsed, exhausted, on the bed.

In the dining room the emperor straightened his purple cloak and rubbed his face. "I wish you could make your sister hold her tongue," he told Theodora. "I have perfectly good reasons to be annoyed with Belisarius, but disloyalty isn't one of them."

"Komito is still jealous of her husband's reputation," Theodora soothed. "She's always sniping at the count; you know her. It doesn't mean anything."

"The count is still very nervous about that charge," Justinian replied. "Lord of All, he was jumping every time you looked at him. I know why you did what you did this summer, my dearest, and it was prudent — but you frightened him badly. And I don't want him to believe that I still suspect him. It might make him actually disloyal."

Theodora ran a finger down the side of her husband's face. "It's virtually certain, you know, that he did say what he was accused of having said this summer. That if you were dead of the plague, he wouldn't submit to anyone I or the household chose to replace you. Whether his ideas about the succession went further than that, I never have found out."

" 'Never while Justinian Augustus lives' would he call himself Augustus," Justinian quoted, smiling at her. "I know, nothing about what he'd do if Justinian Augustus were dead. Oh, what you did was necessary, and I don't quarrel with it. You had to relieve him of his command and attach his retainers to different units of the royal guard, or he would have made himself emperor if I had died. But I haven't died, and he won't try to kill me or usurp the purple. He's served us well in the past, and we don't have another general who can match him. We've given him back his retainers and offered him his command. Why doesn't he want it?"

Theodora laughed. "Antonina. She doesn't want to go back to the Persian frontier, but she'll go to Italy. He doesn't trust her alone in Constantinople. He's simply a jealous husband." She kissed her husband.

"Jealous," the emperor said, thoughtfully. "And for that he's willing to risk our suspicion and give up command of a war. It's a terrible thing, love. But I suppose I could be jealous like that too, and you've never given me any reason."

"And I never will."

The emperor kissed his wife again, then sat up, sighed deeply, and rose.

"You're not going back to work!" Theodora protested, holding the edge of his cloak.

"I promised to meet with Bishop Menas tonight to discuss some theological statements from Rome," Justinian returned.

"Oh, my love, you shouldn't stay up tonight. You're still tired from your illness; you should rest."

Justinian gave her a look of profound affection and took her hands, detaching them gently from his cloak. "Rest wasn't what you had in mind."

She smiled up into his face. "No."

"Well, I promise I will go to bed in two hours — if you want to be there. But I must meet with the bishop first. We must decide this question, settle this dreadful controversy. Goodnight, my life."

Alone in the dining room, Theodora sat on the couch with her knees pulled up under her purple cloak. She took the crown of flowers from her head and set it before her; the roses were wilting. *Like me, like our empire,* she thought. *Spent roses, last roses; the plant knows it's not summer any longer. Belisarius shouldn't have gone to Italy in the first place. We should have hoarded our strength for the winter, not squandered it trying to recover an empire that's lost. But when we were young, anything seemed possible.*

Belisarius certainly shouldn't go back there now. Only I don't trust him in the East, even if my husband does. And I promised Antonina to help him. I owe her a favor.

She touched the roses with a gentle finger, remembering suddenly that John had given them to her. She had not expected him to bring her anything. How sweet he had looked, offering them — like a lover who expects to be refused. "I am deeply grateful."

Diodoros of Bostra was a misty face now, a passion half forgotten, but the child she had borne him was real. *My son,* she thought, with a stab of real pain, *if only you were my husband's.*

III

ḋORSES

JOHN FOUND HIMSELF the subject of enormous interest when he arrived at work the next morning, late and flustered after oversleeping.

"You had dinner with the Augusta last night!" exclaimed Sergius the moment he came in. "What was it like?"

Narses, at his desk as though he had never left it, raised a hand in a gesture precisely between command and supplication and said, "Esteemed Sergius, there will be time for such discussions later. Kindly let us continue our work."

Sergius subsided. John bowed awkwardly to the chamberlain. "I am sorry I'm late," he said nervously. He had had frantic visions of being replaced because of lateness on the second day of the job, and had run all the way from Theodora's palace.

Narses gave him the polite smile. "There is no reason to apologize; I expected it. If you would collect your tablets from the outer office, I need you to take a letter."

John bowed again. "Yes, Illustrious."

The second morning was as busy as the first had been, but again the stream of appointments dried up around noon, and the two scribes finally emerged from the inner office and again invited John to join them at lunch in their favorite tavern.

John hesitated. He disliked Sergius and was not fond of Diomedes, and found both another element of confusion in a world that was bewildering enough without them. *On the other hand,* he told himself, *they are colleagues and I should stay on good terms with them. And they know so much more about the court than I do; perhaps they can explain a few things.* So again he smiled and agreed to come.

"So you had dinner with the mistress and master last night!" said Sergius when they were back at the usual table in the tavern. "Can mere mortals talk to you? What was it like?"

John smiled feebly. "Confusing," he said after a moment. "And very magnificent."

"Who else was there?" asked Diomedes.

"His Illustriousness, of course. And the Augusta's sister, Komito — I think she was curious to meet me. The grandson of her respectable half-uncle, you see. And Count Belisarius and his wife."

"Belisarius was there?" Sergius asked delightedly. "Really? He's out of disgrace, then? Lord, that's news."

"Was he in disgrace?" asked John. The news did not surprise him, he found; it had been plain that something like that must have happened. But he'd had no time to think about it, no time to sort things out.

"Don't you hear about *anything* in Berytus?" asked Diomedes. "When the master was ill, Belisarius was suspected of trying to succeed him. Your patroness found him out. He lost his command and all his retainers, and half his estates were confiscated. He went about the city as a private citizen, looking over his shoulder all the time in case . . . well, you know. So he's back in favor now? That'll be because of his wife. She's a friend of your patroness."

"She did your patroness a favor," Sergius supplied. "Got rid of the Cappadocian for her."

John stared at him, trying to keep the mixture of revulsion and fascination he felt from showing. "The Cappadocian? You mean the praetorian prefect?"

"That's right," Sergius agreed happily. "Your namesake, John the Cappadocian, cleverest and worst man of the age." *Here's a story I can tell our little clerk from Berytus,* he decided. *All it shows is how powerful his cousin is; he'll like that. And maybe he'll let slip a few indiscretions about what Their Sacred Majesties were saying last night, if he's got the sense to realize what's useful.* "Your sacred cousin loathed him with a passion, so they say, but the master thought the world of him because he could always produce whatever cash was needed. But your cousin got him in the end. Didn't you hear about that?"

"I heard in B . . . Berytus that he was deposed from office two years ago, for treason," John said cautiously. John the Cappadocian, formerly praetorian prefect or chief minister, had been hated throughout the East. He had outdone his predecessors in ruthlessness, introducing ferocious economies in the imperial posts and bureaucracy and violently extorting from the citizens every tax anyone had ever heard of and a few they hadn't.

"Caught in the act!" Sergius said with relish. "Your patroness suspected that he wasn't as honest as he could be, but she could never catch him out, because he was so infernally cunning that no one could ever pin anything on him. So the Augusta went to her friend Antonina, the wife of our most successful and glorious general Belisarius. And Antonina went to visit the Cappadocian's daughter. She was a young girl, discreet and modest, and her father loved her dearly" — spoken in a mincing, sarcastic tone. "But Antonina stroked and flattered her, and became her dear friend and adviser. 'O my dear little girl,' says Antonina one day, 'how ungrateful the emperor is to my husband; how cruelly he uses us; how I wish we could do something about it!' 'Well, why don't you?' asks the girl, all agoggle. 'How can we?' says Antonina. 'We have the support of the army, it's quite true, but alas! not the money, and no connections in the sacred offices. Though if your father were to help us, why, we might do anything!' So of course the girl went running and told all this to her father. And her father had a good look at the bait, and bit. Ambitious, her father was.

"They arranged it all, Antonina and the Cappadocian, arranged it through the girl. Antonina and the Cappadocian were to meet at Rufiniae, to settle who was to be emperor when they'd got the master out of the way. Belisarius himself didn't know anything about it till it was over. When it was all set up, Antonina took the mistress and His Illustriousness and one or two others in on it. The mistress arranged it that when Antonina and the Cappadocian met, His Illustriousness was listening behind a wall, together with Marcellus, the captain of the bodyguard, and a force of soldiers. The Cappadocian came straight out with a scheme for getting himself into the purple, and the others arrested him."

"But the master was still fond of him," Diomedes put in, in disgust. "He said that John had served them well, for all his dishonesty, and it would be ungrateful to give him the punishment that everyone knew he deserved. So all that happened was that they made him a priest — very much against his will! — and packed him off to Cyzicus. They didn't even confiscate his property. He was living like a tetrarch on his hoard — until last summer. Then, when the master was ill, your cousin the Augusta got him."

"The bishop of Cyzicus was murdered, and the Cappadocian had quarreled with him," said Sergius. "Investigators were sent from Constantinople. They arrested the unwilling priest and questioned him. He'd been praetorian prefect, he'd been consul, he'd ridden in the curial chair and had games given in his name, and he still wore the white cloak with the purple stripe, but they had him flogged till he screamed for mercy. He didn't confess to having a part in the murder, though, so it was decided to imprison him. They shipped him off like a common thief on a ship all the way to Egypt. They wouldn't let him take his embezzled gold with him; he had to beg for food in every port of call, like any other criminal. 'A crust of bread for the praetorian prefect John, for Christ's charity!' He's now in prison in Antinoopolis — though I suppose the master will have him released before too long." He took a big swallow of wine, and added, "There was some talk of getting His Illustriousness to succeed the Cappadocian. But it was decided he wasn't ruthless enough."

John said nothing. He had no doubt that John the Cappadocian had deserved to be punished, but the story revolted him. He remembered again how Belisarius had looked at Theodora; thought of Diomedes' description of the count as a private citizen, "looking over his shoulder all the time in case . . ." In case the empress had decided to have him murdered, John realized.

But is it true? he asked himself. *I believed that my mother was a common whore, and discovered that she was an empress. Why should I believe that she is a corrupt tyrant? These two men are malicious and dishonest — and much further away from the court than I am myself. They've heard things, but they don't know. I'm in a position to know — if I can only understand what I see! I must learn; I must understand what is happening around me. Otherwise I might just as well be a . . . a lampstand, moved about wherever anyone pleases. Without any power, any will, any . . . self.*

John looked back at the two scribes, who were stuffing their mouths with bread and sausage. Sergius gave a wide smile, bread between his teeth. *He wants information from me,* John thought. *Well, why not? I want it from him; it's a fair trade. But —*

And in imagination he drew a circle about himself, as he had drawn it sometimes in the dust in Bostra, playing as a child: Here I stand, John the Bastard, and no one can touch me. It had been a defense, and he knew it — an attempt to transform a hated isolation into a magic power. But it had been partly successful. He had no power over where he was or what he did, but within his charmed circle he could control what he thought, could assess coolly the demands of a hostile world, and ultimately, bargain his compliance with them.

He smiled back at his colleagues and began his campaign to understand.

·   ·   ·

It took months before he felt even a faint stirring of confidence in his new life. The facts he faced were as numberless as the stars of heaven or the files of the sacred offices. The names and faces of the emperor's ministers and the empress's staff; the correct form of address for a court notary, a silentiary, a scribe from the praetorian prefecture. The streets of the city of Constantinople, and where the chief ministers had houses; the churches, and the problems of who was orthodox and who wasn't. Imperial policies and governors for Africa, Italy, Egypt; the names and rulers of the assorted barbarian tribes across the Danube, and which of them was being paid to be hostile to which. Whom to let into the inner office without an appointment and whom to delay; what sort of wine to buy for Sergius' dinner parties and where to get it; what sort of talk would be most pleasing to the Serene Augusta Theodora. Every small victory of understanding was at once swamped by the army of things unknown; things learned were almost inconsequential in the ocean of ignorance.

The week's trial period elapsed without comment, and he didn't even remember until some days after it had gone that it was over, and by then there didn't seem any point to being pleased about it. He was moved from the guest room in Theodora's palace to a suite of rooms in an elegant house in the city's "Second Region." He discovered to his surprise that he did not have to pay for this. The citizens of Constantinople were required to accept billetings from the palace, and many of them, like the merchant who owned the house John lived in, kept a set of rooms especially for this purpose.

"I am sorry; I would rather have you in the palace," the empress told him when she informed him of this. "But it is customary for junior officials to be accommodated in the city, and to make an exception in your case would raise suspicions." She laughed at his confusion. "People would say we were having a love affair. Never mind, I can still invite you here."

She gave him three slaves to look after his rooms for him — a middle-aged couple and their fourteen-year-old son — and she apologized for not giving him more people: "But you wouldn't have the space for them where you are, and to get you a bigger house would look suspicious just now." He had never had so much space, such luxury, all to himself before, and didn't know how to answer. He was not sure what the slaves thought about the move: both the man and the woman treated him with elaborate and completely impenetrable respect. He eventually decided that the woman was genuinely pleased to have the independence of a house, unsupervised, outside the palace, but the man was resentful, and felt that he had lost status in the change from being the empress's slave to being John's. There was no doubt about the boy, Jakobos — he relished the freedom of the house and the streets of the great city, and he admired John enormously. He made his master uncomfortable.

John discovered that his job carried a salary of a pound of gold, or seventy-two *solidi*, a year; Sergius, Diomedes, and Anastasios each earned fifty *solidi*. It was more money than he had ever dreamed of earning, and there didn't seem to be much to spend it on. The empress was generous. Besides clothing and slaves, she gave him furniture for his house, wine for his cellars, plate for his table, and she pressed money into his hand every time he saw her, commanding him to "go buy yourself something." She liked giving presents; she loved receiving them. Even trivial gifts — flowers, a pair of white doves, a jar of perfume — made her eyes light up and brought exclamations of delight.

She invited him to a private breakfast at least once a week, and occasionally asked him to other meetings as well. One holiday he sailed with her around the city to "enjoy the sea air." The imperial barge had panels of cedarwood and railings of citron, and the oars were gilded; musicians in the stern played on the flute, the kithara, and the cymbals. Theodora stood under a canopy of purple silk on the prow, tossing crumbs to the seagulls to watch them wheel on their flashing wings. The sails were dyed purple. About halfway through the cruise, John found himself laughing at them.

"What?" asked Theodora, throwing a piece of bread at him instead of at the gulls.

"Purple sails," he replied, shaking his head. It seemed absurd, to go dyeing common, workaday things like sails with the precious imperial purple.

She understood at once and grinned. "But how else will everyone know who I am? Look at them all!" She waved an arm toward the city shining on the hill over the sparkling water. "They can all look out and say, 'There goes the empress Theodora on her barge!' It gives them a bit of excitement. And I like purple."

On another occasion he rode with her in her gilded carriage to a monastery outside the city, where she humbly offered gifts to the patron saint. Her entourage was anything but humble — two troops of palace guards and most of her staff, the eunuchs riding white mules or horses, the ladies-in-waiting and their serving girls in enameled coaches. The people of Constantinople cheered as she went past: "Thrice august! Sovereign lady! Reign forever!" She sat stiff in her purple cloak and diadem, her eyes glittering with pleasure. "I love it when they acclaim me," she confided. "I could listen to it forever."

One day she took him to a cellar beneath the throne room of the Magnaura Palace. On a dais in the center was a couch of ivory and gold. Theodora sat on it, swinging her feet over the opposite arm so that her slippers flapped in the air. She grinned. "Stand right here next to me," she told John, and when he had done so, she gave a nod to her attendant, Eusebios. The eunuch smiled and pulled a lever on one side of the room. There was a hushing sound, then a burst of music, and the throne began to rise into the air. John started; the empress caught his arm and held him on the dais, giggling with pleased excitement. The ceiling opened and the couch rose into the throne room above. The jeweled birds on the golden lampstands were singing with the clear, unnatural tones of a hydraulic organ, the golden lions that flanked the dais were lashing their hinged tails and growling, but the room was empty. After a moment there was silence; then the throne gave another lurch and sank back through the floor.

"Isn't it wonderful?" asked Theodora delightedly. "The second

Theodosius had it built. It's called 'the throne of Solomon.' Of course, to get the full effect you have to be waiting in the throne room; they light all the lamps and burn incense, then the curtain goes up and I or Peter arises out of the depths like Aphrodite from the sea, and everyone falls flat on his face. You should see the effect it has on barbarian ambassadors! I love it."

She quite simply loved being an empress, John decided in one of his moments of reflective assessment. All the protocols and regalia of it delighted her, and she was reluctant to omit one fragment of the ceremony that surrounded her. It was the delight of the comic actress given her juiciest role ever. And more than that, it was the poor girl's delight in being fabulously rich, the insulted and abused prostitute's glee at being the fount of all power and honor: she reveled in the contrast, as well as in the thing itself. And she was always aware of the contrast. She loved to be flattered, but was never deceived.

She told him very little about herself, however. One rare revelation came when she casually informed him that he was an uncle.

"Well, I told you I had a daughter who'd died in childbirth," she said impatiently when he goggled at this news. "Her baby didn't die, and he's fourteen now. You may meet him sometime, but I think it's best we don't tell him who you are until he's older. His name's Anastasios, and he's going to marry Belisarius' daughter." She smiled at the thought. "That will make *him* rich and powerful."

"What was my sister's name?" John asked after a silence.

The smile vanished, and her face suddenly looked harsh, older. "Erato," she said flatly. The name meant "lovely," and John tried to picture the girl, fourteen years dead. There was another moment of silence, then Theodora added in a painfully gentle voice, "And she was lovely, too." She stared at John for a moment, a stare almost impersonal in its intensity, then went on. "She was four years older than you. Her father was a charioteer called Constantine. He was a champion charioteer back then, won the gold belt five years running; I was madly in love with him, though I always knew he was worthless. He liked the idea of my having a baby, so I had one. He abandoned us about a month before she was born — I was no fun to sleep with anymore. Mother of God, I thought we would both die, me and the baby! Single girls shouldn't have children; you just destroy yourself trying to look after them. I swore I'd never have another child. When I knew I was carrying you, I went to the market in Berytus and got one of my usual remedies. But I couldn't bear to take it."

"My father never said anything about your having a daughter."

"He scarcely knew. I'd left her in Constantinople with Komito. I was kept for a while, you see, by a fellow called Hekebolos of Tyre, a rich senator. He was appointed to govern the Libyan Pentapolis and wanted to take me with him; he promised me a decent settlement, and gave me twenty-five *solidi* on the spot. I gave the money to Komito to look after my daughter for me and off we sailed. I thought it would be just for a year or so, Hekebolos' term of office. But when we got to Cyrene, he met a girl he wanted more. He offered to set us up in the same house, and when I refused to go along, he turned me out without a penny. I sold most of my clothes and got as far as Alexandria. After . . . after that, I met the bishop of Alexandria, who took pity on me and gave me some money to pay my passage home. "Honest money," he told me. I meant to stay honest, but the ship was delayed in Berytus, where I happened to meet a handsome, shy young Arabian law student and forgot about going home and earning my living honestly — for a while." She touched John's hair, very lightly; he held his breath. "I told your father I had a daughter in Constantinople, but I don't think he really believed in her. She was too far away. Poor little Erato. She was only thirteen when I made her marry."

On another occasion, he sat near her in the imperial box at the hippodrome on a feast day, watching the races. The imperial couple supported the blue team, and all their attendants cheered accordingly. Theodora leaned out of the box and gave a whoop of glee when the Blues won; the emperor applauded and nodded.

"My stepfather worked for the Blues," she explained at breakfast the next day. "My father worked for the Greens; he died when I was five years old. My mother married my father's assistant at once, so as to have someone to provide for us. She thought he'd get my father's job, but the controllers of the faction gave it to another man in exchange for a present. My mother decided to appeal to the faction's supporters over the heads of the men who ran it, and she sent us out into the hippodrome between the races to beseech the crowd. You know, poor little penniless orphaned children, the sort of thing that usually goes down well. She told us what to do and how important it was, and we went out there, me and Komito and Anastasia — she's dead now, Anastasia — wearing garlands and lifting our little hands in supplication. And the Greens just laughed at us. I can still remember it; I thought it must be my fault, and cried so much I was sick. Luckily, the Blues felt sorry for us, and their bearkeeper had died recently, so they took us on. I've supported them ever since. Do you get races like that in Bostra?"

She left the subject quickly, John noted. She must hate to remember it. "Not like that," he answered. "They can't afford to have that many chariots there. And the factions — they're not like that." He couldn't find words to say more precisely what he meant by "like that," and suspected that it was wiser not to try. People had cheered for the Blues or the Greens — mostly the Greens — in Bostra, but the factions had been rudimentary there. In Constantinople the Blues sat in the tier of seats to the right of the imperial box, the Greens on the left. The enrolled men of both factions dressed in tunics with tight sleeves and loose shoulders, which billowed when they waved their arms to urge on their team's horses. They shaved above their foreheads and let their beards grow, and they looked like a tribe of some fantastic barbarians let loose in the middle of the city. They howled if their team lost, screamed with joy if it won, attacked any members of the other faction they happened to find in the streets afterward, and chanted elaborate acclamations to the emperor through trained heralds. Their official duties included the upkeep of the city's parks and fountains, but their functions at the hippodrome had long overshadowed this role. Already John knew that they were dangerous, and at all costs must be avoided at night. Particularly the Blues, who relied on the imperial favor to escape punishment.

"We only had chariot races at the great festivals," John told the empress. "The rest of the time we just had horse races. They weren't organized by the factions but by private citizens who thought their horses were faster than their neighbors'. I rode in one once."

Theodora gave him a delighted smile. "And did you win?"

"I came second. Out of nine, so it wasn't bad. And the horse wasn't in her prime yet; she would have won if she'd been a year older." He paused, thinking of the horse again, with regret, then went on. "They have a different breed of horses here, don't they? Bigger and heavier than the Arabian horses, but not as fast."

"Not as fast? Oh, the horses here are the best in the world! Didn't you see that team yesterday, Kalligonos' team — it went like the wind!"

"I suppose Arabian horses wouldn't be good for pulling chariots," John conceded. "Nor for the really heavy cavalry; they're light animals. But they're faster than the Thracian and Asian breeds everyone here seems to like, and more enduring too."

Theodora gave him an amused look and disparaged horses that couldn't pull chariots. A week later, however, he was given an invitation to see her that evening after work. She was in her audience room, wearing the diadem and surrounded by her confidential staff, when he arrived. "I have a surprise for you," she told him, smiling with pleasure. And she jumped off her couch, and with her throng of silk-clad, bejeweled attendants trailing behind her, she led him through the palace, past a barracks, and to one of the royal stables; the serving girls picked up their long skirts and wrinkled their noses fastidiously at the dung heaps. In front of the stables, held by a groom, was a mare of the purest Arabian breed. She was a dun, one of the rarest and most beautiful colors among Arabians: a silver-gray that was almost white, but darkened to black at nose, feet, and tail. Her nostrils flared red and she eyed the crowd with deep suspicion. She was saddled and bridled with a harness that would have done credit to a Saracen prince. John stared at the empress, suspecting, not daring to believe it.

"She's yours, if you want her," said the empress.

After he had looked at the horse, and touched the horse, and ridden the horse about the barracks, and confirmed arrangements for its stabling, and at last, reluctantly, parted from the horse to return with the empress to the palace, Theodora said, "Now I see that you haven't liked a single other thing I've given you."

John went red. "That's not true. I am very grateful for everything you've given me."

The empress gave him a rueful, undeceived smile. "Not the way you're grateful for that horse."

He was silent for a moment, then confessed, "I haven't been certain what to do with wealth, rank, or power. I have to learn how to appreciate your other gifts. But I know what to do with horses."

The smile lightened. "Ah, I'd forgotten your Persian education. I expect to hear, then, whether your new mount really is faster than the Thracian breeds. What will you call her?"

"With Your Majesty's permission, I will call her 'queen.' 'Maleka,' in Arabic. You would honor the gift more by giving it a name so greatly honored by yourself."

She stopped and stared at him a moment, and he smiled at her. She laughed. "Oh, you're learning!" she told him. "You learn quickly!"

It was after this that he began to feel that he had indeed learned something about how to live in Constantinople. It was early February, and the job no longer weighed on him: he felt confident of his ability to manage any of the routine work, and knew where to turn for help in various sorts of emergency. He had allowed Sergius to cultivate him, but the scribe's gossip was increasingly losing its power either to inform or to perplex: John often found that he knew the truth of something Sergius had learned only in a distorted rumor. When he had the horse he began, finally, to enjoy himself.

The evening after he received the mare, he was in the hippodrome, testing her on the smooth, packed earth where the chariots had spun the week before. The oblong track was crowded, although it was a bitterly cold winter evening, and already growing dark. There were few places to gallop a horse in the crowded city, and large numbers wanting to. But the hippodrome, wide enough for six chariots to race abreast, could contain them all. Young gentlemen of the city, practicing equitation, trotted among the imperial guardsmen out exercising their mounts. The quick hooves of the horses, the flapping cloaks, and the swords or spears of many of the riders gave the ground a bright, hardy, warlike look; the cold wind blew along the empty stands, and the few attendants waiting for their masters huddled into their cloaks. It was quite different from the chamberlain's office, John thought with satisfaction.

The mare was unperturbed by the crowds but eager to run. When she saw the track, she put her ears forward and snorted, then danced sideways, pulling at the reins. John laughed, and took her onto the track at a trot. Slower riders were walking or trotting near the inside of the circuit, he saw; those who wished to gallop used the outer ring. He made one circuit of the track, then eased Maleka into the outside and gave her her head.

After several trips round the turning posts, he heard his name called from the inside ring, and a moment later Diomedes was galloping beside him on a tall bay of an Asian breed. "John!" the scribe shouted again. "I didn't know you had a horse!"

John had been aware that Diomedes did have a horse — the scribe had spent a good deal of time describing its excellence. Diomedes was much more interested in horses, racing, and bearbaiting then he was in Sergius' unending political gossip. John felt a sense of real comradeship with him for the first time. *After all*, he told himself, *I never disliked him the way I dislike*

Sergius. He turned Maleka into the inner ring and slowed her to a walk. Diomedes slowed beside him.

"I just got her," John told Diomedes. "Isn't she a beauty?"

Diomedes looked at the mare doubtfully. *Small,* he thought. *Like our Berytus clerk himself. A pretty horse, though.* "What kind is she?" he asked.

"She's Arabian," John replied happily. "Bloodstock, too; pure Tanukh, a real jewel." He patted Maleka's sleek neck, and the horse flicked her ears back at him.

"I thought she looked Saracen." Diomedes studied the mare again. "Where'd you get her?"

"She's a present from the empress," John said. "Her Serenity kindly invited me to see the races last week, and in the conversation afterward I said I thought Arabian horses were faster than the breeds they use here. So Her Sacred Generosity gave me one."

"What do you mean, Arabian horses are faster?" Diomedes asked indignantly.

"Arabian horses can run faster for longer than any other breed. It's true."

"You think that little piece of prettiness could outrun my Conqueror?"

"I'll race you," offered John. "Standard chariot circuit — seven times round the track."

"Done," agreed Diomedes.

They returned to the starting line, which was in the center of the east side of the track, directly beneath the royal box, and interrupted the steady stream of gallopers to set up the race. It was late in the dusk now, and many of the riders were going home. A few, attracted by any race and eager to see an Asian horse win, paused to watch. Torches had been set up along the spine of the track, and a bright winter moon was rising. The dark bay horse and the pale gray trod the line beside the starting gates. One of the onlookers arranged to give the signal.

John grinned, holding the reins close and waiting; Maleka snorted and jerked her head, dancing with eagerness. *Conqueror indeed!* John thought. "We'll show him, my beauty!" he whispered to the horse in Arabic.

The onlooker dropped his cloak and yelled "Go!" and the horses were out onto the open track in the pale moonlight.

Count Belisarius arrived at the hippodrome during the fourth lap of the race. He had come, with fifty retainers, to exercise his own horse. He reined in his mount near the starting line and watched as the two horses tore past, galloping neck and neck. The count's horse, a white-faced gray of the Thracian breed, fidgeted impatiently. "What's the race?" the count asked at large.

One of his retainers had just been ascertaining this. "Some young citizens," he reported. "One of them is claiming that Arabian horses are faster than Asians — he's the one on the dun."

"Thank you," said the count sharply. "I can tell an Arab from an Asian."

The two horses galloped past again; the gray was now ahead by a nose. "Is the rider on the Arab a citizen?" Belisarius asked doubtfully. "He rides like a Saracen, with short stirrups."

No one answered. At the far end of the track, the light blur of the Arab mare could be seen pulling away from the darker bay. She was a half-length ahead at the turning post, a length ahead coming down the track, two lengths ahead crossing the line, and the seventh lap was over. John reined the mare in to a walk, patting her neck and whispering to her in Arabic, "My beauty, my treasure!" He felt weightless with happiness.

"I know him!" said Belisarius. "That's that cousin of the Augusta, Narses' secretary. I met him at a dinner party in the palace a few months ago."

"Is he an Arab?" asked one of the retainers. "He does ride like one."

"He's from somewhere around there," Belisarius answered, losing interest. He started his own horse onto the track, then paused again. "I remember — he's from Berytus. The emperor commented on it, how he didn't know that the Augusta had any relations in Berytus." He stared after the light gray horse, now walking far down the inside track, the bay beside it. He was not consciously aware of suspicion, of a desire to discover something discreditable to the terrible, omniscient empress, but he remained for a moment, frowning after them. "I suppose Her Sacred Majesty gave him the horse. I heard she'd done a lot for him — a job, a house from the top of the billeting queue. I think I saw him in the royal box with her at the races, too."

"She favors her own family," commented the retainer.

Belisarius looked sour. "She does." *She favors her bastard's son into my daughter's bed,* he thought to himself bitterly. *My daughter, to marry the grandson of a whore and of God knows who — and a boy two years younger than she is, at that! But what can I do about it?*

And now she's favoring this unknown cousin from Berytus. Why does he ride like a Saracen? And why has no one ever heard of this respectable half-uncle of hers, this Diodoros? Would she really pretend this man is her cousin and shower favors on him if he's nothing of the sort?

He glanced around at his retainers. *I'll see if I can settle something about this young man, anyway,* he thought, and he beckoned one of his men over.

"Illahi," he said, "if that rider goes round the track again, ride after him and hail him in Arabic. Try to see if he knows the language, and then tell him I remember meeting him and wouldn't mind exchanging a few words. Invite him to take a few turns of the track with us."

At the north end of the track, the two horses had reached the turning post. The bay started into a canter, its rider waving farewell; the dun Arab mare kept on at a walk. *I'll give her one last time round,* John thought contentedly. At the starting gates he touched the mare to a trot once more; Maleka was more than willing.

As he was rounding the southern turning post, someone be-hind him called in Arabic, "Hai! You on the dun!" and then a rider on a chestnut gelding slowed from a gallop beside him. The horse was Arabian, and the rider grinned at him from under an Arab headcloth. "Peace be with you!" said the rider in the Arabic of the Ghassanid Saracens. "Yours is a fine mare, a true daughter of the dawn wind. I saw you beat the Greek; it was well done!"

John laughed. "Peace be with you! These Greeks thought Arab horses were only good for looking at; they learned!" he replied. It was wonderful to be riding a splendid horse and speaking his own language. "Yours is a fine horse too — are you of the tribe of Ghassan?"

The man grinned, holding his horse steadily beside John's. "Of the tribe of Ghassan, of the clan of Rabbel; my name is Illahi. And you?"

"My name is John of . . . of Berytus." Just in time, he remembered to leave no confusion; he could not be a citizen of Bostra and Berytus both, not even to a chance-met Arab at the hippodrome.

"Berytus? Eheu, I thought certain you were Arabian. How do you speak Arabic so well, if you're from the Lebanon? You sound like a Nabatean!"

John grinned. "My nurse was an Arab woman."

"Ah, so that's it! My master, Lord Belisarius, sent me to say he remembered meeting a John of Berytus at the palace, and, if you were indeed he, to invite you to round the track a few times with him. That is him there, by the gates. Will you come greet him?"

"Belisarius!" exclaimed John. He looked at the group by the gates: the mass of armed retainers sat on their tall horses with the moonlight shining on their helmets, and in front of them was a man in a white cloak which stood out in the faint light. He was surprised, honored — and nervously unhappy. "Of course," he told Illahi.

Count Belisarius on horseback and surrounded by his retainers in the moonlit hippodrome was an altogether different man from Count Belisarius depressed and anxious at the empress's dinner party. He sat proudly on his white-faced charger, his sword's hilt and horse's harness glinting. The stern, strong face broke into an uneasy smile. "It is John of Berytus, then?" he said. "We weren't sure, seeing someone who rode quite so much like a Saracen."

"No Saracen, Your Eminence, and very pleased to be remembered," replied John, and bowed low in the saddle.

Belisarius nodded in return. He turned his charger onto the inner track, starting at a trot, inviting John to follow with a gesture. Maleka laid her ears back, tired of going round and round in the cold. *Just once or twice more,* John promised her silently. *After all, he is Belisarius!*

"You work for Narses, don't you?" asked the count. "How are you enjoying it?"

"It's interesting work, Your Honor," John replied cautiously. "And I am very pleased to have the job. Though it is pleasant to get out on a horse occasionally."

"That's a fine mare, too," the count replied at once. "What is she — Tanukh line?"

"Yes, Excellency," said John, nervously pleased that the famous general knew this.

"The Augusta gave her to you? I thought so; they're hard for private citizens to get hold of here. There's not the call for them that there should be; the bigger horses are more popular. Well, your cousin the Augusta seems to favor you; you're lucky."

"Indeed, Your Honor. I am grateful to her."

Belisarius watched him a moment, assessing. *He rides well,* he thought, *though very like a Saracen, with the knees up and on the horse's shoulders like that. Not so good if you're trying to use a lance, but fine for a bowman. That's not to the point, though, now, for him. He's a fine-looking young man — that could be a resemblance to the Augusta. Or could not. I can't tell these things. And what could I say to find out? He's not giving much away.*

"The Augusta is an exceptional woman," he tried. *And that's perfectly true,* he thought. *Thank God! If there were more like her, mankind would be exterminated.*

John smiled. "The whole world is as sensible of that as it is of Your Eminence's achievements."

Oh, very pretty! Belisarius smiled obligingly. *Not the tongue-tied modest youth you were at the dinner party. You've learned that flattery will keep the Augusta's favor warm for you.* The starting line flickered away, and they approached the turn again. *What can I say now?*

"Do you miss Berytus?" he asked. "Do you still have family there?"

"No, Your Grace. They died in the plague. No, it is hard to miss something that isn't there anymore anyway."

"True." The count rode on a little further in silence, inwardly cursing himself. *Antonina would have had the fellow's life story by now,* he thought, *and what do I manage? "Yes, Your Honor; No, Your Grace."*

"Is Your Eminence going to return to Italy?" John asked. He had to brace himself to ask the question of a man who had been the model of military glory since John was a small boy.

The question came as a relief. "Perhaps in the spring," said Belisarius. "Perhaps not until autumn. I have to recruit some more men. I've lost many of my spearmen to the plague and to . . . domestic upheavals this last summer."

"I am sorry to hear that," John said earnestly. The count gave him a wordless look in return, and he stopped, confused. *He dislikes me,* John thought, *because of my mother. Or am I imagining it? If he dislikes me, why did he invite me to ride with him?*

"Perhaps you'd like to go to Italy?" Belisarius said, trying to force a note of jocularity. "I still need officers!"

John gave a careful smile. *Why is the man saying that?* he wondered. *He doesn't for a moment dream how much I'd like to accept.* "Such an offer from Your Honor is a high compliment. But of course I have obligations to the most illustrious Narses and to my gracious patroness."

"Of course." Belisarius gave a tight smile back. *That's right,* he added silently, *of course your sort never wants to win by honest fighting what you can get by flattering a sovereign.*

They had reached the northern turning post, by the Great

Gate, and John reined in his mare. Belisarius stopped his own horse, and the attendants all reined in at once, fifty horses suddenly standing stock still. John bowed respectfully to the count. "I must beg Your Eminence's leave," he said formally. "My horse is tired, and it's a cold night; I must take her back to her stable."

"Of course," Belisarius repeated. "Much health!"

When the young man was gone, Belisarius set spurs to his horse and rode three times round the circuit as fast as it could gallop. Reining in again, he summoned Illahi with a jerk of his head. "Did the man speak Arabic?" he demanded.

The Saracen shrugged. "Fluently. Like a Nabatean, though, not a Saracen: he's not of my tribe. He said he'd had an Arab nurse."

Belisarius swore under his breath. "Probably it doesn't mean a thing," he said aloud. And yet — what if there was some deception here? Some intrigue on the part of the empress?

Antonina could manage to find out — his brilliant, beautiful, sensuous, cunning, deceitful, faithless Antonina. His older wife who had made a fool of him in front of all the world with a younger man — and with the connivance of the empress. He pictured Theodora, sitting on her purple-draped throne and smiling with half-lidded eyes. *The whore, the bitch, the polluted, unnatural monster!* he thought, silently repeating the names with a hatred already weary from speechlessness and frustration. *Oh God, I wish it had come off this summer — but it wouldn't have, even if my master had died. She found out. She always finds out everything.*

Well, I'll see if I can't find out something myself. Pay some men to go to Berytus and investigate this fellow John; pay someone to dig around the menageries and theaters of Constantinople, to see if this half-uncle of the empress ever existed. And I'll get Antonina to help me. Theodora may be her great friend, but she doesn't want our daughter to marry the son of the empress's bastard — not with Germanus' son Justin still single. She'd like our daughter to marry an emperor.

And why not? he asked himself, putting his horse into a trot for a last circuit of the hippodrome. *I am the one who won Justinian's wars for him. I'm the one who's led two kings captive, whom all the world respects. I swore my loyalty to the emperor, and I'll keep my oath — but no one can say that my child doesn't deserve to wear the purple.*

"You know, Bacchus," Diomedes said to his colleague next morning, "old Berytus isn't that bad after all."

The two young men were alone in the inner office. The chamberlain had a meeting with the master of the offices to settle the week's imperial appointments, and John, as usual, was taking the minutes.

"What do you mean by that?" asked Sergius sourly, stirring his inkwell.

"I met him at the hippodrome last night. Had a race with him, in fact. He has a new horse, a real beauty and fast as a bird, and he knows how to ride it. He beat me and my Conqueror, and that takes something."

"You think the ability to ride a horse confers moral distinction!" replied Sergius. "Berytus is a town clerk's boy who's got above himself. He should have his wings clipped."

"Well, you're a money-changer's boy who's not flying as high as he'd like," retorted Diomedes, stung. "Give Berytus credit: he learns fast."

Too fast, thought Sergius. *Four months ago I thought I could manage him, get some benefit from his connections. I knew the job, I knew the people, he knew nothing. Now he knows more than I do, and I don't think he ever liked me any more than I like him. He's always managed to avoid giving me that introduction to his patroness. It's the same with everyone who tries to cultivate him: it just slides right off old slippery Berytus John. He only takes the bribes everyone expects him to take, and only gives precisely what was expected in return. No one can get near him. You think you're doing him favors, and you turn around and find he's managed to get even with you and owes*

*you nothing, no services, no ties. In a year's time he'll be pro-
moted somewhere big, and I won't even get a word of recommendation to His Illustriousness for the empty chair. Damn
him. I wish I could take him down a peg.*

He bit the end of his pen angrily. "You and your damn
horses!" he told Diomedes in disgust. "That's all you ever think
about."

IV

The Prefecture's Files

A FEW WEEKS LATER, in the outer office, John sat down to transcribe the minutes and found himself staring at the abbreviations on his tablets: *m.off., m.scr.mem., c.s.larg. Magister officiorum, magister scrinii memoriae, comes sacrarum largitionum,* he read them. "Anastasios," he said, "you know Latin, don't you?"

"You have to know Latin in the offices," the old scribe said primly, shuffling a file together and tagging it.

"I can see why," John said feelingly. Anastasios looked up at him and grinned. John smiled back. He had had considerable sympathy for the old man since he first learned that he was a fellow bastard. Proximity had resulted in a joking familiarity closer to friendship than any other contact John had in this dangerous city. "Could you teach me Latin?" he asked.

"Teach it to you? There are plenty of people who could teach it to you."

"Yes, but could *you* teach it to me? At lunchtime a few times a week? I'll make it worth your while."

Anastasios pursed his lips in a soundless whistle. "You'll be terribly bored when you run out of things to learn, won't you? How are you thinking of making it worth my while?"

"By making you eat sausages for lunch. And buying you a new tunic — you've been wearing that old one since I first met you. But I suppose you don't mind that."

Anastasios shook his head, smiling, and put the prepared file onto the rack.

John looked at the stand of files already waiting, each one tagged with a name or codicils indicating whom it concerned and where it should be returned. "I know — what about a new file rack?" he suggested. "Would cedarwood and hammered gold be good enough for the holy objects?"

Anastasios snorted. "Sausages would do."

"A file rack made of sausages? Are you sure?"

The old man gave the long wheeze that was his habitual laugh. "Holy God!" he began, then stopped himself. A visitor had entered the office. He sat down at his writing table and began checking a note of what the next file should contain. John looked inquiringly at the visitor.

It was a woman, a young woman in a black cloak. She wore a tight-fitting black cap over her head, covering her hair, with a fold of the cloak over it as a hood; she had a round, soft, childish face and a pale, blotched complexion. The rest of her was invisible, except for one small hand holding up the edge of the cloak. Three attendants stood behind her — an older woman and two armed men. *Bodyguards and a chaperone,* John thought. *She must be a wealthy widow. Young for that — she's certainly under twenty, and doesn't look much older than seventeen.*

"Can I assist you?" he asked politely.

"I want to see Narses," she told him in a flat, nasal voice. "And the emperor. But Narses first."

Anastasios gave a snort. It was improper in the extreme to refer to the emperor's chamberlain by his bare name.

"Do you have an appointment?" John asked, knowing perfectly well that she didn't. There were no women in the appointment book that morning.

"No," she replied, and gave him a cold stare. Her eyes didn't match the soft, childish face: they were narrow, shrewd eyes, close set, and of an unusual light brown color that was almost orange. "You can put me down in your book for right now: Euphemia, daughter of the most illustrious patrician John of Caesarea in Cappadocia. I've come about my father's files."

Anastasios dropped his file, stared at the young woman, then hurriedly bent over and began picking the bits of parchment off the floor. *Daughter of John of Caesarea in Cappadocia?* John thought, then realized, *daughter of John the Cappadocian. The one who was made an accessory to her father's downfall.*

"Excuse me a moment," John murmured, and looked at the book. Narses was seeing two senators, a barbarian chieftain, a pretender to the Persian throne, and a bishop that morning. Where did the daughter of a disgraced praetorian prefect fit into that? "I don't know that we can manage it this morning," he told the woman. "Perhaps some morning next week?"

"I'll see him now, or not at all!" Euphemia exclaimed. "Tell him it's about the files. He'll see me."

John gave her a formal smile. "Your Charity, His Illustriousness is an extremely busy man. It is customary for even the most exalted personages to have an appointment."

Anastasios was squirming in his seat, trying to catch John's eye.

"You can let that talk rot," the girl replied angrily. "Go tell your master I'm here and I don't intend to stand about talking with some overdressed pen-pusher in the office of a jumped-up valet. You'll be punished if you send me away. Here!" She dropped a full purse contemptuously onto the desk. John had met abuse and bribes before, though not at the same time, and gave her a mechanical smile without touching the money.

Anastasios gave a forced cough, leaned over, and whispered, "Let her in!" John stared at him; the scribe was usually very defensive of Narses' dignity and prerogatives, and it was unheard of for him to pass over so slighting a reference to his superior — though John was fair game. "It's about the files!" he explained in a hoarse whisper, and when this plainly conveyed nothing, "The files her father took from the prefecture, which were lost when he was arrested and have been missing ever since! The tax indiction has been in absolute chaos! Maybe she knows where they are!"

John hesitated, then gave the girl another formal smile. "I will tell His Illustriousness that you are here," he said, and went quickly to the door of the inner office.

Narses was directing one of the senators where to file a petition, newly rescripted by the emperor, for the settlement of a dispute over the liability of some peasants on one of the senator's estates to transport requisitions. He looked up when John entered, holding back the senator's comments with one slight gesture of restraint. "Yes?" he asked politely.

"There is a young woman here, Illustrious, who says she is the daughter of John the Cappadocian, come about some files; she wishes to see you at once."

"Ah." Narses glanced down at the pile of documents on his table, then began carefully to set them into their file. "I am very sorry to trouble Your Excellency," he said to the senator, "but these files have been to the praetorian prefecture what the apple of strife was to Troy, and I would be blamed on all sides if I lost any opportunity to pursue them. If you will take that to the clerk in the outer office, he will register the documents with the respective offices for you. Esteemed John, could you fetch your tablets? I will want you to take notes of this."

John collected his tablets, held the door for the senator, held the door — somewhat reluctantly — for the Cappadocian's daughter and her chaperone, then followed her back in. Narses had risen to greet her, and gave her a precise and graceful bow.

"Most virtuous Euphemia," said Narses politely, "I am at your service."

"Narses," replied the girl in her flat, harsh tone, "you're no such thing. Can we go somewhere quieter? I don't want to talk in front of your whole office."

Narses raised his eyebrows and indicated the purple curtain at the far side of the room. "You object to my secretary's taking notes?" he asked.

"No, but keep them confidential!" she returned, and pushed her way through the curtain.

There was a small anteroom immediately along the corridor, and Narses escorted the girl and her attendant there, offered them seats on a couch, and himself sat down on another couch with an expression of polite inquiry fixed on his face. John took a place on a stool in the corner and readied his tablets.

"I've come about the files," said Euphemia.

Narses nodded, waiting.

"I had a letter from my father, from Egypt. He told me where they probably are. I've destroyed the letter, but I'll tell you what he said — if you drop the charges against him, release him from prison, and let him go back to Cyzicus."

Narses sighed, steepled his fingers. "You think I can get your father out of a prison in Egypt?" he asked.

"Not you. The emperor. I want you to get me an audience, and I want you to recommend my petition to the emperor. He'll listen to you."

The chamberlain sighed again. "My dear girl, your father is accused of having arranged the murder of a bishop; the fact that he also misappropriated files while in office will hardly help him to escape the consequences of that if he is guilty."

"He is innocent!" the girl said passionately. "Immortal God, you must know he's innocent! The charge was just made up by the empress out of malice. She always hated my father."

Narses winced, glanced at John quickly. "Don't write that down," he directed.

"I'm not afraid to speak the truth!" Euphemia declared, still more passionately. "Everybody in Cyzicus hated their bishop; they'd already appealed to the emperor to depose him. And the two men that actually murdered him were caught; they had nothing to do with my father!"

Narses raised a cautioning finger. "They were acquaintances of your father. And one of them insists that your father paid him seventy *solidi* for undertaking the murder."

"He only said that after Theodora's men tortured him."

Narses shook his head. "He said that when he was arrested. His friend denied it. They were both tortured; both persisted in their stories, accusing and denying. They are both still in prison, and their jailers hope that one or the other of them will change his mind. Until that happens, your father is necessarily under suspicion and cannot be restored to his position in Cyzicus." The chamberlain paused delicately, then went on more gently. "His position in Egypt could of course be improved. I believe he is currently being held in the legionary fortress at Antinoopolis in a room reserved for such purposes. He could be given a private house in the city and be permitted to move about freely within the district. And it should be possible to allow him the use of his funds while the matter is undecided. You could certainly petition my master for that."

The girl flushed. "I pitched my demands too low, did I?" she asked bitterly. "If I'd started off demanding that my father get his job back, you'd've been happy to compromise at dropping the charges against him."

Narses shook his head. "My dear girl, it isn't easy to drop quietly the charge of having murdered a bishop. It is particularly difficult when the bishop was known to incline to one of two rival theological sects, while my master Justinian Augustus is known to incline to the other. To give your father a free pardon would damage my master's standing with the churches of the East, just when he has begun to try to reach a compromise with them. I could not, in conscience, recommend it to him."

Euphemia sat still a moment, staring at the chamberlain with loathing. "Damn you!" she said at last. "You always hated my father, didn't you? Envious, like the rest of them. Or do you just hope they'll make you prefect in his place?"

Narses watched her without expression, and the girl's cold glare faltered. "I do not think that Your Discretion believed that accusation even when you made it," he said after a moment. "I am the slave of the Augustus; I have no enemies but his enemies. And I wish him to have no enemies."

"Do you want the files?" snapped Euphemia, slapping the arm of the couch.

"You are perfectly well aware that the staff of the praetorian prefecture are 'eating their hearts with grief' over those files. But I cannot recommend to my master that the charges against your father be dropped."

"How much do you need to make you change your mind?"

Narses smiled. "I do not sell my advice to my master."

"How much did *he* buy you for, then?" the girl asked viciously.

Narses' smile vanished. "I was initially purchased for sixty-nine *solidi*. But that was a long time ago, and under another emperor."

To John's surprise, the girl blushed and looked down. "I . . . I'm sorry," she stammered. "I didn't mean —"

"I am not offended. My dear girl, allow me to advise you — for free. Justinian Augustus likes your father, and feels himself still indebted to him. If you humbly petition for your father to be allowed the use of his money and a lighter confinement, it is very likely that the master will agree. I do not advise any mention of the files, nor any attempt to use them as part of a bargain. Their disappearance caused great annoyance, and to bring them in would only stir up old resentments. They would be much more effective if they were returned as a gracious gesture of thanks for some favor already conferred. You may tell your father I have said this. Do you wish me to make an appointment for you to have an audience?"

The girl looked down, her small hands clenching and unclenching in her lap. "No," she said after a moment. "Not right now." She looked up, and John saw that she was in tears. "I have to think about your advice first."

"By all means. If you wish me to make an appointment, simply send a note and I will see to it. Is that all?"

John escorted the girl back through the offices. At the outer office he saw that the money she had offered him was still on his desk; he picked it up and handed it to her. She stared at him for a moment, blinking, then went red again. "I don't want your filthy money!" she snapped.

"It's your filthy money," John returned. "And it's not usual to give bribes when you're trying to make threats."

"You're an expert on such things, are you?" she asked. She

snatched the purse under her cloak, lifted her shoulders, and strode from the room.

John glared after her.

"True daughter of her father," observed Anastasios. "Euphemia's not a good name for her: 'well-spoken' she isn't."

John nodded. "Dysphemia?" he suggested. "Blasphemia?"

Anastasios wheezed. "That last is a bit strong."

John smiled, then glanced through his tablets. *You might not say that if you could read this*, he thought. He returned to the inner office. Narses was sitting at his desk, not working but staring thoughtfully at the icon on the wall. The pens of Sergius and Diomedes scratched steadily in the background.

"I take it I'm not to transcribe any references similar to the one you had me delete," John said.

Narses nodded without looking at his subordinate. "Tidy it up — you know how it's done," he said. John remained standing where he was, watching the chamberlain, and the eunuch at last looked round and met his eyes. He sighed, steepled his fingers, and rested them against his chin. "The girl is still very young," he said gently. "She loves her father, who is deeply devoted to her. She has suffered greatly since his disgrace — and his arrest last summer was not managed as . . . tactfully . . . as it should have been. It is understandable if she speaks passionately at times."

Understandable, perhaps, but it doesn't excuse her for insulting me and treating you like a slave, thought John. Then, remembering Sergius' story of the Cappadocian's fall, he wondered if it did. "Very well," he said heavily. He looked at Narses for another moment: the chamberlain's face was impassive, distant.

"Yes? Something more?" asked the eunuch.

"Nothing — just that sixty-nine *solidi* doesn't seem very much."

The face relaxed into a rueful smile. "Ah, but it did at the time. Enough to buy a whole clan of penniless Armenians, livestock and all. You had better send in the next name on the list or he'll be offended."

·　　·　　·

A week later, when the emperor Justinian was checking over the day's appointments with his chamberlain, he saw that Euphemia, daughter of John, was near the top of the list. He set the list down on his bed and frowned at it. Wet-haired and unshaven, he had just taken his bath and was dressed only in a towel. Narses stood before him, holding a notebook in one hand and with the emperor's undertunic over the other arm. One of the first duties of any chamberlain was to help his master dress, and it was still a responsibility of the head of the emperor's household staff. The order of the day's business was generally settled in such meetings.

"That's the Cappadocian's girl, isn't it?" the emperor asked Narses. "What does she want?"

The eunuch gave his usual noncommittal smile. "She is petitioning Your Sacred Charity on her father's behalf." The emperor nodded impatiently and lifted his arms for the tunic; Narses slipped it over his head, continuing his explanation as he did so. "She wishes you to give instructions for him to be allotted a private house within the city where he is being kept, and to be allowed the free use of his money while the criminal charges are being investigated. She is a devoted daughter, and it grieves her that her father should be kept locked in a prison."

"Well, that seems reasonable," said Justinian, relieved. He stood so the chamberlain could fasten the tunic. "I was afraid she wanted the charges dropped. I'll be pleased to do what I can for the poor man; he was an excellent praetorian prefect. I do think that whatever he did, he's paid for it already — though we can't say so, with those Monophysite bishops howling for his blood. I'll see the girl privately in the Triklinos reception hall and tell her as much."

Narses nodded and made a note next to the name. He picked up the heavier overtunic with its gold brocade and straightened its folds carefully. The emperor glanced at the other names on the list, then put them aside. "Speaking of men named John . . . ," he began. The eunuch paused attentively.

"I met your secretary, my wife's cousin, at her breakfast table yesterday morning," said Justinian. The voice was casual, but there was a hint of some other feeling in it. Suspicion? wondered Narses, with a surge of apprehension. "How's he managing these days?"

"He is extremely efficient, master," replied Narses. "Very competent, very intelligent, very hardworking. I am entirely satisfied with him."

Justinian grunted. "My wife seems to invite him to breakfast rather a lot."

Suspicion and jealousy, thought Narses. *Mary Mother, how it hits the best of them!* He smiled cautiously. "He is her cousin, master. The sacred Augusta has always assisted members of her own family and been eager to advance them."

"Yes, but . . ." The emperor bit his lip, stopping himself. He glanced around the room, saw that no one was there to hear him except his chamberlain, and resumed. "I would certainly expect her to try to advance a cousin, find him jobs, give him money, maybe arrange him a marriage with a powerful heiress. I don't know why she keeps inviting him to breakfast or has him accompany her about so much. Why does she want to spend so much time with him?"

"He is a pleasant enough young man, master. He is grateful for the favors she has given him, and never asks for more; he does not sell introductions to her or otherwise abuse his position; he gives her the kind of flattery she enjoys, without meaning anything or expecting anything in exchange, and he respects her. She enjoys his company."

"I suppose he is good-looking," Justinian said. The casual tone was gone, and his voice was raw and ugly.

Narses shrugged. "I can hardly judge that, Thrice August. I believe, though, that taller men are generally considered more attractive than short ones, and fair men than dark. And I doubt that the Augusta is overly concerned with her cousin's looks."

"You don't think so?" The emperor looked at his chamberlain suspiciously.

"My dear master, you do not believe that the sacred Augusta

is . . . improperly attached to this young man, do you?" Narses'
voice held a complicated mixture of affection and reproach.

"No. No, of course not. Only . . . only she does seem very
fond of him. And I never knew she had any relations in Berytus."

"Consider a moment, master. He is the son of the relations
who rejected her as unworthy of them, who shut the door in her
face, who despised her. You know yourself how the most pious
empress still suffers in memories the abuses she once endured.
But she has taken the most Christian revenge of assisting this
man to power and wealth. He is grateful and respectful — and
every time he sees her he must prostrate himself on the ground
and hail her as mistress. It cancels the memory of her humilia-
tion without hurting anyone; it delights her. She invited his
company to have more of such delight, and when he proved
himself not unworthy of her attention, she grew fond of him.
But is there any comparison between that fondness and the deep
affection she bears Your Majesty?"

"No," said Justinian, relieved. "I'm sure you're completely
right, Narses. You usually are, aren't you?" He smiled, reached
for the overtunic. "I would be an idiot to suspect my Theodora,"
he said as his head emerged through the neck.

Narses nodded and adjusted the tunic's fastenings. He helped
his master on with the purple stockings and bejeweled slippers
and noted down the places and times for the different bits of
business, outwardly as calm and efficient as ever. Inwardly he was
disturbed. *Holy God,* he though, *thank you for making me a
eunuch! What a deal of trouble love can cause! Here is Petrus
Sabbatius Justinian, Augustus, emperor, master of the world,
Gothicus, Vandalicus, and all the rest, tying himself into knots
with worry over the fact his wife invites my secretary to breakfast! He could find out easily enough if his suspicions were justi-
fied: he has unlimited authority and can hire all the spies he
likes. Instead he looks over his shoulder before breathing a word
even to me, afraid of hurting his wife's feelings. And he's quite
right to be cautious, because the empress would be mortally
offended if he accused her — to say nothing of the damage an*

*open suspicion could do to John. Well, I've succeeded in still-
ing the worry, for now. But anyone else will be able to stir it
up again. And anyone else can see what the master does: that
the mistress favors John rather more openly than is prudent.
Someone is bound to hint as much to the master. I must remember to tell the mistress that she should find that young
man a wife.*

Euphemia was admitted to the audience with the emperor as
soon as she arrived, and merely swept through the outer office
with an icy glare. Before she left the palace, however, she had to
wait while letters were written and forms found to release her
father and his estates. Narses politely introduced her to the
beginning of this business, then, pressed by his appointment list,
left her in the outer office with John and Anastasios. "If you
could," he told them, "explain to her what each of her documents is, and give her a list of them; I am sure it would be helpful. Excellent Euphemia, much health!"

Euphemia gave John a cold look and sat down on the bench
by his desk, folding her hands in her lap. Her chaperone, who
had never spoken a word in John's hearing, sat down next to
her, took out a spindle and distaff, and began to spin. John gave
the girl his mechanical smile and examined the mass of documents she had already collected. "Do you understand these?"
he asked her, expecting an insulting negative.

"Of course," she snapped. "You still need the accounts from
the treasury about the estates. The value of what I'm allowed
back should be about thirty-five hundred and fifty pounds in
gold."

She had, he discovered, an excellent head for figures. He had
not expected this in a young woman, and was taken aback by it.
She had a clear, sharp, critical mind, and a habit of grasping the
gist of a complicated document almost at once and asking awkward questions about it. She also continually suspected the worst
and, it seemed, held him personally responsible for it. It took
over an hour — not including the time spent on interruptions
from new visitors — before the collection of documents was com-

plete and arranged to Euphemia's grudging satisfaction. The chaperone, seeing the file completed, put away the spindle and distaff and sat waiting impassively for her charge to leave. John suppressed a sigh of intense relief.

Anastasios coughed. "Most respected lady," he suggested carefully, "I don't suppose that those files . . ."

"What files?" asked the Cappadocian's daughter.

"The files from the prefecture," said the scribe. "You said when you first came —"

"I didn't make the petition I meant to make," the girl returned. But she hesitated, staring at Anastasios. She looked at John quickly, then frowned down at her own file. "It would be very useful," she said after a moment, without looking up, "to have some contact with the office here. I'd know then when I could petition again. I need to know what's happening at the court, and I have no way of finding out." She looked up, the orange eyes fixing directly on John. "I might be willing to trade information with someone who had access to Their Majesties and who knew what was really going on."

"You are perfectly free to come in and make an appointment with the most illustrious Narses any time you like," John said coldly.

"Narses will call me his 'dear girl' and give me perfectly correct advice which gets me nowhere!" Euphemia said impatiently. "He won't tell me what I need to know."

"His Illustriousness has treated you far more generously than . . . his office obliged him to," John returned. His first conclusion to the sentence, "than you deserve," hung, obvious but unspoken, in the air between them. Euphemia's cheeks darkened with her quick blush.

"Narses wants the information from those files," she said. "He'd like it if you could get it. The whole praetorian prefecture would dance for joy. It would be a real sprig of laurel for you, and sure to be noticed when you look for promotion." She collected her file from John's desk. "If you wanted to . . . visit my house tomorrow evening after you've finished your work, we might come to some arrangement."

"I'm exercising my horse tomorrow evening after work," John returned icily.

"Well then, the evening after!" she snapped. "It's an opportunity for you — think about it!" She rose, pulled her cloak straight, gave John another cold glare, and left the room.

"You ought to take her up on it!" said Anastasios as soon as she was gone. "I think even His Illustriousness would recommend it to you."

"Just what are these files?" John demanded angrily.

"The tax indictions from the last census for Mesopotamia, Osrhoene, Syria, Palestine, and Arabia. To have them missing throws the whole administration of those provinces into chaos. Nobody knows how much is due from where."

"The indictions for the East will be out of date anyway!" John protested. "Between the war and the plague, the whole face of the country will have changed."

"But when they come to make the new indiction, they'll need the old records." Anastasios was plaintive. "They must have the old records. The prefecture can't possibly work without its files."

"Oh, damn you and your files! I don't like that woman, and I don't want to go selling her information."

"She didn't specify any particular information. She may just want you to confirm court gossip," Anastasios coaxed. "Maybe you could talk to His Illustriousness about her offer? Please? I have friends in the prefecture; I know the headaches those files cause."

John groaned and stared at the old scribe in exasperation. Anastasios looked back with an uncertainty that became almost timid in the face of John's irritation. It was embarrassing, disarming, to see the old man so humble. "Very well," John said after a moment. "I will consult His Illustriousness about it, and see if it's considered wise."

"Thank you." Anastasios settled happily back to sorting out another file. John swore under his breath as he set to work on the heap of documents waiting on his desk.

·   ·   ·

Narses approved of the scheme. "I would prefer it, of course, if the young woman simply returned the files to the prefecture," he said, "and you may advise her that I think that would be the wisest thing to do. But if she's determined to bargain with them, I suppose that this is a fairly harmless way to do it. I trust Your Discretion not to give her any sensitive information."

Accordingly, two days later John rode to the quarter of the city where Euphemia had her house.

He had defiantly intended to exercise Maleka before going, but it was a chill, windy, spring evening and raining heavily, so he merely traveled on horseback instead of on foot. The slave boy Jakobos followed him on a sturdy Asian gelding; the boy had been so inordinately impressed by his master's racehorse that John had bought him a horse of his own and arranged for him to learn how to ride it. The horses both laid their ears back and hung their heads in the icy rain, and the riders pulled their cloaks up and chafed their raw hands.

Narses had told John that Euphemia lived in her father's old house, near the Taurus marketplace on the Bosphorus side. The great marketplace was almost deserted in the rainy dusk, and the horses' hooves rang loudly on the cobblestones and echoed as they passed through the triumphal arch. A few sputtering torches in front of one mansion cast red reflections onto the wet stone of the streets; otherwise all was gray. "See if you can find out where the house is!" John told his servant. The boy nodded and trotted across the marketplace, looking for someone to question, and John waited by the triumphal arch. He was dreading the interview.

I don't like the woman, he told himself again; but again he noticed that his uneasiness at the meeting did not entirely match the mere fact of dislike. *She hates the empress, my mother,* he went on, silently testing himself. It didn't satisfy him. *She was wronged by the empress,* he admitted, and the stab of pain was like a flash of lightning, revealing himself and his position out of the rain-dark night.

I want to love Theodora, he thought, *and I almost do. But*

I'm afraid to know what she may have done. She is capable of cruelty, likes revenge. That's all right, within limits — but I don't know what the limits are for her. And I don't want to know. I am her creature now, remade by her, and if she is a tyrant, then I . . .

Jakobos came cantering back across the square. "Second entrance on the right on the third street that goes south," he called. "Most of the house is walled off and let out to people from the palace, but the iron doors are hers."

John nodded and turned Maleka's head south.

The house did in fact front directly on the marketplace, but it was very large, and it was easy to see that this choice part of it had indeed been recently separated from the back. The great iron-bound gates were unmistakable, however, and John knocked on them without dismounting. A dog began barking, and after a moment an old man unlatched a window in the lodge beside the gate and looked out suspiciously. "What do you want?" he demanded.

"I've come to see the daughter of John of Cappadocia about some files. I'm secretary to the most illustrious Narses, chamberlain to His Sacred Majesty."

The window closed, and then a small door set into one of the large gates opened. "She mentioned you," the old man said. "Come in, then."

This door was far too small to ride through. "What about my horse?" John asked.

The man spat, eyed the horses unhappily, eyed the door. "I'll open the gate," he said at last.

The gates were stiff with rust from long disuse, and they had to use the horses to get them open. On the other side was a colonnaded courtyard bordered by a garden and with a fountain in the middle. The garden was a mass of weeds and thorns, and the fountain contained only a few inches of green water. John had the horses tied up in the shelter of the colonnade and covered with rugs; then, escorted by the old man and followed by his slave, he went on into the house.

It was a magnificent house, its walls painted with city scenes or seascapes, its floors covered with mosaics. But it seemed very sparsely furnished, and had a fusty, disused feeling to it, though everything was clean. It was bitterly cold. It had clearly been provided with a hypocaust for heating, but this wasn't running, and none of the lamps on the many lampstands John passed were lit. There were no slaves in evidence; the corridors were empty and silent. Carrying a rush-light, the old man led John along the ground floor, then up a flight of steps and along another corridor. From under a door at the far end of this came gold lamplight. The old man knocked twice.

"Who is it?" came the familiar flat voice.

"The gentleman has come from the palace, mistress," said the old man. "From the chamberlain's office."

There was a moment's silence, and then the door was opened by Euphemia's chaperone. She nodded to John and stood aside. He went in.

Much to his relief, this room was warm. Two charcoal braziers, one on either sde of the window, provided heat, and four glowing lamps hung from a plain wooden lampstand. A double loom stood in one corner, with a girl sitting on a bench before it; another woman next to her was spinning, and a third was carding wool. A baby slept in a cradle by their feet.

They're all the female slaves in the house, John realized, *all here because it's warm. All the men are probably sitting down in one other room on the ground floor. They can't afford to run the hypocaust, and they sold the other slaves and most of the furniture to pay the housekeeping bills after the Cappadocian's money was confiscated.*

Euphemia was sitting on a couch by the brazier, a book in her lap. She was still wearing the black cloak, but had taken off the hat. Her hair was brown and pulled tightly onto the top of her head. She gave him a malicious smile. "It's the expert on bribery," she said. "Welcome!"

"My name is John," he said, fairly sharply. "Of Berytus."

She shrugged. "Your slave can go back downstairs," she told him. "Onesimos, take him down to the kitchen and give him a drink."

John nodded to Jakobos, who went back out with the old man. Euphemia's chaperone closed the door; then, without a word, went over and sat down at the loom and began to weave. There was no other couch in the room, so John reluctantly sat down on the end of Euphemia's. *They give a drink to my slave,* he thought, *but not to me.* "What information were you thinking of trading for?" he asked.

"Coming right to the point," she added for him, and gave an unpleasant smile. "I have the files the prefecture wants, and I'll let you copy them, a few pages at a time. I thought we could make the rate a page a go for the appointment list, and more for any other information that's useful."

"How much more, and for what?"

"How much depends on for what, doesn't it? I just want the usual court gossip — who's in and who's out, whose petitions have been granted and whose refused, who's been caught for corruption, and so on. And if you can tell me something I need to know, I'll add as much more as I think the information's worth. I'll be fair."

"Will you indeed?" asked John. "I will rather have to rely on that, won't I? The most illustrious Narses recommends that you return the files to the prefecture; he said that would be the wisest thing to do."

She shrugged. "I'm not letting go of them for nothing. And I want information over a period of time, so I can't give you all the files at once. But I will be fair."

"What if the prefecture demands the files? After all, your father misappropriated them."

Her eyes flashed. "He did not! He had simply taken them home to work on at the time when he was disgraced. While we were in Cyzicus the prefecture wrote several times asking what had become of them, but we didn't have them there and my father was so anxious and unhappy he couldn't remember where he'd put them. He only wrote me to say that he'd remembered a few months ago."

"But he didn't suggest giving them back to the prefecture."

The mouth contracted. "He is being kept in a tiny room in

the legionary fortress at Antinoopolis. He has no friends in the city, and scarcely enough money to get himself food to stay alive." Her voice was savage. "His wrists are so galled from the chains they keep him in that I could scarcely read his writing. No, he didn't suggest giving the files back for nothing. He didn't suggest throwing them away, either. He wants to get out!" She drew a deep breath, and went on more calmly. "If the prefecture demands the files, then the files disappear. That's final."

John sighed. "Very well. You want the appointment list first."

He took out his pen case and a narrow sheet of parchment and wrote down the list that had occupied the book that morning. Euphemia took it greedily and read it, then asked, "And what about court news? Has Belisarius gone back to Italy?"

"Not directly. He'll be traveling through Thrace, trying to collect some more men; he's expected to get to Italy by the end of the summer."

"Is it true there's another revolt in Africa?"

She questioned him closely for half an hour. To his relief, he found that she did not demand any sensitive information. Like Sergius, she only wanted to hear the ordinary news from someone who could say whether or not it was true.

Eventually her flow of questions stopped and she gave a satisfied sigh and blinked at him. In the lamplight her eyes were darker, deep brown instead of the orange they had been in the sun.

"Now the files?" he suggested.

She nodded and picked up a large red leatherbound book that had been sitting against the far arm of the couch. *She must have been very sure I would come, to have it ready*, thought John bitterly. Without a word she placed it, open, on the couch between them. John saw that it was the census for the province of Syria. He picked up his tablets and took the stylus from his pen case and quickly noted down the information in shorthand. When he finished the first page, he looked at Euphemia. She turned the page, and when he had copied that information, turned it again. "But that will be all for now," she stated.

"That? Five pages? Some of that information is useless anyway. I happen to know that the town council of Emesa had its assessment changed two years ago because of a drought."

She gave him a surprised look. "How do you know that?"

"I was a municipal scribe in Berytus, and I knew some people who'd had dealings with the Emesenes." The news had come to Bostra along the caravan route.

"You were? But . . ." She hesitated, suspicious. "How does one go from being a municipal scribe in Berytus to being the secretary of the emperor's chamberlain within two years?"

"I'm a distant cousin of the Augusta," John said. "I appealed to Her Sacred Majesty for help after my parents died in the plague."

"A cousin of the empress!" Euphemia's expression became one of alarm. "Mother of God!" She slammed the book shut and jumped up. Her slaves stopped their work and stared at John in fear. "I should never have asked you here!" Euphemia exclaimed bitterly. "You've come to spy on me, haven't you?"

"I don't spy on anyone," John replied angrily. "You invited me — and you can hardly claim I was eager to accept. I'm only here to do a favor to my colleagues; I don't care a thing for the prefecture's files. As for all your slanders against the Augusta" — he got to his feet — "I certainly wouldn't report them, if that's what you're afraid of. But I am greatly indebted to Her Serenity, and I would thank you to keep your mouth shut about her."

Euphemia stared at him a moment, very pale. Then she looked down and blushed. "You weren't eager to come," she admitted. "I guess you aren't a spy." She sat down heavily; John remained standing. "I was going to ask you to come back next week and give me more information," the girl said, looking up at him. "Now . . ."

John shrugged. He picked up his notebook. "Invite someone else. Someone from the prefecture."

"They don't have access to the emperor." Euphemia rubbed her face tiredly. "I suppose it doesn't make any difference who your relations are, really," she said. "There's nothing you could tell the empress that she doesn't already know. And I need the information for my father. . . . Come back in a week, then."

"I thank Your Gracious Kindness," said John. "Such a civilized invitation! Such elegant hospitality! If the weather is any better next week, I think I would prefer to exercise my horse, thank you!"

"Please!" said Euphemia, looking up at him miserably. "I'm sorry I was rude, I'm sorry I wasn't hospitable. Please come back next week!" Her lower lip was trembling, and for a horrible moment he thought she would cry. *She is afraid of failing her father*, he realized. *She pictures him there in his prison, relying on her to get information to help him. She's even willing to grovel to me to get it.* He felt embarrassed and disgusted.

"Very well, very well," he said hurriedly. "Next week. Much health!"

He blundered quickly from the room, back through the cold empty corridors, and eventually found Jakobos being entertained cheerfully by a wood fire in the kitchen. He pulled the boy hastily back to the horses. The old man shoved open the groaning iron gates, and they rode back through the dark streets in the fierce cold rain.

V

REVELATIONS

A FEW WEEKS LATER, when John was taking Maleka to the hippodrome for an evening's ride, he noticed that his slave Jakobos looked anxious and unhappy. The boy was usually a model of good nature, cheerful, talkative, enthusiastic about almost everything, but on this occasion, although it was a clear, bright evening and the horses were ready to gallop, Jakobos sat on his bay gelding with his shoulders hunched, looking miserable.

"Is something the matter?" John asked him as they left the stables. "Are you feeling well?"

"I'm all right," Jakobos said sullenly.

John shrugged, and they rode on, out from the palace stables, through the Bronze Gate, the Augusteion market, and the Great Gate of the hippodrome. The racetrack was even more crowded than usual. "You ready to gallop?" John asked.

At this Jakobos brightened up. He could not really control the bay at anything faster than a trot, and tended to lose his stirrups at the canter. But he loved speed, and nodded eagerly. John touched Maleka's sides and she at once leapt off down the track, eager to overtake everything in sight. John held her back, trying to keep an eye on his slave. Jakobos was jolting along behind, bright-eyed and beaming, one stirrup gone already and the reins flapping madly in the air. John slowed Maleka further. "Heels and hands down!" he yelled, and Jakobos obediently lowered his hands and tucked his legs in. He grabbed the bay's mane and grinned at John. "How's that, sir?"

"Better," said John kindly, remembering his own first few months on horseback.

They circled the track three times, cantering and galloping, then five times more at a trot, before turning back toward the stables. Once the excitement of the gallop was left behind, Jakobos again began to look anxious, and shot nervous glances toward John. When they reached the stables, the boy suddenly said, "Master — there's something I want to tell you, but my father said I shouldn't."

"You should obey your father," John told him, automatically repeating the words that he had been raised on.

"Yes, but you're my master, and his too, aren't you? So we ought to obey you first. And you've been so wonderfully kind, too, buying me this horse and having me ride it just like a gentleman. I don't think it's right not to tell you."

John sighed and dismounted. He took Maleka's bridle and stroked her neck. "Well, tell me then, if you think it's wrong not to."

Jakobos scrambled down from his own mount. "It's like this, master. A man offered me a whole *solidus* yesterday to spy on you."

"To spy on me?" John stared in confusion and alarm. "Why? What did he want to know?"

"He said he wanted to know anything — where you went, who you saw, what you said to them. He said he'd give me the whole *solidus* right then, and more later if I was good. I told him to go away before I called my father, and he did. My father said that I did the right thing, but that I shouldn't tell you because it would only worry you and make trouble for the whole house."

"What sort of man was he? Did he tell you his name?"

"No. He was just an ordinary sort of man. Not young but not old, not poor and not rich. He had good clothes, but I think they were second-hand. He talked like a Constantinopolitan, and he had light-colored hair, not really blond but almost. I think he was somebody's slave."

John stood still a moment, frowning. *Who wants to spy on me?* he wondered; then, *Who is spying on me? If he's trying to bribe my slaves, he may have succeeded in bribing someone else.*

"Jakobos," he asked, "your father . . . you don't think he may have been approached himself, do you?"

Jakobos looked shocked. "Oh no, sir! That is, if he was, he'd have done the same as I did. He always says that no good ever came of a slave betraying his master: it's like tearing the roof off your own house, he says. No, he just doesn't like trouble, and masters worrying and rearranging things. That's why he said not to tell you."

"Well, thank you for disobeying him," said John. "If I have an enemy, I'd prefer to know about it."

"Yes, master. Are you going to tell him that I told you?"

John smiled. "Not if you'd rather I didn't."

But who wants to spy on me, and why? John wondered as he walked back out of the palace, followed by a recovered Jakobos. *Does someone suspect my story? Or have I just made some ordinary enemy? Euphemia! Does she hope to find something she can use to blackmail more information out of me? Or* (and the thought brought a stab of cold pain) *does the empress not trust me? Is she afraid that I may betray her or embarrass her? But surely she wouldn't need to offer bribes? My slaves were all hers, and would probably still obey her orders over mine. Who, then? Lord of All, I hate this city.*

He stopped abruptly and looked up at the soft spring stars which hung golden above the mass of the Bronze Gate. *I almost wish I were back in Bostra,* he thought miserably. *I was only a bastard and a whore's son there, but at least I knew where I was. But there's no going back.* "At the limits of the night, Orpheus saw, lost, killed Eurydice." *Maybe Anastasios could tell me what it is in Latin.*

He sighed, and continued on his way home.

·   ·   ·

A few weeks later Anastasios came into work flushed and coughing, and fumbled and dropped files all morning.

"Why don't you go home and rest?" John asked in exasperation. "You're not well."

"I don't like resting at home," said Anastasios. "The only thing to do with a cold is ignore it." He sneezed violently and wiped his face.

He was supposed to provide a Latin lesson that lunchtime, and John duly brought the old man along to a tavern — not Sergius' favorite — and ordered some food. But Anastasios wasn't hungry. "We'll just do the language," he said. "What was it I set last time? 'I send the notebooks to the ministry.' That should be *Mitto libellos officiae . . .*"

"Oh. I thought it would be *officio* or *officiis*," John said.

Anastasios blinked at him with red-rimmed eyes. "Yes," he said after a moment, "it should be."

"Mother of God!" John reached across the table and put a hand against the scribe's forehead; it was burning hot. "You idiot!" he said angrily, getting up. "You're too ill to conjugate 'ministry' properly and you sit here talking Latin. Come on, you're going home."

Anastasios made no resistance as John pulled him from the tavern, but he stumbled on the doorstep and stood staring confusedly at the crowded street. *He's too ill to get himself home,* John realized. "Is it far to your house?" he asked, taking the old man's arm.

It was nearly two miles. The scribe's accommodation proved to be the second floor of a small apartment block near the Market of the Ox; a slave as aged and grizzled as Anastasios himself opened the door to John's knock. He didn't look surprised to see his master. "Told you you weren't well," he said, taking Anastasios' arm from John's shoulder. "Thank you, sir; I'll put him to bed."

"Should he have a doctor?" asked John, hovering uncertainly at the door.

"It's just a fever," said Anastasios, collecting himself with a painfully obvious effort. "I'll be better in a couple of days. You go back to the office, please — and be careful with that file of Priscus'!"

John arrived back at the Magnaura Palace to find Sergius sitting in the outer office at his own desk. The scribe was examining some papers, but he set them down quickly as John came in. "So here you are at last!" he commented. "Where's Anastasios?"

"Ill in bed," John replied tersely. The sight of Sergius' plump dark face above his own notebooks caused him a surprisingly strong stab of resentment. "I had to take him home." He moved around the desk.

Sergius got up slowly. "Well, I'll tell His Illustriousness you're back."

"Thank you." John sat down quickly and looked over the documents on the desk. Sergius had evidently been going through not just the current business but also that from several weeks before. John looked up sharply; Sergius merely smiled sleepily and ambled off to the inner office.

A couple of minutes later Narses came out. "Anastasios is ill?" he asked. There was a note of genuine concern in his high voice.

"With a fever. I had to take him home."

"I trust it isn't serious?"

"He says not. I was thinking of going over there this evening to check on him, though. He really wasn't well."

"That would be wise," said Narses, frowning. "Thank you." He stood still for a moment, tapping his fingers on John's desk, then gave his cryptic smile and went back into the inner office.

John had one of the now regular weekly meetings with Euphemia that evening, and was late checking on Anastasios. The girl treated him with a coldly precise formality that he found almost as irritating as her former dismissive contempt. It was time-consuming, too. All business had to be prefaced with correct offers of food and drink, and conducted in wordy speeches burdened with honorifics. Though he had hurried to her house directly from the Magnaura, it was still almost dark before he was able to leave. When the iron gates closed behind him,

John heaved the sigh of relief that was also a regular feature of the meetings, and rode Maleka at a canter to the Market of the Ox.

Outside Anastasios' apartment block were six armed men, seven horses, and a white mule. The evening was clear and warm, and four of the men sat in a half-circle on the pavement, playing at dice, while the other two leaned on their spears by the entrance. John reined Maleka in and sat staring with surprise, then realized that the men were Narses' retainers. He had been vaguely aware that the eunuch kept a small bodyguard, though the soldiers normally stayed away from the office and he had only met one or two of them once or twice. He dismounted and led his horse over, Jakobos following.

"Greetings," he said, and the four dice players got up. They were all tall, lean, strong men, bearded, clad in chainmail, and armed to the teeth. Of the six, four were dark and two were fair-haired, blue-eyed barbarians.

"Greetings," said one of the dark ones in a thick Armenian accent. "You're His Illustriousness's secretary, aren't you? His Illustriousness is upstairs. We look after your horse, yes?"

"Yes." The Armenian bowed and took Maleka's bridle. John swallowed, nodded to Jabobos. "You stay here and wait," he ordered, and the boy grinned nervously. John went into the building.

On the second floor he found an old woman just entering the door of Anastasios' rooms, carrying a heavy jug of water; she gave him a suspicious look but said nothing when he entered behind her. The old slave he had met before was heaping a brazier with charcoal, and he nodded his head at John, wiped his face, and waved toward a corridor. "That way," he said. "Tell them we'll have the water ready soon."

John followed the direction and found his way to the old scribe's bedroom. It was a very plain room, well lit by good glass windows but almost undecorated, with walls of bare plaster and a floor of cheap Singidunum work. Anastasios was lying on the threadbare coverlet of a narrow bed; he looked feverish and exhausted. Another man, plainly a doctor, stood over him, taking his pulse and holding a cup of some unpleasant-looking dark liquid. Narses was standing by the window with his arms crossed, watching. He smiled when John appeared in the doorway.

"Greetings," said Narses. "As you see, I decided to check on our patient myself. This gentleman is the most distinguished Aetios, my physician. Doctor, my secretary, John of Berytus."

"Greetings," said Anastasios, giving John a feeble smile.

The doctor snorted, not bothering to look round. "You should all go away," he said. "The patient needs rest. What are those slaves doing with the water?"

"They said it would be ready soon," supplied John.

The doctor snorted again, and let go of Anastasios' wrist. "Bad," he told the old man accusingly. "Here, drink this up; it will bring the fever down and help you to sleep." He offered Anastasios the cup. The scribe turned his head away and gave Narses a beseeching look. "Illustrious, it really wasn't necessary . . ."

Narses uncrossed his arms, came quickly over, and took the cup from the physician. "Probably not," he said calmly. "But it sets my mind at rest to know that you are being well cared for. Drink it up, my friend." He held the cup to the scribe's lips. Anastasios drank it and made a face.

"Since the good doctor says that we should let you rest, we'll leave now," Narses told him. "If you want anything, simply tell my slave — I'll send someone round tomorrow morning. Much health! Doctor, if you would . . ." He drew the doctor out of the room into the corridor.

Anastasios groaned, and John went over to him. The old man's eyes were bleared and red, and his face was pinched and flushed. "How are you feeling?" John asked.

"It's just a fever," said Anastasios. "Tell His Illustriousness not to worry." The eyes closed, opened again with an effort. "He didn't need to fetch in an expensive doctor."

"Don't worry about it," John told him. "Just rest and get better. I promise not to rearrange your files while you're ill."

Anastasios gave his wheezing chuckle and closed his eyes again. "Much health!" John told him, and slipped from the room.

Narses was in the entrance hall, talking to the doctor. "I'll leave one of my men to guard your mount and light you home," he was saying when John joined him. "But you'll see that he's attended if he's in any danger?"

The doctor nodded. "I'll have one of my assistants sit up with him. The attendant will have to be paid separately, though."

"Of course. But tell him not to bother the old man about it: he thinks doctors are an extravagance. The payment is entirely my concern. Thank you, most distinguished Aetios, for troubling yourself on my friend's behalf."

The doctor bowed. "It is always a pleasure to be of service to Your Illustriousness."

Narses started down the stairs, and John followed him.

On the pavement outside the house, Jakobos was playing dice with the bodyguard, and greeted his master with a look of disappointment. The soldiers all sprang to attention. Narses addressed one of them rapidly in Armenian, and the man bowed. Another man untied a magnificent white Persian mare from the side of the house and led it over. John was surprised — he had assumed that the eunuch had ridden the mule. Narses mounted and collected the reins: he did not sit the horse like a man who'd been raised to it from childhood, but he did look as though he'd spent some time in the saddle. He smiled at John. "Perhaps you would give me the pleasure of your company back to the palace?" he said.

"Of course, Illustrious." John looked for his own horse and found that one of the bodyguard was already bringing it over. Jakobos ran for his bay gelding and scrambled up, and then all the bodyguard but the one singled out to wait for the doctor were in the saddle and waiting for their commander. John brought Maleka over beside the white Persian mare, and Narses started the party down the street.

"Is Anastasios seriously ill?" John asked.

Narses gave a slight shrug. "Yes. Though Aetios believes he

will recover." He sighed. "I've been afraid that this would happen for a year now. Anastasios hasn't really wanted to live since his wife died; he may fool the doctor."

"His wife? I never knew he was married."

"Oh yes. He married a girl of good family, despite his poor fortune, and they were very happy. They had three children: two died in infancy, and the third, a daughter, is married to a merchant in Smyrna. Anastasios' wife died last spring — one of the first victims of the plague. I'm not surprised that you've never heard of her: he can't mention her without tears, and so doesn't mention her at all. Perhaps I shouldn't even encourage him to live, since he finds life without her so painful. But I am fond of him, and I would miss him."

"I never realized that he cared for anything except his files."

Narses smiled. "He always loved his work. Since his wife's death, he's loved nothing else." They rode on for a moment in silence, and then the eunuch said thoughtfully, "But it seemed to me that he was over the worst of his depression. You cheered him up a great deal."

"I cheered him up?" John asked in surprise.

"You made him laugh. He enjoyed working with you. Well, I pray God he recovers." He crossed himself. "Holy God, Holy Almighty, Holy Immortal." He gave John another unreadable smile. "Crucified for us, have mercy!"

He had used the illegal Monophysite form of the prayer. "Have you known Anastasios for a long time?" John asked him, slightly bewildered by this openness from the inscrutable head chamberlain.

"Years. I met him back when I was treasurer for the privy purse and he was a clerk in the finance ministry. In the Nika rebellion I was given the job of bribing the Blues away from their allegiance to the rival emperor. Most of my own staff flatly refused to come with me — it was frightening, walking out into that howling mob with a purse full of gold. We all thought they would simply kill us and take the money. They'd already killed every imperial official they could get their hands on. I went right through the offices and the household, collecting volunteers, and Anastasios was one of the very few men I could persuade to come. He was a junior clerk paid twelve *solidi* a year, unable to afford to marry, and I put two hundred *solidi* into his hands and told him to risk his life by giving it away in the name of Justinian Augustus — and he did. He's an unusually brave and virtuous man."

John was silent a moment, trying to digest this. "I thought that the rebellion was quelled by Belisarius," he said hesitantly.

"Belisarius and Mundus went into the hippodrome with their private armies of retainers, arrested the rival emperor, and put down the rebellion by killing some thirty thousand of his supporters. I'd been sent out earlier to cause delay and confusion — the usual task of a bureaucrat. No, the true honor of quelling the rebellion must go to the Augusta. If it hadn't been for her, the rest of us would have fled the city. The palace guards were neutral and the populace was hostile: we were afraid for our lives, all of us. Even Belisarius. Her Serenity knew the risks as well as we did, but she was prepared to take them. She is a woman of extraordinary courage and intelligence."

John felt his face go hot; the praise for Theodora was headily sweet, particularly after the doubts bred by Euphemia. "I think she is," he said warmly; then, because the chamberlain was giving so much away, he added uncertainly, "About the Cappadocian . . ."

Narses looked at him expressionlessly.

"I heard a story about the Cappadocian that troubled me," John said, taking the plunge. "And I never know, in this city, whether what I hear is true or not."

"No one ever knows that in this city," Narses replied. "What was the story?"

"That the Augusta engineered his downfall, and that she was the one who had him arrested last summer — and had him tortured too, in defiance of the law."

Narses sighed. "John the Cappadocian," he said after a pause, "is an unusual man. You probably know several stories about him — there are some in every province, dealing with the . . . extreme methods and objects of his fund-raising. Some of what you may have heard is true, and some isn't. It's true that he is of a poor and obscure family. He began his career as a clerk in the office of the master of arms for the East, and the Augustus promoted him because of his sheer ability and intelligence. He is very brave, very bold, clear-headed, capable, and straightforward. He was extremely efficient as a praetorian prefect, and not exceptionally corrupt."

"Not? He has a huge estate. Almost four thousand pounds in gold, and that's only what's left after his disgrace. And I heard . . ."

Narses smiled and looked down. "I said, not *exceptionally* corrupt. He did take bribes, did peculate funds, and was certainly guilty of war profiteering. But that, I fear, is fairly standard these days. And you know the saying, 'All Cappadocians are bad, worse with money, worst in office, and worse than worst in the curial chair.' However, thirty-five hundred pounds in gold — and most of that acquired honestly — is not really very much when you consider the hundreds of thousands he's handled."

"His salary wouldn't have amounted to a tenth of that!" John said hotly.

Narses smiled and made an elegant gesture of concession. "My salary doesn't amount to a tenth of my income either. But there are, as you are aware, perquisites."

John said nothing for a moment. He could not help being aware of the perquisites of an imperial chamberlain. "You waive the fees sometimes," he said at last.

"Sometimes I do. And I still have enough to keep up a few mansions that are too far from the palace for me to use, an estate in Armenia that I've never seen, together with all the slaves and stewards to look after them. Also a monastery, a hospital, and an old people's home here in the city. Of course, my position holds more privileges than a praetorian prefect's; my predecessors arranged that very capably. The Cappadocian's predecessors were gentlemen of independent wealth, on the whole, who had not made such fine arrangements for their enrichment. He had a family, too, and the usual desire to pass his wealth on. And still, when you compare his fortune with the fortune that Belisarius has amassed through his service, it looks very small indeed."

"Belisarius? But I thought . . . that is, everyone says he's so honest!"

"He is as honest as any other general in the imperial service. Certainly he's guilty of nothing criminal, but he has benefited from his position as much as he can. Think a moment. He is able to maintain an army of seven thousand men from his private fortune. He has a moderate estate by inheritance, but a fortune fit for a king through his service. But because he is a soldier and owed much by the state, no one thinks anything of this. John's services were not rated as highly. But without them, Belisarius' wars could never have been fought."

"You're saying that he didn't deserve his disgrace," John said grimly.

The chamberlain shook his head. "No. But you wanted the truth of the story. And part of that truth is the fact that the Cappadocian was not the monster he is frequently portrayed to be. I have met one or two genuinely evil people in my life, and about as many saints, but the extremes are uncommon; most of us are a mixture, and John of Caesarea was no exception. But he certainly did deserve his disgrace. His efficiency was callous, and caused great suffering among the common people — and leaving that aside completely, he had every intention of committing treason against the sacred majesty of our master the Augustus, to whom he owed everything. If you like, you can add that he was a hot-tempered man, often violent and overbearing, and that he had a weakness for the pleasures of Aphrodite and went through mistresses more quickly than most men wear out shoes — though he had fits of repentance for that. He and the Augusta hated each other from the first. There are various absurd stories told about the reason for this. I think the truth is that he felt a deep contempt for women like the ones he kept, and that she had a similar feeling for the keepers. More-over, he thought that women have no place in political life, and resented her power. He never admitted any woman to his schemes, not even his daughter — and he was devoted to her. At any rate, the Augusta and the praetorian prefect opposed each other, spied on each other, and complained of each other to the Augustus whenever they had the chance. His Sacred Majesty, however, though he adores his wife, valued the Cappadocian too highly to dismiss him.

"In the end, Belisarius' wife lured John into an open declaration of treason, to gratify the Augusta. That is perfectly true. And it is also true that last summer, when the bishop of Cyzicus was murdered, the Augusta suspected John immediately and sent her men to arrest him. She was thoroughly convinced that he was capable of anything wicked. And there are perfectly valid reasons to suspect him, and very weighty reasons not to dismiss the charges. It is true that the arrest itself was not . . . handled as it should have been. But you must remember that last summer was a time when the world was ruled by death and chaos. The emperor was desperately ill, and half the city, half the world, was dying. There was no room to bury all the dead. Things were done then which men wouldn't have dreamed of doing at a more normal time — and I'm not sure whether they were done on anyone's orders or from a private terror and hatred."

"And that is the truth?" asked John, frowning.

Narses smiled. "That is the truth as I see it. You were concerned for the honor of your patroness, were you?"

John looked down at Maleka's dark name. "I was," he admitted. "And I have more to do with the Cappadocian's daughter than I'd like." He looked up at Narses; the eunuch's face was still . . . compassionate, he now realized. "Thank you," he said evenly. "I needed to know, and it is comforting."

Narses bowed his head politely. "The most serene Augusta favors you. You are very lucky in that — but I would be careful. Such favor toward an unknown tends to breed jealousy. If you'll take my advice, wear it lightly." And before John could ask him what he meant by that, he went on quickly. "Is that horse the famous Maleka? If you have the time, I'd like to see if she's as fast as her reputation."

The revelations are at an end, John noted — *and is he really offering a race?* He looked carefully at the calm face, then at the white Persian mare. "We're almost at the hippodrome now," he said at last. "If that nag of yours can run."

Narses smiled somewhat less cryptically than usual and touched the horse to a trot.

Maleka won the race by a length, and Narses gave John a smile that was improbably near a grin. "Lord of All!" he said, reining in. "It's a poor omen if an Arab can beat the Romans and Persians both! Ai, but it's a pleasure to be away from the office. I ought to do it more often."

"You ought to. It suits you."

That brought a quick, dark glance and a shake of the head. "Eunuchs are made that way — to sit in offices and look after the household. Though perhaps . . . never mind that. Esteemed John, I must attend the master. Much health, and I'll see you in the morning."

"Much health," said John. The head chamberlain spurred his mare to a canter and crossed the hard earth of the hippodrome, his bodyguard following close behind him. John tried to imagine him taking a purse full of gold into a howling mob of rioters who had proclaimed a rival emperor, butchered Justinian's supporters in the streets, and burned down half the city. To his surprise, he found it was easy. The eunuch had a kind of nerveless courage, a limitless energy, that allowed John to picture him facing the rioters with a polite smile.

Jakobos, who's watched the race with the bodyguard from the starting line, trotted up and followed his master's gaze.

"The bodyguard said that His Illustriousness is a proper man really; being a eunuch doesn't count with him," Jakobos informed him.

"I think they may be right," agreed John, and turned Maleka back toward the palace.

·   ·   ·

Anastasios, gravely ill, looked through the doors of death for a day before reluctantly closing them and recovering. John called at his house early in the morning a few days after meeting Narses there, and found the scribe sitting up in bed and drinking barley broth. The sight was like a sunrise, and he found himself smiling so that his face hurt. A part of himself observed it with surprise: he had not realized how much he liked the old man.

"You've come all this way very early in the morning," said Anastasios. "Stay for breakfast!"

Regretfully, John shook his head. "I've been invited to breakfast with the Augusta," he explained.

"You shouldn't have come," Anastasios told him, shocked. "You'll be late."

"I doubt it. She's a late riser. And it was worth the journey — keep it up!" Anastasios gave a surprised smile, and John grinned at him again, then ran down the stairs and along the streets — he'd come on foot — smiling and wondering at his own affection.

The empress was still in her bath when he arrived, but her staff admitted him to the breakfast room, and Theodora soon joined him. It was a warm, bright spring morning. In the garden outside, crocus and hyacinths were in flower, and the grapevines by the terrace had sent out their sticky green shoots. The empress had her couch moved into the sun before she sat on it, then lounged luxuriously in the warmth, eating saffron bread and grapes preserved in honey. "Have you ever been in love?" she asked John, smiling at him.

"Why?" John asked, smiling back. It was hard not to smile at Theodora, her pleasure in the season was so open and so infectious.

She shrugged, grinning, with half-lidded eyes. "It's spring.

> In spring Kydonian quinces drink
> the river's streams unmixed,
> and the vine leaf's new shadow sinks
> where the vine flower's shoots grow thick;

> But to me love leaves no rest,
> and like a north wind chill from Thrace,
> sweeps with parching madness pressed . . .

You must know what I mean. I used to fall in love every spring, regularly."

He laughed. "I'm not suddenly sleepless with love because it's warm, no."

She tossed him a grape. "Were you ever? Go on, you're a grown man! You can't be a virgin."

John stopped smiling, acutely embarrassed.

Theodora put her hand over her mouth. "Oh Lord!" she said. "You're not!" She gave a peal of laughter and shook her head. "A man, my son, and still a virgin at twenty-four!"

"There is nobody who has to be quite so respectable," John said with a bitter precision, "as the dependent of a respectable family."

His mother stopped laughing. "That's true. No whores allowed, respectable girls are out of the question, and I don't suppose you could afford to keep a concubine. I hadn't thought of that. My poor child! Ah well, chastity is pleasing to God — and prostitution is a wicked trade, where poor girls suffer and pimps get rich. I've been trying for years to stamp it out here in Constantinople. I'm glad you had nothing to do with it." She looked at him soberly for a moment, then the smile crept back onto her face. She stretched, wriggled her toes in the sunlight. "But have you never been in love?" she asked him.

He found himself grinning sheepishly back. "Yes."

"Ah!" She rolled over onto her stomach and propped up her chin on her hands. "Tell me about it?"

He shrugged. "There isn't much to tell. One of the magistrates of Bostra took a concubine a couple of years after his wife died. She was a respectable girl, a freedman's daughter, and he gave her a decent settlement and lived with her openly. I fell in love with her the moment I saw her — I was seventeen at the time, and she was very beautiful."

"What was she like?"

"Like a statue in ivory and gold — she was half Gothic, and fair as the gods. Her name was Chryseis. I used to imagine that her patron would get tired of her, and that when he dropped her I could go up and propose marriage."

Theodora grinned again, like a cat in the sunshine. "But her patron didn't, and you suffered for years in silence. My poor boy! Did you ever get to meet her?"

John laughed ruefully. "That's the worst of it. About a year after her patron established her, my father had some business with him over an estate and saw quite a lot of him. I went along with my father to take notes, and one evening I was put on the same couch with Chryseis during dinner while the elders talked business."

"And you couldn't think of a thing to say to her?"

"I didn't need to. She started off asking me what I'd seen the women wearing on a business trip to Berytus that winter, and went on about how she'd been weaving a new tunic for her dear patron but had run out of the blue wool and couldn't buy more of the same color for all the money in the world. And she told me about her sister's children's colds, and how her brother got a tremendous bargain in a camel-hair rug. I'd adored her like an icon, and I didn't know what to say. I'd been so desperate to talk to her that I couldn't admit that by the end of the meal I was aching to get away from her and hear what the real talk was about. A few days later, the same thing happened at another dinner party, and I had to admit it: Chryseis was beautiful, and a perfectly nice girl, but very dull and not very clever. I was crushed, and swore I'd never fall in love again."

Theodora giggled. "Poor John! And you never have?"

"I haven't had much opportunity. You try not to fall in love if you know that nothing can come of it if you do."

She gave him a bright, mischievous look. "So, like Hippolytos, you've said a long farewell to Aphrodite? What about marriage?"

He stared at her a moment with his mouth open, then closed it. "Marriage? You haven't . . ." He had a sudden horrifying notion that Theodora had already arranged something, that a girl was waiting in an anteroom with her wealthy or important family beside her, ready to inspect the bridegroom, and that he would be matched with the unknown on the spot. It was possible. All of Theodora's old friends from the theater and the hippodrome had had splendid marriages arranged for them by the empress, sometimes to the surprise of their partners. She enjoyed playing matchmaker, and performed the task with relish. But at the thought that she might have done so for him, the limits John had drawn so carefully about himself wavered, and he felt terrifyingly naked, vulnerable. There could be no cautious emotional distancing, no untouchability, in the consummation of a marriage. *I hate this city,* he thought with a surge of almost frightening passion. *It's a trap within a labyrinth, all suspended over an abyss: just when you think you're safe, you're caught. I've had my life remade and myself changed. I'm being spied on, and now I'm to be yoked with some girl of my mother's choosing and driven God knows where. Oh Mother of God, I want out!*

But Theodora laughed. "Lord, what shocked modesty! No, my dear, I don't have anything arranged. I would really like to leave you for a couple of years, give you a chance to concentrate on your career, and arrange something for you when it would be more advantageous. But if you were impatient for love, well, I could find you someone now. Since you're not, let's leave it, shall we?"

Relieved, John nodded, and Theodora laughed at him again and shook her head. "I gather the career's going well," she said contentedly. "What's this I hear about you getting the Cappadocian's files out of his daughter's claws?"

John explained about Euphemia. Theodora listened, munching grapes and waving a sandaled foot in the air. "So he did know where the files were," she commented when John finished. "The filthy hypocrite! Be careful with that girl, my dear. Her father was a vicious brute, and cunning as the king of devils, and it sounds as though he passed it on. If you don't stay on guard with her, you'll find yourself tricked into something and blackmailed. If it were up to me, I'd have the little bitch arrested and the house searched for the files — but I suppose she'll have hidden them."

John looked down at his hands for a moment. *Is it Euphemia who's spying on me?* he wondered. *I could find out. I could mention it now — but what would the empress do?*

He looked up, saw the fierceness of the dark eyes and the ugly twist to the empress's mouth, and remembered what had happened to Euphemia's father. *I can't wish for her to be punished again, and for her father's sake,* he thought unhappily. *I don't like her, but she's innocent of any crime. Would Theodora really put her in prison? And what else might happen to her if she did? I wish I knew what the limits are; I wish I knew where you want me to go, Augusta.* "She'll have hidden them," he agreed. "And I don't really think she deserves to be arrested. She is a bitch, but I suppose she's bound to try to help her father. And from all I can gather, she never knew much about what he was doing anyway; he thought women should be ignorant."

"He was a cunning, greedy, unprincipled brute!" said Theodora savagely. "He used to tell lies about me to Peter. I hated him. But you're right, I don't suppose he told her anything." She lay frowning a moment, her head on her hands, and then gave a malicious smile. "Well, if she tries to seduce you, let her. In fact, you could encourage her. I don't think the experience would hurt you, and it would do her father good to come back and find he's made his daughter into a whore."

John felt slightly sick. Seduce and abandon a girl you dislike, for the sake of revenge on her father? "No thank you," he said quietly.

Theodora looked up sharply. First the malice went out of her smile, and then the smile itself faded.

"You're right," she said, very softly. "It's a cruel scheme. I don't think I'd want to either, in your position. It wouldn't be a very good introduction to love — and if I remember rightly, she's a fat girl with pimples."

"She's no beauty," John agreed. For the second time that morning he felt weak with relief. *There are some limits,* he thought; *she thinks about overstepping them, but she doesn't.*

Theodora laughed at him and offered him the grapes.

The empress had invited the emperor to have dinner in her palace that evening and to spend the night. They dined on oysters and wild boar glazed with figs, washed down by a flask of a priceless Lemnian wine, and then made love in Theodora's great purple-draped bed. A single lamp glowed on the golden lampstand. When young, Theodora had been forced to save lamp oil, and now she liked to leave her lamps to burn themselves out.

Justinian lay on his side next to his wife in a state of complete physical happiness. He studied Theodora tenderly. The purple bedspread, worked with pictures of nymphs and shepherds, lay tangled about her waist; her bare upper body glowed with the wash of golden light. *Beautiful as ever,* he thought, touching her gently. She smiled.

"When we got married, you said we'd spend every night together," she said.

"Well, we did for a few years. But an empress must have her own household — and you like to sleep more than I do, Lazy."

She smiled a fittingly lazy smile, caught his hand, and put it to her lips. She nibbled on the fingers. "You should spend every night with me, even though I have my own household."

"You wouldn't say that if I were coming to bed three hours after midnight after consulting with the bishops."

She giggled. "Spend all night with the bishops, then go to bed with a whore."

"Now, my dear . . ." He kissed her. "You know I don't like you to call yourself that — even as a joke."

"I know — and you know I don't want you to talk about bishops. As soon as anyone says 'Monophysite' or 'Chalcedon,' you go grim as a monk. Let's talk about something else."

"Very well. What?"

Theodora rolled over and propped herself up on an elbow. "Should I get my cousin John a wife now, or in a couple of years' time? I can't decide." Without seeming to, she watched her husband carefully. Narses had given her his warning very tactfully, but she had understood quite plainly what he had meant by it.

"You're thinking of marrying him off, are you?" said the emperor, some of his contentment slipping away. The subject was like a sore tooth, continually poked at secretly by a helpless tongue. On the other hand, a marriage sounded reassuring.

"Mmm," said Theodora, inwardly noting that Narses was, as usual, quite right. *The idiot,* she thought of her husband. *He ought to know better! At least he knew better than to admit it. Here's a challenge, then: can I reassure Peter without marrying John off quite yet?*

"If I find him a girl now," she said earnestly, "she would help to establish him, further his career and give him a decent house. But if I waited a couple of years, I could make a better match for him. I should think he'll be of higher rank in a couple of years than he is now."

"How high a rank were you thinking of for him?"

"As high as possible," she said firmly. "Patrician at least. But he'll have to have a few more offices behind him to get that."

"I'm glad you think so."

"Don't sound so disapproving! I don't want him to hold jobs he can't do. But since he's as competent, or more competent, than most of the candidates, why shouldn't it be him instead of them? He's my cousin and they're not."

"A formidable recommendation," Justinian agreed solemnly. "Who would he marry if he married now?"

"That's the problem. I can think of half a dozen girls I could arrange as a match for him, all rich, all pretty, and a couple of them clever as well. There's my friend Chrysomallo's daughter, or the niece of Peter Barsymes the banker — it would be easy to have John marry one of them. But none of them has any real rank. And he needs respectability more than he needs money.

If we waited a few years, he might manage to marry power as well as wealth." *And I want him to marry power,* she added silently. *Wealth is all very well, but it's power that counts, and if you have power, you have wealth too.*

Justinian laughed. "You incorrigible matchmaker! You've already got your grandson engaged to Belisarius' daughter and your niece to my nephew. Who do you fancy for your cousin John, then? Germanus' daughter, Justina?"

"She's already engaged to Vitalian's nephew," said Theodora. "And Passara would never, ever agree to the match — not that her pimply daughter is worth much anyway."

"What does your cousin think about all this?"

"Oh, I haven't told him anything. It would just worry him."

"Watch out, or he'll go marry some unsuitable girl from the theater!"

Theodora laughed. "I can manage any little slut he might pick up — and if she could hold her own, well, maybe I wouldn't mind. But he'd better not pick some simpering, virtuous, middle-class nonentity, or I'll wash my hands of him. I don't think he's going to marry anyone without consulting me, my dear. He's been very proper and respectful: he knows what's due a patroness."

The emperor smiled. His own jealous uncertainty suddenly seemed improbable and almost unreal; he wondered if he'd really felt like that, and why. "If you want him to make a splendid match, he'll have to have some military experience," he told Theodora. "The household and the offices are all very well, but they're slow roads to advancement. By the time your cousin gets to be patrician by secretarying, he'll be readier for retirement than marriage."

"Mmm. If he doesn't marry now, he should be attached to some general out on campaign." *Let Peter see that I don't mind at all if John's away — and a spell of military service will only be an advantage.* "I was wondering about sending him as an adviser to Martinus in the East. He speaks Arabic, Aramaic, and Persian."

"He would be useful there, then. It's a possibility. I'll bear it in mind when I'm making the appointments. But to tell the truth, my life, I think the war may really be over — avert the omen! We'll have to see what happens this summer. But Chosroes didn't achieve anything to speak of in his invasions the last three years, and he lost a lot of time and money besieging Edessa."

"I pray God the war is over!" said Theodora passionately. "The stupid, pointless, miserable, damnable conflict has lost us so much . . . though I suppose that if it is over, my cousin will have to join Belisarius in Italy or Areobindus in Africa. I'd rather have him in the East; he'd achieve more there, I think."

"There is another possibility," the emperor suggested slowly. "Narses thinks very highly of him, you know; he said he was 'entirely satisfied.' From Narses, that's a high compliment."

Theodora grinned. "It is indeed. Narses himself has no equal."

She had understood two things from the eunuch's warning, besides the main thrust of it: that Narses knew that the suspicions were unfounded, and that he was fond of John. She had always liked Narses, and felt now a flood of affection toward him. *I must do something for him,* she thought.

The emperor raised his eyebrows, then nodded agreement. "I was thinking that since Narses finally has a secretary he's satisfied with, he'd be reluctant to lose him. We need to raise another mercenary force, whatever happens in Persia — the plague has left us weakened. I was considering sending Narses into Thrace to recruit some of the Heruls. He's about the only man who can get anywhere with those savages. Your cousin could help with the recruiting, and then, if he proves competent, help to officer the army. If the Persian war isn't over, we can send them East; otherwise, we could supply them to Belisarius."

"He's asking for more troops already, is he?" said Theodora. "And he's not even in Italy yet! That does sound a good idea, though. Narses would certainly like it."

"Would he?"

Theodora laughed and ran a finger down her husband's nose.

"My life and soul, he simply loves to get out of the city and play soldiers! You must know that! I think that if he hadn't been sold into slavery, he'd have ended up a brigand in Armenia. Captain Narses, the terror of Persian traders! And I think he's better at it than you've ever given him a chance to prove. That disaster in Italy wasn't really his fault."

Justinian smiled. "You have a point. Very well. I'll send him to Thrace and give him some military title."

"It's a good idea for my cousin, too," said Theodora, smiling back. "John can go cover himself with glory among the Heruls, come back in a few years, and marry a lady — and that will be him taken care of. Thank you, my dearest." She lay back into the silk-covered pillows and smiled up at her husband, her eyes half closed. He kissed her.

"I hope for your sake he does just that," Justinian told her. "But I prefer my theater girl to the proudest lady in the empire."

VI

The heruls

Two days later, when John reported for work at the inner office, Narses greeted him with a smile that was stiff with tension; his eyes were unusually bright. "I have something to discuss with you," he announced, and beckoned John to the private anteroom on the household side of the office. John hurriedly collected his tablets and followed.

The private room was dark — it was raining heavily, and the lamps were unlit. Narses stood in the middle and looked up at the half-hidden window, smiling; then, as John closed the door, he glanced over quickly. "What do you know about the Heruls?" he asked.

Of all the barbarian tribes whose letters and representatives flowed through the offices, the Heruls took up the most file space. John hesitated a moment, trying to order the mass of material in his mind, then said cautiously, "They are a tribe of barbarians, related to the Goths, who have settled in Upper Moesia near the city of Singidunum. They provide us with large numbers of allied troops — under Pharas in Africa, under Philemuth in the East —"

"Yes, yes, yes," said Narses impatiently. "What else?"

John again hesitated, mystified by the air of suppressed excitement. *Narses knows as much about the Heruls as anyone in Constantinople,* he thought; *he handles all the delegations and is friendly with most of their chieftains. Why is he interested in seeing how much I know? Is there a crisis? Has somebody leaked sensitive information?*

"Two years ago the Heruls in Moesia killed their king," he said slowly, feeling his way. "His name was Ochos; he'd tried to strengthen his power at the expense of his nobles, and they didn't like it. Last year the nobles decided that they did want a king after all, and they asked us to send them one."

"Not quite," said Narses, smiling again. "First they sent an embassy to Thule. They wanted a king of the royal line, and they believed the family was still extant among the Heruls of the far north. Then, under pressure from Constantinopole, they accepted a king from us — one of our allied commanders, Souartouas. The embassy from Thule still hasn't returned; there may be some trouble if it does and was successful. But for the moment the Heruls are friendly toward us." The chamberlain paused, smiling at John with a bright, secretive gaze. "And we are going to pay them a visit."

John stared at him in blank astonishment. "Who do you mean by 'we'?" he asked.

Narses grinned. "You, me, my retainers, my pick of two hundred guardsmen, and, if the Persian war is over, Philemuth and five hundred allied cavalry. We are to recruit troops either to use in the East or to hand over to Belisarius for his Italian campaign — as many men as possible, ten thousand at the least. We leave this summer, recruit through the autumn, and overwinter in the region. If we do go to Italy, we'll then have to take the troops down to Dyrrhachium and embark them there next spring; otherwise we go back through Constantinople. I'm to have the rank of an acting master of arms and authority to raise and spend money and requisition supplies as I wish. You're to have a position in the imperial guard — the Protectors, not the Scholarians — and possibly a commander's rank later."

"Oh," said John, still blankly. *We leave this summer,* he repeated to himself silently. *We collect troops . . . Lord of All, we're going to war! Away from this treacherous city, and the spies and the cold and the questions, out to the defense of the empire.* "Oh!" he said again, and his blank disbelief began to slough off like a snake's skin. "Is this certain?" he demanded, afraid that it would turn out to be a rumor.

Narses nodded happily, still grinning. "His Sacred Majesty told me this morning. I'd known he was considering such a move, but I thought he would decide to send someone else. I didn't expect the military rank, either. But you mustn't tell anyone else yet. We'll have to rearrange the office before we go, and I want to keep the post-seeking and bribery to a minimum."

"No, no . . ." John didn't know what to say, and stopped himself. He met Narses' eyes; the two men stared at each other for a moment. *He's as excited about it as I am,* John thought.

"Of course," Narses said, "it will be extremely hard work. Moving ten thousand men about is difficult at any time, and it's very much worse when they're barbarians from a particularly wild and undisciplined tribe. And there is a real danger that the embassy to Thule may reappear with a rival king of the Heruls, and our troops will mutiny. And Thrace and Moesia are very poor, wild, and inhospitable regions, where hardship is a condition of life."

John shook his head. "It is absolutely, unspeakably wonderful."

Narses laughed. "Isn't it? Goodbye, Constantinople! But remember, you mustn't tell anyone yet."

The ban on mentioning the mission lasted a month, and was lifted only when the arrangements for the office had been finalized between Narses and his colleagues in the imperial household. The chamberlain's duties were to be divided between two other officials — another of the palace eunuchs to regulate audiences and attend on the emperor, and an agent of the master of the offices to handle the complex mass of financial, legal, and diplomatic business. The three scribes were to remain in the office, and Sergius was given a promotion to act as secretary to both officials in John's place.

"Sergius?" asked John in dismay when Narses informed him of this.

"He is intelligent and competent," Narses said coolly. "I'm certain he'll manage very well."

"Yes, but Anastasios is honest."

Narses sighed and gave John a look of affectionate irony. "The responsibility would kill Anastasios. He's never liked authority, and he would worry himself over what he did until it made him ill again. It has to be Sergius — and he'll stay within bounds since he knows that I'm coming back."

"Very well," John said heavily. The need for an orderly transition of power meant that he would have to spend the next few weeks working closely with Sergius. *Just the chance Sergius is looking for to poke around in my business,* John thought unhappily. *I wish I knew whether he's doing it on his own behalf or whether someone else is paying him.*

Anastasios had recovered by the time the news broke, but he said nothing when Narses made his speech to the office outlining the new arrangements. He glowered for the rest of the day, however, and the following morning abruptly stood up in the middle of preparing a file. "I need to talk to His Illustriousness," he told John, and stamped off to the inner office. John heard his voice raised, demanding to speak to Narses privately, and then silence for half an hour. A bishop and a senator were kept waiting until the old scribe stamped back out again and flung himself down on his stool. The emperor's chamberlain came to the office door and stood there a moment, looking at Anastasios' back with a mixture of anger and regret, then shrugged and nodded to John to send in the next name.

"Damn him!" said Anastasios in an undertone, shuffling his half-complete file. He glared at John. "And damn you too. That's a fine trick to play on me, leaving me to run the office for that slimy Sergius. What a lovely thing to come back to work for!"

"I'm sorry," said John helplessly.

Anastasios snorted. "You I can understand. You're a young man, and any young man with a bit of spirit would rather be out in the field than pushing pens in an office. But a man of the rank of His Illustriousness — and at his age, too! — ought to know better."

"What do you mean, 'at his age'? How old is he?"

"How old do you think?"

"Forty-five?"

"I guessed forty when I met him twenty years ago. He's at least as old as I am myself — he's got no business trying to take up generalship again now. Particularly after that mess in Italy. But no, he just has to prove to the world that they didn't cut off his courage with his testicles — as though anyone with a grain of sense thought he kept it there! Well, I've told him what I think of it, though it won't make any difference to him, damn him," Anastasios rammed the file straight on his desk and jammed on its identifying codicils. "And you can both keep quiet about it from now on."

"Yes, Anastasios," said John meekly, and bent quietly over his work.

Sergius was predictably delighted with the news of his superior's departure and his own promotion, and smirked continuously for a week. "Though a position in the Protectors is quite something," he told John while they were going through the filing system. "You have to pay a thousand *solidi* or more if you're trying to buy your way in. Still, I don't envy you, having to go off and deal with the Heruls. They're the most disgusting people in the world. Though I suppose you think that honor goes to the Saracens."

He's fishing again, John thought wearily. *Somebody suspects something, for Sergius to go on about Berytus and Arabia the way he does.* "I don't know much about Saracens," he replied. "They don't usually come as far as Berytus; we only buy the horses."

Sergius smiled and pretended to study the notes on the filing system. *Slippery as ever,* he thought angrily. *All the money I've spent keeping track of him, and it's got me nowhere. And now I'll have to leave it until he comes back from Moesia. Well, at least I've got promotion.*

·   ·   ·

It was the end of May before John informed Euphemia that he would be leaving.

The girl's big, empty house was slightly less bare and rundown now; some of the restored fortune had gone into it, though John suspected that most of the money would stay with the Cappadocian in Egypt. They had completed the evening's exchange of information, and the Cappadocian's daughter was relaxed and cheerful. Euphemia sat with her legs up on the couch, an earthenware cup of watered wine in her hand, smiling at a list John had given her. Some of her hair had come loose from its usual severe knots, and it curled wispily around her cheek. *A fat girl with pimples,* John thought, remembering Theodora's description. *It might have been true when she was younger, but she's not fat now. She would even be pretty, if she didn't swathe herself in black and clamp herself in hats and hairnets. But she doesn't want to be pretty — the usual things women want, marriage and children, don't seem to interest her at all. Though I suppose she can't marry anyway; no one would take the daughter of a disgraced official who was so widely hated. What does she want, apart from having her father out of prison? Revenge on the empress? Power? Is she the one who's spying on me? And why?*

Euphemia looked up and noticed his stare; she scowled. "What are you looking at?" she demanded. The formal honorifics hadn't lasted long.

"I have to tell you that I will be leaving for Moesia next month," John said simply.

She stared at him for a moment, her mouth going round. "For Moesia?" she asked at last. "Why?"

"His Illustriousness has been appointed to raise a force of Herulian mercenaries in Moesia. I'm going with him. We'll be gone about a year."

The color flooded into her face. "A year? But . . . but what about my information? I had a letter from my father only last week; he was delighted with the information, he said it was invaluable and I must keep it up, and if you go . . ." She stopped and bit her lip, angry with herself for giving so much away.

"You can probably come to some arrangement with my temporary replacement," John said. He tried not to let her see how carefully he watched her response to the mention of Sergius. "He would undoubtedly be delighted to help the praetorian prefecture."

Euphemia said nothing. She looked down, still chewing on her lip. She picked up the thick volume of the tax indiction — still Syria — and held it on her lap. "Who's your replacement?" she asked harshly, when the silence became awkward.

"A man called Sergius, the son of Demetrianos the banker."

She snorted. "I've heard of Demetrianos Golden Thumb. What's this Sergius like? Can I trust him?"

"Do you trust me?" John asked sarcastically.

"Yes," she shot back, quickly and unexpectedly. "I do. I trust you not to lie or cheat me with rumors, and I trust you to know what you're talking about. I know you now; I don't know this Sergius. Would you trust him?"

"No," John answered, off-balance enough to tell the truth. "He's greedy and malicious and I don't trust him an inch. But he is going to do my job at the office, and he should have access to most of the same information. I presume you can come to some arrangement with him if you want to keep him honest."

"I suppose I can," she said, still not looking up.

John hesitated, looking at the precise part on the top of her brown head. "There's also an old man called Anastasios," he said at last. "You met him, I think. He doesn't have the same degree of access to the emperor, but he is honest and scrupulous. And he is deeply offended by the very idea of the prefecture trying to manage without its files; he'd be happy to come if you can't manage Sergius."

"I can manage," she said, sitting up straight and glaring. "You can bring this Sergius next week, and I'll make some arrangement with him. Good night!"

John rose, feeling oddly uncomfortable, as though he had missed something, as though something had been said that shouldn't have been; and yet nothing extraordinary had been said. "Lady Euphemia, much health!" he responded, and walked slowly down the stairs to fetch his horse. *At any rate*, he thought, *I think she really doesn't know Sergius. Perhaps it wasn't she who tried to bribe Jakobos. But if it wasn't she, then who was it?*

He sighed and hunched his shoulders against the unseen watchers, and his thoughts turned eagerly into the road north.

John left the city on a hot, windy morning in early June, riding self-consciously at Narses' side at the head of more than seven hundred horsemen. The Persian war had been ended by a five-year truce, and the five hundred Herulian cavalry trailed down the streets of the city after Narses' twenty retainers and the hundred men of the imperial Protectors; another hundred of the household's Scholarian Guard brought up the rear. The emperor and empress, with another two hundred guardsmen, accompanied the troops as far as the Golden Gate. There the procession stopped on the wide terrace between the two city walls, first the imperial couple and their guard, and then, facing them, the troops bound for Moesia: seven hundred armed men, seven hundred horses drawn up in wide half-circles of light and motion. Behind them, still in the city, the long baggage train of mule carts and packhorses managed by slaves stood and waited in the wide street. The citizens streamed out onto the walls to watch. It was, thought John happily, a magnificent sight and well worth looking at. The light gleamed on the helmets and armor of the men, glittered on their spear points and the fittings of the horses' harness; the enameled shields of the imperial guardsmen, with their monogram of the name of Christ, glowed golden. The emperor rode on a white gelding draped with a harness of purple and gold; the empress sat quietly in her gilded coach. The dragon standard of gold-worked silk fluttered in the breeze as though it wanted to fly from its post and soar off, far into the north. Behind them rose the massive inner city wall and the invincible towers of the gate; before, the road ran through the triple archway of the outer wall northwest into Thrace.

John adjusted the weight of his own enameled shield on his arm and glanced carefully to each side. The empress had told him that he must hire a couple of private retainers, to indicate that he was an officer, and she had found him two sturdy Vandal warriors, Hilderic and Eraric, who now sat on their chargers to his right and his left, looking as though they'd seen it all before. John sighed, and tried to school his own face into a similar impassivity. He found the company of the two Vandals oppressive and their skill at swordsmanship depressing. He had learned riding and shooting in Bostra because they were considered essential even for a bastard gentleman — necessary for examining estates and for the noble occupations of hunting and racing. But how to use a sword or spear, and even how to put on and take off the armor he had acquired, were beyond him. He thought wistfully of Jakobos, who was coming as his personal slave; the boy was with the baggage, and was undoubtedly sorry to miss the spectacle.

Narses, looking unfamiliar in his mail coat and red-crested helmet, dismounted from his white Persian mare. He handed his helmet to one of his retainers, took three steps forward, then gracefully sank down to prostrate himself to the emperor; he rose, then prostrated himself again toward the gilded coach; rose, took one step backward, and again adored the sacred majesty of the sovereigns. John had already discovered how difficult it was to bow properly in armor, and wondered again whether the eunuch was as old as Anastasios had indicated.

The emperor bowed his own head in return. "Most esteemed and truly valued Narses," Justinian said, slowly and clearly so that his voice would carry. "Good fortune go with you."

Narses rose and set one hand on the high cantle of his mare's saddle. "God preserve Your Sacred Majesty in all prosperity until our return!" he exclaimed, and mounted. The trumpets sounded; the household guards all raised their spears and shouted, and on the walls of the city the people shouted the chant from the hippodrome, "Victory to the holy and thrice august sovereigns, Justinian and Theodora! Conquer! Conquer!"

"I haven't liked that chant since they used it in the Nika rebellion," muttered Narses, gathering the reins. He jerked his head to the right and trotted his horse in that direction, past the watching emperor. John looked over at the gilded coach: Theodora was sitting like a statue in her purple robes and the diadem, one hand raised in a gesture of blessing. When John's eye caught hers, however, she gave a quick grin and an unobtrusive but unmistakable wink. John covered his own grin by bowing low and touching his helmet — and then he was past her, and the city was behind him. *Goodbye, Constantinople!* he thought, and patted Maleka's neck. The mare was nervous and unhappy with the weight and sound of the armor, and only laid back her ears at him.

From Constantinople to Singidunum was a distance of more than five hundred miles. For the first four days they rode through the green and fertile countryside of the province of Europa. The fields, silver-green with wheat, were baking to gold in the heat of the summer sun; in the vineyards the grapes were heavy on the vines. The road was in excellent condition, and there was no difficulty in arranging supplies in the prosperous villages along the way. It was a wonderfully pleasant ride, a relaxation much needed after the last month in the city. The work in the office had drowned all his personal preparations. The acquisition of weapons and armor, induction into the Protectors, packing — all had passed in a dream. The reality of departure had seemed confined to requisition orders and innumerable codicils and letters. Now he could catch his breath and look at the troops.

Narses' retainers were mostly Armenians and, with John's Vandals, were the most professional soldiers in the company, skilled, experienced, and impeccably disciplined. They were well equipped as heavy cavalry, and most of them were competent archers as well. The Heruls were all veterans as well, but apart from that were quite different from the Armenians. They were tall, fair men who rode either Thracian or Persian mounts; they were armed and armored in a random fashion and were ferocious fighters, but rough, disorderly, and inclined to drunkenness and quarrels. They were commanded by Philemuth, a brave vainglorious man who fortunately admired Narses enormously and tried to maintain some discipline for his commander's sake.

The imperial guardsmen — the Protectors and Scholarians — were a striking contrast to them. Most were young men of wealthy Asian families, eager to distinguish themselves in war. They were beautifully equipped with standardized arms and armor (mail coat, breastplate, oval shield, round helmet, long cavalry sword, and a spear) and wore brilliantly colored uniforms — green and red for the Scholarians, red and purple for the Protectors. They did not expect to spoil this equipment by doing any of the dirty work of soldiering themselves; they had all brought at least one slave to handle "that sort of thing." They looked very splendid as they rode along through the rich countryside. However, for the most part they were scarcely better trained than John himself. The Protectors in particular were all officers: theoretically, they could serve on the staff of any commander in the empire, though in practice most of them only took a post in the capital for a few years for the look of the thing. The Scholarians, who formed the bulk of the imperial guard, were somewhat less exalted and marginally better trained, but none of them had ever seen a battle. The Scholarians had their own commander, a morose man by the name of Flavius Artemidoros, who had had no desire to leave his comfortable barracks and recruit barbarians in the wilds of Moesia but who hadn't wanted to spend enough to bribe anyone to be excused.

John himself was in command of the Protectors. He had dreaded this, but in fact it required very little attention. Discipline had always been fairly lax for the palace troops, but they instinctively looked up to the secretary of an imperial official and obeyed his orders cheerfully, though he was aware that they regarded him as a jumped-up clerk. The actual business of providing them with supplies and arranging their duties (or, more usually, their slaves' duties) was already part of his secretarial work. The only unusual arrangement he made in the course of the journey was to initiate a training drill in the evenings, and the Protectors welcomed this, as most of them felt as unprepared as John did. The Heruls would watch as the young gentlemen galloped clumsily about their makeshift practice fields, grunting and sweating and missing their spear casts; occasionally one of the barbarians would jump onto his own horse and go through some astonishing feat of skill, and the others would cheer him and jeer at the Protectors.

Around noon on the fifth day they reached Hadrianopolis. It was a grim city, fortified and refortified, tower on wall on moat, gated with iron. Narses gave the order to stop for the night, though they had done only six miles that day. "We'll give the horses a rest," he told John. "The journey will get harder now, and harder again after Philippopolis."

The following day they continued on. The fields were patchier, poorer, and there were few people to be seen working in them. Villagers tended to disappear at the approach of soldiers, and it was harder to find supplies. Partly for practice, John took out his new bow and shot at the pheasants and rabbits the vanguard disturbed from the empty fields. He had always been a competent archer, though never a prize one, and he killed enough small game to treat his fellow officers to fresh meat for supper. Rather to his surprise, both the guardsmen and the Heruls were impressed by his skill. "When did you learn archery?" demanded the Protectors, and John gathered that shooting was not considered essential for gentlemen north of the Taurus mountains. Philemuth asked to see the bow. It was an expensive weapon, a composite one, with layers of horn alternating with wood; it was small, light, and very stiff. "Persian?" he asked in his heavily accented Greek.

"I bought it in the Constantinianae quarter of Constantinople, near the Apostles' Church," John replied. "I assume it was made in the city."

Philemuth sighed, and beckoned over one of his Heruls, whom John had noticed as another shooter of game, and barked an order. The man grinned, bowed, and handed his weapon to John. It was longer than John's own, but made entirely of wood, and far less stiff. "That's the sort of bow we have," Philemuth said. "It is good for small game, and that is all. We are brave men, warriors. We like weapons that will be strong and kill men, so we have never practiced much archery. But the Persians — Mother of God, how they can shoot! Worse than the Huns! And the Saracens as well. In the East, we saw much of the Saracens — some of them had bows like yours. Your horse is Saracen as well, is she not? In the East, most of the Arabian and Syrian troops copied the tactics of the Persians and Saracens; I see it was the same in Berytus."

Narses gave one of his ambiguous smiles. "As to that, we have all copied the Persians. In the distant past, the strength of the Roman state lay in its legions of infantry; commanders these days regard infantry as next to worthless. The Persian *dekhans* were the first to use heavily armored cavalry, and the Romans copied them. Now everyone everywhere tries to get the largest and heaviest horse he can find and piles on all the armor he can afford. I wonder, though, if the infantry isn't underrated. If one had some good pikemen and some archers . . ."

Philemuth snorted. "Heavy cavalry can crush anything."

Narses gave another polite smile and said nothing.

From Philippopolis, which they reached eleven days after leaving Constantinople, the road began to climb into the Rhodope mountains, and as Narses had warned, the journey became harder. Parts of the road were flooded by the Hebrus River and parts were crumbling down mountain cliffs, and the troops had to stop and shore them up before the baggage train could pass over them. Villages were scarce collections of mud huts, fortified and clinging to inaccessible hilltops; even the towns were walled and guarded, clutching desperately at the miserable poverty which was all they had. Larger towns were barricaded with double walls and refused to open their gates to any armed men, even the emperor's. Large tracts of land lay waste and desolate. "This region has suffered invasion almost continually for a hundred and forty years," Narses commented when they failed to find accommodation one night. "The Goths, the Halani, and the Huns, the Vandals and the Lombards, the Gepids and the Bulgars, the Sclaveni and the Antae — they've all been through. And the Heruls, of course. And us — from the peasants' viewpoint, we're almost as bad. It's amazing there's anything left. Make a note that I must talk to the men tomorrow and remind them that we are passing through Roman lands and they're not to plunder."

It was a reminder the men needed. The Herulian cavalry had a tendency to wander off the road looking for loot, and could not be trusted on reconnaissance missions. Even the imperial guardsmen were eager to "shake a few of these hoarding peasants and see what happens," as one of the Protectors put it. "Try it and you'll get shaken yourself," John replied sharply. "They're *Roman* peasants, and we need to keep them sweet. We have plenty of supplies with us and we can get more in Sardica." *Though if it's like this with seven hundred men,* he added silently, *I don't know how we'll manage with ten thousand.*

Narses was already arranging for the ten thousand. On arriving at Sardica he descended upon the governor like a flash of lightning, set up a separate office to handle supplies, barricaded it with requisition orders, fortified it with codicils, and rearranged the tax system for the entire province of Dacia in the bargain. Supplies in kind were to be levied and stored; spare clothing was to be purchased from one tax, spare horses from another. The troops rested in the city for four days; for four days John wrote letters and took notes until his hand ached. He was glad to get back on the road.

Sardica to Remesiana, Remesiana to Naissus, out of the mountains and onto the flat plains of Moesia. The land here was more fertile, though scarcely more populous; the peasants were as suspicious but considerably better off. The region had been partly shielded from invasion by the settlement of the Heruls on the border to its north. "The emperor comes from that village over there," Narses said one morning when they were about two miles from Naissus. John looked toward the village with surprise: it was a small, smoky, dirty place. In the green fields an elderly peasant woman, the only one who had not fled at the sight of the soldiers, was hoeing a field of onions. Her bent gray back was toward them and her hoe flashed regularly in the heavy, hot sun. "You mean his family owned it?" he asked.

Narses smiled. "No. His family lived in it. His mother probably hoed onions like that too." He gave John an ironic look. "You didn't know?"

"No. I'd simply assumed . . . that is, his uncle was emperor; I assumed the whole family was powerful."

"The Augustus Justin rose through the ranks of the army from a common soldier to become a captain of the palace guard — Count of the Excubitors, not the Protectors, I'm afraid. When he found himself a count, he had his nephews brought to Constantinople and educated. He himself was almost illiterate: he had no children, and felt the need for some member of his family to supply his own lack of education. One of the nephews was an able general and popular with the men, but the other was an exceptionally brilliant administrator, an intelligent and original organizer, who managed to get his uncle acclaimed Augustus on the death of the emperor Anastasios. Justin was grateful and adopted him."

"Germanus and Justinian," said John. "Holy God!"

Narses smiled again. "It's not a very noble court, is it? The Senate hates it. Well, we aren't that distinguished ourselves. Philemuth is a chieftain among the Heruls, and well born, but you and I . . . an ex-town clerk and an ex-slave, ex-peasant palace eunuch! Still, our army isn't much either."

"You weren't a peasant!" John exclaimed, grinning and taking advantage of the chamberlain's communicative mood.

"Ah, but I was. Third son of a poor Armenian farmer just over the border from Theodosiopolis. Our plow ox died one winter, and my father was faced with seeing the whole family starve or selling one of his children. He chose me because I was the smallest, and least useful for working the land. The slaver had the cutting done for the same reason. I was still very young at the time, and not worth much. I don't believe the slaver even gave my father enough to buy his ox outright." Narses rode a moment in silence. His smile was gone now. "I still have relations there," he added after a moment. "When I was manumitted and found myself rich, I sent some money to them. Sixty-nine *solidi*. I thought they should at least get as much as the emperor paid."

"Did you never want to go back yourself?" asked John.

Narses shook his head. "There was nothing to go back to, and nothing to say if I did."

John looked down at his own hands, holding the darkened leather of Maleka's reins. "No," he said. "You can never go back, can you?"

Two days' ride north of Naissus and nearly a month after leaving Constantinople, they reached the territory of the Heruls.

The Heruls were officially the guests of the native Roman population, but in practice the native population was sparse and confined to Singidunum and one or two other towns in the region; all the farming villages were Herulian. Heruls did not disappear at the approach of soldiers the way Roman peasants did. Instead, even before the troops reached the first Herulian village the people came swarming up to the road, sullen and suspicious at the sight of the guardsmen and the dragon standard, bursting into sudden cheers when they realized that the bulk of this army consisted of their own countrymen. The Herulian cavalry shouted, beat their swords against their shields, waved their spears in the air, and galloped their horses up and down. Narses gave the signal to halt, and Philemuth conducted a prolonged discussion with the village elders in their own language. Narses sat on his white mare impassively, listening. John already knew that he understood the language, though he preferred not to speak it. Eventually one of Philemuth's men was sent on ahead at a gallop to some local nobleman to announce their arrival.

"Now the tedious part begins," Narses told John — in Persian, so as not to offend the Heruls. "We spend the next three or four months drinking, listening to speeches, and arbitrating Herulian quarrels, and if we're lucky we'll have one chance to bathe during that time."

"Three or four months? Will it really take that long?" asked John.

"Oh yes," said Narses, smiling. "It will indeed."

The Heruls, John discovered, set great store by hospitality, and very little by royal authority. It was impossible simply to go to the king at Singidunum and publish the emperor's request for men. This was a pity, thought John, since Singidunum was the only place in the region where some form of civilized life could be found. The king, Souartouas, had commanded troops for Justinian, and had tried to recreate in the frontier capital a tiny shadow of Constantinople. He held court in the old prefectural palace, and when the army arrived he welcomed them all and invited the officers to an elegant dinner party, where he served imported wine; he also offered his Roman visitors the use of the palace bathhouse (the public baths in the city had been falling down for thirty years). His secretaries wrote out letters to the chief nobles explaining why Narses had come and urging them to cooperate, and he was eager to help with arrangements for supplies and travel. However, all these arrangements counted for nothing with the nobles; they expected to be visited individually. Narses was well known among them: he had dealt with their delegations and arranged positions for their mercenary chieftains, and they respected him. They wanted the honor of entertaining an imperial minister themselves, and it was unthinkable that they should leave it up to their king. So, while most of the guardsmen stayed in Singidunum (and, on Narses' orders, worked at repairing the aqueduct and the public baths), Narses and John and a picked troop rode about the countryside, going to feasts.

Herulian nobles built feast halls as a matter of course. These were usually long thatched barns, with a wooden floor, perhaps, at one end, a fire pit in the middle, and benches round the sides where the chieftain's "companions," or warriors, slept and lived.

They were a considerable improvement over the Herulian house, which was a one-room mud and wattle shack with an earthen floor and a pigsty out the back. Nobody had heard of bathing, and even the washing of clothes was unusual; latrines were dug without drainage in the middle of the village, children and animals defecated in the street, and the stink was atrocious.

Herulian feasts usually began about an hour before sunset and continued until the Heruls were falling down drunk and being sick under the table a few hours later. Women were not allowed at the feasts. The men drank a sour flat beer and a potent yellow mead, and ate great chunks of meat boiled or roasted on spits, accompanied by cakes of a flat, unleavened bread made of barley and millet; wine was almost as unknown as moderation. To a Roman, accustomed to highly spiced dishes, not much meat, and good wheat bread, the food was almost indigestible. For entertainment the Heruls had professional bards, who sang the deeds of Herulian heroes in reedy voices to the monotonous accompaniment of a three-stringed harp. "Some of it is quite fine poetry," Narses said, "though very bloodthirsty, I fear," but it was simply an unintelligible whine to John.

On arriving at a chieftain's village, Narses went to the welcoming feast smiling politely and sat through it imperturbably, avoiding refills of mead with great dexterity. On the next day he got down to business. Every local chieftain had to have the reason for the recruiting mission explained individually; every chieftain had to boast of his military accomplishments and the courage of his followers; the terms of a mercenary contract had then to be explained to the followers themselves, some of whom always agreed to join the force. John drew up the documents and took notes of the conversations in shorthand. Then the chieftain and his companions would invite Narses to come hunting with them — hunting was their other form of entertainment. On the first hunting expedition John shot the quarry, a wolf, with an arrow, only to discover that the Heruls regarded this as surprising, certainly, but unsporting and cowardly. On other expeditions he carried a spear and rode as far from the quarry as he could.

The evening after this enjoyable sport was always the occasion for another feast, to honor the warriors who had decided to join the army. But the following day the whole procedure had to be repeated, because most of the companions who'd agreed to come had changed their minds, and some who hadn't wanted to come now did, and the chieftain wanted to alter the terms of the contract and paid no attention to the written document since he couldn't read it. The major complaint was always that the army in Italy would be commanded by Belisarius. The Heruls all detested the great general, and his offenses against them were detailed again and again: he had men flogged for drunkenness; he paid no attention to Herulian customs, particularly when he allotted punishments; he had once had two young warriors impaled for murder after they'd killed two of their comrades in a drunken brawl, even though the families of their victims had been content to take the blood price and let the matter drop. Narses was infinitely patient. The Heruls would have their own commander in Italy and would not be directly under Belisarius, he would explain. "Who?" the Herulian chieftain would demand. "We would be happy to obey Your Illustriousness. But Your Illustriousness is not going." "The sacred Augustus will provide you with a commander you can trust," Narses would insist. "It will be decided before you leave for Italy, I promise you." And he would signal John to read back his notes of the previous day's discussions, and the chieftain would gape and mutter, considering it either a prodigious feat of memory on John's part or, alternatively, a kind of malignant magic. The contract would be re-examined, more warriors would change their minds about it, and finally there would be a swearing of oaths and another long feast. All the time not spent in feasting, hunting, or consultation found the visitors surrounded by a swarm of men, women, and children who had never seen Romans before and wanted to see if they were human. All Heruls — and, John soon discovered, all who suffered Herulian hospitality — had fleas, lice, and worms. "Tedious" was an extremely mild way of putting it.

After about three weeks of recruiting, John managed to excuse himself from a hunt by pretending that Maleka had a sore hoof. He gave the crowd of sightseers the slip and found some quiet in his horse's stall; it was cleaner than the house he'd been allotted, and didn't smell as much. He had promised to write a letter to the Augusta, and had brought along his pen case, but he sat silently for a long time, staring at the parchment. Constantinople seemed a world so remote that it was hard even to find words to address it. Particularly since the letter would go to Theodora. He pictured her lounging on her couch at breakfast, fresh from her bath, dressed in purple silk, eating . . . it would be apples by now — and listening as Eusebios read her the day's letters. He could almost see the amused glint in her heavy-lidded eyes. He must write her a letter that would flatter her and make her laugh. A letter she would approve of. *But what does she want of me?* he asked silently, and the pleasure of the memory mingled suddenly with an intense but unplaceable dread. It was the fear of discovery, a kind of shame at his pretended importance, and above all the fear of being dragged madly and uncontrollably to some unknown destination. *This is why I wanted to leave Constantinople,* he acknowledged. *And yet I miss it.*

The truth of this surprised him, and he considered it. *I suppose I miss the comforts of civilization most. But I do miss the office, and I miss Theodora; I even miss Euphemia. I wonder how she's getting on with Sergius. . . .*

There was a sudden sound of footsteps coming into the stables, and then a face looked over the edge of the stall. It was a young woman's face, blue-eyed, pretty, and determinedly curious.

"Oooh," she said in a prettily clipped Greek, "you are here, very noble sir. May I speak with you?"

John sat in silence for a moment, wondering how to tell her to go away. But the bare fact that she spoke Greek marked her out as the wife or daughter of someone important, and the success of their mission depended on offending no one important. "Of course," he said, and got up.

The young woman opened the stall door and came in, smiling.

She was about his own age, John decided, and about his own height too — but the Heruls were a tall people. She was dressed in a shift of blue linen and a red cloak worn like a shawl, and she wore a gold necklace and some imported Roman earrings: she was clearly a woman of rank. "I am Datia, the daughter of Rodoulph," she said shyly. "I have been so wanting to talk with you."

Rodoulph was the local chieftain. John suppressed a sigh and bowed slightly. "I am honored, Lady Datia."

"Please, we may sit down?" said Datia, indicating the bale of straw where John had been sitting before. She picked up the tablets and the sheet of parchment and held them while John sat down, and then seated herself beside him. She frowned at the pen case, which was of bronze inlaid with silver. "Always you have this," she said, touching it. "How clever it is, to write! The men say you write as fast as they can talk."

"I am the secretary of His Illustriousness, Lady." John retrieved his pen case and tablets quickly. "Secretaries are supposed to be able to take notes."

"It is very clever," said Datia, folding her emptied hands sadly in her lap. "I wish I could write."

"Isn't there anyone here who could teach you?"

She shrugged. "My father has one man, a priest, who knows writing. But he does not wish I should learn. . . . But I talk sad things. I wished to ask you about the great city, Constantinople. I have never talked to anyone who has been there. It is bigger than Singidunum?"

John couldn't stop a smile. "You could fit a dozen Singidunums into Constantinople and have space left over."

"Oooh. You are joking me."

"No."

"Oooh. How it must be wonderful! And you are from there? Your family is from there?"

"No, I'm from Bostra, in Arabia." The words slipped out before he thought, and he bit his tongue. There was no one else to hear, and this barbarian woman probably didn't know the difference between Bostra and Berytus, but he cursed himself for forgetting the lie.

"Bos-tra. That is a great city too, like Constantinople?"

"Not as great as Constantinople," he said, resigning himself. "But a fine city." And suddenly he saw it in his mind's eye, as he had seen it so often coming home from a business trip with his father: the greenness of the cultivated land, leaping, sudden as a road's edge, from the red and brown wastes of the Syrian desert; the intricate, ingenious irrigation systems that filled all the area with the precious sound of hidden water; the date palms by the walls, and the flowering acanthus; the white-washed houses, the walls of rose-colored stone, the camels watering at the fountain in the marketplace. With a sudden revulsion against the long lie, he added, "It was the capital of Nabatea, of a great kingdom, before it became part of the empire. The caravans come down to it from the northeast, from beyond the lands of the Persians, bringing spices and fine silk from the east." *And I shouldn't be saying this,* he thought, desperately choking off the praise of Bostra that was rising defiantly to his lips. *She may repeat it. The name of a city means nothing, I can easily say she muddled it up — but no one could mistake that description of Bostra for Berytus.*

She stared at him, round-eyed. "I know what is silk," she said humbly. Hesitantly she reached out and touched the red and purple border of his cloak. "That is silk. The king wears it in Singidunum, and some warriors who have been among the Romans, and sometimes their ladies." She fingered it longingly. "I have never touched it; it is so smooth! How it shines! And Bos-tra, your city — it is far from Constantinople?"

"About as far as Constantinople is from Singidunum — maybe farther. But you can travel by sea, so it doesn't matter." The words were safely choked down now, and he remembered that Berytus was a port.

"The sea! I think the sea must be like a plain of wheat, all water, as far as far. But you live in Constantinople, yes? Is your family there?"

John shook his head. "My family are all dead. But I am a distant cousin of the most serene Augusta, Theodora; she was the one who found me my place with His Illustriousness."

She gave him a brilliant smile. "You are the cousin of the empress? Oh, I thought you were noble! The other women, they say you are nobody, even though you command soldiers, because you follow the Most Illustrious and take notes and use a bow instead of a spear. I tell them now, 'He is the cousin of the great queen,' and they will be ashamed. So, you have seen her, the empress Theodora, and you have spoken with her, and with the emperor, yes? What are they like?" She was still holding the silken edge of his cloak, and her fingers locked on it in excitement.

John found himself smiling at her and describing the mechanical throne of Solomon in the Magnaura Palace, with its golden lampstands; he described the emperor and empress rising together on the couch, dressed in purple silk, crowned with diadems, and the attendants prostrating themselves to the sacred majesty of imperial power.

Datia listened open-mouthed, her eyes shining with delight. "Oh, how it is wonderful! Wonderful!" she exclaimed. "That I could see it!" Then, embarrassed, she dropped her eyes and noticed that she had crushed his cloak. Hastily she unclenched her hands and began to smooth it. "Romans are not like Heruls," she said seriously, her delicate hands stroking the silk. "They are so much more knowing, to write and to make beautiful things. So fine, so . . ." She looked up again. Her eyes were a wonderful pale blue, fringed with dark gold lashes. John felt his breath come short and sat very still. Datia's hand lifted from the cloak and touched his face. "You are so different from us," she said regretfully. "You rode to my village yesterday, tomorrow you will go away again. Soon you will go back to Constantinople. You have a wife there?"

"No." John caught her hand and pulled it nervously away from his face. His heart was pounding. *I'm not married, but she must be,* he reminded himself. *Beautiful, over twenty, and a chieftain's daughter: she must have some noble husband off with the hunting party. And it wouldn't be any better if she were a virgin: that would just offend her father instead of her husband. Anyway, she's only curious.*

She held the hand that had taken hers and examined it. "That mark is from the pen, yes?" she said, pointing to the shiny patch of worn skin on his right middle finger. "Show me how you write, please?"

John licked his lips and picked up the pen case and the sheet of parchment. He wrote out the alphabet for her; she leaned her head over, watching. He was painfully aware of her body, the white skin, the round breasts pressing against the shift as she leaned toward him, the warmth of her breath on his arm. *I am a guest here,* he reminded himself desperately. *I must do nothing to offend them.* "Write my name?" she asked, and he wrote it out. She frowned in concentration and pointed to each of the letters in turn, matching it with the alphabet above. "Now I write?" she asked eagerly, trying to take the pen.

"It's easier with these," he told her, and handed her the wax tablets and a stylus. She took them greedily, and clumsily, carefully copied the shapes of the alphabet, again asking the names of the letters, sounding them out. She made a mistake at the zeta and exclaimed angrily; he took the stylus and showed her how to reverse it and erase the error, then guided her hand over the rest of the alphabet. He was surprised that his own hand wasn't trembling by the end. "How it is wonderful!" she exclaimed again when she had finished. She took the parchment. "You let me keep this? I will study the letters."

"Of course. The tablets too, if you like; I have others."

"Oh, thank you! Thank you much! I had wanted . . ." She stopped, looked at him; her fair skin darkened to a wonderful dusky rose. "I thought . . . that is, if you like me . . ."

If I like her! he thought wretchedly. "What do you mean, lady?"

"If you like to sleep with me, yes?" she said, making a helpless gesture. "If you would wish it, I would wish it."

John felt his own face go hot. He looked down at his tightly clenched hands and took a deep breath to calm himself. He remembered how Theodora had laughed at him. He remembered being seventeen, mad with love, lying sweating in his hot dark bedroom in Bostra and dreaming of the fair hair and blue eyes of Chryseis, whom he had never dared to touch. Other girls, too: admired, desired, and never spoken to. He had never dreamed that something like this could happen to him, and it did not seem real.

"Lady Datia," he said formally, "I am most deeply honored, and I am grateful for your offer, but I am your father's guest, and my commander is here on a diplomatic mission. I dare not do anything that would offend your father, or, if you have one, your husband — much as I might like to."

"My husband is dead," she said, and bit her lip. "I have no husband." But she drew away and stood, blushing, ashamed.

"But . . . Lady Datia . . ." He caught her hand, found that he had nothing to say. He felt suddenly terrified. *I don't know their customs about this,* he reminded himself. *Lord of All, I don't know our customs about it!* But he could neither speak nor let go.

"You wish, then?" she asked, her face brightening again.

"Yes, yes, of course!"

She smiled, sat down next to him, and kissed him. "We stay here," she told him. "It will be quieter here than in the houses."

The act of love was not what he had expected. It was relief, not ecstasy; an intense pleasure, but at the same time terrifying. His own body seemed a thing beyond his control, animal and alien, and his mind watched it in astonishment. Afterward, limp and shaken, he lay next to her in the straw, looked down and saw a louse crawling in her fair hair, and felt a wave of revulsion. He sat up quickly and began to pull his tunic on.

She has no husband, he thought bitterly, *but her father will be back in an hour or so. Dear God, this could cause trouble. And it is a sin . . . oh, but she is lovely!*

Datia had sat up and was pulling on her shift; her shoulders were like white marble, her breasts round and rosy. *Like the statue*, he thought, *the Aphrodite of Phidias, on the Middle Street in Constantinople*. She noticed his gaze and smiled at him.

"How it is wonderful," he said, smiling back, and she giggled. She pulled down the shift and stood, picking her cloak up.

"I do not say it right?" she asked.

"You say it beautifully." The mixture of revulsion and tenderness was painful, but to her he could only smile stupidly.

She giggled again, and was about to say something more when there was a sound of horses outside. Quickly she pulled her cloak on and pinned it, and hurried from the stall just as the hunting party rode back into the stables. As soon as she was gone, John found himself wishing that she had never come.

He worried about the possible consequences of sleeping with a chieftain's daughter throughout the feast that night, and decided finally that he must consult Narses. The eunuch had been allotted the finest house in the village, John the second finest; the two were next to each other and were, by Herulian standards, very grand, each consisting of two whole rooms — one for the master, the other for the slaves and the cooking. Accordingly, while they were walking back from the feast hall, John stated that he needed to speak with his superior privately, and was invited into the dark back room. Narses lit the single hanging lamp and waved his attendants out. He sat down on the bed, looking tired but collected. "What is the matter then, Your Diligence?" he asked politely.

John blushed and, stammering with embarrassment, explained what had happened in the stables. Narses listened patiently, saying nothing; then, when John had stumbled to a stop, he sighed.

"You are right to tell me. The Heruls do not regard chastity quite so seriously as the Goths, but this could still cause trouble. Was the girl a virgin?"

"No — she said she was a widow."

Narses looked relieved. "A widow! That's perfectly all right, then. I would suggest that you give her some presents, treat her respectfully, and offer to receive her son, if she has one. Public acknowledgment is undoubtedly what she wants."

"What she wants? I thought —"

"What she wanted beside yourself, of course." Narses gave his polite smile. "She was very courteous in leaving the acknowledgment up to you. Before these people adopted the Christian faith — which was only some fifteen years ago — it was customary for widows to hang themselves by their husbands' graves. A widow who chose to live was treated as contemptuously as we Romans would treat a whore. The custom of suicide is now discouraged by the church, but popular feeling still regards a widow as less than respectable. For your young woman to have an open affair with a Roman ambassador, a commander in the Protectors and a cousin of the sacred Augusta, can only add to her status, and hence her respectability. I hope you told her you were a cousin of the empress? Good. She might even be able to remarry now — though only a man of inferior rank."

"Holy God! Poor Datia." John was silent for a moment, then said, "So she came to the stable with that in mind."

"Probably. Does that offend you?"

"No. But it's confusing." He remembered her dark rosy blush and felt his own cheeks grow hot in sympathy. The actual act of intercourse already seemed curiously blurred, almost irrelevant to all the longing wonder with which he had regarded it before and to the confusion and strangeness of the results.

"Indeed. If it is not inappropriate, coming from me, it would be better if you could refrain from such adventures in the future. There will probably be no difficulty this time, but another young woman might be in different circumstances, and could cause you problems and us embarrassment."

"I don't intend to repeat the experiment," John said. *It wasn't worth the risk,* he thought, *it wasn't really worth all the thought I've given it in the past. And it is a sin. Though not so much for her, I think, not with her family feeling she'd be better off dead like her husband. So that was why she got up so quickly when she told me she was a widow.* "Poor Datia!" he said again. "What savages these Heruls are. Sergius was right: they're the most disgusting people in the world."

Narses shrugged. "They remind me of Homer's heroes. Very brave, very independent, and inclined to boasting. 'Slaughtering the bleating goats and the shambling horn-curved cattle.' "

"Homer's heroes knew how to wash," John said sourly. "And they didn't make widows hang themselves."

"It's probably easier to wash in Greece, where it's warm, than in Moesia. And the Heruls came from Thule, where it's even colder — they say that for forty days each winter, the sun never rises there at all. The Heruls aren't the savages they used to be, either. They gave up the worst of their old customs when they adopted the Christian faith."

"They used to do other horrible things as well?"

Narses did not smile. "They practiced human sacrifice. And if anyone was too old or too ill to look after himself, they killed him."

"God in heaven!"

"It was a brutal custom, but there was a certain dignity to it. When a man was too ill to stand, his family built a funeral pyre and carried him out and set him on it, with the best of his possessions. They all kissed him and lamented and praised his courage and his generosity. Then, since it was forbidden to shed kindred blood, a friend of the family killed the invalid with a knife and the body was burned. They still do all those things sometimes, in villages far from any church — but it's disapproved of."

"And you don't think they're the most disgusting people in the world?"

"No," said Narses sharply. "I would give that title to the Romans, who will do similar things, and worse, for money. And I would say that the Romans are also the most noble of all the peoples of the world, surpassing all others in their laws, their arts, and their faith. Our city is the great whore of Babylon, drunk with the blood of the saints, and it is the city set on the hill, whose light cannot be hidden. That, at any rate, is what I believe."

"You believe in contradictions."

Narses gave a thoroughly ambiguous smile. "Yes, I do."

John was silent for a few minutes, considering the contradiction of civilization and the simplicity of savagery; then, because it was late, he abandoned the consideration in despair. "Well, Roman beds are less of a contradiction than Herulian ones," he said lightly. "Roman beds are made for people to sleep in, but Herulian ones are for bedbugs. But I'll try that contradiction anyway. Good night, Illustrious."

The next morning John went to the feast hall, followed by his two retainers, and openly asked for Datia; it caused quite a stir among the warriors, but eventually one man showed him to the house of Rodoulph. Datia was sitting in the back room, working at a loom with some other women. She looked tired and her eyes were red, but her face lit up when she saw John.

"I wish to thank you, lady, for your kindness," John told her formally. "Please accept these gifts." He offered her his spare Protector's cloak and his pen case.

She jumped up, blushing and beaming, and her friends or cousins began gabbling among themselves. She took the cloak, stroked its silk borders, flung it over her shoulders. She held the pen case and cooed, then flung her arms about John and kissed him. "I hoped you were not ashamed of me," she said happily. "I thought you were angry that I was a widow, and for that you did not say anything. How I was wrong!"

"How you were," he said. In her presence, the issue of love became confusing again; it was less senseless and distasteful than it had been the evening before. And the strange mixture of revulsion and tenderness perplexed him again. He wanted suddenly, intensely, to get away. But he smiled, took her hands, and added, "I believe I should say as well that if there is a child, you can send him to me at Constantinople."

At this she smiled still harder and kissed him again. "And I must attend your father," he added hastily. "His Illustriousness is waiting for me, and we have one or two points of business that must be settled before we leave."

News traveled quickly in the village. When the business had been settled, the packing done, and the visitors were saying farewell to their host, the chieftain, Rodoulph, suddenly turned to John with a grin and said, "I hear that my daughter has made you most welcome here."

John nodded politely, and tried to disguise his embarrassment by looking over the man's right shoulder. "Your daughter is a most charming lady," he said. "An intelligent woman, too: she told me that she was very interested in learning to write."

Rodoulph guffawed. "She told you that, did she? From what I heard, that wasn't what interested her at all! Never mind, she's a good girl. But what's the use of teaching a woman to write?"

John forgot to be embarrassed and looked at Rodoulph directly. "It's as much use as teaching a man," he said in surprise. "She can write letters, read the scriptures . . ." Rodoulph looked tolerantly unconvinced. John remembered how eagerly Datia had seized on the pen case and went on angrily. "I know a young woman in Constantinople — I met her officially, on business. Her father is in Egypt; she manages his estate in his absence, and moreover sends her father all the news of the capital, so that although he is the width of the Middle Sea away, he is as well informed about what is happening in his house as if he lived in the next street."

The chieftain looked impressed. "Do all Roman women learn to write?" he asked.

"All women of rank," John said firmly.

"Well!" said Rodoulph, surprised. "Well!"

Narses gave a particularly mysterious smile and took over the business of saying farewell properly, praising Rodoulph's hospitality, the courage of his warriors, and the fertility of his lands; Rodoulph responded with expressions of loyalty and admiration, and the troops at last managed to ride out of the grimy, stinking village and on toward the next.

When they were safely on the road, Narses slowed his horse until it was walking beside John's and gave another of his smiles. "He will have his daughter taught to read and write," he stated.

"I hope so," John replied, somewhat surprised at the chamberlain's interest.

"The example of the most virtuous Euphemia carried some weight; he will want his own daughter to write him reports on the house while he is off campaigning. And the young woman will do very well, being put in a position of such importance. You have done her a considerable favor. It was good that you paid attention to her . . . literary ambitions." Narses smiled again.

He's pleased with me, thought John, puzzled by it. *He was annoyed that I slipped up by sleeping with a barbarian woman in the first place, but now he's pleased because I've done something that helped her. Why does it matter to him?* Then, looking at the eunuch's quiet satisfaction, he realized, *He is pleased because he likes me; he is concerned at what I do, wishes me to act well, and is delighted that I have.*

It was startling: Narses, the ageless, sexless, remote, and impersonal servant of the sacred majesty of the emperor, had seemed somehow beyond such things as mere human friendship, despite his evident affection for Anastasios. *And yet,* thought John, *I did know there was more to him than that; he as good as told me. "Third son of a poor Armenian farmer" and all that. He's just like me: he draws a line around himself and watches people from the other side of it — but somehow or other he's decided to let me cross it. What in God's name have I done that makes me worthy of his friendship?* And the detached part of him observed, with surprise, his own sense of honored pleasure. *He may be a eunuch, low-born, and a freedman,* John realized, *but I don't suppose there's another man living that I respect as much.*

"Was it the Heruls who taught you to smile like that?" he demanded happily.

Narses looked surprised. "Like what?"

"Like that." John imitated the familiar unreadable expression as well as he could.

Narses laughed. "I don't look like that, do I? No, I learned to smile to hide what I was thinking when I was still a slave. 'For the trial of our faith creates patience,' and a slave's patience is always being tried. But it comes in handy with the Heruls too."

VII

ROMANS AND BARBARIANS

THE PATIENCE OF NARSES and that of his secretary was tried by the Heruls for the full four months that the chamberlain had estimated, but finally, by the end of October, an army of seven thousand Heruls, about half of them the light cavalry the nation was famous for, was gathered at Singidunum, supplied, ordered in companies, and ready to set out. "Far fewer than I would have liked," Narses commented unhappily. "It is the uncertainty about the king that's kept the numbers down. They are still waiting for the embassy to return from Thule."

The other arrangements for the troops had been made by letter. Belisarius was in Italy, but with only four thousand men and unable to do anything against the Goths, who were laying siege to the garrison at Rome. The truce with Persia was holding, however, and Justinian had managed to move another six thousand troops from the East and was sending them to Dyrrhachium, from where they would embark for Italy as soon as the spring permitted them to sail. The Heruls were also to sail from Dyrrhachium, but in order to distribute the burden of feeding the troops more evenly, they were to spend the winter where Narses had prepared supplies for them, in Sardica.

Accordingly, while the last of the harvest was being gathered from the darkened countryside, the army set out from Singidunum, heading back down the road that the smaller force had traveled before. John was sorry to leave the capital. They had had a week preparing the troops before setting out, and by dint of bathing twice a day and using various foul potions from the army surgeon, he had at last managed to rid himself of his assortment of Herulian vermin — but he suspected that he would pick them up again on the journey to Sardica.

Jakobos too sighed when they left the city walls behind. The boy was now riding at the front, between the two Vandal retainers. He had managed to persuade one of the Vandals to teach him how to use a spear, and John had agreed to let him act as a third retainer, provided he still did his work.

"Are you sorry to be going back toward Constantinople?" John asked him.

"Oh no, master!" said Jakobos. "I just wish we could leave all the Heruls behind."

"We came here to fetch them!" John told him. "But I know what you mean."

It was more than two hundred miles from Singidunum to Sardica, and the eleven-day journey was a nightmare. There were seven instances of sheep stealing, four of cattle stealing, four of other theft, and two of rape. The Scholarian commander, Artemidoros, viewed the attempt to control the wild army as doomed from the beginning, and he and his men would watch with a what-do-you-expect air while a company of Herulian cavalry stole sheep under their very eyes. It was difficult to punish the men responsible for the outrages without driving the others into desertion; the only thing Narses could do was bluff and threaten until some restitution was made, and use John and the Protectors to patrol the Heruls and the Scholarians both.

But in Sardica, Narses' office had succeeded in preparing everything perfectly. There were barracks for the Heruls, stables for the horses, spare clothing and weapons, and abundant supplies. A program of drills, games, hunts, and competitions was devised to keep the barbarians out of trouble, and as November ended and the snows fell, John began to hope for a quiet winter.

In early January a ragged survivor galloped from the garrison

at Oescus, on the Danube, to Sardica to report that a huge force
of barbarian Sclaveni had invaded Thrace.

Narses had installed himself and his retinue in the prefectural
palace at Sardica, and called a council there to hear the news.
It was a bleak, chill day, and the huge council room, heated
only by a few braziers, was bitterly cold. Its windows were heavily
shuttered against the wind, and the few lamps on the stand at
one end of the room cast wavering shadows over the damp
patches on the painted walls. Narses sat at the head of the
council table, wrapped in his white and purple cloak, listening
to the messenger behind his steepled hands; his face was in
shadow. The governor of Dacia, an ineffectual man who resented
the eunuch's intrusion into his province, sat on his right, looking
anxious; the other commanders of the army, and the holders
of important posts in the province, were scattered unhappily
around the table. John sat apart from them, under the lampstand, taking notes. His fingers were numb with cold before
he'd written half a page.

"The river was freezing over," said the messenger. "It's been
cold this year, unseasonable. The barbarians dragged some boats
out into the middle of the river and let the water freeze round
them, and then piled trees on top until they had a bridge strong
enough to take wagons. They crossed it and found some people
from Oescus out gathering wood. They killed them and slipped
into the city in their place, threw open the gates, and came in."

"You should have destroyed their bridge before it was built!"
snapped the governor.

"There are thousands of them!" returned the messenger.
"How were we supposed to stop them? We only have two
hundred regulars in Oescus, a few hundred allied troops, and the
militia, which is no good in the winter! They took all the supplies in the city, killed all the men, and carried off the women
and children as slaves. Then they headed downstream, toward
Novae."

"How many thousands?" asked Narses quietly.

"Thirty or forty thousand," the man replied at once. "I can't
be more certain than that. But they filled the city."

"You saw them?"

"Yes, Illustrious. I was posted at a watchtower on the land-ward side. I watched as they took the city, and then went out through the postern and hid in the countryside. I watched until I saw which way they went, and then stole a horse and came here."

"How were they equipped?"

"Too damn well," the messenger said bitterly. "Usually the Sclaveni just fight with a spear and a shield, or maybe a wooden bow and a few arrows. These troops were about half cavalry, and most of them armored."

"They have been copying the Romans," Narses said. "Did they have many archers?"

"Archers? I don't know. The cavalry weren't shooting that I saw. Can Your Illustriousness help? I'd heard that Your Illus-triousness would be here, with troops, and I hoped that you would be able to come quickly and stop the barbarians before they do more damage."

"We have fewer than eight thousand men," said the Scholarian commander, Artemidoros. "And they're almost all undisciplined barbarians. We'll have to send for reinforce-ments."

"By the time reinforcements can arrive, the Sclaveni will have sacked half Thrace and gone home!" wailed the governor. "What if they come this way?"

"How long did it take you to get here?" Narses asked the messenger, who was gaping at Artemidoros in astonishment. He had evidently heard that the army of Heruls was very much larger than it was.

"Three days, Illustrious." The man turned back to the com-mander, sullen with despair. "I didn't dare steal another horse, and the roads are bad."

"The Sclaveni will be traveling slowly if they have plunder," said Narses thoughtfully. "Still, it will be too late to save Novae, unless it can resist a siege. But perhaps they'll turn south to Nicopolis."

"It will take a month to bring the troops from Dyrrhachium

in this weather," said Artemidoros, shaking his head. "There's nothing we can do."

"I would differ with you, commander," Narses said politely. "We could defeat them."

Artemidoros stared at him in shock; the messenger went white. *He doesn't dare believe that Narses means to do something,* thought John, feeling his own heart start to race.

"This is what I would suggest doing." Narses unsteepled his fingers and leaned forward over the table; the lamplight washed over his calm, precise face. "We take the army as quickly as we can to Nicopolis, on the road that goes through Melta. I will take all the archers and all the men who can use a sling from Sardica, Melta, and Nicopolis. At Nicopolis we will try to discover where the barbarians are. If they are besieging Novae, we advance and attack them in the rear; if they are moving on to some other place, we occupy the ground before them and force them to attack us on our terms."

"Illustrious!" said Artemidoros in horror. "You can't mean to attack . . . we have only eight thousand men!"

"Belisarius conquered Africa with twenty thousand and Italy with fifteen thousand. I should think we can manage the Sclaveni."

"Belisarius had regular troops and his private army!" said Artemidoros. "We've got eight thousand Heruls, whom we can't even trust not to join the enemy!"

"The Sclaveni are an entirely different nation from the Heruls," Narses stated calmly. "Their language and customs are quite distinct, and they have been at war with each other in the past. I believe our forces will be quite happy to fight them now. Most valued Artemidoros, we cannot simply stand by and surrender a Roman province to barbarian pillage. If the Sclaveni meet no opposition this year, they will attack again next year — and next year there'll be no large armed forces already in the region. We have to keep troops in the East, and are heavily committed in Italy and Africa: it will be impossible to raise another army to defend Thrace. Unless we act now, we will be abandoning the region for the next ten years. I presume that we have an advantage over the enemy in organization and in equipment; if our men are properly officered, there is no reason why we shouldn't get the victory."

"You're not Belisarius," said Artemidoros.

"That is no reason for doing nothing. John, how quickly can we be off?"

"Tomorrow afternoon, Illustrious?" suggested John, trying to keep an appearance of calm.

"Tomorrow morning," Narses said firmly. "Let's begin on it now."

It was late the next morning, but still before noon, when the army left Sardica. They took no heavy baggage train and left most of the slaves behind, bringing only enough men to control the few packhorses with supplies of journeybread, dried meat, and horse fodder for two weeks. It was a bright, cold morning, and the sun cast their shadows blue on the thick snow; the breath of men and horses was white in the bitter air; armor and harness glittered mirror-bright. The Heruls were delighted with the prospect of fighting the Sclaveni, and beat their shields with their swords and gave loud whoops as they set out.

John was posted at the rear of the army with twenty Protectors to hold it together; he had distributed the rest of his men among the companies of the recruits to keep them in order. He had been up most of the night arranging supplies and mounts for the journey and writing letters to be sent on ahead to Melta and Nicopolis, and he felt almost feverish in the clear morning. *Give us one day to get through the mountains,* he thought, going over the calculations for supplies; *two days to Melta, if we're lucky, and then another two or three to Nicopolis — we can get more supplies there, if we need to — and then? What if they're there, the barbarians? We may be fighting them within a week!*

His throat was tight with a mixture of excitement and terror, and the sun seemed almost painfully bright, reflected from the snow as though from shards of broken glass. *All breaking,* he thought, *with the imminence of death.* He pulled at his helmet strap, then felt for the lump of the bag that held the strings for his bow, which hung around his neck under his tunic, to keep them warm and supple. *I wish I knew how to use a spear. I should have practiced more these past weeks — but we've been so busy trying to keep the Heruls in order.*

Artemidoros suddenly appeared, cantering his horse back along the roadside; he slowed when he saw John, and then pulled up level to ride alongside, his horse fidgeting in the cold and mouthing the bit. "Greetings, Your Honor," he said, and glanced at John uneasily.

"Greetings," returned John, and waited for the Scholarian commander to say what he wanted.

Artemidoros was in no hurry; he sat for a moment in silence, his hands pulled up under his cloak. He glanced at the Protectors, then looked up ahead at the army. "We don't have enough men," he said at last.

John shrugged. "Roman armies have defeated barbarians against worse odds in the past."

"*Roman* armies have," said Artemidoros. "It is absolutely ludicrous to call this ragbag assortment of savages a Roman army. If I had the whole imperial guard here, I wouldn't mind riding out against the barbarians — but these Heruls! They'll run back home as soon as they see how many the enemy are. It's not their lands at stake; they won't get themselves killed attacking forty thousand Sclaveni."

"Forty thousand is almost certainly wrong," John said politely. "It was an upper estimate, and estimates are usually overestimates. There are probably only thirty thousand Sclaveni, if that."

"They won't get themselves killed attacking thirty thousand Sclaveni, either!" snapped Artemidoros. "They'll run, and that will leave us — a hundred Protectors, a hundred Scholarians, and one old palace eunuch with twenty retainers — fighting a barbarian horde all by ourselves. It's suicide. You have some influence with His Illustriousness; please, use it, make him exercise some caution. All right, we have to ride out and look at the enemy, but once we've looked, it'd be sheer lunacy to attack. Make him see· that."

"I don't agree that the Heruls will turn and run," said John. "The one thing they're not is cowards. They have confidence in us and in His Illustriousness, and they're willing to fight. We will have several advantages over the Sclaveni — we'll be choosing the time and place for the battle, we can get guides who know the countryside, and we can always fall back on the fortified cities. The odds aren't as bad as you would imply. This attack is a risk, but not lunacy . . . most esteemed Artemidoros." He added the honorific lightly and smiled on it. "And, as His Illustriousness said, we can't simply surrender a Roman province to pillage. We're here; we must help."

Artemidoros scowled; his lips moved as he swore under his breath. "Young idiot!" he exclaimed. "His Illustriousness is a . . . an official, bred in the palace — what does he know about war? The only time he ever held command before was a disaster, and he was recalled. You've never been to war before, and you think it's all a big horse race, where you make a name for yourself if you win, and if you lose, well, it's a pity, but there's another day. You could get killed. You have no special dispensation from fate because you're the cousin of the Augusta; you'll be just as dead as any bastard Herul if you get a spear in the guts. And wounds will hurt just as much, and crippling be as shameful. Nobody's going to take it out on you or Narses if we go back and call for reinforcements; it won't ruin your promising career or his reputation."

John laughed. " 'Oh my dear, if by a flight from war,' " he quoted,

> " 'We should henceforth be free of age and death
> I'd neither fight myself among the brave,
> nor urge you into glory-bringing battle.
> But since ten thousand forms of death surround
> which mortal none can e'er shun or escape
> let the gods receive a victory's praise, from us
> or from our enemies!' "

Artemidoros snarled. "Very fine! Have you ever thought how many young officers that bit of Homer must have killed?"

"Have you ever thought how many peasants the Sclaveni might kill if they're not stopped?"

"You're a conceited young idiot!" snapped Artemidoros. "And I hope for all our sakes you're right." He pulled his horse away and spurred it viciously, galloping back along the army to the vanguard.

John looked after him and felt again for his bowstrings. One of the Protectors, who had heard the conversation, drove his horse forward. "You don't think he was talking sense?" he asked anxiously.

"I don't think he knows any more about war than we do," John returned evenly. "I've never heard that he's actually seen a battle."

"That's true," said the Protector, but he was still unhappy. John smiled at him. It was surprisingly easy to smile.

"I don't believe it's lunacy, either," he said. "It's a calculated risk — and as for getting killed, you can get killed in a battle with even odds just as easily, and nobody would recommend avoiding that. And people survive lost battles too. Come on, don't let the Heruls see that it worries you; if *they* get worried, the battle really is lost."

That evening, however, when he and Narses had finished sorting out the Heruls' arguments over tent sites, John asked quietly, "What did happen when you were sent to Italy?"

Narses glanced up, then went on putting away his pens. "Was that what Artemidoros was telling you about this morning?"

John shrugged. "He referred to it. But mostly he wanted me to talk you out of this expedition."

"And are you going to try to do that?" Narses closed his pen case and looked up at John with expectant amusement.

"No, Illustrious." John looked steadily at his commander for a moment. "He's a . . ." Artemidoros had begun, then changed it: "an official." What had he meant to say? A eunuch? A slave? *Not a coward: even Artemidoros would never call Narses that.*

Not a coward and not a fool either, thought John. He said carefully, "I know we're taking a risk, but I'm sure you know what you're doing. I have perfect confidence in your judgment."

That brought the smile. "Thank you. I hope I deserve that. My previous military experience is very nearly as bad as Artemidoros indicated. I was sent out to Italy seven years ago, largely as a financial and administrative adviser to Belisarius. The count is of course an incomparable general, but his administration of the territories he conquers tends to be erratic. He understands the need to restrain his soldiers and officers from plundering, but is unable to enforce his wishes once they are out of his reach. I was also in charge of some reinforcements that we had recruited for him — mostly Heruls. You already know the opinion the Heruls hold of the most distinguished count; it caused some trouble before we were finished.

"Well, we arrived in Italy and found that Belisarius was at odds with half his generals — he is a stern disciplinarian but lacks tact, and tends to have trouble with his subordinates. Moreover, a good friend of mine, your namesake, Vitalian's nephew John, had succeeded in getting himself besieged at Auximum while disobeying orders. There was some debate whether to relieve him or not. The most prudent count was rather inclined not: it required a massive advance into territory held by the enemy. But it seemed to me that it was worth the risks involved — we were short of men and could not afford to lose those who were besieged; moreover, a solid victory at that juncture was likely to have a great effect on the support we were receiving from the Italians, while a Gothic victory would provide an enormous boost to the morale of the enemy. I advised as much, and my advice was taken, with results better than I could have hoped for.

"However, when the generals who were dissatisfied with Belisarius' command saw this, they turned to me and said that they would prefer me as a general to the count. I had been sent to advise him, of course, and at first I tried to leave it at that. But the count ignored my advice. We differed on priorities and on methods. I wished the troops to hold more territory than he thought prudent; I was more concerned to safeguard the population, he the men; and so on. And I was very pleased by my success at Auximum, and the generals' offer elated me. I am an ambitious man, my friend, particularly when it comes to military glory." The eunuch hesitated, looked down at his pen case. "Ridiculous as that may be for someone like me," he added softly. "And shameful as it is to want something so useless and transitory, which is acquired by killing one's fellows, which the church regards as morally questionable at the best of times. But even today, if I were offered the choice of becoming a saint or a hero, I'd choose the second without hesitation." He sighed, shrugged. "To my shame, I permitted the insubordinate officers to subordinate themselves to me, and directed them as I thought best, setting off on a campaign quite distinct from the count's. The result, of course, was chaos. The command was divided; no one knew what anyone else was doing; orders got lost in the confusion. But I was contented because my policies seemed to be working. Then Belisarius ordered my friend John, Vitalian's nephew, to relieve the garrison that was defending Mediolanum against a Gothic siege. John refused to accept anyone's orders except mine. Belisarius wrote to me, and I wrote to John with the same order. But by the time it was obeyed, the Goths had taken Mediolanum."

Narses stopped, staring at nothing for a moment, his face grim. "They killed every adult male in the city," he said at last. "Tens of thousands of them — God knows how many died in the end, since no one is certain what happened to all the women and children. The Goths enslaved them and sold them to the Burgundians. We could do nothing to help them, nothing even to redeem the survivors. It was a catastrophe that stunned us all and brought us to our senses — rather too late.

"I yielded my command to Belisarius and ordered my brace of generals to be obedient. In the spring the Augustus recalled me to Constantinople. The Heruls I had brought refused to stay under Belisarius' command and marched home, after selling most of their supplies to the enemy. The count blames me for that as well, though I swear I urged them to stay as strongly as I could." Narses shrugged. "And that is what happened in Italy."

"Dear God," said John. After a moment's silence, he added, "It says nothing at all about your generalship."

"No, only about the dangers of the sin of pride." The eunuch sighed. "I think about Mediolanum every night. Well, God send that we can save Nicopolis from the same fate!"

It took five and a half days of riding hard in the bitter weather to reach Nicopolis. The army arrived to find the city closely shut up and full of peasants from the neighboring countryside; it took some time before Narses could convince the suspicious garrison to let them in.

It seemed the Sclaveni had been laying siege to Novae but, achieving nothing, were expected to turn south at any moment; indeed, they might already be on their way to Nicopolis. "Thousands of them!" the garrison commander told Narses miserably, once the troops had established their identity and been admitted and accommodated. "It's worse than the Bulgars five years ago. More of them, and they're like starving wolves."

"How many thousands?" Narses inquired.

"About thirty thousand," the second-in-command put in quickly. "Judging by the reports of my spies."

"Thank you." The eunuch smiled at him. "How are they equipped? Do they have many archers?"

"They have a surprising proportion of cavalry," said the second-in-command. "Perhaps a third of their total number, and somewhere between a quarter and a third of that is armored — but my spies weren't sure, and most of the reports I've received are exaggerated. The rest of the horsemen seem to have abandoned their bows for the lance, in the Gothic fashion. The infantry have only the traditional equipment: light bows, spears, and no armor to speak of."

Narses nodded once. "Thank you for your precision. I would like to speak with your spies. I wish to determine the best place to give battle, should the Sclaveni make for Nicopolis. John, see that the men get extra rations, and keep them off the drink. I want to leave tomorrow morning."

The second-in-command and John left the commander's office together. "Does he really mean to fight them?" asked the second-in-command. "You have fewer than eight thousand men."

John gave a good imitation of Narses' smile. "Oh, yes. He means to fight them. That's why we have to know our ground."

The second-in-command at Nicopolis stared at him, and John stared back. "Well," said the other man, "and I thought all eunuchs were cowards. Good luck!"

Just as they were leaving Nicopolis next morning, another spy galloped up on a spent horse and announced that the Sclaveni had abandoned their siege of Novae and started south the afternoon before.

"Then we may meet them on the road today," said Narses calmly. "Garrison commander, please maintain a good watch here. I hope we will not have to come back in a hurry — but it's always a possibility." He nodded to the trumpeter to give the signal to begin the march, and once more the wild army started out north along the road.

This time small groups of Herulian cavalry were sent out in advance, followed by a larger group under Philemuth, reconnoitering. The main body of the army followed more slowly, inspecting the ground as they went, checking the various places the spies from Nicopolis had suggested as good for a battle. Around noon, Narses found a site that was satisfactory. The road, descending from Nicopolis toward the Danube, dropped northwest in a long bend before straightening out in the river plain; to the northeast ran a ridge of high ground covered with trees. Narses gave orders for the troops to pitch their camp just back over the hill.

"But let the slaves put the tents up, and tell the men to come here. I want two trenches dug, running at right angles to the road and curving away from it toward the north. And I want all those trees down. We will fix them in the ground before the trenches, facing the direction of the enemy's advance."

"The ground is frozen," objected Philemuth. "The shovels will not be able to dig the trenches."

"Then we must use pickaxes," Narses said calmly. "But we will dig the trenches."

The trenches had just been marked out when some of the advance parties galloped back to announce that the Sclaveni were fifteen miles away, advancing along the road. "Very many of them," reported the Herul captain. "They have much plunder with them, many wagons; also cows, sheep, women, and children. They are coming slowly, not looking where they are going: I think they did not see us."

"Thank you," Narses told him. "Alwith and Phanitheos, take your men back north and keep an eye on the Sclaveni; send someone back every hour to report to me. The rest of you stay here and start digging."

When the digging began, the Protectors and the Scholarians stood by watching, assuming without question that such slavish work was not for them. Narses rode down the long rows of digging Heruls, checking the line of the trench, then stopped in front of the two units of imperial guards, who were standing together by the road. He gave them a long look, saying nothing; then he dismounted from his white mare, tossed his purple-striped cloak over his shoulders, took a shovel — there were no pickaxes left — and began to dig. The Protectors and Scholarians looked at each other, then went over to the trench line and joined the work.

By the time the trenches were finished and the men were warming their blistered hands at the campfires, the Sclaveni were in plain sight in the valley below. It was late in the afternoon, and the early winter dusk left everything slate-colored and white: bare-branched forests and bare fields. The Sclaveni seemed unaware of the Romans until they saw the light of the fires scattered gold in the hills above them. The Sclaveni stopped, milled about, then began to set up their own camp, carefully maintaining the bulk of their force drawn up in the line of battle as they did so. A couple of detachments of Sclavenian cavalry cantered up the hillside, encountered the Herulian advance parties, who were now standing guard, and withdrew.

As the dusk deepened, a party of Sclaveni could be seen coming up the hill, carrying branches of fir and white banners in token of a truce. Narses summoned all the imperial guardsmen, together with Philemuth and some other selected Heruls, and got back on his horse. The select party went to the middle of the road, just before the trenches, and there waited for the Sclaveni. Narses' retainers held torches tied to their spears, which cast a red, unsteady light over the brilliant mass of armed men and horses; the dragon standards leapt in the same wind that made the torches flicker, and the gold Christian monogram on the guardsmen's shields blazed.

The Sclaveni paused when they came up the hill and saw the Romans, but they held their truce tokens high and came on, finally drawing rein when they were only a few feet away. They were tall men, fair-haired for the most part, but darker than the Heruls; they wore long moustaches that mingled with their beards, and long-skirted tunics lined with fur. They were no cleaner than the Heruls, and John noticed with interest that the finest of them wore armor and jewelry of Roman manufacture.

"I am the envoy of Zabergan, king of the Sclaveni and the Bulgars," said their chief, speaking fluent though heavily accented Greek. "The great king wishes to know who it is who dares to bar his path."

"The great king?" Narses asked mildly in his high, sweet, child's voice. "Does your master then serve the king of Persia?"

The Romans laughed; Zabergan's envoy looked annoyed. "My master serves no man living!" he exclaimed. "I call him great king in his own right. I have come to speak not to eunuchs but to the commander of this army: where is your master?"

"My master is the emperor Justinian, Vandalicus, Gothicus, pious, fortunate, glorious, triumphant, ever victorious, forever Augustus, master of the world. And I am Narses, chamberlain to His Sacred Majesty, master of arms for Thrace and Illyricum, and commander of this army. What does Zabergan want in my territory?"

Zabergan's envoy looked at Narses contemptuously. "The emperor of the Romans must be short of generals," he said, "to send you."

"Did you have something you wished to say?" asked Narses sharply.

"I was to say it to a man, a general, not to some slave from a lady's bedroom."

One of Narses' Armenians drove his horse a few steps forward and dropped his spear, torch and all, till its point was directed at the envoy's throat. Without looking at the man, Narses snapped his fingers and pointed back at the ranks; the spear swung up, and the Armenian backed his horse silently into line. The envoy sneered.

"We will meet you again, eunuch," he declared, gathering up his reins. "Tomorrow, when there is light for fighting. Perhaps my master, Zabergan, will sell you back to Justinian Augustus — or perhaps he will keep you. He needs a slave to order his queen's wardrobe." He turned his horse and rode back down the hill, followed by his attendants.

Narses smiled. "Well, gentlemen, I believe we have a battle set for tomorrow. If you will be so good as to join me in my tent, we can discuss how to teach Zabergan and his envoys a lesson in good manners."

The Armenians cheered; the Heruls cheered; after a moment, the Romans cheered as well. Narses smiled again and rode back into the camp.

There was not in fact much discussion when the officers were assembled in Narses' tent. There was instead a rapid series of instructions from the commander.

"The plan is this," Narses declared, drawing a map on the table with his fingertip in spilled wine. "We will draw up our cavalry behind the two trenches — you on the west, Philemuth, and you, Alwith, commanding on the east. At the far ends of the trenches I want all the men who can fight on foot and all those armed with long spears and heavy shields. With them, and lining the trenches toward the center, are to go all the men who can use a sling and all the archers we can muster — not just the ones from the forts, either; if a Herul knows how to shoot, I'd rather have him shooting than fighting on horseback. You are to command them on the east, Phanitheos, and you on the west, Artemidoros, with most of the Protectors and all the Scholarians. I and my retainers, together with some other men, infantry and cavalry and archers, whom I will choose, will take our place in the center. We will let the Sclaveni make the first move. They will certainly attack our center with their heavy cavalry, and I intend to hold them off with the spearmen, slingers, and archers. They will almost certainly then try to pass the end of the trench, and we are to shoot them and hold them back with our spearmen until they are in complete confusion. When their cavalry is in disarray, I will give the appropriate signal, and our cavalry will advance around the trenches and attempt to take the enemy in the flank. The signal will be two blasts on the trumpet. You are not to move until the signal; I personally will shoot any horseman who attacks the enemy before I give him leave. Are there any questions?"

"Where will I be?" asked John.

Narses took a deep breath, his eyes fixed on his map. "I am sending you back to Nicopolis tonight. I want someone to carry a confidential report to the emperor, in case the battle does not go as I would wish."

John felt first a cold shock, then a sense of disbelief, then a merciless, sick rage. His hands were cold, drained of blood, and he rubbed them down his thighs, not daring to speak. *But I thought he liked me!* something inside him exclaimed in anguish. He could feel everyone looking at him, though he had his own eyes fixed on Narses. "Do you think," he managed to say at last, "that I will disgrace myself in this battle, Illustrious?"

Narses hunched his shoulders against the intensity of John's stare, but did not look round. "I have no doubt of your courage. But I want someone to take a confidential report, and I trust you. My report will make it perfectly plain that that is my reason."

"Does that mean you don't trust the others here — these excellent commanders? Artemidoros is senior to me, a more suitable envoy to the Augustus. Surely you could send him?"

"You could!" put in Artemidoros. "I am senior."

"I wish to send John," said Narses, looking up and transfixing the Scholarian commander with a black glare like a bandit chief's. "That is the end of the matter."

"No, it is not!" exclaimed John fiercely. "No one except you, Illustrious, has worked on this army harder than I have; you cannot send me home now, when it has actually come to the war cry. You have no right to take this battle away from me!"

"I am your commanding officer, and I have the right to order you as I please," snapped Narses, turning the glare on all his officers alike. "And I order you to go."

"I will not," returned John. "God in heaven! I am not a coward, I will not turn around and run, and I can hold my place in the line of battle as well as any man here, whatever you may think. And I will not be branded as a coward against my will, not for you or for any man on earth. I resign my commission; I will stay and fight as a private soldier."

Narses took a deep breath. "One moment," he said. "Wait here, gentlemen. John, come with me."

He walked out of the tent and over to the main campfire. His retainers, who were sitting around it, stood up as he came out. Narses said a few flat words in Armenian, and they bowed and withdrew. The eunuch stood still for a moment, staring at the red embers of the fire, then sat own heavily on a log of firewood. John stood behind him; his legs felt unsteady with anger, but rage kept him upright.

"John," said Narses. Then, in a rapid whisper, "Consider what may happen tomorrow; consider it from my position. We fight a battle — we win it or lose it. I die fighting for my emperor, or I achieve a great victory and present it to Their Sacred Majesties, and I am greeted with gratitude and honor. You either share in the luster of the victory or escape the defeat. Now, consider that I give you the place you should have, fighting at my side, and you are killed. I die or, again, achieve the victory; I go back to

Their Sacred Majesties and I say, 'I have defeated the Sclaveni for you, Justinian Augustus, but I am very sorry to tell you, Theodora Augusta, that the young man John — whom you were pleased to say was from Berytus but who wasn't; your only son, whom you loved, on whose behalf you were ambitious — I am sorry to say that he is dead.' Do you think that your mother will be pleased with my victory?"

"Holy God," John said. He sank onto his knees beside Narses. The eunuch looked at him at last, a steady, clear-eyed challenge. "How long have you known?" John whispered.

"From the start, of course. I hear things; I hear everything. A young man called John, an Arabian, was admitted to the presence of the Augusta when he claimed to be her son; it was said that she commanded him to be flogged and imprisoned. Puzzling: she would flog a liar who had insulted her, but not imprison him. And I did not believe, as some did, that she would imprison him if he was not lying. And why did she bother to have the guards who had admitted him posted to Chalcedon? A few days later, the Augusta presents me with another young man, also called John, a native of Berytus, the child of respectable middle-class parents, who has, so I am assured, been at Herion for weeks. The supposed Syrian speaks fluent Arabic and Persian, and when asked to write Syriac, clearly does so by transliterating it from Aramaic. It is not very difficult for me to guess that he is in fact an Arabian and identical with the first young man. But who am I to reveal my mistress's secrets? If you are concerned that others may have guessed it, I can tell you that I do not believe they have; they are readier to believe worse things of the Augusta than I am."

"Sergius and Diomedes told me that you always, always find one out," said John. "They were right." He was silent for a moment, staring at his commander, then said quietly, "But you must let me stay."

"I do not wish to have your mother as my enemy."

"She would understand!"

"Would she? I know very little about love or what it is to

have children, but I do know that people who are subjected to such things are not rational about them. Even the best go mad with these passions. Every time the Augusta saw me, she would think, 'My son died under his command,' and she would detest me. And perhaps she would be right. It is my duty to defend my master and his house, my mistress and her children. I would not be acting as a faithful servant by bringing you into this battle."

"You must let me stay. I'm no more likely to die than anyone else," said John. "Please, Illustrious!"

Narses shook his head, staring into the fire.

"Listen," John told him urgently, "do you know what it is like, growing up the bastard son of a respectable man in a small, respectable city, with everyone knowing that your mother was a whore your father kept when he was a student? Everyone marking you for it, explaining you, knowing you to be venal, weak, shameful, and shameless, before you say a word? You do know, I think. I imagine it's very like being a eunuch."

Narses winced and looked up, again meeting John's eyes, saying nothing.

John went on in a whisper. "And you say to yourself, 'If only I could prove to them that I'm as fine a man as any of them!' And you know the only proof that would really convince them, the only proof that will really convince you — and you need convincing, by now — is to show them that you have courage in war. The test of life and death. You have that proof in your grasp now, Illustrious: you are ready for it, nerved for it, consecrated to it. So am I. And to have it taken away from me because that same whore who abandoned me when I was three months old now wants me back . . . please, Illustrious! I know I shouldn't speak of her so, but all my life I have been her creature, the slave of first my father and now her. But I exist, I am myself, not her; my life is my own if I want to risk it. Don't take that away from me!"

Narses put his hands over his eyes and sat still for a moment. The fire crackled loudly in the silence. "Very well," the eunuch said at last. "Though I warn you, war doesn't prove your worth.

The world will still call you whatever it pleases, and sometimes your soul will bow down and agree." He dropped his hands to his knees.

John took one of the hands and kissed it; he was shaking. "Thank you. I will never forget this."

"As long as you live," said Narses drily. "Very well. Having made a speech about this report, I suppose I shall have to send it, and send Artemidoros. Well, at least he's no great loss."

The day of the battle dawned sullen and overcast; a cold wind blew down the hill from the east, pulling at the standards and tearing the white breath of men and horses toward the Sclaveni like so many flags of truce. The Heruls patted their horses and cast looks of anxiety into the valley, where the light showed the enemy filling the whole plain with spears.

Narses rose early to have another inspection of the trenches and check the disposition of his troops. Seeing the uncertain mood, he had his icon of the Virgin, which he had brought from Constantinople and from Sardica, fastened on the standard. "The Sclaveni are pagans," he told his officers. "God is on our side."

The Heruls looked at the tender smile of the Mother of God and were reassured. The Roman troops were more suspicious — after all, the commander's theology was suspect — but settled unhappily to wait.

John had the place that had initially been allotted to Artemidoros, on the western end of the trench. On his left, in a long triple line that swept from the trench end at right angles and curved back toward the center, was a force of six hundred spearmen — most of the Scholarians and Protectors and two companies of Heruls. To his right, in a line behind the trench itself, were another hundred and fifty of a mixed group of archers from the garrisons of Sardica, Melta, and Nicopolis, together with anyone else from the army who could use the sling and a few Herulian archers with their miserable wooden bows. In the angle between the two groups someone had lit a fire, and some slaves were heating water to mix with honeyed wine against the cold, and arranging quivers of spare arrows.

John had settled the men and given them their orders, and there was nothing more to do but wait. He fidgeted with his own arrows, glancing at the horses tethered behind him. Maleka was already saddled, just in case. Jakobos waited beside her, his sword in his hand, looking anxious. *He wants to save my life in battle,* John thought with affection, *and then be manumitted and become an officer. Maybe I will manumit him. A thanks offering to God for a victory.*

He looked again to his right. Overlapping with his own men behind the trench was the great mass of the cavalry commanded by Philemuth, and far in the distance, in the center of the road, came the gold gleam of the standard. He could clearly make out the tiny figure of Narses, white-cloaked on his white horse. His twenty retainers and some more archers from the garrison stood before him, their bows out but still unstrung, and the pick of the infantry surrounded him, but still he looked very obvious and very vulnerable. John sighed, blew on his fingers, and felt again for his bowstrings.

The Sclaveni had drawn themselves up in a sprawling series of rectangles, heavy cavalry to the fore, infantry to the center and rear. They milled about, shouting; galloped their horses up and down; raced toward the Roman forces and then turned back. A figure in gold armor riding a magnificent bay stallion paced slowly through the horde to the front, and the Sclaveni beat on their shields and howled. The figure paused at the front of his army, looking up the road to where the sun showed plainly the weakness of the force that opposed him. He turned about and lifted his arm several times, striking down at the air, beating his followers with unheard words. Then he turned again, and, faint with distance but terrible still, came an awful, bellowing command. The Sclavenian cavalry roared and began to move forward, trotting at first, slipping up the hill over the white fields, moving quicker now, cantering, hoofbeats like the sea under the whoops and bellows of the war cry.

Hurriedly, John pulled out a bowstring and fitted it, picked up an arrow. His hands were numb and white but perfectly steady.

The Sclaveni attacking the center fell under a sudden hail of arrows and lead sling bullets. Some riders, crashing over their fallen comrades, smashed into the wall of spears and fell; some fell into the trench and were spitted by the trees or by the cavalrymen behind. The road became an impassable mass of fallen men and struggling horses; the cavalry coming up from behind turned from it, going to the right and to the left, galloping with howls of rage along the trench and fanning out, coming closer. A few shot some arrows in the Hunnish fashion, but most were equipped only with spears, useless at this range. John nocked his arrow and drew the bow; he could feel the tension in the muscles of his arms against the stiffness of it, and he tried to breathe slowly, evenly. *They're almost level with my archers now*, he thought. *Why doesn't somebody shoot?* And even as he thought this, the first rider fell, knocked from his horse by the impact of an unseen bullet from a sling. The air darkened with arrows; the steady whirr of the slings and the hiss of arrows leaving the string became mixed with screams of pain. Still the cavalry came on. A Sclavene on a white-faced gray was galloping before the others; his helmet shone with gilding. John set his teeth and waited, the bowstring tight against his cheek, the blood rushing in his ears. The Sclavene turned, grinning, as he saw the end of the trench; the whole world seemed narrowed to his head and chest, and John let the arrow fly. It caught the man in the throat and he fell from his horse; John at once felt for another arrow and shot again. More horsemen were jumping over or swerving past the first comers. *It's up to the spearmen to deal with them,* he thought, and looked back over the trench for another target; found one. "Keep shooting!" he shouted to his fellow archers, and loosed the arrow.

The cavalry hit the row of spearmen like stones falling from a bucket: a few scattered pebbles first, then a smash of rock. There was a crunch of Sclavenian swords on the spearmen's shields, a horrible howl of anguish, another, yells, screams, pounding of hooves. There were no more horsemen galloping past the trench. John turned and stared, unable to move, as the long line of spearmen wavered under the massive force of the cavalry. A horse spitted by a spear and fountaining blood fell onto the man who had speared it; Jakobos ran up with his sword and hacked at the fallen rider. *I'm going to be sick,* John thought in horror. *Dear God, don't let anyone see! Where are my arrows?*

But suddenly it was quiet again, except for a few moans. John looked around, dazed. There were no more horsemen coming. He ran forward and looked down the trench — the enemy had fallen back, and a huge mass of over a thousand of them were regrouping just down the hill. The ground along the trench was littered with the dead and injured cavalry. Some of the Heruls were edging forward, grinning, eager to plunder. "Not yet!" John shouted, with an instinct honed on the march from Singidunum. "They'll be coming back in a moment! Get the archers up at this end of the trench; they'll come straight up the hill next time. Get them up! Immortal God, somebody give me more arrows!"

Jakobos ran up with another quiverful, then ran on to help some of the other slaves with the wounded. John hurriedly arranged the archers so that each would have a clear line of fire, then fixed his attention on the Sclaveni. Besides the horsemen regrouping just down the hill, a larger force was milling about on the road opposite the Roman center; the figure in gold armor seemed to be making another speech. He pointed repeatedly up the road toward Narses. John had no time to be worried before the horsemen down the hill came whooping and howling up in another charge. "Wait!" he shouted at an excited slinger who was wasting his lead bullets while the Sclaveni were still out of range. "Not until you can kill them!"

The second Sclavenian charge was easier to manage than the first: the enemy were slowed down by the piles of their own dead, and there was time to shoot again and again before the crunching impact on the spearmen. The clash itself ended quickly, the enemy retreating almost as soon as they arrived. John was just drawing another deep breath when he heard a thunder of hooves behind him, looked around, and saw that Philemuth and his Heruls were riding down to attack the enemy. "But there hasn't been a signal!" he exclaimed aloud — and then someone gave a horrified shout: "The commander!" And he looked and saw that the figure on the white horse wasn't there.

"Mother of God!" John said; then tore his eyes from the empty pace where Narses had been and looked back at the Heruls pounding past the end of the trench. Down the hill the Sclavenians were regrouping again, and further away the whole road was boiling with men. *It's too soon,* he thought. *Philemuth is making for the center to get the Sclavene king, but we have to get the cavalry out of the way first or he'll be butchered. These damned Heruls are just mad for vengeance, unreliable wild savages! I must stop them.* Even as he thought it, he began running for his horse.

At once his men ran for their horses, and he paused to scream at them to go back to their places and kill Sclaveni the way they were supposed to. He fixed on Hilderic the Vandal and ordered him to see to it. "I'm going to stop those damned idiot Heruls!" he shouted. "You stay here or I'll shoot the lot of you! Jakobos, give me some more arrows!" He was up on Maleka, and Jakobos tossed him another full quiver; he jerked it into the pannier by the cantle and touched the mare to a gallop. "Run!" he told her in Arabic, and she galloped after the Heruls like a winged thing.

As he passed the edge of the trench he heard more horses, many of them. He glanced over his shoulder and saw an indistinct mass of Sclaveni coming up the hill toward him. He leaned over the mare's neck. Spears fell thudding into the ground on his right, and he had a horrifying vision of dying, of his flesh parted with a dozen wounds. *It's the next charge,* he thought, *it's started already and I'm caught.* For a moment he felt so sick with terror that he nearly fainted. *Coward!* a part of him observed, disgusted; and like an echo he heard the voices from Bostra: *What do you expect of a whore's son?*

"I'm not a coward!" he shouted at them. He felt under his hand for an arrow, found one, set it to the bow. *The Parthian shot,* he thought, *that's easy.* He turned, drawing the bow, saw that the first Sclaveni were only a hundred paces behind, let fly, felt for another arrow. Maleka galloped on as fast as she could, snorting, terrified at the scent of blood and fear. John shot again. The Sclaveni were screaming at him in their own language; some threw spears, which missed badly, skewed by the mad gallop. John shot again, his eyes fixed on the Sclaveni; found another arrow, shot again, again and again — found nothing under his hand; turned, saw that the quiver was empty; looked up and saw more horsemen before him; lowered his head against the mare's neck. *Flying,* he thought, *we are flying into death.* The certainty of death was not terrifying; it had been the possibility alone that held fear.

The horsemen scattered before him, shouting his name. He sat up and saw that they were Heruls. Looking back, he found that the Sclavenians who had pursued him were galloping away. He drew rein and Maleka stopped, staggering, her mouth dripping foam. The Heruls had stopped as well and were milling about him, shouting and laughing; Philemuth appeared from their midst, grinning.

"I have seen nothing like that!" he said. "We see them following us, then we see you; we stop to wait. What a sight! She can run, that horse, and you can shoot!"

"What in the name of all the saints of God are you doing here?" demanded John furiously.

Philemuth stopped grinning.

"You were told to wait for the signal!" John shouted, shaking with anger and relief. "He said he would shoot you if you didn't wait; I'd shoot you myself, if I hadn't run out of arrows. Get back to your post at once!"

"They have killed the commander!" said Philemuth angrily, waving toward the road. "We will kill them. We do not stand and wait while they kill our commanders. We are warriors!"

"You are Roman solders, and Roman soldiers obey orders! How do you know he's dead? Come on, back!" He jerked

Maleka's head about. "Back!" he shouted at the Heruls in their own language. He grabbed the bridle of the nearest horse and dragged it about. Looking rather stunned, its rider glanced up the hill. John touched Maleka to a trot and rode back toward the trench, not looking behind him, rigid with rage against Philemuth. *I was nearly killed,* he thought with stunned disbelief, *and it was all that idiot's fault for not obeying orders — the stupid, filthy barbarian. There's not an ounce of self-discipline in the whole stinking nation of them!*

The Herulian cavalry followed like lambs.

When they arrived back at the trench, the Heruls began to shout with joy and point toward the road. The figure in the white cloak was there again, motionless as ever — and mounted on a brown horse. Philemuth rode up and caught John's arm, beaming, and John beamed back, anger all at once forgotten. "It was just the horse," Philemuth said, and sighed. "Good. I go and wait now for the signal."

John nodded. "And I will stay at my post."

At the end of the trench he slid off Maleka; his legs gave way and he sat on the ground, shivering, among his men. "Did they attack again?" he asked at random.

Jakobos was beside him, pulling his cloak about his shoulders. "No, master. They were all chasing you."

John nodded, not really taking it in, then pulled himself up and was sick into the trench. Over his head, golden as summer, came two loud blasts on the trumpet.

As far as John was concerned, that was the end of the battle. On the east, where the steep ridge of the hill had slowed the attackers, the fighting had never been as hard and had stopped sooner. On the west, John discovered, the Sclavenian cavalry had been fatally disarrayed by its futile pursuit of John himself. "It was only a few of them who went after you at first," Hilderic the Vandal told him afterward, grinning. "But you shot their leader, so the whole troop went off for vengeance instead of charging us, and your mare ran so fast they were spread all across the hill and into the Heruls before they knew it. The Heruls had stopped to watch the show, so they were all in line of battle. The enemy knew they were in no condition to fight the Heruls, disorganized as they were, and they didn't have a leader to tell them what to do, so the ones the Heruls didn't get just turned around and rode for home. All that our most illustrious general had to do then was wait until the Heruls were back in their place and give the signal for the charge."

"He was just waiting for them, was he? I didn't need to tell them to come back?"

"Well — no," said Jakobos, who was beside Hilderic. "But you would have if you hadn't gone."

Once allowed the charge, the Herulian cavalry had swept down onto the Sclavenian flank and smashed into the infantry, who were not protected, as the Romans had been, by trenches, missiles, and lances. The king of the Sclaveni, seeing it, had abandoned his attack on Narses and galloped down to help, only to find himself surrounded. The carnage was terrible. When John rode down the valley later that day, he found the road red with blood and strewn with corpses for half a mile. But the king had eventually escaped with many of his men, though all the plunder was left behind.

While the Heruls were still killing Sclaveni, a messenger came from Narses to tell John and his men to come down to the center. Arriving at the road, John found the commander off his new brown horse and lying in the reddened snow while a doctor pulled blood-soaked splinters out of his thigh. The eunuch was very pale and his lips and the shadows under his eyes were quite blue, but the iron composure was still in place.

"John," Narses said when he saw his subordinate, "I am very glad I missed witnessing your escapade. So, have you convinced yourself?"

John stared blankly for a moment. "I suppose so," he said at last. "But I never want to do that again."

"No," said Narses, and smiled tightly. Then he ordered, "Line your men up and have them prepare to assist the cavalry if it becomes necessary. Do you have many casualties?"

The memory of the next few hours afterward seemed to John

like something out of a dream, though at the time it seemed perfectly natural to send Jakobos back to his tent to fetch his tablets, pens, and stylus. The work of detailing the casualties, of assigning some men to care for the wounded and others to bury the dead, and of appointing messengers to bring the news to Nicopolis and to ask for more supplies and accommodation was all very similar to the routine work of running the army. At one point John found himself taking a letter in shorthand, his bow slung over his back and his helmet still on his head, while Narses dictated from a stretcher, stopping once or twice to choke back screams of pain while his wound was cauterized, and down in the valley the Sclaveni were fleeing from the victorious Heruls. Narses had been struck above the knee by an arrow, which had gone clear through the fleshy part of the thigh and into his horse. The white Persian mare had tried to shake the pain off by rolling on top of it, and had broken the arrow and driven it deeper into herself; the bodyguard had killed her, but it had taken some time to cut her rider free, and he had lost a lot of blood by the time they managed it. He had insisted on getting back into the saddle to reassure the Heruls, and the surgeon was vastly displeased with him.

"If you had sat quietly, we might have got the arrow out in one piece!" the doctor told his commanding officer reprovingly, when he had finished pulling bits of wood out of the torn flesh and had cauterized it. "Now look at the mess! It will be months before you'll be able to walk again, even if infection doesn't set in!"

Narses merely nodded impatiently and asked for news of what the Heruls were doing now.

"Taking all the Sclavenian plunder, Illustrious," one of the bodyguards informed him.

"What about the Sclaveni?"

"Gone off north, Illustrious."

"Send Alwith and Phanitheos after them; tell them to keep their distance and avoid an engagement, but to watch where the Sclaveni go. John, go down and secure the plunder in my name.

Promise the Heruls a huge donative, praise them to the stars, point out that things must be divided fairly, and make sure you get everything away from them. Those women and children are Romans, from Oescus and the countryside; they've just been raped and abused by the Sclaveni, and it's not fair to hand them over to the Heruls. Send them to Nicopolis. What time of day is it?"

"About two hours before dusk, Illustrious."

"Nicopolis is too far, then. Well, put them in the camp, then —" Narses stopped abruptly and caught his breath in a ragged whimper: the doctor had just poured a cleansing solution of herbs and vinegar into his wound.

"I'll put them under guard and use the Scholarians," John told him, closing the tablets. "Was there anything else urgent?"

Narses shook his head, blinking back tears of pain.

"Well, then, Illustrious, why don't you rest? The surgeon could give you something to dull the pain, and there's no reason not to take it now. You're entitled to sleep after a victory."

Narses smiled, weakly but without the least ambiguity. "What law code did you read *that* in? Go, then. And if you find that envoy . . ." Narses paused. "Recommend to him that his queen find someone else to care for her wardrobe."

VIII

CRUEL AS THE GRAVE

THE REST OF THE WINTER was one long series of disappointments. As soon as the Sclaveni had recrossed the Danube and burned their bridge behind them, Narses attempted to treat with them. His envoys were received and treated politely but sent home empty-handed; no promises of peace were made. The other tribes in the region were delighted to receive embassies from such a high-ranking imperial minister, and deeply impressed by the victory. They all sent embassies back, and brought several quarrels for Narses to arbitrate, but they were quite unwilling to accept any treaty that left them serving as a buffer against the Sclaveni — even when the treaty was sweetened with offers of land and subsidies. The defenses of Thrace, smashed at Oescus, were crumbling everywhere; Narses struggled with infinite pains to set them up again without barbarian assistance, but the provinces were too battered and exhausted to contribute anything to their own defense, and the rest of the empire had nothing to spare them.

The worst disappointment of all, however, came just before the army was due to start its march down to Dyrrhachium for the voyage to Italy. The troops had returned to Sardica as soon as it was clear that the Sclavenian invasion really was over for the time being; Narses made a journey along the frontier in February and March, carried in a horse litter since he was still unable either to walk or to ride, but the Heruls remained in their barracks. In April, shortly after he returned, Philemuth and the other Herulian commanders arrived at his headquarters together and formally asked to see him.

Narses and John were going over the arrangements for the march in the commander's office when the Heruls arrived. The eunuch was sitting on the couch with his leg up, working through a heap of documents which were piled beside him. The spring sun came warm through the open windows with the thick, sweet smell of the flowering may in the courtyard below. John was sitting at the desk, writing a letter to an obstructive official in Dyrrhachium and finding it hard to concentrate. "In spring Kydonian quinces drink . . ." kept running through his head, and his thoughts kept returning to Constantinople. *I wonder what Theodora made of Narses' report?* he thought. *She'll be pleased, yes, but what will happen? Will Narses still have to return, leaving someone else to take the army into Italy? And what rank will I have?*

I wonder how Euphemia is getting on with Sergius. He smiled, setting down the pen and looking at the leaf-shadows quivering on the sunlit wall. *I wish I could see them! The battle of the slime and the shrew! My money's on Euphemia. Sergius is devious, but hasn't half her brains. I'll bet that he's offended her, and that she's getting information from Anastasios.*

Closing his eyes, he pictured Anastasios and Euphemia in Euphemia's upstairs room, bent in consultation together over the volume of tax indictions while Euphemia's chaperone worked silently at her loom. Grapevines would be budding in the tangle of the courtyard, and the few inches of water in the broken fountain would be green. *They'd get on,* he thought; *they'd even like each other. Both of them go straight at what they want, and they're both efficient. I wish I knew what —*

The office scribe rapped on the door and announced the Herulian commanders.

John rose, smiling, and went to shake their hands. He had been left in charge at Sardica while Narses was journeying, and he felt that he knew the commanders well. However, before he had crossed the floor to them, Philemuth, followed by the others, gave a nervously formal bow. John stopped and bowed back. *Something's wrong,* he thought. *Has there been another murder in the ranks?*

"Most esteemed and illustrious general," said Philemuth, bowing very low to Narses.

Narses sat up, easing his leg round carefully, and inclined his head. John thought he looked marginally older after the events of the winter. The injury had left him even thinner and frailer than before, and there was now more white than black in the fine hair. But the energy was undiminished. "Most esteemed Philemuth — and you, my deeply honored commanders," he returned, "how can I be of service?"

Philemuth cleared his throat, and the others shuffled nervously. "As Your Distinction knows, I was sent with Your Diligence to recruit some of my people to fight for the Sacred Majesty of the emperor Justinian Augustus," he began formally — then stopped. Narses nodded politely and waited.

"And as Your Illustriousness knows, we have already fought for the emperor and endured a savage conflict in the middle of the winter, and won a splendid and imperishable victory." He stopped again, as though he'd forgotten the next line of his speech. "However," he said at last, "now Your Diligence wishes us to go to Italy to fight for Belisarius, while you return to Constantinople. Belisarius has never been a friend to our people. Those of us who have fought for him in the past he has treated very cruelly, and in ways that contradict our own customs completely. We will not have him command us."

Narses sighed. "I understand your concern for your people, most noble Philemuth. However, although I must leave you at Dyrrhachium, you will not be directly under the authority of the most distinguished Count Belisarius. I have received confirmation that you will be commanded by our own friend John, whom I know to be trusted as much by you as by myself."

Narses directed a smile at John, who could only gape back. *All by myself?* he thought in astonishment. *Sole commander, not somebody's subordinate? Holy God, Holy Almighty, Holy Immortal!*

Philemuth smiled at John nervously, but said, "We do esteem John, but we do not wish to fight in a war directed by Belisarius."

"You agreed to do just that in Singidunum," Narses pointed out patiently. "What safeguards do you want, then?"

One of the other commanders cleared his throat. "Your Illustriousness, we have already fulfilled our contracts by fighting for you against the Sclaveni. We wish to go home."

Narses' polite smile faded. He looked from one to another of the commanders, then shoved his pile of documents aside. "What has happened?" he demanded.

They looked at the floor. "We have had enough of fighting foreigners," Philemuth said uncertainly. "We wish to return to Singidunum, to our homes and our wives."

"It's the embassy from Thule," said Narses grimly. "It's come back, hasn't it? It has found a king of the royal line of the Heruls. That's why you want to go home."

There was a moment of complete silence. From the courtyard outside came the sound of a thrush singing. "You can't . . ." John began; then realized that there was no way to stop them.

"Am I right?" asked Narses.

Slowly Philemuth nodded. "They have found us a king," he said. Then, "Illustrious, please understand. The embassy has found a man, Datios, son of Aordos, son of Ochos, son of the sons of the gods, of the pure royal line of the Heruls. Justinian Augustus, though, will support King Souartouas because he appointed him and is sure of his loyalty. Souartouas has been my friend, but he has no more right to be king than I do myself, and neither I nor the people can support him against King Datios. So there will be hostility between us and the Romans, and we cannot go to Italy, even for you, even commanded by John."

"You swore me oaths," said Narses.

"We swore to fight for you. We have done that."

"You swore to obey me! Christ who sees all knows that I've kept my side of our bargain and defrauded you in nothing. You've taken money from me."

"We will return the money, Illustrious. But we cannot go to Italy now."

Narses stared at him intensely for a minute, then looked at each of the commanders in turn. "You know what the Romans say of your nation?" he asked savagely. "That you are a race of liars, faithless, perjured, and inconstant; that you are given to random violence, drunkenness, and fornication; that you are the worst of all men on earth." The officers stared back, shocked and bewildered at first, then angry. One, Alwith, put his hand on his sword.

"Even the Romans," said Alwith, "do not say we are cowards. They have seen too much of our courage in the past."

Narses glared up at him. "I have always defended the Herulian name," he said bitterly. "What am I to tell them now at Constantinople? That my faithful Heruls not only refused to fight for me but wish to run off and plunder Roman lands like their ancestors? I would be ashamed to say such a thing, Alwith — as you should be."

Alwith dropped his hand from his sword, looking bewildered. "Tell them that we are loyal to our own ways," said Philemuth.

Narses snorted. "They will reply that that is entirely evident! You disgrace yourselves, my commanders, and you disgrace me with you."

"Illustrious," said Philemuth in a tone of real distress, "we have no wish to make you ashamed before the sacred Augustus: you have always been our friend and benefactor. But we must have a true king. We will gladly swear to keep peace with the Romans and to respect Roman lands. I myself, when I have gone to King Datios, will ask him to let me return with my men to serve the Romans. But more than that we cannot do. You must see that. We cannot go to Italy."

Narses stared at them for another moment with a concentrated fury amounting almost to personal hatred; then he closed his eyes, pressed his hands against them. "No, you can't, can you?" he said. He dropped his hands, and his face was almost calm again. "Very well, I release you from your oaths. You need not try to repay any money you have received; I will be content if you will swear to refrain from raiding Roman lands. You may return to Singidunum in two days' time, and I will arrange for you to have an escort back to your own country."

The Heruls bowed down to the floor and left. When the door had closed, Narses swept his hand over the pile of documents and sent them crashing onto the floor. He sank his head into his hands, clenching his fists in his hair.

"They're not really . . ." said John helplessly.

"They are," replied Narses. "And we have to let them. Otherwise they'll still go but will have a grievance against us. Mother of God! Patience!" He slammed his fist into the side of the couch.

John sat down at the desk beside his half-finished letter. *No need to finish it now*, he thought numbly. *All that work, a year of it: arranging to recruit the Heruls, enduring their filthy hospitality, bringing them here, paying them, feeding them, worrying over them, sorting out their quarrels, trying to control them . . . all over in a five-minute meeting. Dear God.*

His throat ached, and he sat silently biting his lip and, like a disappointed child, trying not to cry.

"Well," said Narses after a long silence; his voice was calm again. "It was a possibility from the first, and it is considerably better than it might have been. There might have been a mutiny; they might have sacked Sardica. And it is true that we did get one victory for our efforts. We must return to Constantinople. Perhaps I can arrange for us to make some peaceful settlement with the Heruls, or get some more money or troops allotted for the defense of Thrace."

"Is there any hope of that?" John asked bitterly.

"Not much," Narses admitted. "I advised against appointing Souartouas at the time, but the master of the offices was very set on the notion, and the emperor found it appealing. Since he didn't take my advice then, he almost certainly won't drop

Souartouas now. He always supports men once he's appointed them."

"And you know as well as I that we don't have any chance of getting more troops or money for Thrace, not with Belisarius begging for more for Italy and another rebellion starting in Africa. Everything we've done here has been in vain."

Narses got up slowly and limped over to John. He put a hand on his shoulder. "These things must be borne," he said gently. "They are all vanities, anyway: the command of armies, victories, triumphs, the purple cloaks and golden ornaments — gifts of chance, of the earth where all things die. It is wrong that we want them so badly."

John rubbed his eyes. "It was a year's work."

"And not wasted. We saved Nicopolis, at any rate, and those poor women from Oescus. We proved a few things."

"What?"

Narses shrugged. "Heavy cavalry isn't invincible. A man's birth doesn't affect his courage, and an ox is just as good as a bull."

John looked up. "That last was why you set yourself up for Sclavenian target practice in that battle, was it?"

The eunuch smiled. "Of course. Come, we will have to make arrangements for the Heruls' escort back to Singidunum."

The arrangements for the Heruls were not complicated, and the arrangements for their own journey to Constantinople were almost absurdly simple. They arrived back in the city on a bright, windy afternoon in early May. They had sent messengers ahead to announce their arrival, and were greeted with trumpets at the Golden Gate. They rode through: Narses and John with their retainers, then the Protectors, then the small baggage train, then the Scholarians — under the command of a junior officer, since Artemidoros had managed not to be sent back after delivering Narses' letter. *We spend a year recruiting,* John thought unhappily, *and we arrive back with fewer than half the men we set out with and the mission we recruited for abandoned. What a disastrous expedition!*

As they drew closer to the Great Palace, however, people began to come out into the streets and cheer as though the expedition had been an unqualified success. "Narses!" they shouted. "The just, the pious! Conqueror of the Sclaveni, savior of Thrace!" Narses looked surprised.

The Bronze Gate of the Great Palace was also standing open, and before it were drawn up the regiments of the Scholarians and the Protectors, welcoming their comrades home. There was a blast of trumpets, and all the imperial guards shouted as one. Narses stopped his brown horse before the gates, and the commanders of the two troops, the count of the Protectors and the count of the Scholarians, stepped forward together, both wearing the white and purple of patricians, their armor decorated with gold.

"Most Illustrious Narses, we greet you in the name of His Sacred Majesty, our master Justinian Augustus," said the count of the Scholarians formally.

"His Sacred Majesty wishes to welcome you himself, in the Hall of Nineteen Couches, and congratulate you on your victory," said the count of the Protectors.

Narses bowed his head. "Most excellent counts, I am deeply honored."

Each of the counts took one side of Narses' horse's bridle and together led the whole procession through the gate. Narses cast John a backward glance of ironic amusement.

In the open square on the other side of the Bronze Gate, Narses dismounted and handed the reins of his horse to one of the stable attendants who was waiting, and followed by his officers, his retainers, the two counts, and a crowd of palace functionaries, he limped into the palace.

The Hall of Nineteen Couches was an annex of the Daphne Palace, and was the largest of the imperial reception rooms, used for display before a crowd or for state banquets, where each of its couches could seat a dozen people. It was an immense room with a vaulted roof, lavishly decorated with paintings and mosaics and divided in two by curtains of gold-worked purple silk. Light from the windows in the vault slid through the blue clouds of incense that filled the air; all about the walls of the room stood courtiers and high officials, dripping silk and jewels. John had grown unaccustomed to the magnificence of the palace, and was overwhelmed by it. The curtains at the far end of the room were closed.

Narses limped slowly up the length of the hall, climbed the three steps to the dais, and paused. John waited with the other officers before the steps. The curtains swung open, and there were Their Sacred Majesties, Justinian and Theodora, images of purple and gold. Theodora's eyes slid from Narses, rested on John for a moment, then returned to the commander of her army. John prostrated himself, hearing the rustle of silk and the catching of breath all around as everyone in the room did the same.

Narses began to prostrate himself, but moved clumsily because of his injured leg. Justinian rose from the throne and caught his hands, stopping him; he embraced him and kissed his forehead. "Welcome back," said the emperor, smiling. "And many congratulations on your victory."

The troops from Thrace were made much of, showered with praise and money, and feasted magnificently in the Hall of Nineteen Couches before finally being allowed to crawl home to bed. John was glad when the feast was over. The fulsome praise of the victory rang hollow, and the necessity to bow and mutter the correct courtly phrase was an intolerable strain after the hard work, the disappointment, and the long journey. Apart from that one dark stare at the beginning, Theodora treated him no differently from the other officers, and said nothing. *Is she angry with me?* he wondered. *Or has she grown tired of me? No. I'm being stupid; she wouldn't say anything on a formal occasion like this.*

But when he was back in his own house, he found himself worrying again — over the empress's silence, over the unknown spies, over the uncertainty of his own future. "I will recommend you for another military appointment," Narses had told him on the journey back from Sardica. He had also said, that morning, "Don't come into the office tomorrow — take a few days' rest." *And I need rest,* John thought; *I don't think I've rested since I first came to this city. But I can't rest now.*

Exhausted, hot-eyed, and awake, he lay in bed listening to the sounds of the city. In the kitchen, Jakobos was reciting his adventures to his admiring parents, and showing his certificate of manumission to an unending stream of visitors and well-wishers; outside, the carts which were banned from the streets during daylight hours rumbled over the cobblestones. The city seemed like a great weight, pressing down the peninsula to the palace, crushing John. His mind measured the distance from it to Sardica, to Dyrrhachium, calculating rations for two hundred, then for a thousand men, reckoning miles and stops in the journey; it was as though he could look at it from a great height and see the armies crawling across the wilds of Thrace like ants. He groaned and rolled over, trying to shut out the picture.

Narses did not even wait until the next day to resume his work. He left the feast with the emperor and went back with his master to the private apartments, taking up the position of head chamberlain again without a word.

Justinian smiled and dismissed his other attendants, but when Narses took up a valet's stance at his bedside, he shook his head. "Sit down," he ordered. "You're off duty — and I can undress myself, you know. I used to do it all the time." He proved it by sitting down on his bed and taking his purple slippers off. Narses sat down opposite him, on a couch, and carefully rubbed his stiff leg.

"What happened there?" asked Justinian, indicating the leg. "Your letter said that you were slightly injured, but from the look of you the injury wasn't slight at all."

Narses smiled. "I took an arrow through the leg."

"Right through? Immortal God! What were you doing to get an injury like that, fighting in the front ranks?"

"Not quite, master. I never learned how to use a weapon.

But I fear I did indulge in a fit of bravado, and made myself conspicuous by sitting near the front with my patrician's cloak on. I paid for it."

"That was an idiotic thing to do," said the emperor angrily. "I forbid you to take a risk like that again."

"I did not enjoy the experience, and will try to avoid it in future," Narses said, smiling.

Justinian laughed. "You've proved yourself more indispensable than ever," he said. He began peeling off his purple stockings. "It was a magnificent victory, my friend. I did underrate you. I should have recalled Belisarius from Italy that time, not you. Let me reward you for it — go on, ask for something."

Narses bowed. "My reward is in pleasing Your Sacred Majesty."

Justinian looked up and laughed again. "I thought you'd say that. Always the courtier. Well, that leaves it up to me, doesn't it?"

"If you like, master. However, I do have some recommendations for your consideration."

"I thought so! Recommendation number one: that I abandon Souartouas and recognize this new king the Heruls fetched from Thule. Recommendation number two: that I withdraw troops from elsewhere in the empire and send them to strengthen the defenses of Thrace and Illyricum. Am I right?"

Narses bowed. "Entirely, master."

Justinian sighed. "I don't think we can do either. But we can discuss it tomorrow; I've called a meeting of the consistory to consider both those questions. Any other recommendations?"

Narses smiled. "Only one, master. My secretary, John, has proved himself as competent at ordering armies as he was at organizing my office. As you know, I wanted him to command the Heruls in Italy. I now recommend that you make him duke of Syria or Arabia instead, so as not to waste his abilities."

The emperor's expression of good nature vanished instantly. "I didn't mean to discuss your secretary tonight, while honoring you for your victory," he said in a harsh voice. "But I have some questions to ask you about him."

Narses sat very still, letting his face go blank. Inwardly he ran over the letters he had written to Constantinople, and the letters he had received. *Something's happened,* he thought. *I don't know what, but it must have been recent. There was no hint of trouble before.* "If you have any questions, master, I am here to answer them," he said slowly. "I am your slave now as much as I was before you freed me."

Justinian snorted and rubbed his face. He unfastened his purple cloak and dropped it on the bed, then stood and went over to his writing table. "You tried to send him here just before the battle," he said, leaning on the table with his back to Narses. "Artemidoros said that you claimed you wanted him to bring me some confidential information, but all the information you sent was unimportant and could have been brought by anyone. You were trying to keep him out of danger, weren't you? Why?"

Narses sat still for another moment, feeling the hot beat of blood in his wounded leg. "Partly because I wanted to leave the army to someone I could trust to manage it if I was killed," he said at last, "and partly to gratify the Augusta."

"Did she ask you to?"

"No, master. She said nothing to me about him. But I had noticed, as you had, that she seemed fond of him and was eager to promote his career, and I thought she might be displeased with me if he died under my command."

Justinian turned round and looked at his chamberlain. "You thought that." He glanced back at his writing table, picked up a letter, and tossed it over. "Tell me what you think of this!"

To the Sacred Majesty of the most glorious emperor Justinian Augustus [Narses read], Very many greetings. It may concern Your Wisdom to know that no one in the municipal offices of the city of Berytus has any recollection of a scribe called John who left the city a year and a half ago for Constantinople; nor has anyone in the city ever heard of a Diodoros who was half-brother to the bearkeeper Akakios. Moreover, those in Constantinople who were familiar with Akakios say with one voice that he had no brothers, only one sister who died before him. It would therefore seem that the young man John, who claims to be the cousin of the most serene Augusta, can be nothing of the sort, and we wish to alert Your Sacred Majesty to this dangerous imposture.

Narses read the letter, then reread it. It was written with the left hand, he noted, to disguise the writing. Whoever wrote it was afraid his ordinary hand would be recognized. His — or her? It looked like a woman's hand, though that was hard to say for certain at any time and harder when the writing was disguised.

He folded the letter carefully and ran it between his fingers. "Your Majesty should not have received this," he said quietly. "If I had been in my office, you would never have seen it."

"You would have dared to hide it from me?" demanded Justinian angrily.

"I do not usually bring before your eyes charges brought anonymously and without evidence. If the Augustus, the master of the world, listens to such accusations, no one is safe, and justice itself is twisted. If the statements in this letter are true, why hasn't the author signed it?"

"He was afraid of Theodora," Justinian replied at once. "And perhaps he was right to be. If the statements are true, it isn't only your secretary who's been lying, but my wife as well."

"Isn't it much more likely, though, that it is the writer of this who is lying? You know that Her Serenity has enemies, who whisper stories packed with malicious lies about her and look for filth to fling at her. And John has been promoted over the heads of others, which always breeds hatred. When did you receive this?"

"Two weeks ago," said Justinian. His anger was gone, and he sat down on the bed looking anxious and unhappy. "It came with the other letters through your office, but your replacement, Agapios, denied having seen it."

"I will question the scribes about it," Narses said. *And I know which one to question,* he added to himself. *Does Sergius think I haven't noticed him poking about in John's papers?* "Have you investigated the charges at all?"

Justinian made a dismissive gesture. "It is, as you said, an anonymous, unsubstantiated libel. If I have it investigated, I either have to use the offices of the state, which would be the same as accusing my wife publicly, or to hire men privately, which my wife would discover, resent, and probably tamper with. She already guesses that I suspect her of something, though she doesn't know why. She is angry — but sometimes I think she seems alarmed too. Narses, do you think it could be true? That my wife is deceiving me with this —"

"My dear master, do you doubt your wife's loyalty — or her strength of mind?"

"Neither," Justinian said wretchedly. "But she is a passionate woman, and hot-blooded. I'm almost twenty years older than she is, and . . . and I neglect her sometimes. If she met this fellow while I was ill, if he was plausible and she wanted comforting . . ."

"What you are imagining is not true, master," Narses said, softly but urgently. "Theodora Augusta is devoted to you — think accurately of how she acted when you were ill, how she spent all the time she could spare from guarding your empire in sitting at your bedside. She is loyal by nature: a firm friend, a faithful wife, and an inflexible enemy. I am sure that her feelings for John are nothing more than what is natural and proper. And as for his feelings toward her, I am absolutely certain that what you suspect him of has never crossed his mind. He regards her somewhat in the light of a wealthy and powerful aunt, and chafes at her government of his life, though he sincerely wishes to please her."

Justinian stared at his chamberlain for a moment, then let out a long sigh. "Yes," he said. "Very well. You are probably right; it is hard to believe that my Theodora would be unfaithful. But still, there is something wrong here; I can sense it. I don't like it, and I want it cleared up. I put in in your hands, Narses. Theodora has always liked you; she won't be offended if it's you who investigates the matter. And I trust you not to lie to me."

"Speak to the Augusta, master," Narses urged desperately. "Show her the letter. It is only fair to let her know what she is accused of, and to give her a chance to defend herself."

The emperor hesitated a moment, then shook his head. "If I tell her, she will spare nothing to find the writer of this letter and punish him. You know that — you said yourself just now that she was an inflexible enemy. And we both know that she has her spies, her private hiding places, her ships and her soldiers; she might very well find the writer of this before we did, and revenge herself. And if she is guilty, she can cover any trace of that too, so that I would never know. She must know nothing about this until we have determined what the truth is."

Narses stared down at the folded letter in his hands. *What the truth is!* he thought bitterly. *If you asked her plainly, she might tell you, but I can't tell you for her. I'm like the slave in a comic play, caught between my mistress's wishes and my master's orders, trying to serve both.* "May I consult the Augusta, though?" he asked. "You say that she already knows you suspect her; she may have identified some enemy whom she blames for it."

The emperor hesitated. "Very well — but do it delicately, and make sure she knows nothing about the letter. You are to say nothing about this to your secretary, either. Keep him in your office until it's all been settled."

Narses bowed unhappily. "As you wish. Though he is an exceptionally capable and honest young man, and it is a waste to keep him where his abilities are not being used, and where he will be vulnerable to slanders. I would recommend sending him to the frontier all the more quickly because of this."

"He has an honorary rank in the Protectors, doesn't he? He can keep that, and draw a double salary. Tell him that he should have a rest for a while. I want to keep an eye on him. If he is innocent, I will see to it that he doesn't suffer because his enemies told lies about him, and I will promote him as quickly as I can. Will that content you?"

Narses rose, put the folded letter in his purse, then carefully made the full prostration before his master. "It must. I will do all I can to discover who sent this letter, and why."

John woke the following morning with a furred tongue, sore eyes, and a headache; someone was standing over him.

"What is it?" he asked, rolling over.

It was Jakobos. "Anastasios is here from the office, master," he said cheerfully. He seemed none the worse for his celebrations the night before. "He says he hopes you don't mind him coming round so early, but he assumed that you wanted the day off, and he wanted to greet you before he goes in to work."

"Oh!" said John, forgetting the headache. "Tell him to sit down and have some breakfast; I'll be right out."

When he had splashed some water over his head and pulled on a tunic and trousers, John went into the dining room and found the old scribe eating white bread and admiring Jakobos' helmet.

"Got it off a Sclavenian horseman," Jakobos was boasting. "Killed him myself. It fits beautifully — see?" He put it on and fastened the strap. "I killed three Sclaveni after they'd been knocked off their horses. Nothing like what the master killed, but Hilderic says it wasn't bad for a first battle. I'm a real retainer now, with a salary and everything."

"Greetings, Anastasios!" said John, coming forward.

The scribe jumped up, came over, and took his hand, beaming. "So here you are!" he said. "I'm sorry to wake you up."

"If you hadn't, I think I would have gone in to the office to see you. I don't know what to do with myself today."

Anastasios grinned, still shaking John's hand. "It's a delight to see you back. Sergius was even harder to work for than I expected. But I suppose you won't be working with us for very much longer?"

"His Illustriousness is recommending me for a military post in the East. I don't know when that will actually come through, though — or if it will come through at all."

"From what I've heard, it's certain to. You appeared in the report of the battle as glorious as Achilles."

John laughed. "I was 'swift-footed,' certainly. I got chased by a thousand Sclaveni, and ran away from them as fast as Maleka could gallop. Afterward I was sick. His Illustriousness isn't recommending me because of anything like that, but because I can organize troop movements and supplies and keep my temper with barbarians. But our campaign was a disaster, so I don't know how much attention anyone will pay to it."

Jakobos looked annoyed, and Anastasios was taken aback. "But your campaign has been reported as a great victory, a triumph against all the odds!"

"It was!" said Jakabos.

"That's what they're saying here now," John said bitterly. He sat down and helped himself to some bread. "But we didn't manage to do a single thing we set out to do, and somebody's bound to notice it. Let's talk about something else. What's been happening here in Constantinople?" He started smiling again. "What was the outcome of the battle between Sergius and the most virtuous Euphemia?"

Anastasios gave him a surprised look, then laughed his wheezing laugh. "That's a good description of it," he said. "A battle it was. First he tried to sell her false information, and then he tried to seduce her."

John felt a jolt of surprise and, peculiarly, anger. "What happened?"

Anastasios shrugged. "She had him thrown out on his ear. Then she wrote a letter of complaint about him to her father's old colleagues at the prefecture, and gave them half a file free so that they'd pay attention. They are all annoyed with him and believe he's incompetent, to handle her so badly. It's not good for a man's career to have enemies at the prefecture, and Sergius is still licking his wounds."

John laughed. "I thought she'd win. And are you giving her the information now?"

"Yes. She . . . umm, sent me a letter the week after she threw Sergius out, saying that you had recommended me as honest, though less informed." He was silent a moment, then said, "I didn't want to go, but I look forward to our meetings now — she's a clever girl, absolutely fearless, very quick, and a pleasure to work with. I wish my own daughter were as devoted a letter writer! But if you are back in the office for any length of time, I'm certain she'd prefer to see you; she wants to know more than I can tell her."

"There can't be that many files left."

"We're halfway through Arabia, and we have Osrhoene still untouched. I don't usually have much information that she can use, apart from the appointment list. Sergius tries to stop me from seeing anything, just to spite her." The old scribe sighed, and added, "And I must go in to work now — I'll be late, and Sergius will cause trouble about it."

"I'll come with you," John said, grinning. "That will keep him quiet."

When Narses returned to his office from the meeting of the imperial consistory, he found John reinstalled behind his desk in the outer office, hard at work sorting the piles of business from the two replacements into one routine. Anastasios was off happily chasing files.

"I thought I told you to rest today," said the chamberlain.

John shrugged. "This is more restful than wandering about the city and wondering what will happen next, Illustrious."

Narses gave a slight sigh and his usual smile and stood still a moment, resting his fingertips on John's desk. He studied his secretary a moment — the thinness of the face under the neatly trimmed beard, its nervous alertness, the shadows under the eyes. *He is still worrying about the Heruls, and about Thrace,* he thought. *It is so bitter to the young, to discover that their work was futile. I let him overwork himself, too — but he was efficient*

*and I thought he'd receive something back for it. Recognition
wouldn't have canceled the disappointment — he's too intelligent for that — but it would have sweetened it.*

*He has his mother's eyes, and the hands are hers too: long
and narrow, with round nails. If the master would only look at
him, he'd have some idea what the truth is. But "jealousy is
cruel as the grave; its coals are as coals of fire, which has a most
vehement flame." The master can't suspect the truth when he's
suspecting such a falsehood. He said that he trusted me — and
he does. Though he has some doubts, because I tried to protect
John at Nicopolis. What I need to do is produce some results
quickly, showing either guilt or innocence. If I can show neither
— and since everything I could show him would imply guilt, I
don't dare show him that — he will suspect me as well. God
give me guidance!*

"The consistory has decided that there will be no more troops
for Thrace," he said after a moment. "It merely contents itself
with praising the arrangements I made. And Souartouas is to
be supported as king of the Heruls."

"Oh," John said, and paused. "Well, it was what we expected."

"Indeed. I must further tell you that His Sacred Majesty feels
you should rest for a time before taking another military post.
You're to keep your present position here, and have two morn-
ings off a week to drill the Protectors you led in Thrace; you'll
be paid two salaries. I'm sorry."

*Am I disappointed at that, John wondered, or relieved? I am
tired, so tired I scarcely feel this; I do need a rest. The sheer
effort that would be involved in arranging to go to the East, and
in learning a new job, makes me hate the thought of moving.
And yet . . . yes, I would have liked it, to be in my own country
again, and honored. I could do it, too. It would be a routine
administrative post now the war's over, just the usual guard
duties against raids by the Saracens and Isaurians. If someone
asked me to arrange troop movements for Arabia, I could do it
with my eyes shut — it would be infinitely easier than Thrace,
since the province is so much richer. But the emperor "wants*

me to rest." He wasn't impressed by our victory, despite all that talk yesterday.

"Damn Philemuth," he said aloud, smiling ruefully. "And all the Heruls with him. Them and their kings!"

"Indeed," said Narses. He tapped the desk, wishing intensely that he could say more. Unable to think of anything, he sighed again and went on into the inner office.

Sergius was sitting at his old place next to Diomedes, scowling furiously as he sorted some papers from his domination of the outer office. He tried to conceal his anger, however, when his superior came in. "Welcome back, Illustrious!" he said, climbing to his feet and forcing a smile. Diomedes shambled up and grinned.

"Congratulations on Your Eminence's magnificent victory," said Sergius, "We talked about it here for days."

Narses smiled politely and inclined his head. *Shall I question him now?* he wondered. *No, leave it for the present. I need to consult the Augusta first. And it would be useful to have enough on that letter to make a guess at its writer before tackling Sergius.* "Thank you, esteemed Sergius," he said. "And thank you also for your services here in my absence. We will have to do something about them in a few weeks, when we have all settled down again."

Sergius smirked and sat down. Narses took his place at his desk and glanced at the business on it, then looked up at the wall. Hector fought Patroclus in the place normally occupied by the icon. *I shall have to remember to have it unpacked this evening,* he thought, and got to work.

"The most illustrious Narses, head chamberlain to His Sacred Majesty," Theodora's chamberlain, Eusebios, announced to his mistress, smiling. Narses had requested a private audience, and the empress was receiving him in her dressing room after her bath. She was barefoot, dressed only in an undertunic of fine silk, which was worked with gold round the hem; she sat on a low chair, examining her face in a silver mirror while one of her women brushed her hair. Her gown and purple cloak lay across the clothes chest, ready to put on. "You seem to be taking my job," Eusebios whispered to Narses. "But I won't take yours, thank you." He bowed low to Theodora and left the room.

The empress glanced up from the mirror and smiled. "Don't bother bowing," she told Narses. "I heard about your leg. Come and sit down — I won't be too much longer." As he seated himself on a stool by the door, she looked back into the mirror, turning her head from side to side, then made a face at herself and put it down. "I feel like that old courtesan: 'To Aphrodite let this mirror dedicated be: I can't see what I was, and what I am, don't wish to see.' Lord, what a hag I'm becoming!"

She had in fact aged since he had last seen her. The skin of her face had loosened, pulling away from the fine bones beneath, and her eyes were sunken; the heavy lids were more prominent than ever. There was more white in the dark hair. None of this had been noticeable at the feast, and Narses was surprised by it. "Has Your Serenity not been well?" he asked.

"I've not been well or serene either," she said sourly. She snapped her fingers and gestured for her woman to leave her. "I've had a lot of trouble with my stomach," she said when the attendant had prostrated herself and left. "And Peter is worried that I'm being unfaithful to him." She watched Narses steadily, her eyes half lidded, masked. "Do you know anything about that?" she asked deliberately. "He'd tell you if he's told anyone."

Narses nodded once, slowly. "I am very sorry," he said. "Your husband is distressed by some malicious stories he has heard. He has said as much to me and, as far as I know, to no one else."

"Thank God! At last I can find out about it. Peter just asks leading questions and then denies that he suspects anything. Who does he think I've deceived him with, and why?"

Narses hesitated. "He does not actually believe that you have deceived him; he knows Your Honor better than that. But he is concerned by what he has heard. I don't know the origin of the stories, and I was hoping that you could help."

She looked at him probingly for a moment. "He wants you to investigate them?"

Narses smiled and spread his hands helplessly. "Mistress, I am entirely certain of your innocence, and deeply concerned to do all I can to heal this breach between you and my master."

"I believe you," said Theodora, but her teeth were clenched and her eyes hot under contracted brows. "Immortal God! Why on earth has he suddenly started listening to stories? What was the story he heard?"

Narses stared for a moment at her bare feet, which were hooked about the ivory legs of the chair. "I think it would be unwise for me to repeat it, mistress."

She hit the arm of the chair. "What does that mean? Are you not allowed to repeat it?" He looked up at her, and she let out her breath with a hiss, her eyes flashing. "How can I help clear myself if I don't know what I'm accused of?"

"I am sorry, mistress. I thought perhaps you knew of some enemy who might have slandered you."

"I know of lots of enemies, and some friends as well, who might have slandered me! Without knowing what I'm accused of, how am I supposed to guess which one? For the past week I've lived like a nun — I haven't said two words to any man, for fear of Peter's miserable damned suspicions! Can't you tell me more?"

He sighed. "Perhaps, mistress, I should come back when I've been able to make a more informed guess about the source of the story."

"Oh damnation!" She hit the chair again. "If I find the person who's responsible for this, I'll have him flogged and his mouth filled with molten lead to stop his lying! I should just do as I please and let Peter stew in his ridiculous jealousy. Why won't he tell me what he's afraid of?"

"Because he fears that you might have the source murdered and he would never be able to find the truth," Narses said drily.

Glaring, she caught her breath — then laughed ruefully. She shook her head and ran her fingers through her hair. "Lord, what a fix," she said. A few loose hairs were caught in her fingers and she pulled them straight, twisting them across the back of her hand. "What a fix. I haven't even dared to see my cousin

John privately. He's been back two days now, and I was longing
to see him, I was so proud of him. And I suppose he'll be off to
the East now before I can even greet him "

Narses shook his head. *Thank God it came up,* he thought.
"John will be remaining with me for the time being. The master
thought a rest wouldn't harm him."

She looked up quickly, her face lighting with understanding.
"God in heaven, so it's John again!" she exclaimed.

Narses looked at her, saying nothing. *Obeying my orders to
the letter,* he thought, *and violating the spirit of them completely. The old slave's trick dies hard.*

After a moment's stillness, the empress said thoughtfully, "I
thought we'd burst that particular blister. So, who's spreading
lies about John?"

Narses looked down again. *That particular blister — a good
image: a sore on your husband's foot, a place where the shoe's
not quite right and rubs him. He knows that you've lied to him,
and the shoe won't fit till he knows the truth. And surely he
should have it? The results would be far less drastic than continuing the lie. For you, for me, and particularly for John. But
how can I convince you to admit what you've done?*

"I do not believe that the story was entirely a lie," he said
evenly, looking back up into Theodora's face.

The face went still, surprised, alarmed — and behind the
alarm was something else, a rock-hard determination, inflexible
and merciless. "What do you mean?" she demanded.

"The master is not a stupid man, mistress. If he is suspicious
now when he hasn't been before, perhaps it is because he realizes
that you are concealing something from him."

"Oh?" she asked, very softly. "Such as?"

He had heard her use that voice to men before she destroyed
them, but he continued deliberately. "Such as the fact that John
is not your cousin but your son."

She gave him a long, dark stare, then burst suddenly into
peals of laughter. "Oh, Narses!" she exclaimed, wiping her face.
"Oh, I thought you might have guessed it — but my God, you're
a perfect tomb. Not a look, not a word, not a hint, until you

come right out with it. Oh my dear, you should have gone on stage. Holy Immortal, crucified for us, have mercy!"

"Your husband finds the situation rather less amusing."

She stopped laughing. "You want me to tell him, do you? To set his mind at rest?"

"That is the course I would recommend, given the story he has heard."

"I'll settle Peter some other way. I can settle him, now that I know what he suspects. I'll find John a wife."

"Mistress, your husband is a persistent man: he realizes that something is wrong, and he will keep coming back to it until he finds the truth. If you tell him, he will certainly forgive you for concealing it. He will probably even join in concealing the truth, and give your son the promotion he deserves and I recommended. He neither blames nor condemns you for your past, and he is not vindictive."

"Yes — he might let John become a duke, or perhaps even rise to be master of arms for the East. But that would be the end of it. He would keep my son out on the frontier for the rest of his life. And Germanus and his children would stay here in Constantinople, and all the plum jobs would go to them."

"What job did you have in mind for John?" Narses asked, and was suddenly afraid of the answer.

Theodora said nothing. She went instead to the clothes chest and fingered the purple cloak that hung over it, smiling to herself.

"Oh no," he said, shaking his head in disbelief. "No, it won't work."

"Why not?" she demanded, turning on him. "He's cleverer than Germanus' son, he's efficient — you say yourself he's efficient, and you're the expert, the mold, the standard of efficiency. And he's brave, and can handle troops; he learns quickly, he's fair-minded, careful, just — he'd do it well!"

"He wouldn't want it," said Narses. "You haven't told him this. You can't have, or you'd know that the very idea would appall him."

"That's his father's fault," said Theodora, tossing her head.

"He was brought up to know his place, to do what he was told, to behave himself. To be cautious and respectable — twenty-four years old, and still a virgin! But he's capable of it; there's a lot of me in him too. I want my son to have *this*" — she turned back to the purple cloak — "when Peter and I are gone."

"Mistress, he won't want it! The one thing I am certain of about supreme power is that no one ever gets it who doesn't want it, and want it badly enough to pay any price for it. John would simply be afraid of it. He *is* cautious, and he makes heavy demands on himself. He would prefer to work at something that is too easy for him but that he can do well, rather than be promoted and risk making mistakes. He would never accept a position where mistakes are inevitable and can cost lives, cities, and kingdoms. You cannot make him ruthless and ambitious simply by wishing him so."

"I can make him be anything I like!" she snapped. "He does what I tell him. He wants to please me, and he never makes any fuss about doing what I want, even if it's something he doesn't particularly want himself. He didn't want to work for you at first, but he went where I told him and he soon changed his mind. He just needs to get away from his father's shadow."

"Mistress, it won't work. He won't want it and the emperor won't have it — you must see that."

"I see nothing of the sort! I will do as much as I can for John, and if I manage things right, I have every chance of success. You wouldn't understand: you know nothing about love, or what it is to have children. Why are you so against the idea? I thought you liked him."

"I do like him, mistress. I do know nothing about love or children: it makes me pay more attention to friendship. I cannot sit by silently while you discuss a plan that my friend would hate and that is very liable to fail in a way that will injure him."

The empress glared at him furiously; Narses met her eyes and held them. Gradually the glare faded; she put her head on one side, assessing him. Then she shrugged, smiled, came away from the clothes chest. "So you think I'll fail," she said. "I can promise you that if you find the source of that story, I can manage Peter. I won't fail; John won't be hurt. Does that content you?"

"Mistress, I would recommend —"

"I don't want to know what you recommend! Get on with your investigations — and don't tell John what I've told you; I want to tell him myself, when I'm ready. But give him my greetings, and tell him I'm sorry I haven't been able to see him. Tell him why — if you're allowed to."

"I am not allowed to."

She gave him a look of contempt. "Then tell him as much as you can."

"Yes, mistress." Wearily, Narses rose, then bowed down to make the full prostration. Theodora extended her bare foot casually, and he kissed it and backed himself out.

The chamberlain, Eusebios, was waiting in an adjoining room, going through state papers while he waited to dress his mistress. Narses nodded to him as he passed. "You can have your job back," he said. "I don't think I could manage it."

IX

CONQUER!

A COUPLE OF WEEKS LATER, Anastasios asked John casually, "Is your cousin pleased that you're staying here?"

John didn't answer immediately but pretended to concentrate on the letter he was drafting. "What was that?" he asked as he finished and carefully fitted the cap back on his inkwell.

"Your cousin, the mistress. Is she pleased that you're staying in Constantinople?"

John shrugged, cleaning his pen. "I haven't seen her since I got back. I don't know. Narses brought me greetings from her. It seems she hasn't been well lately, and isn't seeing many people." He sprinkled sand over the fresh ink of the letter, then shook it off again into the box on the corner of the desk.

"Oh," said Anastasios, puzzled. "Well, I will pray for her recovery."

John smiled formally, folding the letter in half. *It's true she isn't seeing many people*, he thought, *but she might see me. Should I ask for an audience? But she's always invited me in the past — and if she's annoyed with me for some reason, or has lost interest in me, or for any other reason doesn't want to see me, then I shouldn't force myself on her. I wish to God I knew what was happening!*

He folded the letter again, smoothed the edges with pumice, checked through the signets in their case until he found the correct one, dripped some wax onto the fold, then stamped the sealed letter. It was Narses' seal, a quartered circle with an inkwell in one corner and a sword in the other. He stared at the neat lines as the wax hardened in the air. *And I don't know what's the matter with him either,* he thought. *All that time in Thrace after Nicopolis I could have sworn I knew his mind, that I was as close to him as I've been to anyone in my life. We get back to this city and all at once he goes distant as the sphinx and starts feeding me riddles. "Your cousin sends her greetings" — even when I managed to get to him privately, he just smiled and told me nothing. It's like talking to the Delphic oracle! What have I done wrong? I can't have misjudged them both.*

He pushed the letter onto the heap awaiting delivery, took the cap off the inkwell again, and made a note in the record book.

"Are you drilling the Protectors again tomorrow?" asked Anastasios, trying to make conversation. He had noticed the tension behind the smile.

John snorted, glad of the distraction. "I didn't *drill* them last time. We had to go quell a disturbance at the hippodrome. The Blues and the Greens fell out over a bear-baiting and started smashing the starting gates — and each other. The prefect of the city called us in to keep the peace. Luckily, the factions ran as soon as they saw us coming."

"So long as they confine themselves to smashing each other, I don't mind," Anastasios said. "It's when they turn their attention to the rest of us, or to politics, that I get worried. There've been a lot of disturbances recently." He paused, frowning, then added, "There's likely to be trouble tonight too. Today is the anniversary of the reconquest of Africa, isn't it? There'll have been races all day. The factions will be looking for a fight, particularly since they've had a taste of blood earlier in the week."

"So stay in tonight — or no, you were going to see Euphemia, weren't you? Do you want me to come?"

"Oh, you don't need to come because of that. I'm Constantinopolitan born, I know how to avoid the factions. But she would
prefer seeing you to seeing me. When I saw her last week she
asked about you, and was very eager to see you again. You know
so much more than I do."

"Not just back from Thrace I don't. But I'll come. Should I
meet you at your house?"

"No, I usually go directly from here, and go home afterward."

"Very well — just give me time to collect Jakobos and my
horse, and I'll meet you at the Bronze Gate."

Anastasios grinned and started back to work. "You have to
bring your horse and your retainer, of course," he said slyly.

"Of course! Jakobos would love a try at terrifying the factions.
No, the horse needs exercise, and I may need Jakobos to hold
her."

When he went to fetch Maleka from the stables, however, he
heard shouting in the streets, blurred through the indifferent
reaches of the palace, the words indistinct but the hammerlike
rhythm unmistakable: Conquer! Conquer! He paused, frowning,
and wondered whether he and Anastasios were right to be so
casual. The rioters of the Nika rebellion had pulled down imperial
ministers, burnt half the city, and nearly made a new emperor.
There had been no serious disturbances since they had been
butchered, but that was now a generation ago.

Well, he told himself, *I do have my horse and my retainer to
scare them, even if the retainer is a sixteen-year-old freedman.
I could even bring Hilderic and Eraric — but they'll be off with
their girls by now, and what's the point of troubling them? The
crowd would have no reason to attack me even if there is trouble.
I'll just look warlike and shout "Conquer!" and they'll let me
past.*

He went on to the stables.

The rank of tribune entitled him to keep Maleka, Jakobos'
gelding, and the horses of the two Vandals in the Protectors'
stables. Jakobos was waiting there; both the horses were saddled
and ready to be exercised. "We're just staying on the practice

ground tonight, aren't we?" he asked. "There's been rioting at the hippodrome."

"We're going to see Euphemia," John told him.

The boy's face fell. At the practice ground by the stables he could work at using his spear and hear war stories from the other men. "It sounds bad out there," he urged.

"Well then, take your weapons with you. I'll take my bow. We won't have any trouble if they see that we're armed."

Jakobos cheered up at once. There was nothing he enjoyed more than riding through the streets of his native city dressed in armor and carrying a spear. "Do you want Hilderic and Eraric to come as well?" he suggested eagerly. The longer and more splendid the procession, the better he liked it.

John shook his head. "No need to bother them. Just fetch the weapons."

Jakobos hurriedly fetched the weapons and his Sclavenian helmet from the barracks storeroom nearby and leapt onto his gelding (Hilderic had shown him how to do that), and the two started off.

It was still dusk when they reached the Bronze Gate, but the shops in the Augusteion marketplace were closed, and half of the massive gate itself was closed, with the other half ajar, ready to be bolted shut. Anastasios was standing just inside, talking to the guardsmen on watch; he looked up and greeted John rather grimly.

"It seems that the rioting is serious," he said. "Some of the Blues have been killed, and the rest are out looking for revenge. I think I'd better go directly home."

"I'll see you back," offered John, reluctant to give up the expedition now he'd started. He realized with a sense of surprise that he was eager to see Euphemia. To congratulate her on her defeat of Sergius? he wondered. "We'll stop off at the Cappadocian's house on the way, to set another date."

Anastasios looked up at John, who towered above him on the horse's back. He looked perfectly at ease there, one hand on the reins, the other resting on the unstrung bow beside the pannier of arrows. Nobody would have guessed he'd spent the day sitting at a desk. The shouting was clearer by the gate, and the old scribe suddenly found the thought of company, armed company, immensely attractive. "Thank you," he said.

As they went down the Middle Street toward Constantine's market, the noise grew louder. The great avenue was empty except for a few frightened citizens who'd been caught at work and were hurrying home as fast as they could run. In the market-place itself, the jewelers and goldsmiths were busily boarding up their shop windows, glancing fearfully over their shoulders toward the shouting. Apart from them, the great plaza was eerily vacant. Most of the noise seemed to be coming from somewhere farther on.

"It's a bad riot," said Anastasios, holding John's stirrup. "There hasn't been one like this for years. They may have to call in the troops."

"Why haven't they already?"

"They don't want to provoke the factions. A small squabble can be dealt with by a few troops like yours, but with the big riots, it's all the imperial guard or nothing. It may blow over with nothing."

They crossed the marketplace and passed under the double arch of marble back onto the Middle Street, toward the Taurus marketplace. The shouting grew clearer: "Conquer — the Blues!" in one voice, and then the great roar, "Conquer! Conquer!" A gust of wind brought, acrid and unmistakable, the smell of fire. John stopped Maleka.

"They've set fire to the marketplace," whispered Anastasios. "Dear God. I pray it doesn't spread."

John nodded. His heart was beating very quickly now, and his hands felt cold. *Nothing will happen,* he told himself. *They're not interested in us, they're after Greens.*

But he picked up his bow and strung it. Jakobos grinned at him. The boy was pale under his helmet, and clutched his spear hard.

"Conquer — the Blues!" said John, and they rode on.

The Taurus marketplace too was closed, with every door barred and every window shuttered, but the square was not empty. Its left side was a boiling mass of men, of the barbarously dressed Blues. Some of the mob were smashing the market stalls and heaping the wood against the side of one of the houses; the rest howled and chanted, waving their arms in the air so that their blue cloaks billowed out, black against the red glare of the fire. For a moment John took in nothing more than this. Then he realized that the house was the Cappadocian's.

Almost as he realized this, a window in the front of the house opened and a man appeared in it. The crowd greeted him with a roar of anger. "Cappadocian! Kill him, the beast! Kill him, the oppressor of the poor! Conquer! Conquer!"

The man waved his arms, desperately trying to fan away the smoke, and shouted something to the crowd, something indistinct. He waved toward the side street, the back of the house. John realized that he was telling them that the front of the house had been let, and that it was only the back that still belonged to the Cappadocian — to the Cappadocian's daughter.

John felt cold, sick. The scene before him seemed like something in a dream, colored more vividly than reality and moving with a terrifying slowness. He held the reins tightly, unable to move, staring with horrified fascination. The crowd was slow to understand, too busy chanting. They piled more wood against the house.

"Merciful God!" whispered Anastasios. "They're going to kill her. They wanted to kill her father in the Nika rebellion; now they're going to kill her."

John came to himself with a jerk. He pulled his Protector's signet off his finger and shoved it into Anastasios' hand. "Hurry," he said. "Take that back to the palace and fetch my troop of Protectors here at once."

"You take it!" said Anastasios, trying to give the ring back. "You've got a fast horse."

"It would still be too late by the time I'd get them here. Go on, run. I'll see if I can get Euphemia out."

He touched Maleka into a gallop across the square. Jakobos started after him, shouting, "Master! Wait!" John didn't look back. "Use the side street!" bellowed Jakobos, and John pulled the horse to a stop.

"There's an alley that connects the first street off the square to her house," Jakobos shouted, reining in beside him. "It comes out almost opposite the gate. We can go that way; I don't think they've found it yet."

"Thank you," John said, and turned the mare into the first side street.

It was dark by now, and the wild light cast by the fire swayed between the balconies of the narrow streets. The chanting, trapped by the locked and shuttered houses, seemed to come from every direction at once. The alleyway was almost completely black, and the horses started and trembled at noises in the shadows. The glare of firelight at the alley's end was blinding. The iron gates of Euphemia's house stood wide open, and the mob was pouring in, looking for loot.

"Immortal God!" said John.

"Look!" shouted Jakobos, pointing down the road that led away from the square.

A covered sedan chair was about two blocks away. A few of the rioters had seen it and were running after it; the rest were too busy looting. Even as they watched, the rioters caught up with the chair. The bearers set it down and there was a red blaze of reflected firelight as one of them pulled out a sword — then both men disappeared in a hail of blows, and the chair itself tipped over. John set spurs to his horse again.

It took only seconds to reach the chair, but by the time he had arrived the rioters were dragging a woman out of the chair, and the bearers were lying in bloody heaps on the cobblestones. The woman was old, dressed in black; she kicked, screaming, and was flung aside. Another woman was hauled out, a younger one. She struggled violently, and one of the men caught her hair and dragged her head round while another held her arms and began pulling her cloak off. John drew Maleka to a halt, fifteen paces from the group. *There are about thirty of them,* he thought coolly. His horse, frightened by the fire and the screams, reared up and neighed loudly, and the mob froze and looked round. He saw that the young woman was Euphemia.

"Let her go," he said, loudly and clearly. He held his bow low across the saddle, behind the pannier of arrows.

The rioters looked at him, then looked behind him and saw only Jakobos. They laughed. John tried to breathe steadily, and felt for an arrow.

"Green!" they shouted. "Tax lover! She's the Cappadocian's daughter, the whore! She's going to pay for what her father did!"

"I am a tribune of the Protectors of the sacred majesty of the emperor Justinian Augustus, and I command you to let her go." The arrow was smooth under his fingers, sliding easily onto the bowstring.

"Yaaaa!" shouted the man who was holding Euphemia — a thin, hot-eyed man with a poxed face. "Go back to the palace, whore's son, while you can still ride!"

Euphemia was staring at John, not hopeful, not afraid: angry. Behind her the pox-faced man was grinning. John raised the bow and shot in one quick movement, and the rioter's left eye sprouted feathers, then blood. *Another arrow,* thought John, reaching for it while the rioters were still staring at the first. He shot again; another Blue clutched his shoulder and fell, howling. One of the rioters waved a sword rather uncertainly and ran toward him; John shot again, and he fell. "Jakobos!" he said grimly, and the boy gave a shriek to terror and excitement and charged.

The Blues turned and ran; John pulled out another arrow and killed another to keep them going. Jakobos had speared one and was galloping after the others. "Jakobos!" John shouted again. "Back, you idiot!" He trotted Maleka forward and stopped her beside Euphemia. Jakobos was turning back.

John kicked his foot out of the stirrup and leaned down to grab Euphemia's hand. "Quickly!" he told her. "Before their friends see us!"

Euphemia's cheeks were crimson and she was gasping for breath. "Aunt Eudokia!" she said, looking around her. John looked and saw the old chaperone picking herself up off the street where the rioters had flung her.

"Jakobos, take the old woman!" John shouted. "Hurry!"

Jakobos nodded and jumped from the saddle. "Come on, granny!"

The old woman flung herself at him, spitting with anger. "You filthy beast!" she screamed, tearing at his face with her nails. "You keep your hands off her, you hear? I'll teach you —"

Euphemia ran over and grabbed the old woman. "Auntie! Auntie, they're friends, they've come to rescue us! It's John from the palace, and his slave, don't you see?"

The old woman burst into tears and clung to Euphemia. "Oh, my poor lamb!" she sobbed. "The animals!" The girl pulled her over to Jakobos' horse and tried to shove her onto the animal; the horse snorted and moved away. Jakobos, his face bleeding, watched in amazement.

"Hurry!" shouted John. "The others will notice in a minute!" He urged Maleka beside Jakobos' horse, caught the gelding's bridle and held it; Jakobos and Euphemia between them bundled the old woman onto the horse, and Jakobos leapt up behind her. "Come on!" John urged Euphemia.

Euphemia put her foot in the stirrup and John pulled her up so that she sat sidesaddle before him. "My slaves . . ." she said, looking at the chair-bearers. She caught her breath and looked away again.

"Nothing we can do," John said, already spurring Maleka forward. "Hold on!"

She grabbed his shoulders. Behind him he heard shouts. "The others have seen us!" gasped Euphemia.

John laughed. "It doesn't matter now!" he said. "This horse is the fastest thing in the city. Come on, my beauty!" he added to Maleka in Arabic, and the horse flicked back her ears and broke into her flying gallop.

Euphemia gave a little moan, clutched John tighter, and closed her eyes.

They easily left the rioters behind, and rode quickly through the maze of narrow streets. To their left the black bulk of the hippodrome loomed against the sky; the city smelled of fire.

John turned left as soon as he saw a street he recognized. "We're going back to the palace," he told Jakobos, slowing so that the boy could ride beside him.

Jakobos nodded. The chaperone had fallen half off during the gallop and was now slung across the saddle like a sack of flour, sobbing quietly. Euphemia opened her eyes at the sound. "It's all right, Auntie," she said gently. "In a moment we'll be safe at the palace."

From the hippodrome came the sound of more rioting, but they wove through the backstreets, ignored by the few men they encountered, and emerged at last into the Augusteion market-place. A half-moon lit the great dome of the Church of the Holy Wisdom and picked out the gilding on the towering statue of Justinian on his bronze horse before it; the Bronze Gate stood wide open, dazzling with torches, and through it came the gleam of armor. Maleka broke into a trot, eager to be home.

As John approached the gate there was a shout of challenge, and then another shout of his name, and Anastasios ran out to meet them. "Thank God!" he exclaimed, and grabbed John's foot as the mare stopped. "Thank God! And Euphemia, thank God! You're not hurt? Your troops were going to come, John, but the count of the Protectors stopped them; he said it was madness to go out with just a hundred men into the middle of a riot. He didn't expect you to come back. And he has them all standing there by the gate, not just your troops, but all the Protectors — and half the Scholarians are there as well, and none of them will leave the palace!"

"Oh," said John weakly, looking at the torchlight in the gate. He started Maleka forward again, longing for safety.

The count of the Protectors, a distinguished-looking, silver-haired man of an impeccable senatorial family, appeared in the center of the gate on horseback as John rode in. He looked with a kind of surprised disdain at his troublesome part-timing officer. *Out of uniform, as usual,* he noted, *and my God, carrying a half-*

dressed young woman; his slave is covered with blood; he's a disgrace to the standards. But we have to put up with anything from the Augusta's favorites. "Well, tribune," he said slowly, the rank tasting unpleasant in his mouth, "I see you have been fortunate enough to escape unharmed, and without risking the destruction of all your men in any unsanctioned enterprises. What did you think you were doing, ordering them out?"

"Sir," said John, "the rioters were burning and pillaging in the marketplace, and they nearly murdered this citizen. I thought —"

The count looked down his aristocratic nose. "You would risk the lives of a hundred of my guardsmen to rescue your girl-friend?"

Euphemia sat up, tried to pull her cloak straight, realized she'd lost it, and scowled. "I'm not his girl friend," she declared, and slid off the horse. Her brown hair fell about her smooth shoulders, and her eyes looked enormous, proud and determined in the torchlight. *She's magnificent,* John thought, grinning against his will with admiration. *Her house on fire, her slaves dead in the street, and herself within a hair's breadth of rape and murder, and she comes out of it ready to cross swords with the count. God in heaven, I'm glad I saved her. This alone would be worth it!*

"I am Euphemia, daughter of the patrician John of Caesarea in Cappadocia!" she announced, glaring about her. "Those filthy savages burned down my house and murdered my slaves as I tried to escape. They would have murdered me as well, if it hadn't been for John here, who, though he's no friend of mine, at least has the soul of a man and not a little white rabbit!"

Her words were greeted with a roar of excitement from the troops beyond the gate. John now saw that they were drawn up rank on rank, his own men in the front. "Dirty rabble!" some of the men were shouting. "They run like rats if you charge them. Let us out, we'll 'conquer' them!" "Don't make trouble!" yelled others. "Leave the brutes alone till morning!" And then through the cheers and jeers came another sound, the sudden rhythmic clash of an acclamation. "Thrice august! Reign forever!" The voices joined together now: "Justinian Augustus, *tu vincas!*" And the whole army parted in the middle and sank down on its face as the emperor, followed by his elite bodyguard, walked through it to the gate.

John got off his horse and prostrated himself on the paving-stones; the count of the Protectors was slower, and had only just dismounted when Justinian addressed him. "Markianos Apollinaris," he said angrily, "what is going on?"

The count hurriedly made the prostration before replying. "This young man tried to call his troops out into the city, master, to rescue that woman there."

Justinian gave John a cold look, then noticed Euphemia. The girl, in her turn, bowed down to the ground and rose again. "Why, it's Euphemia, the Cappadocian's daughter," said the emperor in surprise. "What do you mean, rescue her? What has happened?"

"You Sacred Majesty," said Euphemia at once, "the supporters of the Blue faction came to my house in the Taurus market this evening. They set fire to the front part of the building, which I have let out to the imperial notary Alexander. Seeing this, I directed my slaves to leave the house at once, and myself got into my chair and set out, leaving the gates open. Alexander shouted to the crowd that he had nothing to do with me or my father, and many of the men came running to my gate to find me, leaving Alexander to burn in the house — for all I know, he's dead now, he and all his family. Most of the Blues poured in through the gates to destroy my property, but some of them chased my chair down the street, caught it, and killed the bearers. They were on the point of killing me in an outrageous manner when John arrived with his servant. Though no friend of mine, he is acquainted with me, since we have met often to negotiate over some files that my illustrious father mislaid when he left the prefecture. He drove my attackers off, killing several of them, and brought me here at once. Here I learn that he had sent for some troops of the Protectors to help quell the riot, but that this noble count refused to let a man pass the gates."

Justinian looked at the count, his round, high-colored face darkening. "Is this true?"

"Ummm, master, I thought that the troops would be better kept safe . . ."

"What do you think your troops are for?" demanded the emperor. "They're to keep *us* safe, not themselves! That stinking mob is burning an imperial notary alive in his house and assaulting the daughter of a praetorian prefect in the street — can't you think of anything better to do than obstruct those who are trying to prevent such horrors? Lord of All, my own sister lives near the Taurus market!" He turned to Euphemia. "My sister's palace —"

"They weren't attacking your most noble sister's house, Thrice August," Euphemia stated bitterly. "They know that it is well guarded."

"What use are guards against a fire?" asked the emperor angrily, turning back to Apollinaris. "The troops should have been sent out hours ago; they're all to go out now — only the Excubitors are to stay and guard my palace. I want the streets empty in an hour's time, and I want the fires out." He paused to catch his breath, then said to Euphemia, in a kindly tone, "I will have your house rebuilt, my dear, but until it's ready, I invite you to stay in the palace as my guest. My chamberlains can look after you . . . and after your, um, associate." The chaperone had managed to get off the horse at last, and was taking Euphemia's hand as he spoke. "Who are you, fellow?" he added, addressing Anastasios, who was coming over to help the chaperone. "I've seen you before."

"Anastasios, master," said the old man, and bowed to the ground. "A scribe in the office of your servant, the most illustrious Narses."

"Good. Escort the lady Euphemia to your superior's apartments, and tell him to see that she's looked after."

Anastasios bowed; Euphemia bowed down again. "Thank you, master."

The emperor nodded, then looked again at John and at the

count of the Protectors. He stared for a moment, his face expressionless, and then he said calmly, "John of Berytus, I will give you the task of suppressing this disturbance. Markianos Apollinaris, since you wish to stay safely in the palace, you may do so. We will reconsider your appointment tomorrow."

"Master!" exclaimed the ex-count of the Protectors in horror.

"Yes, master," said John, bowing again.

Justinian nodded coldly and walked back into the palace. Anastasios gave John a look of mingled congratulation and sympathy, and took the arm of Euphemia's chaperone. "You need to rest, good lady," he murmured. "Most esteemed Euphemia, it's this way . . ."

They set off behind the emperor. Euphemia walked by herself, her head back and her shoulders straight, making amends for her bare arms and loose hair with a ferocious scowl. John looked after the girl, grinning again. The image of the burning house, the sedan chair toppling in the street, his arrow sprouting from the Blue's eye — they all fell away forceless from that rigid, retreating back. *She's beautiful*, he thought joyfully. *Alive and undaunted; ready to spit in the eye of the world. Absolutely Euphemia, one of a kind, alive. I saved her. And she's beautiful.*

One of the other tribunes of the Protectors moved closer to John and cleared his throat. "Do we go out and patrol the city, then, Excellency?" he asked.

John started, looked around. He became aware that he was profoundly shaken by the night's events, that his hands were numb, and that it was hard even to think of going out into the city again. *Organize it*, he told himself. *Picture it written out. How many troops, how many regions of the city. Leave a reserve for the troublesome areas; start now.*

"Of course," he answered the tribune. "Can we get all the men drawn up in the marketplace? I'll allot the regions."

Narses had a suite of rooms in the Palace of Hormisdas, the section of the Great Palace farthest from the gate, overlooking the waters of the Bosphorus. This far from the city the rioting was only an indistinct noise, half drowned by the crickets in the palace gardens; the air here smelled of sweet thyme and flowering almond. The chaperone, Eudokia, had stopped crying and was merely leaning against Anastasios, sniffing occasionally, by the time the scribe knocked on Narses' door.

The chamberlain was surprised to see them, but didn't show it for more than an instant, and had reorganized his household to accommodate them within minutes of hearing their story. "Tomorrow, of course, we will see about finding more private rooms for you," he told Euphemia politely, as his slaves transformed his study into a bedroom for her and her chaperone.

"And rooms for my slaves," the girl replied. "I sent them out of the house before I went; I think they're unharmed. They'll have to have somewhere to stay." She sat down on the bed the slaves had just brought in. She was very pale with reaction, and gave occasional long nervous shudders, but she still spoke sharply.

"And for them, of course," agreed Narses. "You would be most welcome to borrow my house in the city. Most excellent Euphemia, esteemed Eudokia, would you care for something to eat? Some supper? Some warmed wine and honey cakes, then? The bathhouse is just down the corridor, if you wish to bathe. And you will want some more clothing." He snapped his fingers, and one of his slaves looked up attentively from arranging a clothes chest. "Azarethes, find some clothing for the ladies. Go to the ambassadors' houses for it, don't bother the household of the empress, there's a good fellow."

"We ought to be guests in the empress's household," said the chaperone, with a weak imitation of respectable primness. "It would be more proper for a young lady."

Euphemia smiled to see her recovering, but snapped, "Don't be ridiculous! The empress would prefer it if we were dead." She knitted her hands together, and Eudokia came over and put an arm about her shoulders. The girl ignored her.

Narses sighed, but made no comment. Euphemia looked up suddenly and, with an expression that was painfully unguarded, shy, afraid, hopeful, said, "I'm sorry. I'm your guest, and I shouldn't say such things. John will be all right in the city, won't he?"

"Is John going back into the city?" Narses asked in surprise.

Anastasios grinned. "The emperor gave him command of the Protectors and told him to suppress the disturbance; Apollinaris was told to stay home. Yes, indeed, John will be all right. I think he may get his promotion after all."

"That would be very fortunate," Narses said thoughtfully. "Anastasios, you'll want to stay the night as well — between the rioting and the Protectors, the streets will be deadly. Have you eaten? I'll have the slaves fetch something for you. And perhaps you could have a look at a piece of writing I've been meaning to show you — it's unsigned, and I don't know where to file it. I am certain that the ladies wish to be left in peace to compose themselves. Esteemed ladies, good night. If you require anything, my slaves are at your disposal to fetch it."

Narses' writing desk and a locked chest of documents had been moved into the corridor outside the newly made bedroom. The chamberlain unlocked the chest and took out a folded sheet of parchment, then carefully locked the chest again before showing Anastasios to the dining room.

Anastasios looked at the apartments curiously. He had once or twice visited Narses' mansion on the Golden Horn, which the eunuch kept for entertaining, but he had never been to these very private living quarters. The rooms were severely neat and plain; as part of the palace they had large glass windows and floors decorated with fine abstract mosaics, but no luxuries had been added by their owner. The dining room was small, with a book rack completely covering one of the walls; doors in the other wall opened onto a terrace that overlooked the sea. Anastasios sat down at the rosewood table, and one of the slaves brought him a supper of eggs, goat cheese, cumin bread, and honey cakes, with a flagon of delicate white wine to wash it down.

Narses mixed the wine with water and poured out two cups, then raised his to Anastasios, smiling. The sheet of parchment lay under his hand. He watched as the old scribe chewed his way through the meal. Anastasios ate slowly, and his hands were unsteady. *The old man is tired,* Narses thought. *Too much violence and danger for one night. It's a pity to involve him tonight — a pity to involve him at all. But if the emperor is considering promoting John now, he'll want a preliminary report tomorrow, and my own investigations have so far achieved nothing. Anastasios will be able to identify the hand if anyone can: he knows the writing of everyone in the sacred offices, and can tell the origin of a sheet of parchment at a glance. And he is to be trusted and likes John. Still, I wish I could leave him ignorant.*

With half his mind he noted that the women were going down the corridor to the bathhouse, talking in low voices. *Good,* he thought. *They're out of the way.*

"Thank you, Illustrious," Anastasios said, finishing his supper and pushing aside the plate. "It's very good of Your Kindness to invite me to stay. Is that the writing you wanted me to look at?"

Narses held the still-folded letter before him in both hands and nodded. "This is an unsigned letter which was given to His Sacred Majesty two weeks before I returned from Thrace. The master has charged me with determining the truth of the statements it contains, and I need to know who sent it. Do you wish to see it, or would you prefer not to? If you choose to see it, I must warn you, nothing that it contains or I may tell you must ever be mentioned outside this room."

Anastasios blinked, startled, then hunched his shoulders unhappily. "I think I would prefer not to see it, Illustrious."

"It concerns our friend John."

Anastasios looked still more surprised and unhappy; then his face set grimly. "Is that why he wasn't promoted? Someone sent in an anonymous accusation against him?"

Narses nodded, still holding the letter.

"I will look at it," said Anastasios.

The chamberlain put the letter in his scribe's hands. Anastasios read it under his breath. "Merciful God!" he exclaimed, and looked up at his superior, aghast. "But . . . but it's a lie, a fabrication. It must be. I'd stake my life on it. Surely all you have to do is check the statements in it and prove they're false?"

Narses shook his head. "I have sent men out to investigate the statements. I will eventually report to the emperor that most of the people who knew the bearkeeper Akakios are dead — after all, he was a poor man in obscure circumstances, and has been dead himself for forty years. I will say that those who knew him best — that is, the surviving members of his family and their close friends — claim that he did have a half-brother Diodoros. That is certainly true, since Her Serenity has ordered them to say so. As for the men I sent to Berytus, they will undoubtedly have heard of some scribe called John in the municipality who might or might not have been our friend — the name is fortunately very common. The evidence will be profoundly inconclusive, however, and the emperor will see as much at once. The difficulty is that all the statements in the letter are true."

Anastasios stared for a moment, looked down at the letter again. "Then . . . I don't understand." He blinked rapidly, and his mouth twisted in pain; he pressed his hands against the table. After another moment he said, "John has been lying about who he is? No, I don't . . . he wouldn't . . ."

"Wouldn't what?" asked Narses mildly. "What inference have you drawn?"

Anastasios winced and glared angrily at his superior. "That the Sacred Augusta . . . ," he began, and stopped, swallowed, tried again. "That John . . . no, I don't believe it!"

"Believe what? Never mind, I know! The emperor looked at the letter and drew the same conclusion. A false one, as it happens. John is not the empress's lover, but for reasons she prefers to keep secret, she wishes no one to know his real history. She will not tell it to her husband and does not wish me to do so; her husband has not told her of the letter and has forbidden me to do so. Both of them have forbidden me to mention the matter to John. I am finding my position" — with a smile — "an extremely difficult one."

"But . . . but why would she . . ." Anastasios stopped, blinking, then once more looked at the letter. "But John's innocent?"

He loves him as I do, thought Narses, with a wrench of affection. *He is terrified that John will prove to be an adulterous fortune hunter.* "Unless you hold him responsible for the condition of his birth, which was similar to yours."

"But I'm a bastard — my mother was my father's concubine," said Anastasios in confusion.

"John's mother was somewhere between a courtesan and a common whore," Narses stated deliberately. "She was a comic actress from the circus."

Anastasios stared blankly for a moment. Then the scribe's withered cheeks flooded with color. "By all the saints!" he whispered slowly. "You don't mean . . ."

"Hush," said Narses. "Can you tell who might have sent the letter?"

Anastasios studied the writing, turning the letter and holding it up to the light. "It's been done with the left hand by someone who's not left-handed," he said after a moment.

"I saw that too."

"And it's poor-quality parchment, not any of the sorts used by the offices, and not from Asia or Thrace . . . I know, it's Italian! Yes, definitely Italian: it has that greasy feel that all the documents from the reconquered areas have, and the worn spots where the tanner used too much lye. The brown color of the ink is typical of Italian letters too."

Narses smiled. It was the usual cryptic smile, but his eyes were gleaming. "That should narrow it down. The writer, then, is in Italy or has recently been there; he also knows that his — or her — hand is likely to be recognized, and therefore tries to disguise it." He hit the table suddenly. "I have it! Wait a moment." He left the room and came back a minute later holding a file case with a red stamp on the end. He pulled out a mass of documents, glanced through them, and extracted one letter. He passed it to Anastasios, setting it down beside the first one.

This letter was written normally on the finest Pergamene vellum, and was signed.

Antonina, wife to the ever-victorious commander Count Belisarius, to the most illustrious Narses sends greetings. Your Honor's probity and loyalty have been questioned by none, and we therefore think it fitting to inform Your Discretion of a plot which has been adopted by the most wicked and treacherous praetorian prefect John of Cappadocia to usurp the place of our dearly loved master Justinian Augustus . . .

"It's the same hand," said Anastasios, reading no more of the letter.

"You're certain?"

"Yes. Look at the ligature there — epsilon-upsilon in one stroke, with the upsilon done as a backward hook. She does the same thing left-handed. And the sigma on 'Augustus' is written separately from the rest of the word. Oh, no question of it. But why would she? I thought that she was a close friend of the empress."

Narses sat back in his seat, pulling both letters toward himself across the table. "I believe that she wishes her daughter to marry a more distinguished husband than the empress's grandson," he said after a minute. "She has certainly done everything she can to postpone the match." He sighed, put the anonymous letter back in his purse, and began rolling the old letter up with the other papers from the file. "Of course, her husband hates the empress. But the count is too honest to scheme properly; he may have had suspicions and may have paid men to investigate John, but he wouldn't have sent an anonymous letter. So it comes down to children again. A man, or a woman, may be indifferent to money and honest with authority, but because he wishes to establish his children in riches and power, he may be willing to sell justice, corrupt, lie, scheme, even murder, and think he's doing nothing wrong, because he does it for his children. Dynastic ambition." He tapped the rolled letters on the table, evening out their edges. "I sometimes wish the Almighty had thought of some better way of producing human beings. But of course I owe my career to it. It's to guard against dynastic ambition that men like myself are castrated and put into office." He shoved the letters back into the case.

"Do you regret it?" Anastasios asked quickly, a question he had often wondered over.

Narses looked up quickly, the dark eyes unstartled, the smooth face calm. "Do you regret not being born a woman? Perhaps women regret that they're not men, seeing how many advantages the world bestows on masculinity. But can you really regret being what you are, when to be otherwise would mean becoming someone else — which is the same as not existing at all?"

Anastasios shrugged. "I've regretted it sometimes for you," he said quietly.

That brought the smile. "Ah, but you were happily married; you're no judge. Enough of this. I will question Sergius about Antonina tomorrow, and then make a preliminary report to the master. And I will write Count Belisarius a letter that may prevent further trouble from that quarter. It is awkward, though, that the letter is from Antonina. The master will say, as you did, that she is the mistress's friend and therefore unlikely to act from malice. Still, he dislikes the woman, and may be persuadable. My report will certainly do John's situation no harm, and may help. Thank you for your help, my friend. You should try to rest now: it's late."

X

COUNT OF THE CAVALRY

JOHN KNOCKED AT THE DOOR of Narses' apartments at breakfast-time the next morning. He had spent the night riding about the city, and arrived smelling of smoke and horses. He was dirty and begrimed with ashes; his bow was slung over his shoulder, and a helmet, acquired during the course of the night, was pushed back on his head. Narses' slaves showed him into the clean, neat dining room where their master and Anastasios were breakfasting. The windows of the terrace were open, giving a view over the sparkling blue waters of the Bosphorus to the green bulk of the opposite, Asian shore; the city of Chalcedon could be seen, glowing white in the morning sun.

"I'm sorry to disturb you," he said, and coughed; his throat was sore from breathing smoke and shouting orders. "I just wanted to see that everyone was all right. Greetings, Anastasios — so you are here! I hoped you were. I sent a message to your slaves telling them that you would probably be staying in the palace." He coughed again.

Narses raised his eybrows and indicated a place on Anastasios' couch. He had only just arrived back at his apartments himself, since he had risen early as usual to attend on the emperor. But he had ordered an elegant meal for his guests. "Sit down and have something to eat and drink," he urged John politely. "I gather you were busy last night."

John sat down, unfastened his helmet and set it to one side, rubbed his face with a grimy hand. "Thank you, Illustrious." One of the slaves handed him a cup of watered wine, and he gulped it thirstily, then set it too aside. "Is Euphemia here, then? I checked on her house, and I meant to tell her about it."

At that minute the back door of the dining room opened, and Euphemia and her chaperone came in. Euphemia stopped suddenly when she saw John. The cloak that Narses' slaves had found for her was of yellow linen, bordered with green and gold silk, and her thick brown hair was twisted simply around her head instead of being dragged into a bun and stifled in a net. *She looks a lioness,* thought John, *broken out of her cage.*

But she was very pale and her eyes were red.

John scrambled to his feet. "Esteemed Euphemia," he said, "I meant to report to you on the condition of your house."

"Oh," she said, and blushed crimson. She glanced around the room; Narses rose and gracefully indicated the third couch at the table. She hurried over to it and seated herself there, her chaperone following like a slow and awkward shadow. Narses seated himself again and gave John, who was still standing, a questioning look. John sat down.

"Do I still have a house, then?" asked Euphemia, helping herself to the white bread.

John swallowed, then shrugged. "You have part of a house. The front bit was completely destroyed by the fire, but the part you lived in still has its walls and floors. The wind was blowing north and toward the marketplace, you see, so the fire mostly spread the other way. But between the fire and the looters, your house was gutted. Three of your slaves were found unharmed, hiding in an alley nearby, and I had them sent to the Bronze Gate to wait for your orders. I don't know where the others are. I had your chair-bearers put in the marketplace with the other bodies waiting for burial."

"Did the fire spread far?" asked Anastasios, looking at John's blackened hands.

John shrugged again. "Several of the houses on the market-place were destroyed. The palace there was unharmed, though. And there was another fire in the Fourth Region — the mob wanted to burn the quaesitor's house. We managed to put it out before too much damage was done, and we got most of the inhabitants to safety. Your neighbor Alexander the Notary was killed, though," he added to Euphemia. He picked up his cup of wine and finished it, then reached for a roll of white bread, noticed the ash on his hand, and pulled his hand back and tried to clean it.

"And the rioting?" asked Narses, with some interest. "The master said that it was suppressed within the hour, as he had ordered. You managed to control it easily?"

"More easily than we suppressed the fires," replied John, smiling. "Most of the mob ran as soon as they saw the troops; we only had trouble in a few spots, and that didn't last long. Though I wish the Protectors knew how to shoot. It's dangerous, using foot soldiers and cavalry in those narrow streets: people throw things from the balconies and build barricades. If there had been more of the rioters and if they'd been more determined, we'd have taken a beating. A few more archers and it would have been much safer. I only had three men killed, though, and thirty injured; it could have been much worse." He reached out with his half-clean hand and took the roll.

"Perhaps you can have the Protectors taught archery when you're their count," suggested Anastasios, grinning slyly.

John gave him a surprised look. "Me? Count of the Protectors? There's no chance of that. I may be promoted, but not *that* high."

"I thought you managed to impress the emperor very neatly," said Euphemia harshly.

"Not so neatly as to be made count of the Protectors!" John protested. "His Sacred Majesty is annoyed with Markianos Apollinaris and will move him somewhere else, but he's not going make a secretary and part-time tribune a count. Besides, there's a rumor that he's going to give the job to that Armenian who turned down the position of commander in chief in Africa

— the one who suppressed the mutiny there and rescued the emperor's niece."

"Artabanes," said Narses.

"That's the man. He's the sort who should be made a count. If I'm lucky, the master will reconsider giving me a command in the East."

Narses smiled cryptically. "I agree with your assessment, and I hope you are correct."

Euphemia sat staring at John for a moment. "Where would you go in the East?" she asked at last.

He shrugged. "That would be up to the master."

"Oh. Well, I hope you get your promotion. Last night . . . last night I never thanked you. Let me thank you now, from me and from my father's house, for my life. I hope one day we'll be able to reward you for it."

"It's reward enough to see you still alive," said John, smiling and meeting her eyes. In the sunlight, they were a bright, near-orange color once again.

She blushed. "And more than reward enough if you get promotion," she added sourly.

He stopped smiling and looked down. "I didn't think of that, and I don't care if I get it or not." He climbed to his feet and bowed politely to Narses and to Euphemia. "Illustrious, respected lady — with your permission, I want to go home and rest; it's been a long night."

"Of course," said Narses smoothly, while Euphemia bit her lip. "I was just about to go into the office myself. Anastasios, take your time — send one of my slaves to your house to reassure your slaves, if you like, and to fetch some clean clothing. John, if you will, we could walk together as far as the Magnaura."

When they were out of the Palace of Hormisdas, Narses turned to John abruptly, stopping and catching hold of his cloak. "You are in love with that young woman," he said.

John caught his breath. The long night of violence had left him with a brittle, bewildered feeling, as though the world were a crust of thin ice that he slipped over precariously. At Narses' words, it seemed to break into a thousand shards around him, leaving him plunged deep into freezing water. He caught Narses' hand but could not quite pull it from his cloak, and looked down, trying to find himself again.

"Am I right?" asked Narses after a moment, looking steadily at John's bowed head.

"I don't know," John replied, whispering.

"It is not wise," said Narses. "The Augusta would be very angry. She hates the young woman for her father's sake; she will hate her very much more if she sees her as a threat to her own plans for you. The girl has suffered enough; don't bring more trouble on her."

John looked up, aghast. "The empress wouldn't —"

"The Augusta is a passionate woman. You she loves, and she is willing to work very hard on your behalf. Euphemia's father she regards as depraved and dangerous, and she knows that Euphemia is entirely loyal to him. She would unhesitatingly place the most sinister possible construction on any evidence of romantic attachment between Euphemia and yourself — and punish Euphemia for it."

"The Augusta is tired of me," said John angrily. "She hasn't seen me since we got back from Thrace. And anyway, this is nonsense. Euphemia doesn't like me, and I . . . I don't know what I feel for her. But I've been in love, and this isn't like that at all."

Narses didn't smile. "I will tell you something. More than twenty years ago, when Justin was emperor, I was a subordinate in the office of the treasurer of the privy purse. I was still a slave at the time, and unlikely to be given my freedom, since my superior disliked me. At that time Petrus Sabbatius Justinianus — Sabbatius, we called him then — was the master of arms for the palace and the favorite, but by no means only, candidate for the succession. I and many others of the household staff, the army, and the citizens preferred Germanus. Sabbatius had secured the purple for his uncle and everything he did seemed calculated to secure it for himself: he protected the Blues in the

most atrocious outrages, to gain their support; he bribed and
pampered the palace troops; he had spies and servants throughout the offices, and even his uncle was afraid of him. He was a
calculating, brilliant man, pious in his way, learned, but cold.
He cared nothing for women, food, drink, or anything but power.
Germanus was much easier to like.

"And then one day people began whispering, with disbelief,
that Sabbatius had taken up with a circus girl, the daughter of
a bearkeeper, a comic actress and prostitute called Theodora. It
surprised everyone. And it grew more surprising by the day. He
installed his mistress and her bastard child in the Palace of
Hormisdas; he showered her with wealth; he gave her the rank
of patrician; he wanted to marry her. The emperor Justin was
outraged, though his nephew bullied him into bestowing the
rank; the empress was adamant that no nephew of hers would
marry such an impossible creature; both were furious at the
slight to the imperial dignity. Germanus, of course, had married
a daughter of the Anicii, the most illustrious family in the empire; Germanus was much approved of, and began to be preferred. Many people, myself among them, were pleased.

"One day I was sent to the emperor with some accounts. He
was in consultation with his nephew Sabbatius — Justin was, as
I may have said, an illiterate, and Sabbatius explained everything to him. As I came up to the curtain that covered the door
of the room where they were sitting, I heard them talking, low
but angry, and I stopped, afraid to interrupt. 'Have you no respect for us?' the emperor was asking. 'It was bad enough to
dress that . . . that *creature* in white and purple, and now you
want to crown her with the diadem! It's illegal for a man of
senatorial rank to marry an actress!' 'Then change the law!' said
Sabbatius. 'You can do it. Make an edict declaring that if the
actress has given up the stage and obtained high rank . . .' 'It
would make us a laughingstock!' the emperor replied angrily.
'Your aunt is very distressed.' 'My aunt started out as your concubine; she's got no right to be so proper now,' said Sabbatius.
'With her courage and intelligence, Theodora would make a

great empress. It's sheer hypocrisy and prejudice to call her "that creature" and sneer at her. One of the troubles that has plagued this empire is that men are promoted for their noble ancestors rather than their abilities. What use are genealogies when you're trying to get something done?' 'I will not have that whore as the next empress!' said Justin. 'You'll just have to make up your mind. Which do you want more, the purple or your Theodora?' 'Theodora — *and* the purple,' said Sabbatius furiously. But he said 'Theodora' first. I was astonished. I stood outside the curtain, listening while Justin swore, and I wondered. I'd thought I understood what men were like when they were in love — it was partly just a pleasure for them, I'd thought, and partly a need. But only weak-minded men let it dominate them. And yet here was Sabbatius, the coldest and cleverest man in the city, forswearing everything he had been and all he had worked for, for the sake of a whore. Love, I thought, must be much stronger and more terrible than I had believed. I thanked God I was well out of it. But I felt some pity for poor demented Sabbatius.

"They finished their argument, so I went in and prostrated myself and handed the emperor the accounts; he shoved them back at me and told me to get out. 'I'll do them,' said Sabbatius, and took them. Outside the room, though, he paused and looked at me. 'Your name is Narses, isn't it?' he said. 'You've done some fine work,' and he mentioned some work I'd done for my superior. 'Come with me,' he ordered, and led me off to the Palace of Hormisdas. I thought he just wanted me to check the accounts, but when we arrived he went straight to his mistress's quarters and presented me to her. She was, of course, an extremely beautiful woman, and when we found her she was reading. 'This is Narses," he said, 'and he is the only intelligent man in the office of the privy purse, as well as the only honest one. Be nice to him, my dearest.' And the infamous Theodora, the prostitute, the unnatural monster, got up and took my hand. As she put her book down, I saw that it was a volume of history — Malchus of Philadelphia, in fact, serious recent history, not a chronicle patched up to entertain. She smiled and said, 'Welcome. If what Peter says is true, we'll make you treasurer when he wears the purple.' 'We can do the accounts now,' said Sabbatius, and we did. Theodora stayed with us, leaning on her lover's shoulder and asking questions — very shrewd questions. She was learning how the finance of the empire worked, and she learned very quickly.

"After we had finished the accounts, Sabbatius took me back outside — we stood about where you and I are standing now. 'Now,' he said, 'say that she is a common whore and that I'm a middle-aged idiot besotted with lust and can't think straight.' 'It is not my place to say anything to you,' I replied. 'But do you think it's true?' he demanded. And I had to admit, no, I could see that it was not true; that she was a brilliant and able woman whom I would not have hesitated to promote had she been my subordinate. He knew I was saying nothing less than the truth, and was contented. 'I'm not offering to bribe you,' he told me, 'because I don't think I can, and there wouldn't be any point since you have no influence. But I know your superior's incompetent and that all the work that comes from his office that's of any use is yours. When I am emperor, you'll have his job, and your freedom, and the rank of a patrician. And I will be emperor — my uncle can't manage without me, and if he doesn't know it now, he soon will. And Theodora will be empress, whatever the world says about it. There's more to love than the world thinks. Sometimes passion alone lets you see clearly.' "

John was silent for a moment, looking down at the eunuch's face. "And you think I'm in love like that?"

"What do I know about love?" asked Narses. "But you looked at Euphemia the way Justinian looked at Theodora. Not just with lust, but with enchantment, pride, the discovery of an equal mind. And she is intelligent, self-reliant, and courageous. I can see that you would love each other. If I were able to love a woman, it would be a woman like her. But you would destroy her."

John was silent for a long minute, his cold hand on Narses' wrist. In the palace gardens the birds were singing, and the air smelled of flowers and the sea. "I'll stay away from her," John said at last, quietly. He dropped his hand.

Narses let go of him. "I'm sorry," he said after a moment. "But I would recommend just that." He sighed deeply, looked up at the clear sky. "It would be best now if you went home to rest — and I have some important business at the office."

Very important business for you, he thought to himself when he had threaded his way through the Magnaura Palace to his office. It was empty — it was still early, and the rioting would naturally delay the scribes. The icon of the Virgin was back in its place on the wall above his desk; Narses stood for a moment, contemplating her calm face. *"Blessed stem that has budded and been brought forth from a thirsty earth!"* he thought. *Human who gives birth to divinity; Mother of God, make us like you, to live where the contradictions are all resolved.* Carefully, he bowed down to the ground before her, then took his place at his desk. The first thing was to write his report.

Anastasios arrived not long afterward, Diomedes about an hour later, and Sergius an hour later again.

"Sorry I'm late, Illustrious," he declared, coming into the inner office. "But the rioting was bad in my quarter."

Narses nodded graciously. "You live in the Fourth Region, don't you? I gather you had fire there. I trust your family is unharmed?"

"The troops stopped the fire before it spread too far," Sergius replied. "They diverted water from the aqueduct. They were pretty quick last night — better than usual. I suppose John was with them? I notice he's not with us."

"John was in fact charged with quelling the disturbance; I am pleased to hear you approve his direction. It is very likely that His Sacred Majesty will see fit to award John the promotion that he so richly deserves — in which case I will need a new secretary." Narses smiled politely. "Perhaps this would be a good time to reassess your own position here, most esteemed Sergius?"

Diomedes looked up enviously from his copying; Sergius caught his breath. He rubbed his hands down the sides of his tunic, trying to calm himself, and smiled eagerly. "If you think so, Illustrious."

Narses rose and indicated the curtain over the entrance to the imperial apartments. Sergius grinned and made his way to the private anteroom, and Narses followed him.

"Of course," said Narses, closing the door behind them, "I shall miss John a great deal. His abilities have made my own work much easier — the shorthand alone is invaluable — but more than that, I shall miss him as a person. His integrity is a quality I will find difficult to replace. Still, I can only be pleased if he is promoted. It will be a relief to me if he manages it despite a certain malicious letter."

Sergius' smile faltered only for the barest instant, but the smirk went out of his eyes. "A letter, Illustrious?"

"An anonymous letter of accusation, which was delivered to the emperor. It should not have been; the emperor himself long ago directed that he should see no charges that their authors were not prepared to sign, and we have always obeyed that policy. When Agapios was shown the letter by the master, he had no recollection of its passing through this office, though it must have done so. I was wondering, Sergius, if you could help me to understand how it could have done so."

"Oh, now I know what you're talking about!" said Sergius. "Yes, Agapios asked me about it too. But I've never seen the letter, I'm afraid, and I have no idea how it reached the master. Did it concern John?"

Admirable, thought Narses. "It did, I fear — but we were to discuss your own position here. Yes." He sat down, steepling his fingers. "The difficulty is, Sergius, that I do not know whether you are simply dishonest, or whether you are dishonest and rash as well." Sergius stopped smiling, but Narses went on smoothly. "If the first, I will recommend that you have a place in the letters office, where your undoubted intelligence will be put to good use and the dishonesty will be of little significance. If the second, I fear I can recommend no other place for you at all, and you will have to go back to your father's house."

"What . . . what do you mean?" said Sergius. "What about your secretary's place?"

"You've been a little too eager for that, don't you think?" asked Narses mildly. "Investigating the papers while another man still has the job? Who asked you to spy, Sergius?"

"I don't know what you're talking about," said Sergius, his face like a shuttered house. "But if you accuse me of anything, I can appeal for justice."

"Accuse you? I am trying to work out what would be the best thing to do with you. Did you read that letter?"

"I've told you, I don't know anything about that letter!"

Narses took the letter out of his purse and handed it to Sergius. "Please read it for me now."

Frowning, suspicious and angry, Sergius took the letter and unfolded it. "I haven't seen it," he reminded Narses, and moved over so as to hold it under the light. He read it aloud, slowly; the frown deepened. Narses watched him carefully. Sergius stumbled over the final phrase and stared at the paper, his brow deeply creased. *He hadn't read it,* thought Narses. *I thought as much. He was after John, and would not dare offend Theodora.*

"But . . . ," said Sergius, "but this . . . this accuses the empress. It says she was lying."

"Indeed. And the empress is aware that she has been accused, though she does not know that there was a letter. In my presence she swore that if she found who was responsible for the story, she would have him flogged and his mouth stopped with molten lead. She was not joking. And she might spare her friend Antonina, but she certainly would not spare you."

Sergius went white. "Oh my God." He sat down, dropping the letter to the floor.

Narses bent over and retrieved it, folded it carefully, and put it back in his purse. "She doesn't know that there was a letter," he repeated. "She need never know. But I want some honest answers. When did Antonina hire you?"

Sergius looked up, white and sick. "You know about that?"

"I know something of it. Go on, answer the question."

"She . . . she invited me to her house the spring before you went to Thrace. It was the ides of March. She said that she and her husband were worried that John wasn't what he appeared to be — it seems her husband thought he rode like a Saracen and spoke Arabic like a Nabatean, and wanted him investigated. She said that she feared that the empress was being taken in by a clever imposter, that she hoped it wasn't so, but that she wanted to be certain. I thought she wanted to show John up and win some favor from the empress in return. She wanted me to find out what I could about him, and she promised me a position in the treasury if I could prove anything."

"So you spied on him."

"So I looked for a way to show him up. But I never found anything. I spent a lot of money trying to bribe his slaves and the people round him, but it didn't get me anywhere; Berytus doesn't give much away. I didn't tell any lies about him, I swear it! Antonina said she wanted facts, not rumors; rumors would just offend the empress and prove nothing. This spring, just before you come back, I got a letter from Antonina saying that her husband had completed his investigations of John and that the results were worrying but inconclusive. She said she didn't want to write the mistress, who might be offended to receive unproved allegations against a man she regarded as a friend and cousin. But, she said, she thought the master ought to know in case he was thinking of promoting John. She enclosed that letter, sealed with wax and unstamped, and she asked me to be sure that the master saw it. I put it in the pile of letters to go in, but I swear by all the saints I would have cut my hand off before I put it there if I'd known that it accused the empress."

"I believe you," said Narses. "Dishonest, then, but not rash. Of course you cannot stay here in my office after such a serious breach of confidence, but I will recommend you for a position in the letters office. But I advise you as strongly as I can to say nothing about that letter or its contents to anyone; it would be very likely to come to the empress's ears if you did. I will write a letter to Count Belisarius, and I think you will find that the most distinguished Antonina will not interfere with you again. If you are interested, I have investigated the statements in the letter myself, and the evidence is indeed inconclusive but tends more to refute than to support the statements. I believe that the wife of the most glorious count is concerned principally to prevent a marriage between her daughter and the empress's grandson. That is all; you may take the rest of the day off."

He waited until Sergius was gone before he rose and went back to the office. *That letter to Belisarius will be extremely difficult to write,* he thought unhappily.

Belisarius had written Narses a letter of congratulation on the victory of Nicopolis. Most of the letter had been concerned with the need for more troops for Italy, and hence fewer for Thrace, but there had been two or three glowing paragraphs at the beginning which had been surprised, honest, delicious.

He can have no idea how much I relish his praise, Narses thought. *His more than anyone's. He is the absolute master of the art of war and a man who takes courage for granted: if he was impressed, then the victory was impressive. Anastasios and his questions! If I've ever wished to be other than what I am, it's been because I wanted to be another Belisarius — absurd as that is for a man in my position. And now I must offend him . . . I could simply write to Antonina, but she would undoubtedly show him the letter, and that would be more offensive than writing to him directly.*

He sighed and went back to his office. Diomedes was sitting motionless at his desk, staring in bewilderment at the door through which Sergius had departed. *I will have to borrow some staff from the offices,* thought Narses; *I can hardly manage on one copy clerk and one file clerk.* He smiled vaguely at Diomedes and checked the outer office. The usual queue of appointments had been reduced to two or three; the rest were waiting to see if the riots were really over. Anastasios was grinning to himself as he worked. He glanced up as his superior appeared briefly in the door, and grinned more widely. "So much for Sergius," he said.

Narses smiled back. "Now I make my report to the master. Say a quick prayer for me, will you?"

The emperor Justinian was sitting by himself on the throne of Solomon, reading a report on the riots. The mechanical throne sat motionless in a pool of sunlight, and the lamps on the golden lampstands were unlit. All around the room the closed curtains of purple silk glowed with deep color: the emperor might have been sitting inside a crystal of amethyst. He turned a page, glanced up, and saw his chamberlain waiting by one of the curtains. He nodded, and Narses came forward and made the prostration.

"Well," said Justinian, "there is after all something to be said for giving command of troops to a bureaucrat." He ruffled the pages of the report, which Narses saw was in John's clear, precise hand. "This was ready first thing this morning. It has a complete list of casualties, a record of damages classified by region, and an assessment of the probable cost of repairs, listed in order of urgency. Count Apollinaris would have waited three days and then handed in a panegyric on his own conduct, done in beautiful Attic prose and entirely useless. You're right to value your secretary. He's evidently a very capable young man."

Narses smiled. "I have certainly always found him so, master. Here, if you have time for it, is a preliminary report on the letter you received about him."

Justinian grunted, took the report, and began to read it in a rapid undertone. At the end he looked up in surprise. "Antonina?" he asked.

"So it would seem, master. I surmise that she wishes to prevent the marriage between her daughter and the grandson of the most serene Augusta."

The emperor frowned. "I have always said that that woman

was capable of anything. Because she makes a fool of her husband by running after men half her age, she finds it likely that my wife would do the same — and decides to tell me so! I think you may be right: she and her husband have been dragging their feet over that marriage for a year now, though their daughter would be perfectly happy to go through with it tomorrow. Well, the marriage is to go ahead. In fact, it's to go ahead as soon as possible, whether or not the girl's parents can manage to return to Constantinople for the ceremony. I'm losing patience with Belisarius. He's been in Italy a year now, and what's happened? The Goths have taken Rome, that's what! Belisarius hasn't even managed to land on Italian soil except where he has one of our fortresses there to receive him. And Herodian has been writing me, complaining that the count keeps demanding money and threatening him if he won't pay. So much for conquering the Goths out of his own pocket!"

Narses was silent a moment, then said carefully, "The count is desperately short of men and supplies, master. Even Belisarius cannot be expected to conquer a kingdom with only four thousand men. He made promises rashly, and is ashamed to admit to you that he can't keep them. Many of the other commanders in Italy — Bessas and Herodian in particular — have acquired considerable sums from their territories, which they have not spent . . . in the way Belisarius would wish. I find his position only too easy to understand."

Justinian snorted. "It was a mistake ever to go into Italy," he said bitterly. "And it was a worse mistake to go back. Between us and the Goths, the city of Rome has been virtually destroyed and its citizens exterminated."

"But having gone in, master, we have no choice but to see the war to some kind of end."

Justinian snorted again. "Perhaps. But when it comes to that, Belisarius may well find that he is not indispensable. And as for the suggestions of Belisarius' wife, I place no reliance on them at all. From the evidence you have here, there is no justification for the conclusion that Theodora is lying when she says John is her cousin. The evidence won't support any conclusions at all. But why should I disbelieve my wife? I know she's loyal to me, more loyal than anyone else in the entire empire. I would have to have very strong evidence that she was lying, and instead I have one malicious letter based on an *argumentum ex silentio*. There's no proof that John is not who he claims to be, and I can trust Theodora if I can trust anyone. She guessed that it was John I suspected of intriguing with her, you know."

Mary Mother, did she work this change? Narses thought in astonishment. "Did she, master?" he said cautiously.

"She guessed it from the fact that I hadn't promoted him. We've talked it through now. I was an idiot to suspect her, Narses. A cruel idiot — she's not well, and this business has worried her." The emperor picked up Narses' report and folded it in halves, in quarters. "My beautiful Theodora!" he said softly, looking at the parchment. He crumpled the report up and handed it back to his chamberlain. "You can burn that, and the letter with it. I don't want to hear any more about it unless there's hard evidence. And I will assume that there is none." He smiled tightly, his eyes glinting, and added, "My wife now wants her cousin to marry. Do you know who she wants him to marry?"

"No, master," said Narses. He remembered John looking at Euphemia with wonder in his eyes. With a sense of regret amounting almost to guilt, he tried to blot out the image.

"She wants him to marry my niece Praejecta! She was very annoyed when I told her that it was out of the question. That's why she's so keen on Cousin John, though: she's seen that he's capable, and she wants to enter him in the race for the succession."

"But that's out of the question, is it?"

The emperor considered. "Not entirely, I suppose. Germanus is my heir now, as he always has been. By the time I'm ready to die, of course, Germanus will probably be dead too, and perhaps some of my other nephews as well, so the husband of one of my nieces would have a chance. But even if Theodora does patch up a splendid match for her cousin, he'd still be very much an outside chance, and would have to do something that proved him outstandingly more capable than any of the others to get the purple. The fact that he was a member of her family, even of a respectable branch of it, would count heavily against him, particularly with the senate. And I have no intention of antagonizing popular opinion by supporting Theodora's family. But leaving speculations aside, a marriage between John and Praejecta *is* out of the question. She wants to marry your countryman Artabanes, who rescued her in Africa after her husband was murdered. And Artabanes is desperately eager to marry her — it was why he turned down the position of commander in chief there. He wanted to escort her home and ask for her hand. He's likely to get it, too."

"I am pleased for my country's sake," said Narses smoothly.

Justinian laughed. "How old were you when you left Armenia?"

Narses smiled. "Your Sacred Majesty knows very well that I don't know how old I was, since I can't say when I was born or how long my first owner kept me. But I have never forgotten my origins."

"Which in itself is typically Armenian. Well, Artabanes would also be very much an outside chance for the succession, but he should make yet another distinguished Armenian general. He displayed considerable courage and initiative in suppressing Guntarith's mutiny. I am going to make him count of the Protectors."

Narses bowed. "I had heard a rumor to this effect. Shall I have his codicils of rank drawn up today?"

"Do that. And for your friend John . . ." The emperor paused, studying his chamberlain. Narses' face was still as ever, but Justinian noticed how the fingers of the right hand curved with tension. *He likes the young man a great deal*, thought Justinian, *which in itself is telling: he despises disloyalty and the pleasures of Aphrodite, and values integrity.* "For your friend John, you can draw up codicils giving him the rank of count of the household cavalry. He can command the imperial guard in conjunction with Artabanes. Your countryman is a bit inexperienced when it comes to paperwork, and will need someone to help him with the accounts."

Narses smiled, his eyes very bright, and bowed to the ground. "Yes, master."

That will please Theodora, thought Justinian when the eunuch had left. *It will do something to atone for my suspicions. And the young man is able.*

He flicked through the report again, appreciating the ability it displayed — then paused, looking up at nothing. *And if the young man is guilty,* he thought, half against his will, *if he has been deceiving my wife, or if they have deceived me together, then he will be here in Constantinople, and I will know where to find him.*

The following morning a messenger from the palace brought John an invitation to breakfast with the empress.

He had slept badly, and the messenger's arrival woke him from a confused dream of riot and fire. Jakobos came into his bedroom and relayed the invitation, and he lay in bed for a few minutes, staring blankly at the wall.

So Narses was right: she isn't tired of me, he thought, and the thought brought a wave of the familiar dread, together with an equally strong flush of pleasure and gratitude.

He got up and dressed hurriedly, pulling on the red tunic she had given him. His Protectors cloak was still having the ash washed out of it, and he had to be satisfied with the red civilian one. In five more minutes, washed and with his hair trimmed, he was accompanying the messenger back to the Daphne Palace, where he had to wait in the breakfast room for half an hour while Theodora finished her bath.

When she appeared, though, she was smiling. "John, my dear!" she exclaimed as soon as she saw him, and giving him no time to bow, she ran over and hugged him. "It's been so long! Let me look at you — why, you haven't changed. I expected you to be the complete soldier by now. Sit down — no, here, next to me. I have a present for you." Her eyes were glittering with pleasure.

When he had seated himself on the couch beside her, he noticed how she had aged. Her hands were like the claws of some large bird, he thought, all bones under the jeweled rings, and her face was haggard. "You haven't been well," he said, shaken by it. "I'm sorry . . ."

She waved it aside. "I'll be better soon — and it doesn't mean anything, just a stomach upset. Lord, how good it is to see you! I suppose Narses told you nothing of all our alarms?"

"What?" he asked, confusedly wondering if she meant something to do with her illness.

"Peter took it into his head that you and I were deceiving him. I've put a stop to that notion, but we'll have to be cautious in the future. Still, I had to see you today!" She snapped her fingers, and her chamberlain appeared. "Eusebios, fetch John's present."

John stared at her. "The master suspected that —"

"Somebody told him some story. If I find out who, they'll pay for it. Never mind, it's over now, except for being cautious." She leaned over and began unfastening his cloak pin. "I've got you a new cloak," she told him, her eyes dancing. "Here, stand up, let me take this one off . . . there! Eusebios?"

The eunuch returned, smiling; across his arm hung a radiance of white and purple silk. Theodora laughed, jumped up, and took the cloak from her chamberlain. "Here you are," she announced, holding it up.

"But . . . but it's a patrician's cloak," said John.

Theodora burst into peals of laughter. She sat down, crushing the new cloak against her sides. "Oh Lord, the look on your face!" she exclaimed. "Yes, my dear, of course it's a patrician's cloak. There's nothing strange about the count of the household cavalry receiving the rank, and I'm awarding it to you."

"I . . . I'm not —"

"You . . . you are. Peter appointed you yesterday, and Narses has drawn up the codicils. Here, put it on!" She was back on her feet, pulling the cloak over his shoulders. She looked around for something to pin it with, and Eusebios came over with a brooch of gold and garnet. "There," she said, fixing it firmly in the silk. "Immortal God, you look wonderful! That cloak is the second-best color in the world."

He stared down at himself and hesitantly touched the wide stripe that bisected the cloak: pure sea purple.

"Yes," said Theodora, "that's the best." She ran her hand down her own cloak, smiling.

He looked back up at her, confused, as he always seemed to be in her presence. Her haggard face was flushed, and her eyes glowed with a delight in the gift so great that he began to smile as well. "Thank you," he said.

She laughed, and once more sat down on her couch, flinging her feet up over the end of it. He sat beside her, cautiously arranging the cloak.

"I'll tell you something that's very unusual about that cloak," said the empress, reaching for her cup of goat's milk. "Where do you think the silk in it comes from?"

"Where does silk come from? From the Silk Country, east of Persia."

Theodora shook her head, putting the cup down. Her lips were rimmed with white; she licked them with a pink tongue. "Not that silk. That is Asian silk, made here in Constantinople. I have the first cloak ever made from Asian silk, and you have the third one — Peter has the second, of course."

He examined the silk again: it looked like any fine silk. "How? What's it made from?" he asked.

She giggled. "Worms."

"Worms?" He stared at the glowing fibers as if he expected them to wriggle away.

She giggled again. "Caterpillars, then. They turn into a little brown moth, and before they do, they make a silk cocoon for themselves. The silk workers take the cocoons and spin them into raw silk. There were some Christian monks from the borders of the Silk Country who were visiting Roman lands to see the holy places, and they told Peter and me all about it. We promised to reward them if they could bring us some of the worms and raise them, and they smuggled out some of the eggs in a hollow staff — the rulers of the Silk Country have always guarded their secret jealously, knowing how much it's worth. But we've got the silkworms now, and we can say a long farewell to the Silk Country and the Persian traders both — and Mother of God, will the great king feel that! All those hundreds of thousands of *solidi* that have been paid for silk every year . . . and now Peter and I can make it ourselves, and it will all come to us. That will pay for a few wars."

"It will kill Bostra," said John, staring at it in horror. "We lived off the silk caravans."

The empress shrugged. "But the war had already stopped those, hadn't it? And anyway, what do you care for Bostra now? You're a native of Berytus and an inhabitant of Constantinople, remember."

"Yes . . . yes, of course." But he frowned unhappily at the white and purple cloak. "I dreamed of Bostra last night," he said on impulse, "and my father."

She looked at him. The smile was gone from her face, leaving it skull-like. "What was he doing?" she asked after a moment.

"Dying." He had been again in the darkened room, in the summer heat, watching helplessly as the plague claimed another victim. He shivered. "I went into our house in Bostra and saw him dying. And when I went out, I was in Constantinople, in the Taurus marketplace during the riots." *And Euphemia was there*, he thought with a stab of misery, *burning in the house, dying, I couldn't help her. Mother of God, I wish I could see her again, just to be sure!*

"What a horrible dream," said the empress, and crossed herself. "God avert the omen! I expect, though, that you simply had too much to do during the riots. Though," she added, beginning to smile again, "I can't complain of what you did, since it convinced Peter to promote you. I can't even complain that you risked your life to rescue that girl — that impressed Peter more than anything, since he knew I would never have sanctioned it. Why did you do it?"

"I don't know," he answered slowly, Narses' warning beating in his mind. "I was actually on my way to see her when we ran into the riot. My colleague Anastasios had been trading information for a look at those files while I was in Thrace, but she thought I knew more, and I'd joined him that evening. When I saw the house on fire, I just thought I had to try to get her out. Fortunately, she wasn't in the house; she was a couple of blocks away in her sedan chair, so it wasn't too dangerous for me."

"I heard that you charged the whole mob! Well, things get distorted in the telling. What happened to the files?"

He smiled. "I don't know, but I'm sure I'm not going to see them again — and good riddance! The prefecture will have to manage without the tax indictions for Osrhoene and southern Arabia. I doubt that the administration will grind to a halt."

She laughed, sat up straight, and touched the side of his face. "I love you when you smile like that," she said tenderly, smiling herself. "My own dear boy. I was so proud of you after Nicopolis — I wanted to tell everyone that you were my son. But of course that would have spoiled everything." She dropped her hand and twisted one of the rings on it, staring at it sadly. "I thought of a girl for you to marry, too, but Peter has engaged her to someone else. I'm sorry — I'll find you another. When you're married I'll be able to see more of you without raising anyone's suspicions."

"I wish you could tell everyone who I really am," he found himself replying. "I would rather be free to see you as I pleased, to live honestly, with everyone knowing I'm yours, than have any number of promotions."

She looked up. "Oh, that is sweetly said — but you don't mean it, I hope. As my acknowledged son you would be an embarrassment — a far worse one now than if we'd done it at first. Your friend Narses thinks I should tell Peter, but Peter wouldn't like it at all. No, my dear: you stay a citizen of Berytus, and I will look after you." She yawned, stretched, and added, "And you had probably better run along now and pick up your codicils of rank, before Peter turns up and starts worrying about your being here. It's traditional to give the emperor's chamberlain a present for drawing up the codicils. Narses thinks drawing yours up is a present in itself, of course, but I've got him a present anyway; Eusebios will give it to you on your way out. And I'll give you some more slaves, too. You get quarters inside the palace with your new job, and you'll want some more people to look after them."

XI

THE PROTECTOR'S WIFE

THE NEW COUNT of the Protectors returned to his luxurious quarters beside the Bronze Gate, gloomy and irritable after his first meeting with his staff.

Artabanes was a tall, athletic man, deeply tanned by the African sun; he wore his mail coat and helmet without even noticing their weight. But when he entered his dining room, he unfastened his sword belt and flung the weapon with a clatter on the floor; he sat down on the end of a couch and put his head in his hands. "Levila!" he shouted to his servant. "Fetch me a drink!"

Levila, a blond Vandal retainer, appeared at once with a flagon of wine and a sympathetic expression. "Didn't it go well?" he asked, pouring his master a cupful neat.

Artabanes took the cup and tossed off half of it at once. He unfastened his helmet and dropped it on the floor beside the sword. "They're a lot of damned clever pen-pushers, and they think I'm an uneducated soldier who knows nothing about anything except fighting. And the trouble is, they're right."

Levila grinned. "If they think you're stupid, master, they're going to get a nasty surprise."

Artabanes snorted and took another gulp of wine. "This isn't

Carthage, and they're not your Vandal and Herul friends, Levila. The staff for the Protectors are mostly Constantinopolitan born, raised with a copy of the *Iliad* in one hand and an account book in the other. I may not be stupid, but I hardly got beyond alpha-beta-gamma, and you know I can't do mathematics to save my life. I'm willing to take oath to it that that quartermaster has some little game going over money for provisions, and I'd bet that the purser is up to tricks as well, but they were *laughing* at me! They know *I* can't catch them. No, the man who scares the staff sick is the count of the cavalry. He's a prizewinner, he is."

"He's new too, isn't he?"

"Appointed the same day as me, and not even as old. John of Berytus. Came to the meeting dressed like a prince in white and purple, and not carrying so much as a sword. He did carry a set of wax tablets, though, and he started making notes while the staff explained the bookkeeping system, and as soon as they were finished he began on the questions: Which book did they record payments of traveling expenses in? Did they keep a record of members attached on special duties? And you know what he'd done? He'd written down everything they'd said; he quoted it at them, and compared it with the way they do things in the sacred offices. He had the staff in a sweat in five minutes; they started falling over themselves to explain things to him and cover their tracks. *That's* the sort of soldier who does well here. I couldn't think of anything to say. I still don't have any idea how the pay structure works. I'm going to make a fool of myself, and that clever Syrian is going to make it look even worse. We should've stayed in Africa."

"Wax tablets wouldn't be much use in a battle," said Levila.

"There's not likely to be a battle here," replied Artabanes. He finished his wine. "Sometimes the Protectors get posted to the front, but they can always get out of going if they give up a few years' pay, which most of them are perfectly happy to do. And why not? Their families are mostly filthy rich, and they're only soldiers for the prestige and the benefits. The most fighting they have to do is to chase rioters. Count John did a good job of that, it seems. That's why he was promoted — that, and being the empress's cousin." He held out his cup.

Levila filled it, frowning. "Perhaps you could make a friend of him?" he suggested. "If he wanted to, he could be useful to you — and you're senior to him, and could make it worth his while. Was he respectful?"

"He was very correct," said Artabanes gloomily, taking another swallow. "He kept smiling and piling on the honorifics. I had no idea what he was thinking." He sighed. "I suppose I could invite him to dinner."

John arrived for the dinner late, nervous, and exhausted. He had spent most of the day going over the books for the household troops, the rest of the day trying to remember the names of his new slaves and the arrangements he had made for his new house, and most of the previous night in tormented dreams of fire, battle, and Euphemia.

"I'm very sorry to be late," he told Artabanes as the Vandal Levila ushered him into the dining room. "But I've been moving house — I'm sure Your Excellency knows what that's like." He smiled politely up at the count of the Protectors, who was a full head taller than him.

Artabanes had lived in barracks since he was sixteen and had never moved house in his life, but he tried to smile back. "No need to apologize," he said. "Sit down and have something to drink."

John reclined on the indicated couch and took the cup of wine Levila offered him. It was mixed with only a quarter water, which was stronger than he usually drank it, and he sipped it cautiously, looking around. There was a rack of armor in one corner of the room, but otherwise all the decor and furniture had come with the apartments. *Well,* he thought, *Artabanes is a proper soldier — not like me.* He smiled again to hide his nervousness, and lifted the cup to his host. "Much health!"

Artabanes reclined opposite and swallowed some of his own wine quickly. "You were going over the books today, weren't you?" he asked, then wondered if that was too blunt.

"Yes, Eminence." John gave the books a dismissive wave. "Such as they were."

"Have they been cooked?" asked Levila with interest. Artabanes shot his servant a look of angry reproach.

"No more than you'd expect," John replied without blinking. "I don't know when the cavalry last had a count who understood accounting, and naturally the clerks have taken advantage of it. They're not very well paid."

"You don't mind it?" asked Artabanes, too surprised to be indirect.

"Oh, I'll put a stop to most of it." John looked down at his cup. "But of course if you get rid of the clerks, you have to get others, and they're unlikely to be any more honest and won't be familiar with the work. I thought perhaps if Your Excellency and I could agree on who the worst offenders are, we could juggle the staff we have. Then we'd only need to replace one or two at the most."

Artabanes grunted and finished his wine. "Who do you think the worst offenders are?" he asked cautiously.

"Well, the quartermaster, for one. He's been charging the offices three times for the same supplies, once each to three different departments. And then he sells half the supplies he finally buys with the money, and that at twice the rate he paid!"

"Oh," said Artabanes. He tried to imagine how much the quartermaster must have amassed in a year of this; the sums swam madly through his head, and he took a deep breath. "What about the purser?"

"Him? He's not too bad. He's diverted some funds to his private pocket, but he hasn't stinted anyone. I would've thought he'd be all right if we just keep an eye on him."

"Oh. I never learned accounting." *Better to say it*, Artabanes thought, *than try to pretend I understand and have this smooth Syrian sneering behind my back.*

John smiled. "I rather thought Your Honor hadn't; Your Eminence looked a bit lost yesterday, if you don't mind my saying so. Well, I never learned soldiering, which is generally considered more important for a commander." He hesitated, wondering if Artabanes would be offended if he offered to help him with the accounts. He decided he might be, and wondered how to show willingness to be of service tactfully. "Your Eminence's own achievements are of course known to all the world," he ventured at last. "It is an honor to serve with you."

Artabanes blinked. *Does he mean that?* he wondered. *Or does he just want something?* "I'm glad one of us knows accounting," he said, deciding to leave the subject for the time being. "Did you learn it in the sacred offices?"

"No, with my father. I haven't actually worked in the offices; I've been private secretary to the most illustrious Narses, the head chamberlain."

"Oh," said Artabanes in a different voice, and gave John a second look. *He doesn't look soft,* he thought with a surge of hope, *and they say he's a good horseman. Perhaps he knows something about soldiering after all. Narses must look an even more unlikely commander, but if half the stories are true, that affair at Nicopolis was worthy of Belisarius himself.* "You wouldn't have gone with him to Thrace, by any chance?" he asked, and, at the nod, "Could you tell me precisely what happened at the battle of Nicopolis?"

John told him, arranging bread rolls and plates on the table to show the disposition of the forces; Artabanes hung over it eagerly, asking questions.

"Lord, that's pretty!" he exclaimed when John finished. "I'd heard about the battle, of course, but nobody could quite believe it — that your general had managed to defeat a force of heavy cavalry with pikemen and archers. Mother of God, I'd like to try that against the Persians! You can tell that His Illustriousness is an Armenian — that idea about the archers is something only a countryman of mine would come up with. And though I say it myself, Armenians are the finest soldiers in the empire — the bravest and the best disciplined. Only an Armenian would still manage to be a proper soldier even after he's been made a eunuch."

John looked down to hide another smile: Artabanes suddenly

reminded him of the Heruls and their refrain of "We are warriors!" "His Illustriousness is the bravest, the most intelligent,
and the best man I know," he said quietly. "And I think he
probably agrees with your assessment of his countrymen."

Artabanes grinned. "Levila," he said, "give Count John some
more wine."

"I haven't finished what I have!" John protested.

"Then join me in a toast. To Armenia!"

John drank to Armenia, and Levila refilled the cups.

"And to the beautiful Praejecta!" added Artabanes, finishing
his cup at a gulp.

John took a couple of swallows and put his hand over the top
of his cup. "I'd heard that Your Honor was to be congratulated
on that," he said.

Artabanes sighed. "Unfortunately, I'm not — not yet. She's
still officially in mourning for her murdered husband. Though
I've been given permission to hope. She's like the princess in the
old tales, kept in an inaccessible gold palace, and I'm the seventh
son, out to win her hand by killing monsters. I killed one in
Africa, but there don't seem to be many around in Constantinople, and those there are seem to be more vulnerable to the
stylus than the sword."

John smiled. "My stylus is at your command, then, Count."

Who would have thought it would be so easy? wondered
Artabanes. "Count," he said, grinning with pleasure, "my sword
is at yours!" And he raised his cup for some more wine.

Sorting out the accounts for the Protectors as well as the cavalry
took a great deal of time and an even greater deal of attention.
John was glad of this. Since the riots he had felt an almost un-
bearable tension between his past and his present, between what
he appeared to be and some immense interior revelation that he
tried desperately to ward off. He buried himself in the work,
piling up account books and tablets as a barricade; but at night
his mind spun through the figures that had occupied it all day
and ran off down obscure paths into nightmare. He dreamed

again and again of being chased by an unseen enemy through a labyrinth which was sometimes the Great Palace, sometimes the dark streets of the city, and sometimes the irrigation channels of Bostra. Always the paths ended blindly at a locked gate, which he beat at frantically while the blackness closed in behind him. Sometimes he saw Euphemia beyond the gate, pinned to the ground with Sclavenian spears, burning in her house, once holding up her arms out of a mass of quicksand; always dying. He would wake from the nightmares shaken and sweating, and get out of bed trembling. Usually it was an hour or so before dawn, and he would go to the lavish bathhouse attached to his quarters and try to steam the tension away, and then either take his horse out for a gallop or sit down at once to the paperwork. He longed to see Euphemia. Only the fact that he would have to explain himself to Narses prevented him from visiting her to reassure himself that she was alive and unharmed.

And then, one morning three weeks after his promotion, he looked up from an account book to find her standing in the office door.

He caught his breath, staring at her. She was wearing the yellow cloak again, and a hat bordered with gold; she stood framed in the sunlight that fell in behind her and sent the dust motes swirling above the tiled floor.

"Euphemia," he whispered.

She smiled the old sour smile. "I have some business for you," she said. Then, looking at the pile of documents on his desk, she added, "Not that you seem short of it. May I come in?"

He stood up hurriedly. "Of course. Do sit down."

She smiled again, and seated herself on the chair by the wall. As she entered he saw that she was followed by one of her slaves — her old gatekeeper — but not by her chaperone. "Is your aunt not well?" he asked, standing nervously by his desk.

Euphemia shrugged, pulling her cloak straight. "She's quite well, thank you; she's resting at home. She's needed a lot of rest since the house was burned down. And she's not really my aunt, she's my grandmother's sister's daughter. I just call her Auntie."

"Oh," he said. He sat down again. "I . . . I hope the house is now on its way to being rebuilt? Were your slaves all right?"

She nodded. "My chair-bearers were the only ones killed. The master's workers say it will be another month before we can move back in." She hesitated, then added, "I'm sorry if I was rude to you the day after the riots. I . . . I was very upset about my chair-bearers. They'd been members of the household since before I was born. They used to give me rides on their shoulders when I was tiny and they were just boys. It was very . . . very distressing that they were dead — and the whole night was so unspeakable, I didn't know what I was saying. But I am very grateful to you, and shouldn't have let my tongue go."

"Please don't apologize," said John, staring at her, trying to memorize the sight — the orange-brown of her eyes, the turn of her head — keeping it to hold against the dreams. "I quite understand."

Euphemia gave another sour smile. "In token of my gratitude I've brought these." She nodded to her gatekeeper, and the old man walked over and set five thick red leather volumes on John's desk. *God in heaven*, he thought, staring at them in astonishment, *not those wretched files again!*

"I thought they must have been destroyed," he said uncertainly.

She shook her head, smiling not-so-sourly. "No. I kept them in a secret compartment in the gatehouse; Onesimos went back to check the rebuilding yesterday and found them still in their place. You can take them to the prefecture whenever you like." She nodded to the old man, and he grinned, bowed, and went to wait for her outside the door.

"Oh. Why don't you take them? It would strengthen your own position to return them as His Illustriousness suggested, in gratitude for a favor already conferred by His Sacred Majesty."

She scowled. "Don't you want them? Perhaps they're not much, but they'll make you friends at the prefecture. You can get the credit for recovering them. That's the only gift I can give you that's worth anything."

"Your thanks are worth something, to me," he said.

She glared. "Don't make fun of me. I don't like pretty speeches."

"It isn't a pretty speech, it's the truth," he said, stung. "I was pleased to save you because I'd rather have you alive than dead, and I never cared a copper drachma for these damned files: I was rather pleased to think the miserable things had burned." He pushed them aside impatiently.

She bit her lip, her face going red. "I'm sorry," she said. "I always say the wrong thing to you." She pulled at her cloak. "I . . . I wanted to give you something valuable. I don't have the money to buy anything — my father is keeping almost everything with him in Egypt. I thought that those . . ." She stopped, and held the edge of her cloak to her face. He realized that she was crying.

"Oh Immortal God!" he said, and hurried round the edge of the desk. He stooped uncertainly by her chair. "I'm sorry — of course the contact with the prefecture will be valuable. I only meant —"

She wiped at her face with the cloak's silk border, shaking her head. "I know: you never really wanted anything to do with me or the files. And why should you? You don't need them or anybody. You've got the favor of the Augusta and enough ability to get yourself any position you like. I can't give you anything. Nobody can — nobody can touch you. Very well, do what you like, be what you please — but don't condescend to me!" She glared up at him, red-eyed.

"I . . . ," he said, and swallowed. His throat hurt; it was difficult to stay still, stooping with his heart beating in his ears. He crouched beside the chair, holding to one arm of it to steady himself. "I . . . I dreamed of you last night," he told her in a low voice, not sure what he was saying or what he meant to say. "I dreamed you were trapped in your house, burning, and I couldn't reach you. I would never condescend to you — please believe that. And I think you could give me one thing that I want more than anything in the world. But I can't receive it."

"What do you mean?" she demanded, white with astonishment.

He looked away. "Honesty. I think you're the most honest person I know, the most direct, the most fearless. When I saw your house on fire, I realized that your death would leave the whole world the poorer — that's what I meant when I said it was reward enough to see you alive."

"I've treated you like dirt!" she said, shocked. "You can't mean that!"

He swallowed. His legs hurt, and he leaned back on his heels, looked up into her shocked, confused eyes. He looked down again, then started to stand, saying nothing. Euphemia leaned forward and caught his arm.

"No, you must explain what you mean!" she told him. "You can't just say something like that and then retreat into your shell again!"

"Most excellent Euphemia, please believe that I esteem you very highly and am entirely content merely to have been of service to Your Discretion. However, you are bound to your father, and I to my sacred patroness the Augusta, and any . . . association . . . between us is now necessarily at an end. You've returned the files; I have another job. It would be better if you accepted my esteem and demanded no explanations."

"You sound like Narses," she said savagely. "Spouting the jargon of official letters, locking your secret mind up in a box somewhere and burying the key."

"I admire Narses more than I've ever admired anyone," he replied coolly.

"Oh, you're two of a kind, you and Narses," she agreed bitterly, letting go of him. "Infinitely admirable — brave, brilliant, unreachable. You ought to get yourself castrated like him, too. Then you'd really be untouchable. I love you. I realized that I was in love with you when you went away to Thrace, but I was in love with you a long time before that. There: I've said it. It horrifies you, does it?"

He closed his eyes, crouching on the floor with his shoulders hunched over and his head bowed. Not looking up, he was aware of how she sat, leaning forward, gripping the chair arm beside his hand; aware of the shape and the warmth of her body; aware of her breath coming quick and her legs twisted underneath her, tense with the revelation. Her words seemed to have become a hard angular shape inside his chest, something that choked the breath painfully in his lungs.

She leaned back in the chair. "It horrifies you," she repeated, with a mixture of bitterness and tenderness.

He shook his head, looked up at her. "Not the way you think," he whispered. "Narses advised me to stay away from you. My mother would punish you, he said, if she thought I loved you."

He had not meant to say it, was not sure for an instant that he hadn't after all said "cousin" — but her eyes opened very wide, the pupils contracting in shock, taking it in. "Your mother," she said after a long silence, in the flat, nasal voice that was the first tone he had heard from her.

"I meant, my cousin," he said, quickly. "The Augusta."

"That's not what you meant at all. Your mother. It's perfectly obvious now. Hence all the favors — Mother of God, you even look like her. Narses is undoubtedly right, as he usually is, and I'd be punished for looking at you cross-eyed." With bitter sarcasm she added, "A girl like me can't be permitted to fall in love with the empress Theodora's precious bastard! And you, of course, will do exactly what your dear mother tells you to!"

"You do what your father says," he pointed out, shocked and confused by the sudden change.

"She *destroyed* my father, the tyrannical whore! She had him flogged like a slave and chained and starved like a dog, for nothing, for one of her lies! And she used me to help her!" She set her teeth and pulled herself up very straight. "You're absolutely right. Any association between us is now at an end."

He stood, slowly. "Then we're agreed," he said heavily, and became afraid. *Lord God,* he thought, *I've given it away, my mother's secret, into the hands of her enemy.* "You said you were grateful to me," he said urgently. "Let me ask you then to leave this meeting out of your weekly letter to Egypt."

She went crimson. "What do you think I am, a whore like your . . . patroness?" She jumped to her feet, staring at him, then caught her breath with a sob. "I'm sorry," she said, low and wretchedly. "I've said unforgivable things to you, as usual, and you've been more than generous in return, as usual. I'm sorry, I'm sorry, I'm sorry. And . . . and of course you haven't said anything to me that you shouldn't have said; I never heard anything. Let's part with . . . with esteem, as friends." Still flushed, her eyes shining with tears, she held out her hand to him.

He took it slowly; it trembled in his. "I'm sorry," he told her. "I wish —" He stopped himself, and stood a moment holding her hand and watching her face, feeling that they stood in one solid moment in a sea of chaos and darkness. He bent his head and kissed her hand. "Esteemed Euphemia, much health!" he whispered.

"Much health," she returned, drawing back her hand. She took a deep breath, then pulled up her cloak and left the room.

He sat down at the desk, his mind in such chaos that it was several minutes before he could frame a coherent thought. *What am I doing*, he wondered at last, *here in this city which I hate, living a lie, rejecting love? For what? It's not for anything I want. I would be happy . . .*

He realized that he had never even considered what would make him happy.

I have no spirit, no independence, he thought despairingly. *"Of course" I do what my mother tells me. But what's the alternative? Oh, I suppose I could find work, even if I simply disappeared from this city and went back to Bostra, Diodoros' bastard come home none the wiser. It would be hard to go back to being a town scribe, but I could get used to it. More realistically, though, I could go to His Illustriousness, or to some of the others in the offices, take a demotion, and escape out of this city full of lies, to somewhere I could shape my own life. But what family do I have, apart from Theodora? I have wanted to please her, to belong. I must belong to her because I don't belong anywhere else.*

And Euphemia? That's impossible: she's seen now herself that it's impossible. Too much has passed between our parents, and our loyalties are in opposed directions.

But I want to get away from here, from this terrible city that presses on me — yes, that I want. To have a post in the East, perhaps, doing some useful work with my own people. If Theodora would permit it.

The door of the office opened and Artabanes came in, carrying another load of accounts. He stared at John in surprise.

"What's the matter?" he asked.

John sighed and cleared a space on his desk. "I was just thinking how much I hate Constantinople."

"What, you too?" Artabanes grinned and set the documents down. "As soon as I've been married a year I want to set out for the East. Reorganize the frontier defenses at least, and worry the Persians if they break the truce. You'd be the perfect man to take along."

"Better than an Armenian?" asked John, managing a smile.

Artabanes laughed. "Most Armenians don't speak Arabic. No, you could show me how to do the paperwork — I wanted this explained, by the way. We could be co-commanders of the East!"

"It sounds good," said John, smiling more naturally. "I'll take the job."

Artabanes grinned again and stretched. "God send it comes soon! Lord, I wish there were some whores in this city. Your sacred patroness is undoubtedly pleasing God by stamping the trade out, but it's hard on a man who wants to marry and has to wait."

Artabanes' marriage to Praejecta never took place. One evening in late August the count of the Protectors came knocking at John's door and demanded to be allowed in at once.

John was in the sweat room of the bathhouse when Jakobos announced Artabanes' arrival. He was on the point of giving orders for Artabanes to be entertained when the count himself pushed into the room, fully dressed and in armor. "I need to talk to you," he told John. "Do you mind if I join you?"

John hurriedly pulled a towel around his waist. "Certainly — though I was just about to come out . . ."

"Oh, I could use a bath myself," said Artabanes, and began to take his armor off.

"Jakobos, take Count Artabanes' things. Put the mail coat somewhere dry," John ordered, feeling helpless. Artabanes stripped himself with the carelessness of a man accustomed to living in crowded barracks. His body was several shades paler than his face, hairy, and scarred with the marks of old wounds. He made John feel like a deskbound slug.

Artabanes sat heavily on the bench opposite John, grasping his knees with his large square hands. "I need to ask you a favor," he said. "You have influence with the Augusta, don't you?"

John felt his heart sink. "Her Sacred Majesty has been generous enough to favor me," he said cautiously. "I wouldn't say that I can influence what she does."

Artabanes waved the quibble aside impatiently. "Her staff will let you in to see her, though; that's more than most men can claim. Could you speak to her for me? A dreadful thing has happened. My wife has turned up, and she says she's going to appeal to the Augusta."

"Your wife?" said John, staring in astonishment. "I thought you were going to marry Prae —"

"I intend to marry Praejecta! But I was married to Shirin back in Armenia when I was fifteen."

"I don't understand," John said. "How can you mean to marry the emperor's niece when you're already married?"

Artabanes struck the bench. "I'm not married to Shirin, not by any reasonable interpretation of marriage. It was arranged between our families; I was just a boy and went along with it, but we never got on. She's a useless creature. Hated to sleep with me — just lay there like a sheep waiting to be slaughtered. She thought I should drudge in the fields all my life, and she should drudge beside me, not saying more than three words a day, and this was our lot and to be endured. She's lazy and dirty. I joined the army after nine months of her, and was glad to get away. I haven't seen her from that day to this; I thought she was probably dead. Well, she isn't. She heard I was made a count and has come to take her place as a grand lady and my wife. She arrived this morning at the Bronze Gate, barefoot and stinking, asking for me — she hardly even speaks Greek, but she came right out with "count of the Protectors, my husband." I told her I'd give her a divorce and a rich settlement, but she won't agree. She's my wife, she says, and that's that. She'll appeal to the Augusta, who protects poor women — that's another of her Greek phrases, 'poor women.' And you and I both know that it's true, the Augusta always listens to any bitch who goes to her complaining that a husband or a pimp has mistreated her. I'm not saying anything against the Augusta! I'm sure it's very charitable to defend poor women who have been abused. But Shirin has no claim on me, and the Augusta doesn't always listen to both sides of the story. If you can put my case to her, John, I'll remember it with gratitude for the rest of my life."

"Wouldn't it be better if you put your own case to her?" suggested John. "After all, I don't know much about it."

"I've just told you all there is to know. I was married to the woman by my father; we didn't get on; there were no children; I left; I haven't seen her for close on twenty years. If that's not grounds for divorce, what is? But I'm not likely to be admitted to Her Sacred Majesty and allowed to say that, and no one would listen to me if I were. She'd listen to you, though, if you went on behalf of a friend."

"I'll go, of course," John said unhappily. "But —"

"Thank you! I knew you'd help!" Artabanes leaned back against the sweat-house wall and ran a hand through his hair, grinning with relief.

"But it's . . . it's very bad luck," John went on.

"The worst possible!" agreed Artabanes. "If she'd waited a

few months, I would have been married to Praejecta and I could have laughed in her face."

"That wasn't exactly what I meant," John said sharply. "Praejecta's family is very conservative. They won't like it that you've been married before — or that you neglected to tell them so."

"Praejecta's not a virgin," Artabanes pointed out.

"*She* was rather publicly widowed," John said acidly. "*You* have an abandoned wife who's just turned up on your doorstep. You can tell everyone it's not your fault, but it doesn't look very good and isn't much of a recommendation for the position of nephew to the emperor. Even if your wife is unsuccessful in her application to the serene Augusta, you may find your marriage called off. I'd suggest that you go and explain the situation to Praejecta and her family immediately."

"I'll go straight there," said Artabanes soberly. "Just let me wash myself off." He stepped directly into the plunge bath and rose out, shaking the water from himself like a dog. "Though Praejecta will understand — she knows I love her. I've sworn it to her often enough. And nobody will believe I ever loved a creature like Shirin." He looked around for a towel; John handed him his own, the only one in the room, and called Jakabos.

The next morning John went to the Daphne Palace and applied for an audience with Theodora.

He had seen the empress at intervals throughout the summer: he had arranged escorts for her to her summer palaces and back; he had been to her dinner parties, her sister's dinner parties, her friends' dinner parties; he had accompanied her to the races and sat near her in the royal box. He had been a privileged guest at the wedding of her grandson, his nephew, to Belisarius' daughter — a quieter occasion, that, than the empress would have liked; the bride's parents were still in Italy. But he had not seen her privately since she gave him his rank.

The eunuch who kept the appointment register recognized him at once and escorted him with smiles to a private anteroom before going to notify the empress of his arrival. He remem-

bered, briefly and like something from a dream, the first time
he had applied for an audience: the strangeness of everything
that was now so familiar, and his own terror. He stood impatiently and walked about the waiting room. He had charge of
an escort duty later that morning, and wore his mail coat and
sword; they weighed uncomfortably on his shoulders.

Artabanes should have told someone that he was married, he
thought for the hundredth time since the Armenian had explained the position. *I can't blame him for wanting a divorce,
but he should have done something to formalize one years ago
and not just left the woman, forgotten like an old shoe. Still,
he's my friend, as much as anyone is, and he asked me to speak
to the empress for him. The least I can do is put his case.*

The chamberlain Eusebios appeared at the door. "She's just
finishing her breakfast," he told John, smiling. "She'll see you
at once."

Theodora was reclining on her couch in the sunlit breakfast
room, listening while one of her eunuchs read her a letter. Her
health had not improved over the summer, though it had grown
no worse. She was thin and haggard, and there was yet more
white in her hair. But she smiled brightly when she saw John,
and held her hands out.

"Don't bow," she commanded, and he came over, took her
hands, and kissed them. Perplexed by a sense of tenderness, he
stood a moment holding them and looking at the worn, shadowed face that smiled up at him.

She giggled. "Lord, don't you look military!" She moved over
on the couch, making room for him to sit beside her; he took
a seat facing her, leaning against the armrest. "Let's see if I can
guess what you've come about," she said, her eyes sparkling.
"The most beautiful Praejecta?"

He smiled. "Indirectly. I'm here on behalf of my friend Count
Artabanes."

She laughed. "On Artabanes' behalf! That's good. I saw his
wife yesterday."

He stared. "What, already?"

"Indeed." Theodora grinned. "She appeared yesterday afternoon, applying to see me. I couldn't believe it at first; it seemed
too good to be true. But I had her brought in and questioned,
and there's no doubt of it. She is his wife, and she has letters
to prove it. That puts a stop to Artabanes' ambitions!"

John hesitated. "I . . . I don't approve of the way Artabanes
treated his wife. But he was very young when he married her,
it was never a successful marriage, and he hasn't seen her for
nearly twenty years. He's very much in love with Praejecta, and
this is a great blow to him."

Theodora snorted. "I'm sure it is!" She grinned at John again.
"And I'm sure he was very much in love with the idea of being
Peter's nephew. What do you think of Praejecta, then?"

"I've only met her once. Artabanes introduced us. Is she very
distressed?"

"She's furious!" said Theodora with relish. "Though, surprisingly, she'd still be willing to marry the dirty schemer. But I
think she could be persuaded to change her mind." She gave
John a sly look under half-closed eyelids.

What on earth is she thinking of? wondered John. He licked
his lips and tried again. "Artabanes wanted me to intercede
with you for him — to tell you his side of the story."

"Did he? I'm not sure I want to hear it. Do you realize that
poor woman walked most of the way from Armenia? Her family
wouldn't support her in her claim on her husband, so she saddled their one mule and rode off. She had to sell the mule
halfway, to have enough money for food; she's been sleeping in
haystacks and living on journeybread. When her husband saw
her, he tried to pretend he didn't know who she was. He may
well wish he didn't!"

John was silent for a moment, then said hesitantly, "He says
he's offered her a divorce and a rich settlement."

"That's what he offered to make her go away. If he'd offered
it years ago, I'd have some sympathy for him. The poor girl was
sent back to her father's house like damaged goods when he ran
off to join the army. She's been living for the past twenty years

as a disgraced maidservant to her father. Worse off than a maid-servant: she's a wife, and can't remarry. She's been poor and wretched and despised. Everyone blames her for what Artabanes did to her. He's had a grand time, fighting and whoring in Carthage, winning promotion, becoming rich and powerful. Well, he didn't divorce her when he joined the army, and he didn't even check to see whether she was still alive when he proposed marriage to Praejecta. But now it's her turn. He can have her back and treat her with the honor she deserves — and if he doesn't, he'll have me to reckon with. I'd see her treated right even if I wasn't pleased that Praejecta is free for you."

"For me?" said John, shocked. "What do you mean?"

She laughed. "Oh, my chaste Hippolytos! Why not for you? She's about your age, a rich young widow, tolerably pretty, not stupid — and Peter's niece. I wanted her for you before, but Peter insisted: Artabanes had saved her when her husband was murdered; she loved Artabanes; Artabanes should have her. Well, Artabanes isn't in a position to marry anyone, but you unquestionably are. You should go talk to her. She's bitterly disappointed in Artabanes, and feels insulted because he would have made her something little better than a mistress. You could appear as his friend to console her — flatter her, listen to her — and let her get a good look at you. I can get Peter to agree to the match if she agrees. And she was never really in love with Artabanes — it was just that he's a handsome man and she was grateful to him for rescuing her. She does want to marry again, and she knows it will be hard for her to manage it. She knows I've opposed matches for her in the past; she knows I haven't wanted to give anyone else that power. Well, now I'm making an exception, and there you are, a count, a patrician, good-looking, and a very able young man whose prospects are obvious to anyone who takes time to think about them. She'll agree. Be courteous and respectful, give her her due of flattery, and she'll agree."

"But I don't want to marry her," John said stupidly.

"Are you in love with someone else?" she demanded, alarmed.

He thought painfully of Euphemia; pushed the thought aside. "No, but —"

"Then don't be ridiculous! She's Peter's niece!"

"But . . . but she was going to marry my friend," John said, helplessly trying to fight off a rising tide of panic. "It would be disgraceful for me to abuse my position as a friend to take his place."

"You dear scrupulous innocent!" Theodora took his hand and looked up smiling into his face. "It's not his place. He's married, and wouldn't be Praejecta's bridegroom even if you'd never been born. If he's really your friend, he should be pleased that it's you rather than someone else."

John pulled his hand away, in such turmoil that he was unaware what he was doing. *Praejecta,* he thought. *The emperor's niece. An heiress to Justinian.*

Theodora wants me to inherit the purple.

As soon as the thought was framed, he realized that he had known it for a very long time. This was the destination to which she had been driving; this was the revelation that had pursued him in his dreams. He had turned now; he saw it plainly, and the panic fell away into a cold clarity.

"No," he said desperately. "I don't have it in me. I can't."

Theodora's smile had become a look of impatience. "Can't what? Can't love a woman? You should try; I'm certain you'll find you're as able as any young man."

"Not that. Can't be emperor. I'm not a match for Praejecta. Find me someone nearer my own rank."

The look of impatience became a frown, the brows lowering over the fierce eyes. "Don't be absurd. Your rank is what you make it — what *I* make it. And Praejecta's grandfather was a peasant. You're a patrician and a count; that's as high as rank goes."

"I don't have it in me," he repeated, the words painful and distinct. "There are others who've grown up hoping for the purple: Germanus and his children; Praejecta's brothers — they all want it, and the Senate would prefer any of them to me.

Even if I were legitimate, I'd still be an outsider. I'd have to fight my way to the purple over their heads, and I don't have the will to fight like that. And I couldn't do it even if the others were dead. Immortal God! The empire of the Romans, the whole East, Asia, Egypt, Africa, Italy, Thrace — God have mercy! All that to be ruled by someone like me — by Diodoros' bastard?"

"*My* bastard!" declared the empress angrily. "Not his, mine! I rule it all; why shouldn't you? You're more able than any of the others — cleverer than Germanus' children, braver and more patient than Vigilantia's. Look at me! I tell you now, quite plainly, that you can have it, all of it, the purple and the diadem and the title of Augustus. You can do it, it is possible and within your grasp."

"I don't want it! I wouldn't know what to do with it. No. It's not for me; it would destroy me to try. No."

She slapped him across the face. "What sort of spineless talk is that?"

One of her rings had torn his cheek; he put his hand to the stinging wound blindly. "I don't want it. Supreme power is too much. I couldn't use it well. And there are too many other people who do want it, who want it badly. I couldn't fight for it, not even to please you. It would kill me. And even if it didn't, I don't think I'd recognize myself or want to by the time I got it. No. I will not marry Praejecta; I do not want to make any attempt at the purple."

She drew in her breath with a hiss. "Your father did this to you! I know you have courage; that was made plain enough at Nicopolis and in the riots. Don't let your miserable respectable father turn you into a coward now!"

"You were the one who left me with him," said John evenly.

She slapped him again, then pulled herself up at the opposite end of the couch, panting and pressing a hand against her side.

"I'm sorry!" he said wretchedly. "But I am what I am: probably a coward, certainly afraid to touch half what the world offers me, miserably respectable — like my father. But I am his bastard too, as much as I am yours. I can't help it, and it's too late for me to change. I don't want the purple, and I won't take any steps to compete for it."

She leaned forward and caught his cloak. "I gave you this," she said, shaking it in a clenched fist. "I got you your position. Shall I take it away again, since you don't like power?"

"You can do whatever you like," he replied. "I didn't ask you for the cloak or the position. Send me away, if you like. Send me back to Bostra. I wouldn't tell anyone where I'd been. I could live with that more easily than I could live with the purple."

"Oh, God, you!" She struck his shoulder with her clenched fist. The blow thudded harmlessly into the chain mail. She pulled her hand back and cradled it, glaring. "You're impossible! Get out of here! If anyone else insulted me like that, I would have him killed! Get out!"

He got up, pale but steady, and made the full prostration before walking out past the horrified eunuchs and stumbling through the palace back to his own quarters.

He told his troops that he had been taken ill and excused himself from the escort, then went into his luxurious quarters and lay down on his bed, still in his armor. He could hear the slaves working about the house; from behind the house, in the exercise yard, came the shouts of some of his men, who were tilting.

Could I really bear going back to Bostra? he wondered. *Go back to being a scribe, after having so much authority? Go back to lodgings and sneers after luxury and power?*

More easily than I could take up the purple. I suppose I am a coward. Perhaps Euphemia was right, and I should have been a eunuch. I'm certainly no good at love, and I'm disqualifying myself for power as well — even His Illustriousness has never gone that far. "There are some who are eunuchs from their mother's womb, and some who have been made eunuchs by men, and some who have made themselves eunuchs for the sake of the kingdom of heaven." Only it isn't for the sake of the

*kingdom of heaven; it's from fear. I don't have it in me to wear
that color, and I'm afraid of it. There's nothing in it that I can
see in myself. She expects too much of me.*

No — I've failed her.

He lay on his back, staring up at the ceiling, feeling exhausted
and sick. After a time Jakobos knocked on the door and announced that Artabanes had called and wished to see him.

"Give him my compliments," John said, without getting up.
"Tell him that my meeting with the Augusta was not a success,
that I quarreled with her, and that he's going to have to take his
wife back. And tell him that I'm not well and will see him
tomorrow."

Jakobos went. About half an hour later he knocked on the
door again.

"I won't see him," said John impatiently. "Tell him tomorrow."

"It's His Illustriousness this time, master," Jakobos announced.

John sat up. "Ask him to come in."

Narses entered at once; he must have been standing beside
Jakobos. He glanced about the bedroom, looking small and un-
ruffled in his white and purple cloak. Then he nodded to Jakobos, who was waiting by the door. "See that we're not disturbed,
there's a good fellow," he directed, and sat down on the clothes
chest. Jakobos bowed and closed the door.

"You're the one person I want to see just now," said John.

Narses gave his cryptic smile. "Although the Augusta sent
me?"

"I thought she probably had. What did she tell you to say to
me?"

The eunuch sighed, regarding John steadily for a moment. "I
am to explain her intentions to you."

"I think I understand them. Did she tell you what they
were?"

"Oh yes. Some time ago, in fact. I advised her then what the
probable outcome would be, but she refused to listen; she is
very ambitious for you. But I'm not sure you do understand her

intentions. You know what they are, but that's a different matter."

John sat still a moment, his arms on his knees, his fingers twisting restlessly together. "Very well, explain them," he said at last.

Narses hesitated, then steepled his fingers. "How much has she told you of her past?"

"Not much. A little about her father's death. And that my . . . my sister's father was a charioteer called Constantine, and that she was abandoned by one of her lovers in Cyrene. That's about all."

"More than she tells most. Her mother died when she was ten. Theodora was already on the stage by then, assisting her sister Komito in comic mimes. A certain wealthy gentleman of the city took an interest in her and offered her stepfather some money for the use of her; the stepfather agreed, and by beating her forced her to agree as well. The gentleman really liked boys, and used her as one. He kept her for a few years and then returned her to the stage when her body began to change. She has always insisted that he was kind to her, and perhaps he was. But she has since sought out any wealthy man accused of abusing boys in that fashion and had him punished with the utmost severity.

"It is generally expected that a comic actress is willing to prostitute herself on the side, and this Theodora did. Though some of the tales told of her are quite absurd: she never slept with a tenth of the men she's alleged to have slept with, and she obviously preferred to be kept by one man at a time. Which didn't save her from contempt, abuse, and occasional atrocious ill-treatment. Imagine her, if you will, as a seventeen-year-old girl who's learned to laugh when her lover beats her — laugh because she must, if she's to feed the child she has at home. If she enjoys power now and uses it too freely, it's because to her power is the only alternative to being weak and abused; it is the ability to revenge injury, to protect the weak and to humble the strong. Can you understand this?"

John was silent for a long time. "I understand it," he said at last. "But it's not the only alternative."

"So you believe. You, more than most men, are interested in obtaining dominion over yourself, and in having complete control over your own actions. Being given responsibility for others merely threatens that."

"I've never had control over my own actions! I've always, all my life, done what someone else tells me!"

"You know perfectly well what I mean," Narses said impatiently. "A man can be a slave, under another's orders, and still define for himself an absolute dominion over his own soul. That's what I've wanted, and that's what you want. Every responsibility you've accepted since you came to this city has been taken in the confidence that you could put it down again if you had to, that you weren't bound to anything. Marriage or the purple would bind you, and so you won't accept them."

"Because I'm afraid of power. I'm a coward."

"My dear friend! I thought we proved something at Nicopolis."

"I was sacred sick at Nicopolis, and I'm scared sick now. Narses, I don't want it. I think I would probably be destroyed in a struggle for the purple — and even if I could have it without effort, I wouldn't want it.

"Why should you want it?" asked Narses. "It is not true that everyone wants power; there are at least as many people eager to avoid the possession of authority as to acquire it. The position of supreme power is dangerous, can consume everything else its possessor loves, and is probably exercised in futility, vanity, and vexation of the spirit. To want it earnestly requires a degree of confidence few men possess — though there are always more men wanting it than can be satisfied. You are neither ruthless nor confident. You don't want it, and you sense that in a struggle with men who did want it, you would probably be killed. That does not mean that you are weak or foolish, or a coward."

John looked up at the eunuch with relief. "Thank you."

"I haven't finished. The Augusta directed me to explain her position, not my own opinions. You may not want power, but she cannot understand that. She finds it difficult to believe that anyone would refuse power except through cowardice or corruption, which plainly do not apply in your case. She blames your father for imposing too many restraints on you, and expects you to change your mind. You know, I suppose, that she bitterly regrets that she has had no children by her husband?"

"I . . . that is, she hasn't mentioned it."

Narses smiled briefly. "No. She doesn't. But she has grieved for it, nonetheless. And she resents fiercely that the succession will go to Germanus and his children. She has done all she can to obstruct Germanus and his family and to provide the emperor with heirs elsewhere. She favored the son of the emperor's sister Vigilantia and married him to her niece, Komito's daughter; she has tried to secure herself by this match between Belisarius' daughter and her grandson. But she has been unhappily aware that her candidates were no more distinguished than Germanus'. Then you appeared. She was at first uncertain — determined to advance you, but doubtful of your ability. She gave you to me; I was delighted with your efficiency, and she began to hope. You distinguished yourself in battle; she was overjoyed. At last, she thought, she had a horse to outrace her rivals', an Arab colt who could carry the race. Now she has discovered that it perversely refuses to run."

"I'm not a horse," said John.

Narses smiled. "No. And a contest for empire isn't a race. Those terms were hers, just now. Allow me to restate the position in a way we will both understand better. This empire is the greatest in all the world, but its government is delicate, chaotic, and corrupt. It's like a chariot with its horses bolting and half the reins broken. The man who drives it must know something more than simply how to urge the horses on, demanding that they win the race: he must understand how to steer gently, because if he doesn't, he will find the reins of power breaking in his hands and the state crashing against the turning post or flying into the stands. I would rather see you in the purple than any of the other candidates."

"What do you mean? You can't think I'm fit to —"

"The empire has suffered rulers who are incompetent or even insane. Emperors are not gods. When I consider the other young men who aspire to the purple, I find myself agreeing with the Augusta that you would be preferable. Germanus' son, Justin, is an amiable young man but not very bright, and impatient with detail and with the offices; his reign would breed corruption. And the other Justin, Vigilantia's son, who was the Augusta's favorite until you appeared, is clever but conceited, hot-headed, and unstable; he might put the whole state at risk by unnecessary wars. You would be careful, prudent, and moderate — the very qualities that our poor battered empire needs most. That you do not want power is all to the good."

"Don't." John groaned. "Narses, I couldn't do it. And the state doesn't want me — the Senate would detest me as an outsider, and the people and the army would prefer a member of the house of Justin. The emperor himself distrusts me already and wouldn't want me as an heir. As I said, I certainly couldn't survive a struggle to get the purple."

"You couldn't," Narses said evenly, "unless you were determined to win."

There was a long silence. John stared at the chamberlain in shocked disbelief. Narses stared back without expression.

"If you entered a contest for the purple," Narses went on at last, deliberately, "you would have a number of advantages over your rivals. The first is your mother, whose influence is very great. The second is a familiarity with the offices and an understanding of them which you could use to win support there. The third advantage consists of your own abilities, which are, I believe, greater than those of your rivals. The fourth, if I may add it, is my own support, which is not altogether inconsiderable. If you were determined, and ready to work hard to obtain the support of the people and the army and to conciliate the Senate, you would have an excellent chance of winning."

"Is this what you believe I should do?" John asked.

Narses spread his hands. "I have explained what the Augusta wants. My own opinions are of no consequence."

"They are to me! When you advise something, you're nearly always right. What do you advise?"

"It is not my place to advise you on this. I have stated that if you did seek the purple, I would prefer you to the other candidates."

"Oh, damn you! That isn't the same thing as saying you think I should seek the purple, and you know it."

"No," said Narses, smiling. "But it would be enough to lose me my rank if the emperor were aware of it."

John was again silent for a long moment. "Working to win support means what?" he asked at last. "Scheming for places, getting money and giving bribes, doing favors? Influence-peddling, making friends for the advantage I could get from them?"

"All of those. I hope it would be possible to get by without slandering, injuring, or otherwise obstructing your rivals, but I couldn't possibly promise that. It would also mean marrying Praejecta."

John slumped back against the wall, shaking his head.

"I have been assuming that it is not principally Praejecta you object to," Narses said slowly. "I trust that Euphemia —"

"There's nothing between me and Euphemia, though I admit I wish there were. Narses, I don't have it in me to do it. I couldn't. I don't want the purple, and I can't pay the price I'd have to pay to get it. You can tell that to my mother."

Narses bowed his head, lifted it. "I will tell her."

"What . . . what do you think she'll do?" John asked as the eunuch rose to go.

He paused, looking mildly surprised. "Do? What do you think she's likely to do?"

"Strip me of my rank. Send me back to Bostra. Even imprison me. I don't know — only she's very angry."

Narses shook his head. "She wishes you to have the highest rank; she is hardly going to take away the rank you have. She still cherishes her ambitions — and beneath them she is fond of you. I believe that she will simply try to convince herself that you will change your mind. You are quite right that she is very angry, and will certainly refuse to see you unless you beg an audience and prostrate yourself with apologies. But more than that . . . no. Anything she did would hurt her more than it hurt you, and she knows it."

"Oh. Narses, tell her I'm sorry. And I am sorry. But I can't."

Narses smiled, then leaned over and touched John's hand. "I know. I expected your answer would be what it is. Don't be sorry that you are you and not someone else: there's no sense or virtue in that. My dear friend, much health!"

XII

The Prince of This World

THE FOLLOWING SPRING, the scribe Diomedes was showing a new acquaintance the hippodrome when John rode in with half a dozen retainers to exercise his horse.

It was a clear, warm evening in early May and the track was crowded, but the crowds parted for the young man in the patrician's cloak with his armed followers, and they trotted, glittering, on the packed earth in the heavy horizontal sun.

"I used to know him," Diomedes said, reining in his tall bay by the Great Gate and waving down the track at John. "He was His Illustriousness's secretary for a while. Promoted beyond all recognition now."

The acquaintance, who had arrived in the city only the week before and was hoping to find a job, looked after the much-promoted secretary with interest. "What rank does he have now?"

"Count of the household cavalry, and patrician with it. Of course, he's a distant cousin of the sacred Augusta — clever, too, but connections are everything. He's from Berytus. That's your native city too, Elthemos, isn't it?"

"No, I've just been living there for the past two years, studying law. My native city is Bostra."

"Where's that?"

"Capital of Arabia." Elthemos was sour. "A very fine city."

"Oh. Well, I never was much good at geography. Count John is from Berytus. You know what his father was? Municipal scribe. So was John, until he appealed to the Augusta. Connections are *everything*."

Elthemos sighed and looked down. He was painfully aware of his own lack of connections. *I've got some money, though,* he thought hopefully. *I should be able to buy some kind of place for myself. Maybe this fellow Diomedes will help, if I make him a present.*

"He's got a horse like yours, though," Diomedes observed as John and his retainers rounded the turning post at the far end of the track. "An Arab — and she's fast, too. That was why I asked you if you wanted to sell yours when I saw you unloading it at the docks."

Elthemos patted the neck of his black Arab gelding. "I can't sell you Lucky. He's a jewel. But if you like, I could write my brother and ask him to see if he couldn't find you a horse in Bostra and have it shipped. We buy plenty of horses from the Saracens in Bostra; they're the fastest things on four legs." He looked down the track again, noticing the beautiful flowing gait of the dun Arab mare. "I don't know that I could get you one like that, though," he conceded ruefully.

"That one was a present from the Augusta herself. I wouldn't expect ordinary mortals to be able to buy one. Do you suppose your brother really would be able to find me some fast Saracen horse? A mare, maybe, that I could cross with my Conqueror? I'd send him the money for it, of course. It's just that you can't get many of the pure Arab breed here — I've been trying to for a year now."

"Well, they're Saracen horses. You don't find many of them outside Arabia. The Augusta was probably given some by King Harith. That mare is bloodstock, all right." The mare was trotting toward the gate again, and Elthemos drew his own mount's reins tight, studying the animal. The rider's cloak of white and purple silk fluttered with the horse's motion, and Elthemos looked at him enviously — then jumped, frowned, and stared as the horse passed them and went on up the track. "Holy God!" he exclaimed.

"What's the matter?" asked Diomedes absently, engrossed by the image of a speeding foal by his Conqueror out of an Arab mare.

"Your Count John looks exactly like my bastard half-brother."

"Does he?"

"Yes, exactly. It's an extraordinary likeness — your count has a beard, of course, and John didn't, but they could be twins. And my brother's name was John, too. Holy Immortal! What a peculiar thing!" He sat watching, waiting in fascination as the gray moved into the outer track, broke into a flying canter, and rounded the post to come back toward him. The rider leaned over her neck but straightened slightly as he passed the Great Gate, glancing over the milling mass of men and horses to make sure his path was clear. "Exactly!" Elthemos repeated, shaking his head in amazement.

Diomedes snorted sympathetically. "I saw a woman once who looked exactly like my aunt; I even ran up to her in the street to greet her, and it wasn't till she slapped me that I realized she was a complete stranger."

"But it's amazing! I've been looking for my half-brother for years, on and off, and to see a man, a count, with his face — it's extraordinary."

"Looking for him? Why, did you lose him?"

Elthemos laughed. "He disappeared two and a half years ago. He used to be our father's secretary, but when our father died in the plague, John went off to Berytus; he said he was going to look for work there. I tried to look him up while I was in the city, but I couldn't find him. My brother and I both regretted that we ever let him go — nobody realized how much work he'd done or how good he was. If we'd known, we'd have made him steward and paid him a fat salary. We had to hire two different scribes to replace him, and buy a slave as well. He was a damned clever bastard, and knew shorthand, and Persian and Aramaic as well as Arabic and Greek. And he did all the accounting and had his own filing system, and was never caught out by anybody."

Diomedes, who'd been listening with only half an ear, suddenly frowned and stared at Elthemos. "Shorthand, accounting, and filing?" he said, surprised. "That's exactly what Count John used to do in our office — and he knew Persian and Aramaic and Arabic. Everyone always commented on it, how unusual it was for a Syrian to know Aramaic better than Syriac, and to speak Arabic."

"I never met anyone in Berytus who did," said Elthemos, now frowning as well. "You don't think . . ."

The gray Arab mare galloped up to the gate again; her rider pulled her in, grinning, and waited for his retainers to catch up with him. He didn't notice the two men watching him among the crowd not far away.

Elthemos swallowed, reaching over, and caught Diomedes' wrist. "It *is* him," he whispered.

"It has to be just a coincidence," said Diomedes.

"No — he has a scar at the corner of his left eye. He got that in a fight with me and my brother, when he was ten and Diodoros and I were nine and seven. It is him."

Diomedes sat still for a moment. "When did you say he disappeared?" he asked at last.

"Two and a half years ago. He set out for Berytus in late July."

"That would fit. And what was your father's name?"

"Diodoros of Bostra."

"He says that his grandfather was a Diodoros who was half-brother to the father of the most serene Augusta. It's all jumbled around, but it fits." He took his eyes off John and turned them, solemn and troubled, on Elthemos. "You say he isn't even legitimate?"

"He's the son of a Berytus whore my father kept for a while when he was a law student."

"And he claims . . . it's not right. It's not proper, for a fraud like that to be wearing white and purple and have the confidence of the empress. We ought to tell her."

Elthemos swallowed. "Wait a minute. I can't just —"

"Well, do you think it's proper?"

"No, but . . . but what if I've made a mistake?"

"Have you?"

"I don't think so, but —"

"Then we ought to tell the mistress. Or the master. They say the mistress isn't well and is seeing even fewer people than usual. We could tell the master, and he could get rid of John and tell her gently."

"Yes, but . . . but I can't . . . that is, what would happen to John? I'm sure he deserves whipping, but he is my half-brother, and I wouldn't want him killed. It would be better just to go to him privately and tell him the game's up and he should come home at once."

"He'd make sure you never got near anybody to tell them. You'd be discredited before you said a word. He could even have you killed — people who have influence with the Augusta can do anything. Anyway, they wouldn't kill him; he'd probably just be flogged, paraded in public, and sent home. That's the way they do things here. It's not proper for a bastard impostor to be taking in Their Sacred Majesties. He should be punished. Come on, I'll get us in to see the master tomorrow morning, and you can tell him."

"Me tell the emperor that the count of his cavalry is a fraud?" squeaked Elthemos. "I . . . I can't . . ."

"Come on! It will bring you to his attention, and maybe you could ask him for a favor afterward. We'll have to be careful how we do this, though. John is a friend of His Illustriousness, and His Illustriousness would make sure you never got to see the master with news like that. I know, you can say you're appealing on some business connected with an estate. I can make sure your name gets near the top of the appointment list, and I'll go in with you. Then you can tell His Sacred Majesty. If you do it tactfully, you won't come to any harm even if you are mistaken."

· · · ·

Shortly before noon the next day, two men of the Excubitor guards came to John with an order for him to attend the emperor at once.

John was in the middle of a long argument with the count of the stables about the supply of fodder for his men's mounts, but when the Excubitors arrived, his colleague bowed, set another date, and John started off with them for the Augusteion. He was not alarmed; requests to attend the emperor at once were not uncommon, and usually meant a guard of honor was required unexpectedly. He merely ran his fingers through his hair and settled his sword behind his hip, wondering which ambassador it was this time.

It was a brilliant sunny morning, and a breeze from the Bosphorus rippled the new leaves in the palace gardens, shaking the last petals from the apple trees. John found himself smiling, almost happy. The autumn and the winter had been a time of black misery for him, when he had been sunk in a depression so profound that he sometimes felt he was buried alive in the dark earth. Theodora had not seen him since he refused the marriage to Praejecta, and he felt her contempt and anger across the whole width of the palace. The city pressed on him, a huge weight of humanity he had somehow left behind; the palace pushed back, and he felt crushed. He alternated between contempt for himself and anger at Theodora and his father. Everything he did seemed pointless, contaminated by his own weakness. He thought sometimes of Euphemia, and the memory scalded his mind. The only pleasure he could find was in work, good hard work that held his thoughts firmly and left him exhausted and dazed by the end of the day, wanting only to sleep.

Outwardly, his situation was better than it had been a year before. He was used now to the splendid quarters and the possession of twenty slaves to look after him. He had hired some more retainers, and became accustomed to riding through the city with either his own six men or a troop of imperial guardsmen at his back. He kept the friends he had made, and saw Narses occasionally, when the chamberlain had time, and Anastasios fairly often. The old scribe's daughter had been visiting the city with her husband during the winter; one of the few bright moments that season had been when Anastasios arrived at the Bronze Gate with a seven-year-old grandson, whom John was delighted to escort round the barracks. Artabanes believed that John's quarrel with Theodora had been on his own behalf, and swore eternal gratitude despite the mission's failure. The Armenian was now doubly eager to leave the city. His wife had been installed in his house and given her own slaves by the empress. "They spy on me," Artabanes complained, "watching to see if I treat the bitch well. If I so much as raise my voice to her, they tell the Augusta. I wish the Augustus would send me to the East, or even to Italy. Belisarius is still begging for reinforcements." The Augustus, however, was busily negotiating with Persia and moved no troops anywhere.

But he may post us somewhere this summer, John thought as he followed the Excubitors into the private apartments of the Augusteion. *Probably Italy — but even that's better than staying in Constantinople. Well, I can only hope.*

The emperor was waiting in the Triklinos reception hall, one of the smaller of the palace audience rooms, less grand than the Augusteus or the throne of Solomon but still magnificent. Its walls were of jasper and carnelian; the columns that supported its vault were of porphyry; its floor was decorated with a mosaic of the fruits of the earth; and its ceiling was covered with golden stars. Justinian was sitting upright on his purple-draped couch, crowned with the diadem; he looked impatient and angry. John noted that there were a few others, guards and some civilians, standing near the walls of the room, but he did not immediately look at them. He walked the regulation distance toward the emperor, then made the prostration. The emperor did not extend his foot to be kissed, and John lay still on the mosaic branches, wondering who had annoyed Justinian enough to make him forget to do this.

"Get up," said the emperor coldly. John rose and met the eyes under the gold of the diadem. The pupils were contracted to a pinpoint of bitter rage, and fixed directly on him. He stared back in shock and bewilderment.

"Do you know this man here?" the emperor asked, indicating a person on his right.

John paused, staring at the emperor in confusion for a moment before he turned his head and saw Elthemos standing beside Diomedes.

Time seemed to slow down. He recognized his half-brother and had time to notice that he had put on weight since they had last met and that he had bought his red and white silk cloak very recently, because the nap of the cloth was standing up on the collar and Elthemos was fidgeting with it, nervous and miserable, out of place. John felt no fear and scarcely even any surprise, only a sense of profound displacement, and beyond that, an immense relief that it was, or soon would be, all over.

"Yes, master," he answered quietly.

"Who is he?" demanded Justinian.

"He is my half-brother, Elthemos son of Diodoros, of the city of Bostra in Arabia."

"Is he?" said Justinian, the anger breaking through his cold tone. "And who are you?"

"Who Elthemos told Your Sacred Majesty I was."

"Not who you said you were — a citizen of Berytus, the legitimate descendant of a relative of my most esteemed consort?"

"No, master."

"What lies did you tell my wife?"

"None, master."

The emperor rose and took a step forward. From the dais of his throne he towered over John. "Don't tell stories now," he said, slowly and savagely. "Your tricks have all been exposed now, and you will be punished for them. Tell the truth, and your punishment will be less severe. What lies did you tell my wife?"

"Master," John said, the distancing of shock beginning to wear thin at Justinian's rage. "Master, I told no lies to the most serene Augusta."

Justinian hit him, a straight blow with a clenched fist that knocked John sideways. He stumbled against the edge of the dais and fell. There was a thick silence in the room; he could hear the Excubitors moving forward to guard the emperor in case John drew his sword.

John pulled himself up by the edge of the dais and stood, unsteadily. His mouth was full of blood, and he swallowed repeatedly, carefully feeling his teeth with a sore tongue.

"I knew that you were lying from the first," said the emperor, still in a slow, savage tone. "I tried not to believe it, for my wife's sake. I gave you your position and your rank, I tried to look at nothing but the quality of your work — but I knew. Now I want the whole story. Tell it to me."

"Master, it is not my place to tell you the mistress's secrets. And it was she, not you, who gave me my rank. Ask her."

"I will ask her — after I have heard it from you."

John was silent. *The lie was hers,* he thought. *She commanded me to keep to it, she warned me not to embarrass her. No, by all the saints, I will leave it in her hands; I will show her that I am loyal to her. I will put it to the test again to see whether I'm a coward. And if she wants to deny me, she can. That is her choice, and perhaps it will be for the best.*

"Master," he said, meeting Justinian's eyes, "it is not proper that I reveal something that the Augusta has commanded me to keep secret. Ask her." Justinian struck him again; he staggered and straightened, swaying.

"Y-your Sacred Majesty," said Elthemos, wavering forward, "f-forgive me for . . . for speaking, but . . . but he must have lied, and he must be out of his senses with fear now to deny it. Surely Y-your Sacred Charity c-could . . ."

Justinian glared at him, and Elthemos fell silent. Diomedes grabbed his arm and pulled him back to the side. *Poor Elthemos,* thought John vaguely, *trying to protect me, not realizing that the emperor knows that his wife was lying too.*

The emperor nodded to the guards, and two of them came forward and took John's arms. "Take this man out and give him twenty lashes," Justinian commanded. "Then bring him back."

"Master," said John as the guards began to obey, "you should ask the Augusta."

Justinian nodded to his men again, and they pulled John out.

The room was absolutely still. The emperor sat down again upon his throne, looking at nothing.

Out of respect for his rank, the Excubitors did not flog John in the middle of their barracks square but in the prison behind it; it was too embarrassing to take a patrician's cloak and a Protector's uniform off a man before chaining him to a post to whip him. The pain was surprising, penetrating even the deadening dedication with which he had prepared himself. By the fifth blow he began to wish he had spoken out. By the fifteenth he no longer cared, and clung to the post, letting his mind go blank. The Excubitors unchained him and he leaned against the stained wood. With an extraordinary clarity he remembered the battle of Nicopolis, flying into death. *It should have been then*, he thought. *It would have been better then, without this last year to endure first.*

"Can you walk?" one of the Excubitors asked him with an incongruous air of polite concern.

"I don't know," he whispered, and pushed himself away from the post. He staggered, and the guards caught his arms again. They pulled his tunic on him and walked him back to the Triklinos hall. One of their fellows joined them halfway, running from the prison with John's cloak, just in case.

It seemed that no one had moved in the hall. John walked between his guards up to the dais again, seeing himself through the shock in the faces round him. His tunic stuck to his back, soaked with blood. The guards let go of him when they reached the dais. He swayed unsteadily a moment, then deliberately made the prostration. He found he couldn't get up again, and crouched on his hands and knees. Every muscle in his body seemed to be trembling.

"What lies did you tell to my wife?" Justinian asked again.

"I told no lies to her," John said quietly. "Ask her."

Someone on his left made a choked noise of horror. Elthemos, he realized.

"I will have the truth from you before I trouble her with so much as a whisper," said Justinian. "You probably know that flogging is mild compared to some of the things that can be done."

John knelt with his head bowed. *I won't have the strength,* he thought despairingly. *I will give in. And probably I'll be disbelieved.*

"Master," he said, looking up, "please ask her."

There was a sudden commotion at the entrance to the room, and the sound of a blow. Justinian's eyes left John's and widened with astonishment. John pushed himself up on his knees, tried to look round, and checked as the movement tore at his lacerated back.

"What is going on?" demanded Theodora.

John closed his eyes with relief. The empress stopped beside him, staring down at him, and he was able to look up and notice that Narses was standing just behind her before he fixed his eyes on her face. He had seen her at a distance from time to time during the autumn and he knew that she had still not recovered from her illness, but her face shocked him. It was colorless, like a skull set in the jewels of the diadem. Only the eyes blazed as hotly as ever.

"What has he done?" demanded Theodora, of John now. She dropped to her knees beside him, her face crumpling in pain and anger. "Oh my God!" She caught his arms and held him against her, his blood soaking onto the purple cloak. The pressure of her arm against his back was excruciating, but even the pain was joyful.

"Theodora!" said her husband in a voice of anguish.

She did not move, merely glared up at the emperor. "Yes, Peter? Do you want to accuse me of something?"

He was shocked speechless. She glared fiercely about the room, then looked back at Justinian. "Did you have something to ask me?" she demanded.

The emperor had gone white. "Who did that young man tell you he was?" he asked, slowly and distinctly.

"He told me he was the son of Diodoros of Bostra. And Narses has just come running to tell me that a certain Elthemos son of Diodoros was the one who stirred up this trouble. Which is he?"

Someone pointed Elthemos out. Theodora pulled away from John very gently and advanced on him, stopping a few paces away. "I am the empress," she told him, while he gaped miserably. "Greet me as one!"

Elthemos staggered, then went down on his face. He was not adept at the prostration, and did it clumsily. When he rose, Theodora slapped him. "You miserable busybody!" she said. "Elthemos — named after your grandfather, aren't you? I remember your father telling me that name, the name of the father of the woman he preferred to me. You'll pay for this."

She turned away abruptly and stepped onto the dais, standing over her husband, breathing quickly, one hand pressed to her side. "You idiot," she told Justinian. "Did you really believe that I would be unfaithful to you? John is my son, by Diodoros of Bostra, who was the last lover I had before I met you. I met him on my way back home from Egypt, and I lived with him for a year, then left him and his child in Berytus. I said John was my cousin in order to be free to further his career. I kept this from you for fear that you would insist on my sending him away, and because I had ambitions to settle the succession on him. He, however, is obstinately and perversely unambitious. You know that he refused to marry at my direction; he refused also to agree to take any steps for his own advancement beyond count. Why on earth did you have him whipped?"

The color came back to Justinian's face in a flood. He stared at John, then stared at Elthemos.

"Go on," said Theodora, sitting down heavily on the throne, her hand still pressed against her side. "Ask him who John's mother was."

"What . . . what do you know of this?" asked Justinian.

Elthemos looked sick. "Sh-she was a whore," he said. "A whore my father met in Berytus . . . oh God. Oh God. Her name . . . it was Theodora."

"You see?" said Theodora. She bent over, her whole arm now

clutched against her. "Why did you have my son whipped?" she demanded again. "You could have asked him."

"I did ask him," said Justinian, almost plaintively. "He refused to say anything; he said it was your secret, and told me to ask you."

Theodora looked at John. Her face was gray, beaded with sweat. It was only then that he realized that she was in great pain. He made a wordless sound of protest and used the edge of the dais to pull himself up and over to her.

"Very well," said the empress, reaching out one hand for his. "You did it to show me, did you? To punish me? Well, I take the point. Darling, do what you like. You're my son, anyway." She clutched his hand and folded over in a long spasm of pain.

Justinian was suddenly crouching at her other side, his arm around her. "My life and soul!" he said. "I'm sorry! You shouldn't have been disturbed with this, you're ill! I'll do what you like about John. No one outside this room will ever know what happened today, and I'll make certain that none of them ever tells. Go back to bed and rest!"

Theodora shivered, straightened a little, and spat blood onto the tiles of the floor. She stared at it bleakly for a moment: it lay bright and red on the green mosaic leaves. She turned her head to meet her husband's eyes. "You might as well know it now, Peter," she said quietly. "I'm not going to recover."

"Don't say that. It isn't true. You won't die, you mustn't die!"

"We must all die, Peter. Everyone born is a corpse someday. Have the guards fetch a litter; I don't think I can walk back. And for mercy's sake, get a doctor for my son!"

John afterward discovered that Narses had learned from one of the guards what was happening when John was taken out to be whipped. The chamberlain had tried to go at once to the emperor, but was refused admission and given instead an order to go back to his office and wait. He had disobeyed the order and run like a message boy to the Daphne Palace to fetch Theodora.

"And she came at once," Narses said when he visited John

at his house that evening. "The guards didn't want to admit her either, but she cuffed them like disobedient children and marched in. I didn't realize how ill she was — she'd kept that from everyone, and I would never have guessed it from watching her."

John said nothing for a moment. He was lying on his stomach on his bed, his back covered in lotions and light bandages. "How ill is she?" he asked at last.

"As ill as she said. Dying. Her doctor says she has a growth, a tumor, in her side. She apparently has had episodes of vomiting blood for the past month, but she'd commanded her doctor and her attendants to tell no one. She doesn't want to die, and hoped perhaps to put it off by keeping it secret."

John clenched his fist and bit on the knuckles. "When I caught the plague," he said slowly, "I saw for the first time that my father loved me — and he caught it from me and died. Here it is, three years later, and the same thing happens with my mother."

"She has been ill for a year," Narses pointed out. "That has nothing to do with you. Don't trouble yourself about it, my dear friend. You could hardly have behaved better through the whole affair."

John shook his head, setting his teeth against the tears. "I disappointed her."

"You acted with great integrity. And she has disappointed you. You know, when my family sold me, my mother wailed over me as though I had died, but when I tried to cling to her, she handed me over to the slaver. It has been a lifetime since that happened. I have rank, power, riches, and even respect because of it; when people curse eunuchs, they make an exception for me — but I cannot remember that betrayal without bitterness, even now. Your mother offered you power when you wanted love. You were right to reject the lesser gift in favor of the greater."

"Perhaps. But everyone I finally manage to love dies."

Narses sighed. "That is the condition of all humanity, to love what dies. Death is the prince of this world, and love is the only thing of durable value in all the chaos and futility. We can only try to have faith in God's word that love will prove more durable in the end. Rest, please. Your mother won't die tonight; you'll have time to say goodbye."

It took Theodora two months to die, and she fought bitterly to live right to the end. Justinian abandoned theology, Persia, and all but the most rudimentary mechanics of running his empire, and sat for hours by his wife's bed. John spent time there as well, sometimes sitting beside the emperor. They talked to please the empress, about the state of the provinces, the gossip of the court and the church. Theodora said nothing more about John's future, or indeed any serious matter. She was content to have him beside her, and the emperor was eager for anything that would make her smile. During the first month she wanted to smile. She latched eagerly onto the smallest doings of the palace slaves and laughed over old jokes. Gradually, though, as the pain grew worse, she grew less interested in gossip and began to send for her priests and settle her affairs with her staff. Then she took the opium her doctor offered her and slept more and more of the time.

John's troops were told that he had tripped going into the palace and injured his back, and had been given leave from his duties for a few months to recover. No one questioned this story openly, though it was common knowledge that he had been disgraced in some way and that the empress had interceded for him. Of his slaves, only Jakobos knew that he had been whipped.

"You'll never be able to use the public baths again in your life," Jakobos said sadly when he was changing the dressings one morning. He studied the red and yellow scabs and shook his head. "It looks awful for a count to have the scars of a whipping. Can I ask you a question, master?"

"Ask away."

"Did they do this because you were the mistress's lover or because you're her son?"

John turned on his side and stared at the boy. "What do you know about that?"

"Well, I thought it had to be one or the other. I know how

much she's favored you, and I was brought up in her household. I know it's unusual."

John rolled back onto his stomach. "The master thought the first; the second is true, and the matter has been dropped. But it's very secret and you're to tell no one."

"Yes, master," said Jakobos with satisfaction, and began to put the salve on. "I just wanted to know."

The Excubitors who had witnessed the scene were bribed with fat sums and threatened with death for disclosing a word of it. Diomedes was transferred to another post and also bribed and threatened to keep his mouth shut. John interceded quietly for Elthemos, and the threats against him were dropped. He came to John's house to thank him.

"I didn't know," he explained. "I thought you'd turned trickster."

"You should have guessed," John told him sourly. "You knew enough to guess. You always were a fool. And what reason did I ever give you to make you believe I was that dishonest?"

Elthemos looked down and shuffled his feet. "Everyone always said to watch you. You were too clever, they said, and a clever bastard's a danger to honest men."

"You don't need to tell me what everyone always said; I heard them for myself." John looked at his half-brother with a sudden sense of surprise. In the past he had learned to give way to the legitimate sons of the house; only occasionally had he exploded into violent rage against his superior brothers and fought with them. Now he was speaking with the tired impatience of a superior, and Elthemos was giving way. "Why did you come to this city?" he asked.

"I wanted to find a job," Elthemos answered at once. "Dio's got the estates, and he's tied to the council. I thought I'd try my luck at the court and see if I could earn some money. But it looks as if I'm lucky to escape with a whole skin."

"I'll try to find you a job," said John. "But mind you, I'm no connection of yours. Embarrass Their Sacred Majesties and I drop you flat."

"Yes, John," said Elthemos humbly.

John found him a position in the praetorian prefecture by trading on the good will acquired by the Cappadocian's files, and Elthemos was gratefully silent.

Theodora lost consciousness for the last time on the twenty-sixth of June, and died in the evening two days later. The emperor stayed beside her from the moment she lost consciousness, and when she died had to be carried out of the room, sick with grief, by her staff. John was left alone with the body; he had been admitted, in a silent recognition of his status, even to the end. He remained alone beside the body for a few hours, trying to pray. The room was very quiet, though from elsewhere in the palace came the wailing of the mourners. The lamps on the golden stand sent soft light glowing on the purple silk of the bedspread, and the smell of disease and death was swallowed by the incense. The body had been arranged for death even before the breath left it, and lay with the clawlike hands folded on the breast, the heavy lids shut over the now glazed eyes. The aging that the disease had set on her had fallen away, and she looked fragile, beautiful, young. In the morning, John knew, the slaves would dress her in her purple cloak, set the diadem on her head, and place her in the Church of Holy Wisdom for the people to gaze on. *It is over*, he thought, kneeling by the head of the bed. *It is over — and it never really began. I have been too cautious. I thought if she was a tyrant, I couldn't love her. She was, and could have been much worse, and I still would. I still do.*

He kissed the cold cheek and left the room.

The whole city was plunged into extravagant mourning, every statue draped with black, every church resounding with hymns for the dead. After lying in state for a day beneath the dome of the Holy Wisdom, the empress's body was carried in a long procession through the streets to the Church of the Holy Apostles, where she was buried in the mausoleum that held the bones of all the emperors since Constantine. The emperor laid aside the purple and the diadem and followed the coffin dressed in black, and behind him in their thousands walked the staff of the palace, from the ministers of state down to the junior clerks and guardsmen, dressed in black and mourning as though for a member of their own families. For a week afterward no business was conducted, and the shops in the marketplaces were allowed to open for only a few hours every day. "You'd think the plague had come back," said Artabanes in disgust.

When the shops were allowed to open again and the work of governing the empire was resumed, one of the first things the emperor did was summon John.

John found himself escorted not to any of the audience rooms but to Justinian's private study, a small room on one of the upper floors of the Magnaura. Justinian was sitting at a desk, dressed in black, with his hair cropped short in mourning. The walls of the room were lined with books on theology. There was scarcely room for John to make the prostration.

"You can get up," the emperor said when John was halfway down. "And you can sit down, there." He indicated a couch by the window."

John sat, nervously aware that even the highest ministers did not sit in the presence of the Augustus, and the emperor stared at him bleakly for a moment.

"I should have seen it before," he said. "You look like her. I should have known better than to suspect her — but she shouldn't have lied to me." He sighed and rubbed the back of his neck. "I knew she had her secrets, her monks and her heretical priests and a few private prison cells for her enemies as well. I gave her authority and she didn't always do what I would do with it. That's what you expect, though, if you make a forceful and intelligent person your colleague in power, and it's what you have to accept if you want the love of an equal instead of that of a slave. But I didn't ask too many questions, and she didn't lie to me or cross me openly — except about you — and we were happy. I always thought she would outlive me." He looked up at John again. "So, she wanted to settle the succession on you."

"She wanted a son by you and couldn't have one," John replied.

The emperor nodded. "Oh, I don't blame her. And I didn't say anything to her when she was dying. But I cannot settle the succession that way, not even for her. Not on the son of a man who rejected her, who's no relation of my own."

"I don't want the purple," said John. "I quarreled with her about it, as she said. I don't have the will to desire it or the nerve to work for it, and I am perfectly content to let the matter drop."

Justinian studied him a moment, then nodded again. "No, you're not the ambitious type, are you? She found it hard to believe that anyone was unambitious, but I've always been certain that most of the men I promote will stay loyal. Belisarius, Narses, Tribonian, Germanus — I've always been sure that they wouldn't betray me. Nor, I think, would you. And you are very able, and her son. You can keep your rank and that cloak she gave you. But I don't think I want you here in Constantinople, reminding me that once she slept with your father. She was my wife, not his. No one else ever recognized what a jewel she was; no one else ever loved her as I did."

"She told me that you were worth a dozen of my father, even leaving rank aside," John said slowly.

The emperor smiled painfully. "And she never loved anyone as she loved me. That I believe. Thank you. Very well, what do you want?"

"Master?"

"I've told you that you can keep your rank but that I want you to leave the city. You've inherited some of her abilities and could undoubtedly be useful somewhere. Pick your position."

John swallowed, licked his lips. "I would like a position in command of troops in the East. A dukedom in Arabia or Syria."

Justinian nodded once. "Very good. You're a Nabatean Arab, aren't you? You speak Arabic and Persian?"

"Yes, master," John stared at the emperor, slightly confused by the speed of events.

"And you're undoubtedly familiar with the situation in the

East and, I think, a cautious man, unlikely to start any wars. Very well. I can hardly demote you from count of the cavalry to being a mere duke of Arabia. I will make you count for the *strata Diocletiana*, the frontier from the Orontes as far as Arabia Deserta. I'll give you personal command of some of the troops already there, and you can try to control the dukes and the phylarch — who, I warn you, are a very unreliable and insubordinate collection of generals. The most I hope for from you is that you manage to put a stop to the raiding we've suffered from the Lakhmid Saracens; the least is that you don't start a war, the way your predecessor did." The emperor took the pen from his desk and wrote a few lines on a piece of parchment, then picked up a stick of sealing wax stained with purple, lit it, and dribbled it onto the document. He sealed it with the signet on his right hand and gave it to John. "There you are," he said.

John stared at the codicil in astonishment, then looked up at the emperor. "Thank you, master. It's more than I wanted; I'll try not to fail you."

Justinian winced. "Don't. You look like her. Leave as soon as you can — within the month. Narses can help you arrange the money and the troops you'll want to take on the journey. Now leave me alone."

Narses was quietly delighted for him, Artabanes was jealous but pleased, and John's staff were grateful to be rid of such an exacting superior. John spent the day trying to determine what the new position would entail. By the time evening fell, the excitement was wearing off, and he felt tired and depressed and wanted intensely to be by himself. He fetched his horse from the stables, sent his retainers away, and rode out into the city. It was a hot, dry day, and one of the dusty Constantinopolitan winds gusted from the north, stinging the eyes with grit from the city streets. He rode to the hippodrome but had no heart for the track. *In a few months,* he thought, *I can take Maleka for a gallop along the edge of the Syrian desert and into the gardens of Nabatea. Home again.*

He turned the mare and rode instead past the porticoes of the

Middle Street as far as the Taurus marketplace. He stopped the horse under the triumphal arch in the middle of the market and stared across it. The front part of Euphemia's house was being rebuilt as a separate building, and was covered in scaffolding. The back portion was invisible from the marketplace, but he knew that it was intact and that the girl had moved back in.

And that is why I came here, he thought. *Of course.*

He touched Maleka's sides and rode forward, into the third side street. The iron gates had not been damaged by the fire, and he knocked on them firmly. After a moment the porter, Onesimos, stuck his head out the window.

"It's you!" he said in a surprised tone. Then, "I mean, it's Your Honor."

"Is your mistress in?" asked John, and the porter nodded, flustered.

"I'll get the gates open, sir . . . there we are. I'll take the horse. Is the mistress expecting you?"

"No. No, I was out riding, and I thought I would stop . . . Announce me to her, will you?"

The old man nodded, secured Maleka in the overgrown courtyard, and escorted John through the house. He could hear voices from the back — most of the slaves must be in the kitchen garden, enjoying the evening sun. But Onesimos led him up the stairs to the usual room and knocked on the door.

"What is it?" came Euphemia's voice.

"It's Count John, mistress, from the palace, come to visit."

There was a silence, and then Euphemia opened the door and stared at John with her eyes wide in astonishment. Her hair was loose, and she was wearing the yellow cloak.

"I . . . I was out riding, and I thought I'd stop," said John. "May I come in?"

"Yes — yes, of course." She stood aside from the door, and he entered the room. It was empty. "Auntie's in the garden," Euphemia explained. "I . . . I was just writing a letter."

"To your father?"

"Yes. I don't have much to tell him these days, but he doesn't need the information as much. He's made a position for himself in Egypt; he has hopes that the charges will be dropped soon, for lack of evidence."

"Particularly since the Augusta is dead?"

She blushed. "He doesn't know that yet. Though it will help." She stared at him a moment, then touched the edge of his black cloak. "I'm sorry for your sake, if not for my own."

"Yes." John glanced about the empty room, then sat down on the couch. "Yes, I understand that. I did love her, you know."

"You have to love your parents," she said, blushing again, sitting on the other end of the couch. "I . . . I love my father. Maybe I shouldn't. I know he did things that made people hate him, hate him justly. But he loved me, and he was all I had."

John looked down at his hands. "I'm going to go to the East," he said after a long moment of silence. "I've been promoted — given charge of Arabia and the Syrian frontier. I'm to leave within the month."

"Oh," she said, staring at him. After a moment she added, "Congratulations."

He shook his head and looked up at her. The evening light streamed through the window, gilding her hair, bringing out the orange in her close-set eyes. Her hands were linked together in her lap. *I've been too cautious all my life, and left things too late,* he thought. *I might as well be reckless now.* "Come with me?" he asked, in a whisper.

"Come . . . what do you mean? Come where?"

"Come with me to the East. As my wife."

She went white. "You don't mean that."

"I do."

"You . . . you're saying this to make fun of me."

He shook his head slowly. "I love you," he said, finding that the words he had never said came easily, surprisingly sweet.

She stared in anguish. "You haven't thought about it."

"No, not really. I didn't know I was going to come here to-night and say this. But I have thought about it — thought about you, anyway."

She looked away, twisting her hands in her lap. "What did

your mother think of that?" she asked at last, finding a shaky and unsteady sarcasm.

"I never told her. She had ambitions for me that I couldn't fulfill. But she's dead now. I have no parents, and don't need to consult anyone but myself."

"Who was your father? A bearkeeper, a charioteer?" she demanded, trying desperately to defend herself with anger. "He wouldn't care?"

"He was a gentleman, a magistrate in the city of Bostra, by the name of Diodoros. He died in the plague the summer before I first came here. He was a highly respectable man, if that's any help."

She bit her lip. "I have a father," she said. "I have to consult . . . and he wouldn't approve. Even if I say nothing about your ancestry, and I'd have to say nothing, he wouldn't approve."

"He'd accept it, though, wouldn't he? My rank is respectable enough." He did not say that the daughter of a minister who was hated so widely would not have many offers of marriage from patricians; there was no need to.

"You'd still be the empress's cousin. He had reason to hate her, and he'd hate you for her sake. Bad blood, he'd say."

"Well, you're the Cappadocian's daughter, which is generally reckoned worse blood, and I don't care. If you're willing to marry me, I'll go to the emperor and say so. I have some influence just at the minute, and I don't think His Sacred Majesty would object. He could give consent in your father's place. I'm not bothered about any dowry; your father can keep his money. I'll have enough for both of us."

Euphemia was twisting the edge of her cloak in her hands; now her mouth twisted as well. "I can't," she said, "not break with him. Not after being responsible for what happened to him."

"You weren't responsible. You were deceived, just as he was himself."

"I was used; it shouldn't have been possible for me to be used! I have to obey him now!"

He reached over and took her hand, and she looked up, angry

and wretched. "The world is ruled by death and futility," he said. "The plague and the wars have destroyed whatever anyone has tried to build in the past thirty years. People die — my father, my mother have; I might and you might. You did say once that you loved me. Isn't it worth grabbing at that while we're still alive and have time to love each other?"

"I love my father too," she said. "I have to keep faith with him."

"You said yourself he's made a position for himself in Egypt now, and the charges are likely to be dropped. You've been faithful for four years. Isn't that long enough?"

She pulled her hand away and went to the window. "You either keep faith or you don't. Anyway, you don't need me."

I need you; I've needed you all my life, he thought, but he couldn't say it. "Do you want me to go, then?" he asked instead, staring at her back.

After a moment, her bent head moved once in a nod.

Maleka was standing in the courtyard, chewing on a piece of weed. John untied her, and Onesimos opened the gate. John was just setting his foot in the stirrup when he heard his name called, and he turned to find Euphemia running toward him.

"No!" she said, meeting him, flinging her arms about him. "No, don't go! I will come, I want to come. I will leave the city with you if I have to go as your mistress!"

He was not sure afterward if he cried for her or for Theodora, but he kissed her, and went back into the house with her in tears. Onesimos stared after them a moment in surprise, then shrugged, tied up the horse again, and closed the iron gates. The evening sun gilded the iron indifferently along with the golden cross on the high dome of the Church of Holy Wisdom, indifferently along with the rough waters of the Bosphorus, the wilds of Thrace, and the mile upon mile of the long frontier that remained to the empire of the Romans.

epilogue

Procopius of caesarea, the great historian of Justinian's reign, tells a story of the empress Theodora and her illegitimate son, whom he says she had murdered. However, Procopius says this in his *"Unpublished"* or *"Secret"* History, and like everything else in that lurid compilation, the tale is hedged about with absurdities, impossibilities, and outright lies. It is impossible to know how much, if any, of what he says is true, and a responsible historian is obliged to use the *Secret History* only with extreme caution.

Fortunately for me, a historical novelist is under no such obligation. As Sir Philip Sidney observed, the historian, "affirming many things can, in the cloudy knowledge of mankind, hardly escape from many lies. But the poet . . . never maketh any circles about your imagination, to conjure you to believe for true what he writes." If I researched this book, it was for the pleasure of it; when I wrote, it was for the pleasure of telling a good story. When the solid ground of historical knowledge gaped open or quivered beneath my feet, I "called the sweet Muses to inspire me to a good invention," spun myself a bridge of gossamer, and went whistling on. This is a work of the merest fiction.

The rough framework, however, is true. The bubonic plague, which ravaged the world under Justinian, struck Constantinople in A.D. 543; a group of allied Herulian troops commanded by the chamberlain Narses defeated a "much larger" (no numbers are given) force of Sclaveni around 545; and the empress Theodora died on June 28, 548.

Belisarius did return from his futile command in Italy, in the year of Theodora's death; he was given the rank of commander in chief in the East and high office in the palace, and did no more fighting until almost the end of his life. The emperor's cousin Germanus was given charge of the reconquest; however, he died before the army he had raised could set sail. Narses was appointed in his place, led the force to Italy, defeated the Goths, defeated the Franks, got rid of the Lombards, and ruled the province with great efficiency for the next fifteen years. The Balkans, however, were virtually abandoned and suffered almost annual devastation by the Sclaveni and Bulgars until these people set up their own kingdoms in the exhausted region.

The Armenian Artabanes succeeded in divorcing his wife after Theodora's death, but was not successful in his proposed marriage to Praejecta, and frustrated love — or ambition — eventually propelled him into a plot to assassinate the emperor. The plot failed, but Artabanes was pardoned and eventually even restored to command. Justinian was always forgiving where he apprehended no threat.

Belisarius and Antonina also succeeded in procuring a divorce for their daughter Joannina from Theodora's grandson (whom the girl reportedly adored). But their hopes too were blighted, and it is not even recorded what became of the unfortunate Joannina. When Justinian died in 564, his successor was Justin II, son of his sister Vigilantia and husband of Theodora's niece Sophia. Justin was a disaster, and under his megalomaniac leadership most of the territories Justinian had reconquered fell back into barbarian hands, leaving the empire, after countless lives lost and lands and fortunes ruined, no larger, and almost certainly weaker, than it had been at Justinian's accession.

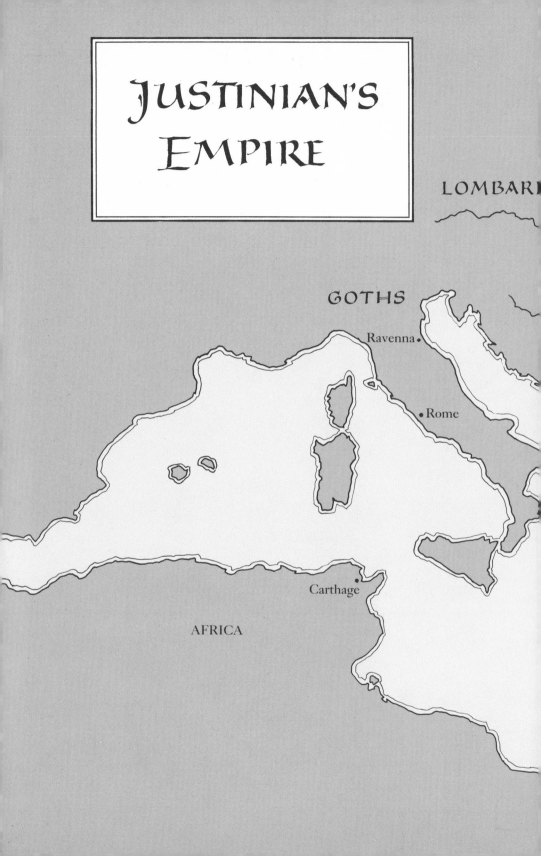

JUSTINIAN'S EMPIRE

LOMBARD

GOTHS

Ravenna

Rome

AFRICA

Carthage